MY EVIL FUCKING NEIGHBOR

MY EVIL FUCKING NEIGHBOR

EDITED BY

R.E. SARGENT & STEVEN PAJAK

CRYSTAL LAKE PUBLISHING
SINISTER SMILE PRESS

MY EVIL FUCKING NEIGHBOR
Edited by R.E. Sargent & Steven Pajak

Published by Sinister Smile Press, LLC, a Division of Crystal Lake Publishing
P.O. Box 637
Newberg, OR 97132

Trade Paperback ISBN: 978-1-964398-38-9

www.sinistersmilepress.com
www.crystallakepub.com

CONTENTS

"Man knows not what evil lurks in the heart of his neighbor until it's too late. But when that time arises, when it comes down to me or him, it will always be me."

—REX RYKER

FOREWORD

DUNCAN RALSTON

We've all had bad neighbors at one point in our lives.

When I was young, really young, I read Roald Dahl's *The Twits* —a children's tale about the probably most despicable couple ever imagined—and it inspired me to write a little story of my own about what it might be like to live next door to them. We'd had some pretty mean neighbors prior to that—according to my mom, one woman kept calling us "feelthy people" after we moved in, whenever we happened to be outside while she was tending her garden—so I was already familiar with bad neighbors by then. I imagined The Twits would make for the worst neighbors anyone could ever possibly have, and the story I wrote was gleefully macabre.

Then I got older and moved off on my own, and... well, let's just say The Twits have got nothing on some people. From the house-mate who scammed me out of a thousand bucks, to the landlord's son-in-law who smoked crack in my bathroom, to the elderly woman who opened up her window several times a day to shout a string of random epithets and immediately slam the window shut, to the 'roided-up dude who'd do pull-ups on the stair railings, dripping with sweat and shouting inspirational slogans at himself practically right outside my door... I've had my share of bad neighbors. And those are just a few examples I remembered off the top of my head.

Or maybe... maybe *we've* been someone's bad neighbor ourselves.

I'm sure there have been times, particularly in our late adolescence and early adult years, when we've annoyed the people living around us, inadvertently or deliberately. When *we've* been the problem. When we've had the cops called on us for partying too loud or doing drugs or playing pranks or... what have you.

But *evil* neighbors, and *evil fucking* neighbors, at that... *those* are thankfully quite rare.

Very few of us, I imagine, have actually lived next door to a serial killer, like Glenda Cleveland, the woman who called the police multiple times about her neighbor, Jeffery Dahmer. Or the neighbors of the friendly man who hosted parties at his nice little suburban bungalow and often dressed as "Pogo the Clown," John Wayne Gacy. Or the people who lived next door to Ariel Castro, a man who'd kidnapped and raped multiple young girls.

Very often, these people are deemed to be "nice" and "quiet" by the people they live amongst, like wolves in sheep's clothing. It's said that psychopaths like these derive a sense of superiority and control from being able to so successfully deceive their neighbors.

But serial killers are just the tip of the iceberg. We've also got spousal and child abusers, human traffickers, drug lords, pedophiles and sex criminals of various ilk, secret cannibals, torturers—the worst kind of scum, hidden in plain sight. Often not even hidden, just living there, an open secret, like a suspicious stain nobody wants to acknowledge, and the cops don't have the wherewithal to deal with.

Even Hitler had neighbors, after all.

Like I said, we've all had bad neighbors. But *truly evil* neighbors, the neighbors from Hell, those *evil fucking neighbors* like the people I've just mentioned... we like to hope they're rare, but maybe they're not as rare as we think.

Even so, the stories you're about to read, from some of the best indie and mid-sized press authors of dark fiction working today, will make your experiences with bad neighbors seem like you lived next door to Mr. Rogers.

Many of these writers have given us not just evil neighbors but evil *houses*. Imagine you lived next door to the dangerously insane house in Brian Asman's mindfuck of a novella, "Man, Fuck This House." Or to the extremely haunted Brackenby House in MJ Mars's terrifying "The Suffering." Or the Exorcist's House from Nick Roberts's wildly popular and aptly-titled "The Exorcist's House." Or the childhood home harboring a very evil entity within an unfinished painting in Steven Pajak's "The Devil's Doorway."

These authors, and the other excellent horror writers in this anthology, are very familiar with evil.

So, come. Let me show you around, introduce you to our neighbors from Hell. People—and *things*—who'll make your skin crawl, who'll disgust and disturb you, who'll leave you wondering if you really know your own real-life neighbors.

Or maybe you'd rather stay at home.

Lock your doors.

Shut the lights.

Pretend that you're safe.

But if you're brave enough, if you've got the stomach for it, follow me a little while. Prepare yourself to face the terrors that lurk *right next door…*

D.R.
12/2024

PINE RIDGE HOMEOWNERS ASSOCIATION

JAY BOWER

1

"Just put it downstairs," Melanie said to Josh. Sweat beaded on his forehead. He struggled with the oversized box. Breathing heavy. Arms aching. He wasn't known for his physical prowess and Melanie knew this.

"Where?" he replied.

"I don't know. Under the stairs?"

He let out a grunt but trudged down the blue-carpeted stairs to the fully finished basement. White tile floor. Wood paneling on the walls that was now painted white. A drop ceiling with a couple of tiles broken. The redeeming quality of the main basement space was the sliding doors that opened to the backyard and a wood-burning stove in the corner. At least if the weather got bad in the winter, they'd have something to keep them warm.

Josh turned to go under the stairs. Cobwebs painted the corners. Dust covered the floor. Just one more thing for them to take care of after they got everything moved in. He placed the box on the floor with a great exhale, then rubbed his arms and shoulders. There appeared to be a bad patch job on the paneling under there, as though someone had replaced it with a piece of thin plywood.

Coming from St. Louis to small-town southern Illinois was not on his agenda in life. Ever. But when Melanie received a job offer for a full-time tenure-track position from the university in Carbondale, they had to jump at the chance. Those positions were notoriously difficult to come by. There weren't many options for historians.

Josh didn't need to move for work. As a freelance social media marketer, he'd built up a significant client base and earned the ability to work out of their home. In St. Louis that meant a two-bedroom apartment. The only requirement he had for the move was that they had decent internet. It was difficult to run his business without it.

The new house was massive. Three bedrooms, a dining room, a living room, a family room, and two full baths. All on the main floor. The upstairs was once an attic but had been partially finished, turning it into one massive room.

The basement, other than the wood stove, also had two rooms, a partial bath, and a laundry room. Their little nine-hundred-square-foot apartment could fit down there with room to spare.

It was in a quiet neighborhood called Pine Ridge just minutes from the university campus, though it felt like they were out in the country. The entrance to the community was flanked by two brick walls with the name Pine Ridge carved in a central stone on both sides.

Josh wasn't looking forward to maintaining the 1.25 acres of land when his previous experience with yard work consisted of a push mower on a tiny plot of grass. But it was the place Melanie wanted, and because they were moving for her, he gave in.

He wiped the sweat from his forehead, cursing under his breath about having to move in the middle of summer. Classes started in mid-August, and Melanie was adamant that they move sometime in July. The heat and humidity were bad in the city. Josh discovered when they stepped out of the rented U-Haul truck that it was far worse in Carbondale.

Still, he had grown excited for the move. It was their first house together, and from everything he'd read online, the area was a great place to raise children. If they ever had any.

2

Two days after moving in, Josh and Melanie went for a walk through their new neighborhood to get their bearings and famil-iarize themselves with the new area.

They lived on a dead-end road with only four other houses past them before the road ended within a stand of enormous pine trees. It was toward that part of their neighborhood that they walked.

"Seems nice enough around here. The lack of traffic is different," Josh said. Less than a week ago they couldn't escape the constant drone of cars and horns and exhaust fumes living within the bowels of the city. The loudest thing now were the birds and squirrels scampering across the detritus amongst the trees.

The last house on their road had a unique feature. The garage was built into a small rise that flanked the road so that the roof barely poked above their level. The driveway sloped downward in a curve, the middle of the curve leading to the front door of the house. The garage door faced the house so that all they saw from their vantage point was a gray-shingled roof.

"That's interesting," Melanie said, indicating the garage.

"I bet it's great as a tornado shelter," Josh replied. "With the front facing east and the back built into the ground toward the west, it's a perfect place to hide if a storm comes."

"We've got a basement now, so I think we'll be good." Melanie smiled at him, and they continued past the house toward the large circular end of the road. They held hands like when they used to date, and Josh felt a warm, fuzzy feeling inside. Thick trees lined the end of the road. Tall, silent sentinels guarding the neighborhood from outside influence.

"This is such a huge difference from the apartment," Josh said.

"But you like it, don't you?" Melanie asked. "You're okay with this?"

"Of course. As long as I'm with you, that's all that matters."

They reached the end of the road and followed the curvature to turn back toward where they came from.

"You know, St. Louis is only a two-hour drive if we really need a city fix," Josh said. "What I'm trying to say is, I like it here. It's peaceful. Maybe..." He smiled, tugging her hand to his heart. "Maybe we can raise a family here."

Melanie's cheeks reddened. "It's not off the table."

They walked closer by the house with the unusual garage, Josh taking note of the wraparound porch and the view into a small ravine on the back end of the house.

"I've dreamed about a place like this all my life," Melanie said. "I still can't believe we're here. It seems so perfect." She gave his hand a squeeze. It felt like love, like the bond they shared could never be broken.

"Perfect? Maybe not. But it is—"

Josh was cut off when the two of them heard a muffled scream.

"Did you hear that?" Melanie asked.

"Where'd that come from?"

"It sounded like the garage," Melanie said. "But that can't be right."

"Maybe someone is hurt?" Josh asked.

Melanie let go of his hand and headed down the curved driveway toward the front of the sunken garage. Josh hurried after her.

"What are you doing?" he asked, stepping closer to her.

"We should probably see if someone needs help."

"But we don't know anyone here," Josh said. "For all we know, they could be doing some kind of weird sex fantasy thing."

Melanie gave him that look she did when he said something asinine, which was given often. "What better way to introduce ourselves than to offer help?"

Melanie peered into the glass on the garage door, cupping her hands against the sunlight streaming through the trees above.

"I don't see anything. Just a car."

"Excuse me?" a man called out. Josh's heart leaped into his throat. He and Melanie both turned to face the man.

Older, maybe in his mid-fifties, and with thick graying hair. A slight paunch. He walked slowly but carried himself with confidence, something that struck Josh as being academic, kinda like how Melanie was when around her colleagues.

"Hi, sorry," Josh said. "We thought we heard something."

"Probably just a cat. There's a few feral ones around here."

Josh approached the man and noticed a woman at the door, though she remained in the house. From what he could see, it seemed like she was wearing a long black skirt and a long-sleeved shirt. Odd, with the summer heat bearing down on them.

"Hi, I'm Josh Jordan, and this is my wife, Melanie." Josh stuck out his hand, and the man shook it. "We're the new folks in the neighborhood."

"The old Royce house, right?" the man asked, not offering his name.

"Yeah, that's us," Melanie replied. "We just moved in a couple of days ago."

"I expect Martha will be over to your place soon," the man said.

"Martha? Is that your wife?" Josh asked, nodding toward the house.

The man chuckled. "Hell no. I'd rather shove sticks in my eyes than have to wake up to that woman every day. Martha is the head of the greeting committee for the homeowner's association. She's also a hell of a busybody, so you might want to be careful what you say around her." He chuckled again.

Josh had forgotten all about the HOA. They had $200 annual dues for the privilege of living in this neighborhood, a scam he remembered telling Melanie, but she quickly stifled his opposition.

"Anyway, my name's Dan. I'm guessing you either work at the university or you're a doctor. That's all we get in this neighborhood."

Josh laughed. "Neither. Well, for me anyway. I'm a social media marketer. My wife, on the other hand, she's the newest history faculty member."

"History?" Dan said. "I wish more of the youth would take an interest. What's your specialty?"

"Early American Colonialism and Comparative Religion. Are you a doctor or will I see you on campus with me?" Melanie asked.

Dan smiled. "I teach in the Mortuary Science program."

Josh's smile didn't leave his face, but inside he recoiled. The man played with dead bodies for a living? That was a bit creepy.

"Oh," Josh said. "I'd heard that was a good program here."

"One of the best in the country. I've got five more years until I can retire, but I enjoy my work too much to give it up. My wife,

Patty, she wants to travel and see the world. I don't care much for that. I've got too much to do here."

Josh was ready to move on. He was all about being social until he wasn't, and the revelation that his neighbor taught something like "Playing With Dead People: 101" was something he wasn't prepared for.

"Good to meet you, Dan," Josh said. "I hope the cat gets out of your garage."

"Huh? Oh, right." Dan nodded and offered a welcoming smile. "Nice to meet the both of you."

3

While Josh was pouring a glass of water and enjoying the frigid temperature of the fully functional air conditioning, the doorbell rang. Melanie froze, her glass touching her lips. They didn't expect anyone. Melanie's parents weren't planning on coming for a couple of weeks, and Josh's mom lived three states away in Pennsylvania.

It rang again, breaking them from their temporary paralysis. Peering down the hall toward the front door, Josh could see two older women through the glass, one of them with a black binder clutched to her chest.

"Oh, I think that might be the welcoming committee," Josh said. They both answered the door to greet their new neighbors.

"Hello! Are you," the woman looked down at her notebook, "Mr. and Mrs. Jordan?"

Josh smiled, the formality of her aswords feeling out of place. "Yes, but you can call us Josh and Melanie."

"I see," she said. Josh noticed she was wearing a full button-down shirt with her arms covered and a black skirt that fit tight around her and went down to her ankles. It was similar to what

Dan's wife wore. Her long peppery hair was pulled back and in a ponytail. The other woman was similarly dressed.

"Well, here's the rules of the Pine Ridge Homeowners Association. We've taken the liberty of adding your contact information in the directory at the back."

"Oh. Okay."

"If you need anything or have any questions about the association, please refer to the rules first. Welcome to the neighborhood. Praise the Lord, it's so nice to have a new family." She smiled and turned to walk away with the other woman at her heels.

"Hey, what's your name?" Josh asked, realizing that they hadn't introduced themselves.

"I'm Mrs. Martha Williamson, and this is Mrs. Regina Thomas," she said. "Check the directory if you have any further questions."

She turned away and scuttled down their sidewalk toward the quiet road. Both Josh and Melanie stared at them as the odd couple turned the curve and went out of sight.

"That was strange," Melanie said.

"Praise the Lord," Josh said, mimicking Martha. "What the hell kind of place is this?" he asked. He tossed the notebook on the dining room table and went back to get his water.

Later that day, he sat at a recliner in the family room at the front of the house to watch outside and observe his new neighborhood. It was something he'd done every night since they moved in, and every night it was a parade of people.

An old man and his wife walked by their house, the old man mumbling while the woman peered in Josh's direction. They each carried a brown paper bag clutched tightly to their chests. Like Martha, Regina, and Dan's wife, she wore a similar outfit. He considered checking the rulebook for the association to see if he needed to buy Melanie new clothes and jokingly imagined Martha telling him, "It's in the rules."

A younger couple, maybe just a few years older than he and

Melanie, walked their dog. The woman was dressed like the others, too. They'd pass going toward the dead end. The man carried a milk jug filled with something dark. Close to half an hour later, they came by again, but this time without the jug.

Regina rode by on an old bike with white wheel walls, while her skirt fluttered behind her comically. She had a basket in the front, and it was filled with something wrapped in brown butcher paper. On her way back, it was empty.

He'd seen something like this every night. It didn't make sense. It seemed to him that all these people were going toward Dan's house, but why? What was he taking from them?

4

On their walk the next day, Josh and Melanie headed toward the dead end again at Josh's insistence. Melanie thought he was crazy when he shared his previous observations, but she went along with it to appease Josh.

They passed by Dan's place in total silence. Josh was convinced he'd hear something. When it remained stubbornly quiet, they walked past toward the circular end of the road to turn around.

"Are you convinced now?" Melanie asked. They reached the tall trees and turned to go back.

"I swear to you, something weird is going on."

"I doubt it. We're in a new place. They just do things differently here. Nothing to freak out about."

"You think so?" Josh replied. Melanie nodded.

"Let's try not to piss off the new neighbors too soon, okay?" She smiled and bumped her hip against his. Melanie had a way of diffusing difficult situations, and Josh appreciated that about her.

They approached Dan's house, and in the warm silence of the

summer day, a muffled cry split the air. The hairs on Josh's neck bristled. Melanie stopped dead in her tracks.

"Oh hell. What was that?" she asked.

"Do you believe me now? Something's wrong," Josh said.

The cry rose up again, and Josh pointed at the garage. "That's not a cat. I don't care what he says. Someone is in pain. We have to do something."

They walked closer to the driveway when Dan came out of his house, hurrying toward them.

"Hey, neighbors," he said, waving a hand. "How are you today?" He stopped at the edge of his driveway and glanced toward the road. Josh wondered if he was looking for the people that had been a constant parade.

"We're fine," Melanie said, placing a hand on Josh's arm. A move meant to deter him from doing or saying something stupid that would get them both in trouble. Josh decided now was not the time to confront Dan. But an idea had already formed in his head, and he'd wait until they were alone before sharing it with Melanie.

"Glad to hear it," Dan said. "I bet you can't wait to start your new job," he said to Melanie. "Classes start in two weeks. If you need help navigating the campus, I'm more than willing to show you around."

"That's very kind of you," she replied.

Josh barely listened to their conversation. His focus remained on the garage and the horrific cries he'd heard from there. They had settled down since Dan approached, but that didn't mean anything.

"We must get going," Melanie said.

"You folks have yourselves a great day."

Melanie pulled Josh away, though his thoughts remained on the situation. Something was wrong. He couldn't put his finger on it, but he knew that his new neighbors were up to something. They were all acting strange.

When they got out of earshot, Josh spoke in a quiet tone. "I think they're hiding someone. What else could it be?"

Melanie let out a nervous giggle. "I'm starting to think that the move has got you rattled."

"Wait. Didn't you hear those screams? Haven't you seen the people going toward Dan's house? It's freaking weird."

"Hun, I know you think you heard something. I did too, but my interpretation is far less nefarious than yours."

"What, so now you believe Dan and his cat story?"

"It's plausible. We have no reason to suspect otherwise."

"What about all the people and how they bring things his way and leave without them? What about all the old-time skirts?"

"Maybe you just didn't see the things in the first place? There's got to be a rational explanation for what you *think* you're seeing."

Josh's irritation grew. Where had this come from? Melanie was always on his side. Always.

"Why don't you believe me?" he asked.

She let out a sigh. "Because I think you're making it up as a coping mechanism to deal with our move. I know you didn't want to come here at first, but I'm glad we did. It's an amazing opportunity for me. For us." She stopped, turning him toward her. "Let's not do anything rash. Besides," she said, offering a sultry glance and biting her bottom lip, "I have something in mind that might ease your tension."

5

After dinner and then enjoying a wild session in bed, both Melanie and Josh fell asleep. It was early evening, but both were exhausted.

Around ten at night, Josh woke with an aching in his groin. He got up to relieve himself, and after flushing the toilet, he heard a strange noise coming from the basement. At first he thought it was their air conditioning unit. They hadn't lived there long enough to acclimate to the normal sounds of the new house. But the more he listened, the more worried he became. It didn't sound like anything mechanical.

Leaving Melanie in bed, he dressed in pajama pants and a t-shirt, then crept down the basement steps, flicking on the lights at the bottom. He stood still and listened.

The sound came from under the stairs where he'd put the box when they moved in. *Is it mice?* he thought. But it was louder, like a deep thudding noise.

Adrenaline pumped within him. His heart thudded in his chest. Josh slowly walked toward the source of the noise. Peering under the stairs and expecting to find... what? A monster? A rat? An evil being?

There was nothing. Just the box. But the sound persisted, and it seemed to come from the patch in the wall he'd seen when he dropped off the box. Three feet high and just as wide, it was built into the wall facing the front of the house.

The sound was coming from the other side, as though someone was lightly knocking inside the wall.

"What the hell?" he whispered. Should he open it? What if someone was on the other side? What if it was an animal like a raccoon or something? Melanie would be pissed if he let a trash panda loose in the house.

Knock. Knock. Knock.

That wasn't an animal.

Josh swallowed hard, then pried the wood from the wall. A man, maybe college aged, leaped out at him and knocked him over.

"What the fuck!" Josh screamed. The man was naked and covered in mud and dried blood. His large eyes were moons on his crust-covered face.

He rolled away from Josh and stood on shaky legs. Thick chunks of flesh were removed from his thighs, leaving deep crevasses of exposed muscle. The wounds were fairly fresh as they weeped blood.

"They're fucking crazy! The shit they're doing. Get out. Get out!"

"What are you doing in my house?"

The man struggled to stand, backing away toward the door. "They'll get you. They're insane!"

He bumped against the sliding glass door. Realizing his chance at freedom, the man slid the door open and ran into the darkness.

Josh stood like a statue. His mouth hung open and his brain took a moment to process what the hell he'd just witnessed.

Melanie rushed down the stairs. "What was that? Are you okay?"

Josh turned to his wife, unsure of what to say. Instead, he just pointed at the open door. Melanie pursed her lips, then walked toward the door to close it. "What's all over the glass? Is that... is that blood? Are you hurt?"

"No. I'm okay," he said. "There was a man in our basement."

"Our basement? Did he break in? We need to call the police!"

"There's a door under the stairs. He was inside. When I opened it, he rushed me, then warned me that 'they're fucking crazy.' He warned me to get out. What does he mean?"

Melanie's face went from fear to confusion. "I have no idea. You said there's a door under there?" She approached the stairs and peered in. "Damn." She crouched to get a better look. "I think it goes pretty far back."

"What do we do?" Josh asked.

"I think we need to call the police," Melanie said while still peering into the tunnel. "What if there's more people in there? They've got underground access to our house."

"He said they're crazy. What if he meant our neighbors?"

She stepped out from under the stairs to face him. "Our neighbors? Come on, you've been trying to find a fault in them since we moved in. They seem normal enough."

"Are they? You and I both heard screams coming from Dan's place. Plus, there seems to be a lot of our neighbors that go there and leave after dropping something off."

"I highly doubt he's doing anything that involves this," she said, waving toward the tunnel.

"Maybe we should look inside," Josh said.

"Are you insane?"

"That's what that guy said they were, whoever 'they' are."

She looked to him, the tunnel, and back to him. "I still think it's better if we call the police."

"Let's look inside first, and then we can call them. Deal?"

Melanie let out a deep sigh. Josh knew she was on his side, but she was searching for a reason not to be. "Fine, but we're not going far. As soon as we're done, we're calling the police."

"Deal."

6

After changing into jeans and a t-shirt and grabbing a flashlight, Josh headed into the tunnel with Melanie right behind him.

"I can't believe we're doing this," she said.

"I just want to see where this goes," Josh replied.

After crawling on their hands and knees for about twenty feet, the tunnel's ceiling rose high enough for them to walk upright. All sides of the tunnel were hard-packed dirt. Spiders had made their home there, cobwebs decorating the upper reaches of the tunnel.

"This is nuts. We must be under our yard right now," Josh said. "Why do you think this is here?"

"I don't know, but I'm starting to get a really bad feeling about this," Mel replied. She pulled her cellphone out of her pocket.

"Don't call the police yet," Josh said. "Let's see where this goes first."

"I'm not. I pulled up the maps app. We can track where we're going and if your wild theory is right."

Josh smiled. "I knew I loved you for a reason."

"And all this time I thought it was because of my nice ass."

The brief moment of levity helped calm Josh's nerves.

Josh followed the tunnel until it ended at a crossing where they could go left or right. If his bearings were correct, going left would take them toward Dan's house.

"This is crazy," he muttered. "I can't believe this is under our neighborhood. Why was that guy in here?" He looked left and right, then took the left path.

"This is going toward Dan's place," Melanie said. "What do you think it's for?"

"I'm honestly surprised it hasn't sunken in yet. What's holding it up? How far underground do you think we are?"

"It can't be too far if I can still get a cell signal. I mean, it's weak, but there."

They pushed on, Josh deciding to remain quiet to keep from being discovered. Ten minutes into their trek, they came upon another branch in the tunnel, this one going left.

"Where are we?" he asked Mel. She glanced down at her phone.

"This is the house right next to ours. Holy shit, this is crazy! Do you think these go to all the houses here?"

"I'm starting to suspect that. But why? Who needs this?" Josh followed the path straight ahead. Everything pointed to something odd going on at Dan's place. The tunnel *had* to go there.

Moving with a purpose, he followed the tunnel until they came to the end where it branched to either side of them.

Melanie spoke before he asked. "If we go left, we'll be at Dan's place. I'm guessing if we go right we'll be under the road and headed toward the houses over there."

Josh headed to their left. Melanie grabbed his shoulder and he turned to face her.

"Are you sure we should be doing this?" she asked. "What if, I don't know, what if something bad is going on?"

"We have to find out. That guy wasn't running from the dark. He was scared. You should've seen his legs. They took out chunks of muscle. I have no idea how he even stood, to be honest with you. Do you still have reception?"

Melanie looked to her phone and nodded.

"If we run into something bad, dial 911. Got it?" She seemed to accept his decision and didn't counter his argument. Josh took that as a sign to continue.

Following the tunnel, they reached the end. Unlike at their house, the tunnel's ceiling didn't get lower. The door at the end wasn't small like at their house, either. It was a normal-sized wooden door. Cobwebs and dirt covered the outside, but the door-knob was clear of anything as though it had been used frequently.

"I don't think we should go in there," Melanie said. "It's trespassing."

"We have to know. Where did that guy come from? Is something happening in there? What about those screams? You and I both know that wasn't a cat. Just make sure you're ready to make that call if we need to," Josh said.

"Shit," she replied. "I don't have service here. We really should turn around. There's got to be a logical explanation to this."

Josh's heart thrummed in his chest. Maybe Melanie was right. Maybe they should just turn back and forget that there's an elaborate system of tunnels under their neighborhood that led to every-one's houses. *No*, he thought. He couldn't leave. Not when someone had access to their home whenever they wanted.

Without saying a word, Josh grabbed the doorknob and turned. To his surprise, it wasn't locked.

7

Inside the door was a cavernous room. Old overhead fluorescent lights bathed the space in a soft, yellowish glow, illuminating cages built into the earthen walls.

"What the fuck?" Josh said.

"I don't like this," Melanie added. "We need to turn back. This is crazy."

There were two kinds of cages that Josh could see. Some were tall enough for a person to stand in and wide enough to remind him of a jail cell. The other kind were smaller, like four feet by four feet in size. Both kinds had metal bars, again mimicking a jail cell. Josh walked toward one of the small cages and peered inside, shining his light into the darkness.

A set of eyes looked back at him. Deeply set on a man's dirty face, they conveyed a mix of shock and fear. The man's legs were missing. The bottom of his cage was soiled with shit and piss. The naked man had one arm while the other, like his legs, was missing. Blood crusted over the wounds, making Josh think they weren't that old.

"Holy shit!" Josh said.

"No more, please," the man begged. "I don't want to feed it anymore. Please let me go." His voice was weak and strained. The voice of defeat. The man had been resigned to his fate but latched onto Josh as though he had a say in his freedom.

"Oh my God," he heard Melanie say from across the room. She had gone to one of the taller cells and looked inside.

17

Josh couldn't tear his gaze off of the mutilated man in front of him. The pain and fear inside the cage a powerful attractant.

"Josh, what's going on in here? Who are these people?" Melanie asked.

"I won't say a word about who did this," the man in front of Josh said. "Just let me go. My parents... they need me. Please."

Josh had no words. No comfort. No way to ease this young man's pain.

From the far end of the room, a door opened, and Josh nearly pissed his pants. He tore his gaze away from the man and faced Melanie, the sheer terror on her face evident.

"We need to leave," she whispered. Josh nodded.

The soft crunch of footsteps on the dirt floor grew closer. Josh glanced at the far end of the room and realized that it turned, L-shaped, into another section. That was where the sound was coming from. And it was getting closer.

They couldn't go back through the door without giving themselves away. Instead, Josh spotted an open cell door near the end of the room and nodded toward it. Melanie saw what he was indicating and shook her head no.

"We have to. It's our only option," Josh whispered. She continued to shake her head no, a small tear running down her cheek. Josh knew it wasn't ideal, but they had no choice. He gently nudged her in that direction, and they entered the cell, clicking off their lights and pushing themselves flat against the inner wall.

8

Footsteps drew closer, and Josh worried that maybe going into the cell was a bad idea. But then they stopped. Metal clanged as one of the cell doors was opened.

"No. Please. No more. You can't. This is wrong. Please. Please!" Josh recognized it as the man he'd just seen moments ago.

"Shut up. You're on the menu today, and there's nothing you can do about it." The voice. It was Dan's. Josh pushed his lips together to keep himself quiet. Dan! He knew the bastard was up to something. What did he mean the other man was on the menu? Images of Dan and his wife sitting down to feast on the man's leg flashed in front of him. Is that what they did to the man he discovered in his own basement? A sickening, nauseating feeling settled in his gut, twisting and curling inside. What the fuck was going on?

"What about those other people? Why not get them? You don't have to do this anymore. Get them instead!" the man cried out. Josh's face lost all its color. If Dan listened to the man, they would surely get caught.

"Shut your mouth," Dan growled.

The footsteps grew closer again. Josh and Melanie slowly scooted to the back of the cell, crouching low and praying to remain hidden.

Across the hall from them, a light flickered to life. What Josh thought was another cell turned out to be a much larger room. In the center was a metal table big enough to fit a body with a single light bulb dangling from a cord above it.

On either side of the table were metal cabinets and on the far wall, a large silver refrigerator.

Dan walked by with the mutilated man in his grasp. He heaved the man up to the table and slammed him down. The legless and nearly armless torso thrashed, but Dan was clearly in control. He pulled straps across the man's chest and lower abdomen, securing him tightly to the table.

Melanie let out a yip, and Dan turned toward them, though Josh was certain he didn't see them. The faint light from the other room didn't reach that far, and they remained in the shadows. Josh spun his head back toward her. She'd covered her mouth, another tear rolling down her cheek.

Josh turned back toward Dan, who had frozen in place with his attention toward them. Several paralyzing moments ticked by. Josh was sure they'd been caught. Finally, Dan turned back to the man on the table.

"Please, no!" the man cried out. Dan smacked him hard.

"Shut up," he growled. Reaching in a cabinet behind him, Dan grabbed what looked like a hacksaw.

"No. No, no, no, no!" the man said. "Why don't you take it from Brock instead? He's got more to offer than me."

"I'll worry about him. Your time is now."

"He escaped, didn't he?" the man on the table asked. "I heard him. He's out there, isn't he?"

Dan grabbed hold of the man's remaining arm, pulled it out to the side, and started to cut into his flesh near his shoulder.

"No, please!"

Dan snarled.

The man screamed as the blade dug in. A sickening sound like meat being torn was barely discernible above the man's cries for mercy. Blood leaked out of him. The stump of a body wriggled on the metal table. But Dan kept going.

The sound of the blade in the meaty part of the man's arm suddenly changed sound as Dan cut into the bone. The man howled terribly, his trunk shaking wildly.

Melanie whimpered, clutching Josh's arm in a vice-like grip. The two of them watched in rapt attention as Dan continued to cut through the muscle and bone.

"Almost," Dan said, more to himself than to the man on the table. Then with a few more cuts, he set the saw to the side and hoisted up the severed arm. Blood drained onto the table. Dan sniffed it like a fine wine. He set the arm on top of the cabinets, then pulled several wooden sticks out of a glass container. They were coated at the end with a silvery substance.

The man on the table groaned and whimpered, blood leaking from the fresh wound.

Dan applied the wooden sticks to the wound. Once he did, the man screamed loudly. His body convulsed. Dan continued to touch the silvery substance to the bloody wound.

"We gotta make sure you don't lose any more blood. Preserving what's left is important to my Lord."

Josh's insides were roiling. His jackhammering heart felt like it was going to explode.

When Dan was done, he took the arm to the refrigerator. When he opened it, Josh could see plastic containers filled with various limbs and internal organs such as hearts and livers. There was even a brain. He shut his eyes tight, hoping that it was all a nightmare. He hoped that when he opened them, it would all be gone, but it wasn't.

Dan unstrapped the man from the table and hoisted him over his shoulder. With no limbs left, he was no threat at all. He carried the man back to his cell and locked him inside. Returning to the operating room, he cleaned his tools at a sink that Josh hadn't seen earlier, put the tools back up, then turned off the light as he left.

9

When Josh turned to Melanie, tears were running down her face. Her lips quivered. Her body shook. Josh was speechless. What the fuck had they stumbled upon? Who were these sick bastards?

He wrapped his arms around Melanie, and they waited several moments until Josh thought they were cleared to leave. Standing and helping Melanie to her feet, he spoke in a whisper.

"I think it's clear. We need to get out of here."

She nodded. Josh's heart broke for those in the cages and for the trauma he'd just witnessed. He wanted to free whoever might be kept prisoner, but what if Dan came back? What if there were others with him? The man was clearly capable of horrendous things.

This was something the police would have to handle. It wasn't for him to be the hero, and that felt sickening. Leaving those poor souls behind crushed him, but his priority was getting him and Melanie to safety. Once they were free, he could worry about the others.

"Let's go," he whispered.

"What about them?" Melanie said, indicating the cages. Her heart was in the same place as his, but he couldn't let that sway him.

"We'll call the police and let them take care of it. We have to get ourselves out of here first."

"No. We have to help them." Melanie broke from his embrace and rushed to one of the cages. She grabbed the bars with both hands and shook, but they didn't budge. "There's a girl in there!" she said to Josh. He shoved a finger against his lips in a gesture to remain silent. "Help me! We have to free her."

"Mel," he said in a quiet voice. "We have to leave. Please, let us get the authorities to help."

Melanie glanced into the cage, back to Josh, and then back to the cage. Large tears rolled down her cheeks. "Oh God, I'm so sorry," she said to whoever was inside.

Forcing herself to back away, Melanie reached out and took Josh's hand.

"I know this sucks, but we aren't equipped for this. We need to get to safety," Josh said.

A door flung open. A beam of light bobbed against the earthen walls. "Oh shit," Josh muttered. Adrenaline flooded him, spiked with fear. He was frozen like a deer in headlights, unable to get his legs to move. The light turned the corner at the end of the tunnel and suddenly it blinded him.

"What the fuck?" the person said. It was Dan! Josh pulled Melanie toward the exit out of instinct.

"You shouldn't be down here!" The light bobbed as Dan ran toward them. That's all the motivation Josh needed to spur into action.

"Come on, let's go!" he yelled. Pulling Melanie with him, he reached the door where they entered and flung it open. He shoved Melanie ahead of him and slipped through, slamming the door closed just as Dan reached it.

"Go, go!" he yelled.

The tunnels were dark and stunk of rotten earth, of putrid decay, of death. Melanie ran ahead in the dark, and Josh followed. Behind him, he heard the door open, and he glanced back to see Dan outlined by the glow of the lights from the other side, but his flashlight was off. Then the silhouetted figure vanished. Josh didn't know if that meant Dan left or was coming after them, but he didn't want to wait and find out.

They reached a crossroads, and Josh desperately tried to remember the way back. They'd used Melanie's phone earlier, but there was no time now.

"Which way?" he asked, his voice carrying the panic timbre of someone on the edge of death.

"I don't know," Melanie admitted. "This way?" she said, indicating their right. Josh followed her suggestion. If Dan was after them, waiting around to decide the correct path was not an option.

They followed the tunnel to their right and discovered another crossroads about ten feet in.

"Shit!" Josh said. He didn't remember this from their way in. They must have gone the wrong way. He and Melanie stood silently contemplating their predicament when footsteps sounded in the tunnel behind them.

"Come on," Josh said. Then he guided Melanie to their left. He only hoped it was the right way to get the hell out of there.

10

Josh's decision turned out to be a terrible one. The tunnel extended straight for about fifty feet and then the ceiling dropped low, just like it had from his basement. The smaller tunnel meant they needed to fall to their knees and crawl on all fours.

"Son of a bitch!" he said. Behind him, a quick burst of light illuminated the darkness and then flooded the tunnel.

"Get back here," Dan growled.

There was no time to wait. They had to push on.

"Mel, go!" Josh said. His heart had leaped into his throat.

"Where does it go?" she replied.

"I don't care!"

Melanie crawled into the smaller section of the tunnel. Josh couldn't see what was ahead of her, but he could see Dan closing in on him.

Melanie struggled to make much progress, getting about ten feet in before she slowed. "There's a door!" she called out.

"Get through it. Hurry!" Josh replied. He'd just gotten to the edge of the smaller section and was crawling inside after her.

"I can't open it. The door is stuck!"

"Push harder!" Josh said. He glanced back and saw Dan only feet away from him. "Hurry! You have to get out!"

Melanie beat on the door, the sound echoing in the small, confined tunnel. Josh tried to crawl faster to catch up, but Dan grabbed hold of his ankle. A bolt of fear raced through Josh's body.

"You can't go," Dan said. "You're gonna be given over to our Lord, just like all the others. Don't you understand that?"

His voice was strong but calm. There was no question he meant what he said. Josh just had no clue what the hell he was talking about.

"Get off me!" Josh said. He kicked his feet, and Dan held firm. Josh pulled back with his free leg and put everything he had into the kick. Dan's arm snapped when Josh's foot connected with his wrist.

Dan howled in pain, instantly releasing his grip.

Melanie had broken through if the sound of snapping wood meant anything. Suddenly the tunnel ahead of him had grown brighter. A quick thought of *Go to the light* crossed his mind.

Behind him, Dan growled and snarled. "You will never escape. Our Lord will get what belongs to him."

"Fuck your Lord," Josh snarled. Dan crawled in after Josh, but with his injured wrist, he moved much slower. Josh scurried toward the light.

"Come on, hurry!" Melanie called. Josh followed her voice, glancing back toward Dan to make sure he wasn't closing in.

When he reached the small door, he grabbed the sides and pulled himself out, a rebirthing man exiting into a new world. Melanie pulled him to his feet, and Josh stumbled but caught himself on a dresser.

"Where are we?" he asked, but didn't wait for an answer. Dan was crawling closer to them, snarling and shouting about "their Lord."

"You're both dead now!" Dan yelled. "Dead!"

"Help me with this," Josh said as he shoved the dresser closer to the door. "We can slow him down if nothing else."

Melanie helped as they pushed the five-drawer dresser over tiled floor until it blocked the little door. They finally got it into place. Dan beat on the backside of it.

"I'll carve you both myself! This is not over!"

"We need to get the hell out of here," Josh said. He took a

moment to get his bearings straight. They were in a basement similar to his own, though the door was not under the stairs, but along the open wall. Opposite them was a sliding glass door. It was a way out, and that was good enough for him.

"Call 911," Josh said. "We're getting out of here."

11

It was pitch black outside. Josh had no idea where they were. In the dark, the backyard and the house didn't look familiar. He half expected Dan to come bursting from the shadows with a bone saw. The images of him carving that poor man burned into his memory. The ranting about his "Lord" adding another layer of fear.

Melanie trembled as she spoke to the 911 operator. Her words were barely intelligible, but that wouldn't matter. Help was on the way.

She didn't stay on the line as the operator asked, instead clicking off the call. Her face had gone pale and expressionless. Josh wondered if she was in shock. He stepped to her, embracing her.

"I'm so sorry I brought us here. This is all my fault," she said.

"What? No. How could you know? These people are crazy. It's not anyone's fault but theirs."

Melanie sniffed and wiped the snot from her nose on her arm. "I can't believe this. It's insane."

A streetlight to their left indicated they were close to the road. Josh still wasn't sure where they were, but it was better in the light than not.

"Let's get out of here and hope the police find us." They walked across the yard until they reached the road. Sirens in the distance were a welcome relief. Their nightmare was nearly over, and crazy Dan would be exposed for the lunatic that he was.

12

As the sun rose while the police questioned them in their house, several officers had entered the tunnel in their basement.

They found nothing.

They claimed the tunnel only went fifty feet in and then ended. There were no connecting tunnels, just a wall of dirt.

"That's impossible!" Josh said when they reported back to Officer O'Neil, the man that had been talking to them. "I swear, it's there! We followed it to the end of the road. There was a massive room filled with cages and people were trapped in them."

"I'm sorry, but my officers haven't found a thing. I'm not sure what's going on here, but wasting department resources is not a great way to introduce yourself to the neighbors."

"Fuck!" Josh said. He knew they weren't making this up. He and Melanie had seen the same horrors underground. The image of the limbless man clear as day in his mind.

"Next time, you better make damn sure you know what you're talking about," Officer O'Neil said. "All right, boys, let's get out of here." The remaining police officers gathered up all of their gear, packed into their squad cars, and left.

Josh and Melanie sat at their dining room table staring out toward the road, speechless. It took Josh several minutes before he could gather the words to speak.

"This was real, right?" he whispered. "We didn't make it up. We both saw it. Tell me I'm not losing my mind."

Melanie blinked and composed herself. "It was real. We're not staying here. I don't care what the police say. Something evil is happening around here. Something—" Melanie went quiet, her gaze fixated out the window. Josh followed her lead, and his mouth dropped open.

It was Martha Williamson and Regina Thomas. Both were dressed as before with long-sleeved shirts and long skirts.

"What the fuck," Josh whispered. It was only seven in the morning, and after the nightmares they'd just been through, seeing these two walking toward their door sent a shiver down his spine.

Martha knocked.

Melanie and Josh exchanged a worried glance. Martha knocked again, louder.

"I know you're in there. This is an urgent matter."

"Maybe... maybe they know something," Melanie said.

Josh went to the door and opened it, Melanie standing just behind him.

"Hello?" Josh said.

"Mr. and Mrs. Jordan, you have violated the most sacred of all the rules of the Pine Ridge Homeowners Association. You have angered our Lord. Do you know what that means for our neighborhood?"

"Lady, I don't have any clue what you're talking about. Sacred rules? We discovered Dan is butchering people in underground tunnels that go all through the neighborhood! Are you gonna tell me that it's not real, just like the police?"

Martha and Regina shared a look, and Josh was sure that they knew it was true.

"You know, don't you? You fucking know!"

"Mr. Jones, this cannot stand. I'm afraid as a violation of rule number 1.3 of the homeowners code, you must pay a fine."

"What?" Melanie said over his shoulder. "You're crazy!"

"Crazy, ma'am? It's in the rules. Have you read them?"

Both Josh and Melanie shook their heads no.

"Had you taken the time to acquaint yourself with them, you would have known," Martha said.

"Fuck you," Josh said, then slammed the door. Who were they to legitimize the evil they'd experienced? They were all crazy.

When he turned around, he froze. His legs trembled. A warm stream of urine unleashed itself and soaked his pants.

There stood Dan with one arm around Melanie's neck, keeping her silent. In the other was the saw from before.

"Our Lord always gets his due," Dan said.

Behind him on the porch, Martha and Regina started to chant in unison, their words shaking him to his core.

"Praise our Lord. Praise Satan. Give us our strength as we give you your blood. Praise our Lord. Praise Satan." They repeated the phrase over and over.

Josh stepped toward Melanie, and as he did, the door opened behind him and something hard smashed the back of his head. He crumpled to the floor.

The last thing he remembered was Melanie screaming, the women chanting, and an arm landing with a meaty thud on the floor, splashing blood on his face.

"Praise our Lord," he heard, then it all went black.

THE MOONDIAL

MJ MARS

Lennie flicked her ankle, the ball whacking against her shoelaces and arching perfectly to meet the top of her other boot. She juggled from foot to foot three more times before switching tack, so the ball landed on her knees, her thighs nudging it higher and higher until she ducked forward and caught it on the back of her neck. Just like the TikTok tutorials had shown her, she raised her shoulders and hunched a little. The ball remained stationary for a moment, squashing her chunky ponytail against her sweaty skin.

In her mind, she pulled off the maneuver with expert precision, the ball slipping down the front of her body and landing on her left foot, where she recommenced the keepie-uppie game without missing a beat.

In reality, the ball went wayward, sliding back off her shoulder and thudding onto the grass directly behind her. Frustration burst out of her in a chest-deep growl, and she turned and kicked it with all her might. She intended to smash it into the fence, enjoying the thud of her frustration shaking the wood in the posts, but it sailed directly over the top. Lennie watched in horrified slow-motion as the soccer ball disappeared into the next door neighbor's garden. A second later came the noise of a pot shattering.

Heart sinking, Lennie ran to the fence and peered through the hole in the wood, formed by a natural ring rather than a cut-out. It just so happened to be at eye-height so Lennie could peer through. Not that she ever did. The neighbors were creepy as hell, and the ring of strange, unpainted, and semi-formed gnomes that stood around their sundial were the first thing she saw when she stood at eye-height to the hole.

Sure enough, her ball had hit the sundial. The metal prong at the top had been dislodged so that it rested flat on the clockface, and when the ball had bounced off it, it had landed on one of the gnomes. The gnome lay in three pieces, jagged brown shards sticking up like a lethal weapon on the concrete.

Lennie swore loudly. Now that she was fourteen, her parents let the odd word go, but she knew not to make too much of a habit of it. This was definitely a suitable occasion to drop the f-bomb. She said it again, a little louder this time, feeling a rush of exhilaration that momentarily overrode the anxiety she felt at damaging the Sinclairs' gnomes. The Sinclairs were the weirdest people Lennie thought she'd ever meet in her whole life. It sucked to be living next door to them. Staring through the hole with her heart jumping at the thought of her parents making her go next door to apologize, Lennie swore again for good measure.

An eye appeared in the hole on the other side of the fence.

Already on edge, Lennie squealed and fell back, biting the side of her tongue when she landed on her butt.

"Leonora?" came a sharp-sounding voice from next door's garden.

"It's Lennie," Lennie grumbled, clambering to her feet and dusting grass from her shorts.

"Are your parents home?" the voice behind the fence said.

Lennie's felt her stomach drop. "Yes."

"I'm coming over. Tell them to expect me, Leonora."

Expect her? What did that even mean? Lennie dragged her feet through the grass as she made her way reluctantly to the house. She found her mom working at her laptop in the kitchen, and her glasses immediately fogged from the steam coming from the ever-running coffee machine.

"Mrs. Next Door is coming over," Lennie mumbled, reaching into the fridge and grabbing a jug of orange juice.

At the table, Lennie's mom looked up from her work in confusion. "Huh? What did you say?"

"Mrs. Sinclair, from next door, is coming over," Lennie clarified, closing the fridge door. She took three gulps of juice and swiped her arm across her mouth. The juice left a sticky trail that clung to the hairs of her arm.

Lennie's mom spun her office chair around so that it faced her. "Why is Mrs. Sinclair coming here?"

"I think she's bringing my ball back."

"And why hasn't she just thrown it back over the fence?"

"I may have hit one tiny thing..." Lennie winced.

Mom threw her hands up. "Lennie! We've talked about this."

The doorbell chimed, saving her from the onslaught of her

mother's exasperation. Following her mom to the door, Lennie hung back, sheepish, in the hallway.

"Mrs. Sinclair. How nice to see you."

The woman was tall and wiry, her nails long and polished red. She wore her hair in an old-fashioned style, coiled around and pinned at the back, and her silken shirt was buttoned high up on her neck. To Lennie, it always seemed as though Mrs. Next Door had stepped through a portal directly from the 1800s. The old woman spoke in clipped and angry tones. "I regret it isn't under the best circumstances. Leonora has caused criminal damage on my property."

"Criminal?"

"Criminal?" Lennie echoed, stepping forward with her fists balled. "I only broke a stupid gnome."

"That gnome was in my family for generations. Besides which, I'm referring to my moon dial."

"You mean sundial?" Mom asked.

"It is a moon dial. More precious even than the gnome itself."

Lennie could tell that her mom was keen to nip the argument in the bud and get the strange neighbor far away from their doorstep. She reached for her purse. "Of course, we'll pay to replace both, er... items."

"Unfortunately, they are both priceless."

Lennie watched her mother's hands flutter around her purse, thrown off by the statement. "Well then, is there something else we can do to make it up to you?"

"Yes. There is. I have been called away to an emergency this evening and would like Leonora to watch over my father."

"Father?" Lennie blurted. She couldn't believe Mrs. Sinclair still had a living father. She looked about eighty years old herself.

"You do know that Lennie is only fourteen, Mrs. Sinclair. That's a big responsibility for a little girl."

"Nonsense. Mr. Sinclair has suffered with a number of health issues over the years, rendering him immobile and without his senses. And I assume that you and your husband will be here next door the whole time?"

"Well, of course, but that's not the point," Mom told her, growing more flustered. "I can come and take care of him."

"He doesn't know you!"

"Does he know Lennie?"

"Well, no, of course not. But she is a small girl. He gets frightened around adults that he doesn't know."

"Then I don't think it's such a great idea," Mom said softly.

Mrs. Sinclair's eyes blazed under fine-plucked white brows. "Well then, you shall be hearing from the police regarding a criminal damage charge."

"Wait!" Mom cried, looking from Lennie to the neighbor and back again. "How long are you expecting her to stay with your father?"

"Mom!" Lennie protested but closed her mouth when her mom held back an upturned palm like a traffic warden. That was a sure sign to quit talking and let her handle it.

"Three hours. The errand I am to run will take place between seven p.m. and ten p.m."

"Lennie goes to bed at nine-thirty," Mom said.

"I believe it's the same at the juvenile detention facility. Lights out promptly and all that."

Lennie watched her mom's back lift and fall in a heavy sigh. She knew that she wouldn't really be sent to juvie for breaking a gnome, but Mrs. Sinclair was notorious on the street for keeping enemies and escalating issues until the nice neighbors either moved away or avoided their side of the road altogether. Mom loved this house. There was no way she was going to allow this crazy woman to spoil it.

"He's quite easy to care for. He won't say or do anything. He remains seated in his chair. Leonora simply has to keep an eye on him and the property until I get back."

Mom turned to Lennie, her expression grim. "We'll be here the whole time. You can FaceTime me and I will run right over if you need me."

"Mom!"

"It's just for three hours, Lennie. You owe them your time for breaking their property."

"Indeed, she does," Mrs. Sinclair said. "Which reminds me. Here."

From behind her back, she produced Lennie's ball. It had been popped, the leather sphere drooping around her hand like a melted clock in a surrealist painting.

When the old woman had gone, Lennie sulked over the kitchen counter, purposefully preventing her mom from going back to work.

"I don't want to go."

"You should have thought about that before you got too close to their fence. We've had this talk over and over, Len. You must be more careful."

"It was just a stupid gnome!"

"Well, it obviously meant a lot to her. Perhaps now you'll treat other people's belongings better."

Lennie glared at the back of her mom's head and waited until she was in the middle of typing a sentence onto her laptop. "What if I hadn't broken the gnome today?"

Mom stabbed at the keyboard with agitated fingers, then slowly spun the chair around. "What?"

"She said she had an errand to run and there couldn't be a strange adult. Who would look after Mr. Sinclair if I didn't?"

Mom took a sip of coffee, biding time while she thought about it. In the end, she shrugged and said, "I guess she was planning on asking you anyway, but instead of being paid for it, you now have to do it for free."

Lennie mulled that over, fingering the puncture wound in the ball. Instead of a crack or a small hole from where the sharp shards of the gnome's pottery had gouged the leather, the break in the ball was sleek and fine. The width of a kitchen knife.

The old man was sitting in a large, leather-bound armchair. Lennie's eyes were drawn to his feet, which looked too large for his frail frame. He wore brown slippers with tan socks and his trousers were hitched up, revealing inches of pale-yellow ankles that were marked with multiple age spots. Bruises dappled the prominent shin bones, as though Mr. Sinclair spent a lot of time walking into things. His hands were equally bruised and marked, however, resting gently in his lap. Lennie quickly looked away from his nails, which were ridged and stained, the whites at the tip turned black from the grime that had collected between the nail and his skin.

His blue-and-white striped shirt was far too large for him, gaping at the neck and revealing a sallow chest and sagging chicken neck. There was a puffy, pink scar on the front of the old man's throat, and Lennie wondered if he had been in an accident. Her cousin had needed a breathing tube when he got injured in a football game in college and, although his young skin had now healed so well you could barely see it, the scar from his tracheotomy was in the exact same place.

Lennie lifted her gaze to his face, then wished she hadn't. The old man's chin was unkempt with wiry stubbled whiskers, two tracks of dried and crusty white drool framing his chin. His eyes were open but unseeing and glazed, reminding Lennie of watered-down milk. He wore a funny little smirk on his thin, dry lips, and his bald head looked like a map of the world, age spots and bruising creating continents and islands across his scalp.

"This is my father, Mr. Sinclair," Mrs. Sinclair told her.

If it had been any other human on the planet, Lennie would have found it weird that she called him "Mr.", but she was more than used to the stuck-up ways of her next-door neighbor.

"Do I need to, you know... do anything with him?" Lennie asked, eyeing the old man warily. If Mrs. Sinclair mentioned anything about diapers, Lennie was going to head straight for the door.

"No. As I already stated, my father is completely incapacitated and quite happy where he is. He does not leave the chair, and so all you have to do is stay in the room with him and make sure he is all right while I'm gone."

There was a static-like tension in the room, and Lennie didn't like it one bit. But she'd promised her mom she would stick it out and take it as a "life lesson," so that was what she was going to do. She was torn between wanting Mrs. Sinclair to leave and go to whatever event it was that couldn't possibly wait, and simultaneously hoping she would stay so Lennie didn't have to deal with the creepy old man on her own.

It wasn't just the man himself who was creepy. The room was oppressive with shadows, the blinds tilted so that only thin slivers of light hit the far wall. There was no color or comfort in the furniture and fittings of the living space. The colors were muted, a throwback to the '70s; grubby-brown carpet and a dark velvet three-piece suite of furniture backed up against the walls. The TV table was dark walnut, as was the chunky coffee table that stood in the center of the room, presumably where Mr. Sinclair picked up most of his bruises. The walls and ceiling had a yellow hue, as though someone had smoked heavily on the premises but, instead of smoke, the house smelled of artificial sweetener and dust.

"I'm leaving now. You know where the kitchen and bathroom are. You have no reason to either go up or down stairs, and I implore you to certainly not go down. It is very unsafe." Mrs. Sinclair fixed Lennie with a hard look, as if she was daring her to argue. She didn't have to worry. Lennie's plan was to sit and play on her phone for the nightmarish three hours ahead of her, then get the hell out of there as soon as Mrs. Sinclair got home.

For the first hour, Lennie lost herself in a game. She occasionally looked up and checked on the old man, but each time she did, he was exactly the same. He didn't move a muscle. After a while, Lennie started to feel kind of bad for him. Here was a man who had no quality of life whatsoever. Judging by what Mrs. Sinclair had told her, he was unable to think, speak, hear, or see. He couldn't get up and move around on his own. Lennie knew that as soon as she was able to replace her ball, she'd be back out in her garden playing kick around all day if she wanted to. Mr. Sinclair couldn't even go to the kitchen to make himself a snack if he wanted.

Being so young, Lennie hadn't had much cause to consider being empathetic to anyone. Her world moved too fast, her thoughts mainly circling around her own wants and wishes. Even though she was getting bored out of her mind and the old man creeped her out a little, she was starting to understand why this kind of chore was considered a life lesson. She guessed Mrs. Sinclair had a lot to put up with. No wonder she was so uptight. When Lennie eventually got home that night, she vowed to think better of it when she caused noise or fooled around too close to the Sinclairs' fence.

Closing her game, Lennie switched to catching up with her friends to pass the time. The next time she checked the clock, there was only an hour and a half to go. It wasn't a huge amount of time, in the big scheme of things. Lennie finally began to relax.

Mr. Sinclair stood up.

There was no warning, no sound. One moment, Lennie was messaging a friend on Snapchat, showing her the weird furniture in the room. The next moment, she was aware of a shadow looming across her phone screen. She raised her head and saw that Mr. Sinclair had stood up, his eyes still blank and milky, that weird smirk still twisting his lips.

Lennie felt her heart drop into her stomach.

She watched, frozen, as the old man stayed on the spot, swaying slightly, his huge feet looking like a concrete block holding down a gangster's victim at the bottom of the sea.

"Um... Mr. Sinclair?" Lennie said. It was a stupid, instinctive move, since the man was unable to hear her.

The crazy old woman had told her he wouldn't move. So what the hell was this crap?

She took her phone off her knee and held it with her thumb ready to FaceTime her mom, just in case Mr. Sinclair started to get weird. It was a relief her parents were only mere feet away and would come to her rescue the moment she asked. But still, having the old and frail man who lived in his own world standing stock-still in front of her with that peculiar grin on his face was unnerving. Worse still, it seemed like his eyes were directly on her, even though his pupils weren't visible. His head was tilted down toward where she sat on the armchair, the eyeline of his gaze in perfect alignment with her own.

He was still standing stock-straight, so Lennie got cautiously to her feet, intending to guide him gently back down into the chair. But, as she stood, his head raised, as though those milky, unseeing eyes were constantly trailing hers.

His smirk became a triumphant smile, and he turned and strode to the door.

"Wait!" Lennie called, although she knew it was futile.

She reminded herself just how difficult losing your senses must be. As a fourteen-year-old, she felt invincible, as though nothing in her rapidly changing body could ever go wrong beyond the nightmare of puberty. But here was a man who couldn't hear, couldn't speak, and couldn't see. Just the thought of any one of those sped up her heart. For the first time in her life, she was conscious enough to be grateful that she had her health.

Despite her discomfort, she tried to stop thinking of herself and considered what might have caused the man to stand. She peered around to the armchair. Everything looked to be in order. There was nothing on the seat, nothing amiss that might have caused him to become uncomfortable. Although the thought of his toilet needs had freaked her out earlier, she checked that there were no wet patches or stains that needed to be tended to and realized that she was in fact fully capable of dealing with that kind of thing if it had happened. For the first time ever, she felt responsible for another human, and all she wanted to do was make sure he was comfortable.

Mr. Sinclair strode purposefully to the far side of the room.

Lennie dropped another f-bomb, although it felt less satisfying than the three she had used earlier that day in the garden.

Although she knew he couldn't see, Mr. Sinclair's hand struck out and landed perfectly with the door handle. Trying to gain her bearings, Lennie realized the door led to the basement. The place that Mrs. Sinclair had told her was off-limits for being dangerous.

"No, no, no!" Lennie pressed her thumb to the phone screen and brought up her contacts. She FaceTimed her mom and watched the old man tug open the door, panic growing, as her mom failed to pick up.

She rushed after Mr. Sinclair, tugging at the almost-closing door and looking down the stairwell to find him already halfway down.

"Oh, shit!" she yelled, the liberation at being able to swear dampened by the sense of pure panic she felt as she watched the frail old man striding down into the black.

Mercifully, her phone began to chime, her mom's picture showing on the screen.

She swiped to answer, but instead of her mom's grinning face flooding the screen, all she could see was their kitchen at home. The table was laid for two and she guessed her parents had planned some kind of loser date-night with Lennie being out of the house. It looked as though her dad had cooked up a storm, laying out shrimp and sauced pasta with a huge green and red salad and garlic baguette pieces. The food was untouched.

"Mom?" Lennie spoke into the phone, hoping the urgency in her voice would stop her parents cuddling or kissing or whatever they were doing. She watched the screen, and the phone began to move as though it was being held by someone behind the lens. "Mom, I can't see you. Turn the screen around."

Lennie frowned down at the livestream, wondering what the hell her mother was doing. They'd FaceTimed on countless occasions, so she knew how to do it. Granted, her dad was pretty useless when it came to technology, but Mom was usually a bit of a whizz.

She watched her screen as the phone moved through the house, away from the kitchen and down the hallway to the front door. *Thank goodness,* Lennie thought. *At least she's coming over.* She wondered if her mom was speaking, trying to explain what was going on, and so she turned her volume up high and lifted the phone close to her ear.

There was no sound, no footsteps or chatter from her mother. Instead, a low, rattling breathing came through the speaker.

It didn't sound like her mom.

Looking back at the screen, she watched as their front door opened as though it had been pushed by an invisible hand. A streak of red marked the white wood underneath the door handle.

Fear was creeping through Lennie's limbs, giving her whole body a static electricity feeling that set her arm hairs on edge and caused her knees to shake as she carefully followed Mr. Sinclair down the steps. Although the breathing through the phone's speaker hadn't sounded right, she figured something must be wrong with Mom's iPhone. That would not only explain the weird sound, but also the fact that Mom must have thought she was Facetiming, when all Lennie could see was the camera view.

Rationalizing her thoughts in this way made it a lot easier for Lennie to resist the urge to bolt for the door and leave Mr. Sinclair to it. Besides, her mom was already halfway between their house and the Sinclairs's, judging by the hedges and gate that now passed by the screen.

She hopped down the final step and turned the corner.

The basement wasn't what Lennie had imagined. Instead of a dark and dingy space with open rafters and piles of discarded junk, the Sinclairs had converted theirs into an extra room, with a coarse red carpet, white-washed walls, and rows of bookshelves stuffed neatly with all kinds of books. There was a faux chandelier–style light hanging from the ceiling. The wiring must have been faulty, because the light flickered, plunging the room into darkness every few seconds.

Mr. Sinclair was standing under the light, his arms straight by his sides, the weird smirk still plastered on his face. Once more, it seemed as though his eyes were fixed on hers, although it should have been impossible to tell where his attention lay.

"Mr. Sinclair, we aren't supposed to be down here," she said.

As though he could hear every word, his grin widened. His teeth were rotten brown stubs, the gums coated in creamy white paste.

"Come on, Mom," Lennie begged, looking back to her screen. Her mom's phone was moving through the Sinclairs' home, heading right toward the basement steps. Relief was a wash of cool over Lennie's clammy skin. She called out loud, "Mom! We're down here."

Mr. Sinclair turned to his side and began to make mumbling

noises. He moved his hands around, as though he was trying to communicate with someone.

"I'm over here, Mr. Sinclair," Lennie told him, empathy keeping her feet planted to the ground while she waited for her mom.

The old man continued to grunt and murmur, his movements growing bolder as he got more and more excited.

She looked down at her screen and saw her mom descending the basement steps, the phone lifting and falling slightly with each step taken.

The video-like image on the screen turned the corner, and suddenly Lennie could see herself.

On her own phone, Lennie was standing in the basement, her eyes like saucers behind her glasses, staring in the direction of what should have been her mom with her iPhone. But there was nobody there. She stared hard at the stairwell, scanning the area to see whether her mom was holding out the phone to check if she was down there before heading down herself. Still, all Lennie saw was the empty entrance to the basement room.

She looked back at her display and screamed.

The "phone" that wasn't a phone had moved closer to her. As well as seeing herself onscreen, panicked and disheveled, she could see Mr. Sinclair behind her. He was still trying to animatedly converse. Now, Lennie could see what he was talking to.

Beside Mr. Sinclair stood a strange beast with horse-like legs. It wore tattered gray rags over a hairy body, and it was coated in a dusty substance that reminded Lennie of Mrs. Sinclair's stupid gnomes, the damned reason Lennie was here in the first place.

She whipped around and scanned the room but through her naked eyes could only see Mr. Sinclair, jabbering away with visible pleasure.

When she looked back at her phone display, the creature had turned from Mr. Sinclair and was staring right at Lennie. Its eyes were yellow orbs, as milky and unfocused as the old man's, but filled with menace and determination. Its head was smooth as if it had been roughly formed in mud and, when it opened its mouth, it dripped the slick of watered-down clay.

Panic overcame Lennie as she struggled to reconcile the fact that she could only see the creature on her phone screen, through Face-Time with a mother who wasn't even there. Every time she looked up with desperation, trying to focus on the threat in the room with her, she saw nothing but the old man, who was now clapping his hands with glee.

When she looked back at the screen, the monster was right next to her, looming over her. She felt its hands on her shoulders and saw smears of clay daub her skin.

The new family burst like a whirlwind through the house, three teenagers clattering out into the garden. Mrs. Sinclair watched from the upper window, her mouth pinched in a thin line as the youngsters began throwing a football around. Shortly after, the father came out and began installing a tetherball stand.

For a moment, Mrs. Sinclair regretted getting rid of Leonora and her parents.

Just for a moment, however. Breaking one of the gnomes was unforgivable. It had set Mr. Sinclair back years. He was only just regaining his full strength, thanks to the girl. She cast her gaze down to the moondial and the statuettes that surrounded it. Leonora's golem had replaced the broken figure, returning Mr. Sinclair to some of his former glory.

"Oh dear," he said from behind her, tugging back the curtain so he could get a better look at the garden next door. "How noisy."

Mrs. Sinclair leaned back into the strong chest of her husband

and peered up at him. His eyes were now sharp and clear, his hair thick and lustrous. When he wrapped his arms around her, it pleased her that his skin was now soft and full of youth, not marked with age spots and bruising.

Below them, the football sailed into the garden, missing the dial by mere feet.

Mrs. Sinclair sighed and picked up a kitchen knife from the windowsill. "Excuse me, dear. It's time I went and welcomed the new neighbors."

THE GIRL NEXT DOOR

STEVEN PAJAK

The summer heat clung to Jordan's skin like a second layer as she stood at the edge of her driveway, watching the Millers load their car. At seventeen, she was caught in that strange, in-between space between childhood and adulthood. The neighborhood was unusually still, as if it were holding its breath.

Mrs. Miller's voice broke the silence. "Jordan, are you sure you're okay with this? Two weeks is a long time."

Jordan smiled—her most practiced, reassuring smile, one she'd perfected in front of the mirror over the years. "Of course, Mrs. Miller. I'm happy to help."

Mr. Miller chuckled, the sound, as usual, grating on Jordan's nerves. "She's not a kid anymore, Helen. I'm sure she can handle feeding Whiskers and watering a few plants."

Jordan nodded, her gaze briefly flicking to the upstairs window of the Millers' house. She knew every inch of that place, every corner, every hidden nook. The thought of having it all to herself for two weeks brought a rush of excitement that she quickly buried beneath her calm exterior.

"We really appreciate this, Jordan," Mrs. Miller said, handing her an envelope. "Here's half the payment upfront. Feel free to use the house—watch TV, swim in the pool. Just no wild parties, okay?"

Jordan accepted the cash, which was earmarked for the MacBook she'd been saving for since last Christmas. Between the money she'd received from the holiday and her birthday that just passed, she almost had enough to buy the new model when it came out in September.

"Have a great anniversary cruise," Jordan said, waving as the Millers' car pulled away. She lingered there, watching them disappear around the corner, her mind already spinning with ideas.

Later that evening, as the sky deepened to a shade of bruised purple, Jordan sat on her bed, staring out her window at the Millers' house. It seemed different now, almost as if it were inviting her over, promising fun and maybe even a little danger.

The next morning, the house buzzed with the energy of her parents' preparations for their weekend trip to Chicago. Jordan sat at the breakfast table, half-listening to her mother's excited chatter about the Metallica concert they were attending, while her mind raced ahead.

"You sure you'll be okay on your own, sweetheart?" her father asked, his concern evident as he poured himself a final cup of coffee.

Jordan nodded, flashing a practiced look of teenage nonchalance. "Dad, I'm seventeen. I think I can handle a weekend alone."

Her mother laughed, ruffling Jordan's hair as she passed. "Our responsible girl. We're so proud of you."

A few minutes later, Jordan watched from the porch as their car pulled out of the driveway. She waved, maintaining the smile until they turned the corner. Then, with a surge of exhilaration, she realized she was truly alone.

She stood for a moment, soaking in the silence, before turning her gaze toward the Millers' home. The key they'd given her felt heavy in her pocket, a tangible symbol of the freedom she now held. With a quick glance down the street to ensure no one was watching, Jordan crossed the lawn to the Millers' front door.

Inside, the house greeted her with an inviting stillness, the air charged with possibilities. Jordan moved through the rooms, ticking off her responsibilities: feed Whiskers, water the plants, adjust the thermostat. But her mind was already wandering to what she could do with this space that was now hers to explore.

As she ran her fingers along the spines of books and the edges of picture frames, she imagined the freedom to do whatever she pleased—sip from the liquor cabinet, try on Mrs. Miller's jewelry and cocktail dresses, maybe even invite a friend over without anyone knowing. The thoughts made her pulse quicken with excitement.

With her chores complete, Jordan allowed herself to indulge. She ran her fingers along the spines of Mr. Miller's vinyl collection before settling on a worn copy of Pink Floyd's *The Wall*. As the music filled the room, she closed her eyes and swayed to the rhythm.

But the music wasn't enough to quiet the restless energy building inside her. She needed something more, something to match the freedom she felt. Her eyes snapped open, locking onto the liquor cabinet across the room.

"It wouldn't hurt to sample a little," she whispered to herself, her heart quickening as she approached the cabinet. Her fingers closed around a bottle of Jack Daniel's, the glass cool and solid in her hand.

Pouring herself a generous measure, Jordan felt a thrill of excitement. This was just a taste of the freedom she had been craving.

She raised the glass to her lips, the scent of whiskey sharp in her nostrils. "Here's to new experiences," she toasted quietly.

The first sip burned, but it felt good. With each swallow, the carefully crafted image of the good girl next door began to slip away, revealing a side of her she was eager to explore.

As the warmth of the whiskey spread through her chest, Jordan felt the last of her inhibitions melt away. She wandered from room to room, the glass in hand, feeling more at ease with each step. The quiet of the house no longer felt eerie; it was a blank canvas, ready for her to leave her mark.

Jordan found herself in front of Mrs. Miller's vanity. The polished wood gleamed under the soft light, and she reached out, touching the assortment of delicate bottles and brushes. She picked up a bottle of perfume, inhaling the floral scent before dabbing a bit on her wrist. The fragrance was different from her own, more sophisticated, and she smiled as she imagined herself as the elegant woman Mrs. Miller appeared to be.

Feeling emboldened, she opened a drawer and found a collection of jewelry—nothing extravagant, but each piece carefully chosen. She selected a pair of earrings, slipping them on and admiring her reflection. The girl staring back at her was different—more daring, more confident.

This was what freedom felt like.

Returning to the living room, Jordan settled onto the plush couch, the glass of whiskey still in hand. The music from the vinyl played softly in the background, creating a perfect backdrop to her thoughts.

She had two weeks. Two weeks to explore, to indulge, to let loose in a way she never had before. The thought made her heart race with excitement.

As the afternoon sun began to dip, casting long shadows through the windows, Jordan felt a contentedness settle over her. This was her time—no parents, no neighbors, just her and the endless possibilities that lay ahead.

She set the empty glass on the table beside her and stretched luxuriously on the couch, her mind lazily drifting through the potential adventures of the next two weeks. The music from the vinyl continued to play softly in the background, its rhythm matching the slow, steady beat of her heart.

The warmth of the whiskey left her feeling pleasantly drowsy, but instead of letting herself drift off, she shook herself awake. Tonight was no time to sleep—she had plans to make, things to explore.

Pushing herself off the couch and grabbing her empty glass, Jordan decided to head to the kitchen and see what she could whip up for dinner. Maybe she'd pour herself another drink, enjoy the feeling of being completely in control of her own little world.

The music pulsed through the house, classic rock drowning out the bubbling of simmering pasta sauce on the stove. Jordan swayed to the rhythm, whiskey glass in hand, feeling the warmth of the evening settle into her bones. She felt a thrill of satisfaction as she moved through the kitchen, reveling in the freedom she had now that the house was all hers.

As she poured another measure of whiskey, her thoughts drifted to Billy, the boy from drama club who always seemed to watch her with those intense blue eyes. The thought of having him over crossed her mind—a playful idea that made her smile. Maybe a little teasing would be the perfect way to get his attention. If she sent him the right kind of photo, he might just drop everything and come running.

Setting her glass down, she pulled out her phone and snapped a quick selfie, her hair tousled, her eyes half-lidded in the warm kitchen light. But as she looked at the photo, she felt a rush of boldness. This wasn't just about getting his attention; it was about pushing boundaries, seeing how far she could go. The idea of luring Billy to the house thrilled her, even if she didn't fully understand why.

She adjusted her top, pulling down one strap just enough to make the photo a little more daring. With a mischievous grin, she snapped another picture. But that wasn't enough.

Jordan set the phone down momentarily, her heart racing with anticipation. She took a deep breath, then pulled her top down farther, exposing her small breasts to the camera. She posed in front of the kitchen counter, her heart pounding, as she snapped a few more photos, each one more risqué than the last.

But just as she was about to take another, she noticed something in the background of the screen. Her heart skipped a beat, and she turned quickly, her breath catching in her throat.

There, standing at the kitchen island, was a man. His eyes were wide with surprise, and for a moment, neither of them spoke. The realization that he might have seen her topless sent a strange mix of embarrassment and thrill through her. She quickly grabbed her top and pulled it back up, her face flushing.

He held up his hands, his expression one of shock and awkwardness. "I'm sorry, I didn't mean to frighten you."

Recognition dawned on Jordan. The man was Wes Miller, the neighbors' son. The teenage crush she hadn't seen in years, now standing before her, looking both apologetic and intrigued.

Did he see my tits? she wondered. The thought both embarrassed and excited her.

"What are you doing here?" Jordan managed, her voice steady despite the adrenaline coursing through her veins.

Wes's brow furrowed as he tried to compose himself. "I could ask you the same thing. This is my parents' house."

"Oh!" Jordan felt a slight flush rise to her cheeks, suddenly hyper-aware of how she must look—caught in the middle of something she wasn't ready to explain in the middle of her neighbor's kitchen. "I'm Jordan. From next door? Your parents asked me to house-sit while they're on their cruise."

Wes's eyes flickered with recognition, followed by a slow smile. "Jordan? Little Jordan from next door?"

She nodded, quickly slipping her phone into her pocket with a calm smile. "Yeah, that's me."

"Wow," Wes said, his smile widening as he took her in. "You've... changed."

Jordan felt a thrill run through her at the appreciation in his gaze. Gone was the gangly teen she'd mooned over. In his place stood a man, mature and undeniably attractive. The idea that he might have seen her tits lingered in her mind. She wondered if he liked them or if he thought they were too small.

"They never said you'd be coming home," Jordan said, keeping her voice steady as she tried to steer the conversation away from the awkwardness.

Wes shrugged, moving further into the kitchen. "Last-minute decision. Needed a break from the books." His eyes roamed over the scene—the music, the whiskey, and Jordan herself. "Looks like I'm interrupting quite the party."

Jordan kept her composure, offering a slight smile. "I'm sorry, I can leave if you want—"

"No," Wes cut her off, his smile widening. "No, please. Stay."

"Well," she said, gesturing to the stove, "I was just making dinner. There's plenty if you'd like some."

Wes's gaze lingered on her for a moment longer before he nodded. "Sounds great. Let me grab a shower and change, and I'll join you."

Jordan glanced up at Wes from beneath her lashes, her gaze lingering on the sharp angles of his jawline as the kitchen light cast soft shadows across his face. He took a bite of the food she prepared, and she found herself mesmerized by the way his throat moved as he swallowed, the muscles shifting beneath his skin.

"This is incredible," Wes murmured, his voice low and appreciative. The compliment sent a small thrill through her, though she quickly hid it behind a modest smile.

Silence stretched between them, taut as a wire. Jordan could feel the weight of something unspoken pressing down, a tension that seemed to thicken the very air around them. She sensed that Wes was struggling with something, a battle waging behind his dark eyes. She waited, her pulse quickening with anticipation, her thoughts racing with the possibilities.

A flicker of thought reminded her of Billy. The photos she'd taken, the teasing messages she'd considered sending to lure him over. But as she looked at Wes now, that plan seemed distant, almost irrelevant. There was something about Wes, something more immediate, more real, that pulled her in. The idea of Billy faded into the background as Wes became her focus.

Finally, Wes set down his fork with a soft clink, the sound almost too loud in the charged quiet. His gaze drifted past her, settling somewhere beyond her shoulder as if he couldn't bear to meet her eyes.

"I should explain why I'm here," he began, his voice carrying a note of vulnerability that caught Jordan off guard. "My girlfriend and I broke up last week. It was... ugly."

Jordan's breath hitched slightly. She leaned forward, drawn closer by the raw emotion in his voice, her own heart twisting in response to the pain she could hear so clearly.

"I couldn't stand being on campus anymore," Wes continued, his words tumbling out in a rush now, as if he needed to expel them before they choked him. "Everywhere I looked, I saw her. I needed to get away, to clear my head. That's why I came home."

For a moment, neither of them spoke. The room seemed to hold its breath, the only sound the faint hum of the refrigerator in the background.

Suddenly, the vulnerability of the situation hit her, and she stood up abruptly, her chair scraping against the floor in a sharp, discordant note.

"I should go," she whispered, her voice barely audible, thick with the weight of what she felt. "You came here for solitude. I'm intruding."

Before she could take a step, Wes's hand shot out, his fingers wrapping around her wrist with a firm but gentle grip. "No," he said, his voice steady, almost pleading as his eyes locked onto hers. "Stay. Please."

Jordan hesitated, caught in the magnetic pull of his gaze, the warmth of his touch spreading through her like a slow burn. Her skin tingled where his fingers pressed against her wrist, and for a moment, she couldn't move, couldn't breathe.

"Are you sure?" she asked, her voice a mere whisper, hardly daring to believe that he wanted her to stay.

Wes nodded, his grip on her wrist loosening slightly but not letting go. "I thought I wanted to be alone," he admitted, his voice softening, "but having you here, it helps."

Slowly, almost reluctantly, Jordan sank back into her chair, her movements tentative as if the spell could be broken at any moment. Wes's hand slid away from her wrist, the loss of contact leaving her feeling oddly bereft, as if something vital had been taken from her.

"Okay," she said softly, her voice filled with an emotion she couldn't quite name. "I'll stay."

Jordan's mind whirled with the unexpected turn of events, her thoughts racing ahead, wondering what might happen next. Billy was forgotten, at least for the moment. Wes was here now, and that changed everything.

The living room was bathed in the flickering blue light of the television, shadows dancing across the walls like restless spirits. Jordan perched on the edge of the couch, hyperaware of Wes's proximity. His arm, draped casually along the back of the sofa, radiated heat she could feel even without touching.

On screen, the movie played out—some mindless horror flick Wes had chosen—but Jordan barely registered the plot. Her senses were overwhelmed by Wes: the subtle scent of his cologne, the sound of his steady breathing, the way the TV's glow caught the sharp planes of his face.

"Hey," Wes's voice cut through her reverie, low and conspiratorial. "Want to make this more interesting?"

Jordan turned, pulse quickening at the mischievous glint in his eye. Without waiting for an answer, Wes reached into his pocket and produced a small, tightly rolled joint.

The lighter flared to life, illuminating Wes's face in sharp relief for a moment before fading back to TV-glow twilight. Jordan watched, transfixed, as he took a deep drag, held it, then released a cloud of sweet-smelling smoke.

He offered her the joint, eyebrow raised in silent challenge. Jordan hesitated for a heartbeat, then reached out. The paper was warm where Wes's lips had touched it.

The first inhale burned, acrid smoke filling her lungs and making her eyes water. She coughed, cheeks flushing with embarrassment, but Wes just smiled and guided the joint back to her lips.

"Easy," he murmured. "Small sips, like you're drinking through a straw."

His hand on her arm steadied her, and this time, the smoke went down smoothly. Heat bloomed in her chest, spreading outward until her whole body felt warm and loose.

Time seemed to stretch as they passed the joint back and forth. The movie became a kaleidoscope of color and sound, and Jordan found herself laughing at things that shouldn't have been funny. Wes's arm had migrated from the back of the couch to her shoulders, and she leaned into him, savoring the solid warmth of his body.

In the hazy, smoke-filled room, with the boundaries of reality softening at the edges, Jordan felt a surge of reckless courage. She turned her face up to Wes's, close enough to count his eyelashes, to feel his breath mingling with hers.

The room swam in a haze of smoke and dim light, the movie's dialogue a distant murmur. Jordan's skin tingled, hypersensitive to every point of contact with Wes. His arm, draped across her shoulders, felt like a brand of heat.

Wes shifted, turning toward her. His eyes, dark and intent, locked onto hers. Time seemed to slow, each heartbeat stretching into eternity. Then, with agonizing slowness, he leaned in.

The first brush of his lips against hers was electric. Jordan's breath caught in her throat, her body rigid with surprise and want. Wes pulled back slightly, searching her face. Whatever he saw there must have satisfied him, because he dove back in, kissing her with an intensity that made her head spin.

Jordan's hands found their way to Wes's hair, fingers tangling in the soft strands. He groaned, the sound vibrating through her, igniting something primal in her core. His hands roamed her back, pulling her closer until she was practically in his lap.

"We should, " Wes panted between kisses, "move this somewhere more comfortable."

The world tilted as he stood, lifting her with him. Jordan wrapped her legs around his waist, marveling at his strength as he carried her up the stairs. The journey was punctuated by pauses where Wes pressed her against the wall, stealing breathless kisses.

Wes's bedroom was a blur of shadows and moonlight filtering through half-drawn curtains. He deposited her on the bed with surprising gentleness, then stood back, drinking in the sight of her. Jordan felt exposed under his gaze, vulnerable in a way that both thrilled and terrified her.

"You're beautiful," Wes murmured, voice husky with desire. He joined her on the bed, his weight dipping the mattress.

Clothes were shed with fumbling urgency, hands exploring newly revealed skin. Jordan arched into his touch, gasping at the sensation of skin on skin. Wes trailed kisses down her neck, across her collarbone, lower still.

She was vaguely aware that she should feel something more—guilt, perhaps, or fear. But those emotions were distant, muffled.

Instead, she felt powerful, alive in a way she'd never experienced before.

The room was filled with the sounds of heavy breathing and creaking springs. Moonlight filtered through the half-drawn curtains, casting eerie shadows across the tangled sheets. Jordan lay beneath Wes, her body moving in rhythm with his, but her mind was elsewhere.

Her eyes, once clouded with feigned desire, now sharpened with predatory focus. As Wes lost himself in the throes of passion, Jordan's gaze fixed on the trophy perched above the headboard. Its metallic surface gleamed in the dim light, beckoning to her.

Time seemed to slow. The world narrowed to a pinpoint, all sound fading except for the thunderous pounding of her own heart. With a fluid grace that belied her slightly intoxicated state, Jordan's hand shot out. Her fingers closed around the cold metal of the trophy perched on the small shelf above the bed, its weight solid and reassuring in her grasp.

Wes, oblivious to the shift in atmosphere, continued his rhythmic movements. His face was buried in the crook of her neck, leaving him completely vulnerable, utterly unprepared for what was to come.

In one swift motion, Jordan raised the trophy high. For a split second, she hesitated, watching how the moonlight glinted off its surface. Then, summoning all her strength, she brought it crashing down onto the back of Wes's head.

The impact was sickeningly loud in the quiet room. Wes's body went instantly rigid, a choked gasp escaping his lips. His movements ceased abruptly as he collapsed onto Jordan, suddenly a dead weight.

Silence fell, broken only by Jordan's ragged breathing. She lay still for a moment, feeling Wes's unconscious form pressed against her, and eventually his cock softened inside of her. Slowly, almost reverently, she pushed his limp body off to the side.

She looked down at Wes's still form, his chest rising and falling with shallow breaths. A small trickle of blood matted his hair where the trophy had struck.

A strange calm settled over Jordan. She should feel something—horror, revulsion, guilt—but instead, she felt oddly detached, as if watching the scene unfold from a distance. Her lips curved into a small, secret smile.

Wes groaned, his head pounding as he drifted back into consciousness. He blinked against the sharp pain at the back of his skull, trying to orient himself. When he tried to shift his weight, the realization hit him like a bucket of ice water—his arms and legs were bound, his skin brushing against something cold and slick.

He looked down, panic gripping his chest as he recognized the large sheets of black plastic beneath his feet. His heart raced, each beat thudding loudly in his ears as his eyes darted around the room, searching for an explanation.

The sight of Jordan standing in the doorway sent a chill down his spine. She wore nothing but her underwear, her small breasts rising and falling with each breath, but it was the kitchen knife in her hand that seized his attention. The blade tapped rhythmically against her thigh, a hollow sound that echoed in the otherwise silent room. Her eyes, once warm, were now devoid of any familiarity, replaced by a coldness that sent a wave of dread washing over him.

"Jordan... what... what is this?" Wes's voice trembled, his earlier confidence stripped away. He tugged at his restraints, testing them with mounting desperation, but the bonds only tightened in response.

A smile played at the corners of Jordan's lips, but it didn't reach her eyes. She said nothing, just continued tapping the knife.

"Seriously, I'm not playing. Cut me loose now," Wes demanded, fear edging into his voice.

Jordan pushed off from the doorframe, approaching, her movements slow and deliberate, almost seductive. As she neared, her demeanor shifted, the playful facade dropping away to reveal something darker. She stopped directly in front of him, the knife glinting in her hand.

"Oh, Wes," she purred, her voice low and dangerous. "This was never a game. You have no idea what you've gotten yourself into by showing up here."

She circled behind him, her fingertips trailing across his shoulders. Wes shuddered at her touch, his mind racing to understand what was happening.

"Jordan, please," he whispered. "Whatever this is, we can talk about it. Just untie me, and we'll figure this out."

Jordan laughed, a chilling sound devoid of humor. She came back into view, crouching to meet his eyes. "There's nothing to figure out, Wes. This is who I am. Who I've always been. You just never saw it before. No one has."

The knife glinted in the dim light as Jordan raised it, letting it hover near Wes's cheek. He flinched away, eyes wide with terror.

"What do you want from me?" he asked, his voice barely audible.

Her face hardened, and the smile vanished. "You raped me," she said, her voice low and venomous. "You hurt me. You stole my virginity."

Wes felt a rush of fear unlike anything he'd ever experienced. His mouth went dry as he tried to defend himself, stammering, "You... you wanted it! You were totally into—"

The words were cut short as Jordan plunged the knife into his thigh. Wes screamed, the pain blinding him, tearing through his leg like fire. Tears streamed down his face as he sobbed, struggling helplessly against the tape.

Jordan ignored his cries, her expression cold and detached. She went to his dresser and pulled out a pair of balled-up socks, stuffed them into his mouth and wound the duct tape around his head as he whipped it wildly, trying to stop her.

She knelt in front of him, yanked the knife from his flesh. She slowly raked the bloody tip of the knife across his chest, relishing the look of terror in his eyes.

"Huh," she said, the knife pausing. A curious look fell across her face. "I didn't notice when we were fucking, but you have weird nipples."

Suddenly, she plucked Wes's left nipple between her thumb and forefingers and lopped it off. "There, that's better."

With Wes gagged and whipping his head wildly, she began to carve a heart shape into his chest, her knife slicing through flesh with methodical precision. The room filled with the sound of his muffled screams, each one more desperate than the last, but she continued her work with unrelenting focus.

"Stop moving or you're going to ruin it," she said as she finished with the shape. She picked at the point of the heart with her fingernails until she lifted a small section of the skin, then with a great ripping pull, she tore the skin from his muscle.

"Eww, that's gross," she said, looking at the flap of skin. She tossed it, and it landed against Wes's thigh with a wet smacking sound and stuck there, like a bloody slice of bologna thrown against a wall.

Finally, she moved her attention lower, the knife tracing a path that made Wes's heart seize with terror. Before he could fully comprehend what was happening, she made a final, brutal cut. His severed dick fell to the floor with a sickening thud.

Just as she was about to retrieve it, the cat darted in, its sudden presence a jarring intrusion into the grisly scene. In a flash, the cat snatched the bloody cock in its jaws and bolted from the room.

Jordan froze, her breath catching in her throat as the absurdity of the moment clashed with the horror of what she'd done. A slow, incredulous laugh bubbled up from her chest, a laugh that quickly turned into a humorless, unhinged cackle as she watched the cat disappear into the hallway.

"That pussy snatched my dick!" she said incredulously.

She dropped the knife and rushed after the cat, leaving Wes alone, bleeding out on the cold, slick plastic, the horror of what had just happened sinking in as his vision began to fade.

Jordan's breath came in short, frustrated huffs as she hauled the heavy, plastic-wrapped bundle through the narrow hallway, her bare feet sliding on the cold tile of the kitchen floor.

Every few steps, she paused, adjusting her grip on the slick plastic that encased Wes's body. It wasn't just the weight—it was the awkward, uneven distribution of it, the way his lifeless limbs flopped and twisted with every tug, making her struggle all the more maddening.

By the time she reached the door to the garage, Jordan's arms were burning. She leaned against the doorframe for a moment, catching her breath, before yanking the door open and dragging the bundle over the threshold. The smooth concrete of the garage offered less resistance, but the task was still a grueling one.

"Should've just done it down here," she grumbled, her words punctuated by the sound of the plastic scraping across the floor. "Would've saved me all this trouble."

She reached Wes's mom's car. With a deep breath, Jordan popped the trunk and stared at the empty space inside. It looked smaller than she remembered, and for a brief moment, she wondered if the body would even fit.

She wrestled with it, hoisting it up and angling it awkwardly as she tried to stuff it into the trunk. The plastic rustled loudly, filling the quiet garage with a grating sound that set her teeth on edge. Finally, after what felt like an eternity, she managed to shove Wes's body into the cramped space, slamming the trunk shut with a force that echoed through the garage.

Jordan leaned against the car, wiping a sheen of sweat from her brow. Her hands trembled slightly from the exertion, but she couldn't afford to rest. Not yet.

She slid into the driver's seat and started the engine. The garage door rumbled open, and she eased the car out, the headlights slicing through the darkness as she pulled onto the street.

The night was still, the only sound the steady hum of the engine as she navigated the quiet suburban roads. It wasn't long before she merged onto the expressway, the car gaining speed as the houses and streetlights blurred into a dark, featureless landscape.

Nearly an hour passed, the road stretching out endlessly before her, until a weathered sign appeared, illuminated briefly by the headlights: a faded marker for a rural Indiana town.

Jordan's eyes narrowed as she pressed down on the gas, the car surging forward into the night.

Jordan pulled the car to a stop beside the towering silhouette of the abandoned silo, its rusted, corrugated walls standing like a sentinel in the middle of the flat, desolate Indiana landscape. There was nothing around for miles—just fields of corn stubble and the occasional cluster of trees.

She turned off the engine and sat in the stillness for a moment. With a slow, deliberate movement, she unlatched her seatbelt and stepped out into the night. She moved to the back of the car, hesitating only briefly before popping the trunk.

She grabbed the edge of the plastic and began to pull. She grunted with effort as she dragged the wrapped body across the rough ground. The entrance to the silo loomed closer, a yawning black mouth ready to swallow her secret whole.

The inside of the silo was pitch-black, the kind of darkness that made you forget there was ever such a thing as light. Jordan fumbled with her iPhone, turning on the flashlight and sweeping it across the circular, empty space. The beam caught on an old, rusted lantern hanging on a nail in the wall. She set the edge of the plastic down just inside the doorway and walked over to retrieve the lantern, her footsteps echoing off the curved walls.

She lit the lantern with a match, the small flame flickering to life and casting a dim, yellowish glow around her. With the lantern in hand, she returned to Wes's body and resumed dragging him toward the center of the silo, where a ten-foot hole gaped like an open grave. Her breathing was ragged by the time she reached the edge, her muscles burning with the effort.

She took a moment to steady herself before rolling Wes's body into the hole. It landed with a dull thud, the plastic rustling as it settled among the other shapes down there—two blackened mounds that had been there long before Wes.

Jordan crouched at the edge of the hole, holding the lantern out over the darkness. Wes's body lay twisted at the bottom, his face obscured by the layers of plastic, but she didn't need to see it—it was already forever etched in her memory.

She set the lantern down carefully on the edge of the hole and walked over to a corner of the silo where a red gas can waited where she'd left it on her last visit. The smell of gasoline filled the air as she poured it over Wes's body, the liquid splashing onto the other mounds in the pit. Once the can was empty, she tossed it aside and pulled a box of wooden matches from her pocket. Her hands were steady as she struck a match and watched the flame flicker for a brief moment before she tossed it into the hole.

The fire ignited with a whoosh, a pillar of flame consuming Wes's body and the remnants of the past. Jordan stepped back, the heat washing over her face, as she watched the flames dance and twist, devouring everything in their path.

The light from the fire illuminated the interior of the silo, casting long, eerie shadows on the walls. Jordan turned away from the burning pit and walked over to an old folding lawn chair she had left behind on her last visit. Beside it sat a wooden box, its paint faded and peeling from years of neglect. She sat down, the chair creaking under her weight, and pulled the box onto her lap.

Inside were two items, both familiar, both leaden with memories.

The first item was a missing persons flyer, the edges yellowed with age. A grainy photo of a thirteen-year-old girl named Melissa stared back at her, the smile frozen in time. Jordan knew her well— they had been in seventh grade together. The memories flooded back, sharp and vivid.

She and Melissa in the woods behind the school, the sunlight filtering through the trees as they talked and laughed. Jordan had felt something then, something she didn't understand but couldn't ignore. When she kissed Melissa, it felt like the most natural thing in the world. But Melissa's reaction was totally unexpected. She freaked out, called Jordan gross and disgusting. "I'm going to tell everyone that you're a nasty lesbo!" Melissa shouted. Jordan's world had shattered in that moment, and the next thing she knew, she grabbed a large rock that rested against the base of a nearby tree and smashed it against Melissa's skull, caving it in.

Melissa's body was one of the two charred mounds in the hole below.

The second item was a plastic boutonniere, the white petals faded and brittle. Robbie had given it to her on prom night earlier this year, a night she had been so excited for, so full of hope.

They had danced, laughed, and for a brief moment, she had felt like she belonged. But after prom, in the back of the limo, Robbie had convinced her to let him finger fuck her. It was her first sexual experience, and she flushed with hormones, moaning as a cozy warmth spread in her vagina and bloomed in her stomach.

The next week at school, Robbie told everyone about what they'd done and claimed his finger still smelled like rotten tuna even after washing it like twenty times. The humiliation had burned deeper than anything she had ever felt.

That weekend, Jordan invited Robbie to her house with the promise of letting him stick more than just his finger inside her. She lured him into the storage shed behind the house where her parents stored the lawnmower and gardening stuff. She used a shovel to knock him unconscious.

When Robbie came to, he was bent over a block table, his hands and feet tied off so that he was spread eagle. Jordan used a pair of pruning shears to remove his index finger, the one he'd awkwardly used to plunge around inside her pussy. She jammed the severed digit up Robbie's ass like she was a proctologist, rooted it around a bit, then pulled it out and made him smell it.

"Does it smell like rotten tuna or shit?" she asked. Robbie tried to pull away, but Jordan held his head down as she poked the fingertip into his nostril, making sure he got a good whiff.

"Maybe you should taste it," she said and forced the soiled finger into Robbie's mouth as she laughed. Robbie gagged and spit the severed digit out.

"I'm going to kill you, you sick fucking whore!"

Jordan smiled. "Not if I kill you first," she said, bringing the shovel down hard on his skull. Many, many times.

He was the second charred body in the hole.

Jordan placed the cherished items (and memories) back into the box, her hands trembling slightly. She stood, the chair creaking as she rose, and walked back to the car. She opened the front door and reached inside, retrieving a glass jar filled with a murky liquid. Floating inside was Wes's dick. She shook the jar slightly, watching as the contents swirled, a twisted smile tugging at the corners of her lips. There were small teeth marks where the cat bit into Wes's junk.

She returned to the lawn chair, placing the jar carefully into the wooden box alongside the other mementos. Then, with a deliberate slowness, she pulled a joint from her pocket and lit it, the sweet, pungent smoke filling the air. She'd stole it from Wes's dresser drawer. He wouldn't need it anymore.

As she inhaled deeply, she pulled out her phone and began scrolling through her photos, looking at the selfies she'd taken earlier. She had wanted to send them to Billy before Wes had interrupted her. She picked two of the best and sent them off with a quick tap, a rush of satisfaction filling her as she imagined the reaction they would provoke.

She smiled as she took another drag from the joint, her eyes narrowing as she pictured Billy's reaction. She hoped he would share the photos, let everyone see them. And maybe, just maybe,

Billy's gorgeous blue eyes would look nice in a jar, right next to Wes's dick.

Jordan sat back in the lawn chair, exhaling smoke into the night, the fire crackling behind her. The flames danced in her eyes, a reflection of the darkness that had consumed her—a darkness that she fully embraced.

TODDLER TOY GRAVEYARD

CANDACE NOLA

"Keep your goddamn kids off my lawn." Virginia's shrill voice pierced the quiet like a gunshot. Lynn sighed and set her book down on the arm of the couch before she rose and went to the door. The kids were playing out front, as usual, in the muddy creek that ran between their property and their not-so-pleasant neighbor's property. It filtered down from the stretch of forest that bordered their homes and the cornfields on either side. Lynn stepped on to the deck, letting the screen door slam shut behind her. As she did so, she spotted Virginia along the row of bushes that split their yards, running along their property line. The kids were nowhere near her yard; they never were.

"I see you, you lazy cow. In the house all day, not watching them damn kids. You mark my word, something bad going to happen to them. You just wait." The woman spit venom like bullets. Each shrill word clipped and hostile. The sound of her voice was enough to set off a migraine any day of the week. The woman bent down, scrabbled around the dirt by her feet for a moment, then heaved something toward the kids, who were barely paying her any attention. Her screaming had become background noise over the hot summer days.

The rock fell flat, landing with a heavy splat a few feet from where the kids were playing in the creek. Muddy water splashed them, and they scrambled away, startled by the sudden projectile. Kasey, Mitch, and Drew looked toward the neighbor's yard, then at their mom waving at them from the porch. The kids started moving toward the house, not quite running but walking quickly with a wary glance cast behind them as if another rock was going to launch from the other side at any moment.

"Come on, kids. Time for supper anyway. Let's give Miss Virginia some peace and quiet for a bit, okay?" Lynn called to the kids, her voice gentle and calm. Inside, her blood boiled in her veins. That woman pissed her off to no end, but yet, there they were, neighbors. Lynn barely knew the woman, had never said an unpleasant word to her before they moved there. Hell, for all that mattered, she didn't speak to her now. She let her husband deal with that particular nuthouse. He was better equipped than she was for confrontations.

She watched the kids as they came up the stairs, sweaty and muddy, but she didn't care. There was a hose out back. She ushered them through the house to the backyard, hosed off their grimy shoes and feet, then had them sit on the back stoop to dry in the sun. As they settled down, Lynn disappeared inside and returned a moment later with a handful of popsicles. Popsicles on a hot day always brought back smiles.

"Mom, why does Miss Virginia hate us?" Kasey asked. The youngest of the three, and the most inquisitive.

"She's just a witch," Mitch answered, making Drew snort with laughter.

"Now, now, we mustn't be mean," Lynn said, failing to hide her own smile. "Some folks are just unhappy, and they don't know any other way to be."

"How come, Momma?" Drew asked. "Why can't she get happy? She can't make friends?" Drew frowned at the empty popsicle wrapper, then sucked the last of the blue syrup from it before handing it back to his mom in exchange for a second ice pop.

"Well, I don't know if she has friends or not. Don't know much about her, but it doesn't seem like she wants any friends," Lynn replied. Her middle child was the most thoughtful, more sensitive to the needs of others. She ruffled his curly hair, then dropped down to sit on the stoop beside the kids.

"There's a saying that hurt people hurt people, if you understand what that means," Lynn said to the kids. They all looked confused and shook their heads no, so she continued. "It just means that sometimes a person is so hurt on the inside, by life, by family, by hard times, that they don't know what to do with all that pain and anger, so they take it out on everyone around them."

"Oh, so she likes to make everyone else sad too," Mitch said matter-of-factly. "Isn't that what a witch does?" He snorted, then mimicked the evil cackle of a witch. The other kids laughed, and Lynn sighed again, though she wasn't upset. She didn't blame the kids at all. Her neighbor was a nightmare straight from Hell.

"Well, yes, to the first part. But stop calling her a witch. It's not nice. You know the rule," she said. "If you don't have nothing nice to say..."

"Don't say nothing at all," her kids finished in unison.

"That's right. Now, come inside and wash up. You guys can watch a movie or something while I finish dinner." She herded the kids into the house, picking up popsicle wrappers as she went. She shut the door behind her, feeling Virginia's eyes on her the entire time.

She looked through the window in the kitchen door once the door was securely locked, and sure enough, the woman stood just behind her own house, on the sloping bit of hillside that formed both backyards, sneering at her. The rage in her gut roiled and churned, pumping acid into her throat. Lynn took a deep breath, rolled her eyes, and went to get the kids settled, exhaling on the way.

Later that night, after the kids were in bed, Lynn told her husband Don what had happened. Already tired from his afternoon shift at the factory, Don listened with a weary expression on his face as he settled into his easy chair.

"I just don't know what to do anymore," Lynn said. "The kids don't bother her. They don't go over the property line. I've never once seen them in her yard, not even Mitch, and you know as well as I do the trouble he gets into." She looked at him from across the room, her book on her lap, one finger still holding her place. "It wasn't just a small rock she threw, Don. It was big and heavy. If she had hit one of the kids, we'd be at the hospital right now instead of having this talk here at home. Can you please do something about it?"

"What would you like me to do, Lynn?" Don asked, tapping the mute button on the television remote control. "I have talked to her and to Tim. Tim just nods and backs her up. Honestly, I think he's afraid of her." Don snorted. "Hell, I guess I would be too." He shot Lynn a boyish grin. "Not all men got as lucky in the wife pool as I did."

Lynn chuckled. "I guess I can see that, but seriously, I'm afraid she's going to hurt one of the kids one day."

"All right, I'll try again. I'll go have a word with her before work," Don said. He gave Lynn a wink and turned the volume back up on his monster movie.

Lynn smiled back, tight-lipped but not willing to fight right now. He was right, anyway. He had tried several times. Virginia just kept right on with her bullshit. She'd take the kids to the park pool tomorrow, get them out of the house and away from their neighbor for the day. They could all use the break, anyway.

The next day, Lynn got the kids up early, pouring juice and cereal as they trudged sleepily to the table. She was already dressed for the day, in a loose t-shirt style dress with her swimsuit beneath it. Her sandals sat by the door, next to their beach bag packed with towels, sunscreen, and snacks.

"Hurry up and eat, guys. I want to get a couple decent chairs at the pool. You know it'll be crowded by eleven."

"Pool day?" Kasey asked, the remnants of sleep making her voice huskier than normal.

"Yep, pool day. Then I thought lunch by the mini-golf course, and we can play a round or two before we come home." Lynn smiled at the kids, watching their faces light up. Even Mitch seemed enthusiastic about the idea, even though at ten, he thought the park pool was for babies. The heat and their neighbor must have soured him on the prospect of another dreary day at home.

"Cool!" Drew said. He made quick work of his cereal after that, even drinking his glass of juice before putting his bowl in the sink. The other kids followed suit soon after, and they took off down the hall toward their bedrooms to change.

"Make it snappy," Lynn called. "Train leaving in fifteen minutes!"

She heard their muffled replies, then a laugh from Drew as doors slammed and dresser drawers banged open. Lynn smiled to herself, wiped the table down, then went to make a quick check of the house, locking and relocking doors and windows. As she reached the windows that faced Virginia's house, she peeked out. Sure enough, the woman was there, standing on her porch and glaring at their house. She held something green in her hands. Lynn moved to the next window, then looked again, trying to get a better angle. A green-tinted bottle was in her hands, like an old Coca-Cola bottle.

As she watched, Virgina lifted the bottle and let it drop, smashing it on the concrete steps below her. She picked up another from her porch railing and let it smash to the ground as well. Lynn just stared for a moment, utterly baffled by the woman's behavior. As the third bottle smashed, Virginia looked up and over, directly at her, then lifted a hand in a one-finger salute.

Lynn stepped away from the window, but not before she saw the sinister smirk on the woman's face. She heard the tinkling of more glass as another bottle broke. Lynn's guts clenched and acid rose in her throat, hot and sour, burning the inside of her throat along the way. Lynn placed a hand against her throat, smothering the stream of bile that threatened to launch from her mouth, and hurried to her bathroom for the antacid medicine she kept there.

This woman was going to give her ulcers or a heart attack. The stress alone from the bizarre behavior was enough to make anyone snap. The kids being threatened only added more stress on top of an already steaming pile of it. She reached her bedroom just as the kids were emerging from theirs. Hearing their happy voices allowed her to take a breath and calm herself for a moment before she popped several of the tablets in her mouth and chewed them. A glass of tap water to wash them down, followed by several splashes of cool water on her face, and she was ready to go.

Lynn plastered on her "mom" smile, took a couple more calming breaths, then breezed from her room to join the kids in the dining room. Once there, she slid her feet into her sandals, then snagged her purse and the beach bag.

"All set?" she asked the kids as they finished putting on their own shoes. Old sneakers for Mitch with fat laces, canvas low tops for Drew, his comfy ones, to hear him tell it. And Kasey had black flip-flops on like her mom. All of them wore the unofficial summer uniform of ripped jean shorts of various colors and simple t-shirts. Kasey had some pastel-colored bears on her shirt, some video game character for Drew, a blue hedgehog or something, and Mitch had a basic white t-shirt on.

"Out to the car then. I'm right behind you." Lynn shooed them out the door, then followed, pausing to slide her key in the lock to turn the deadbolt. As it clicked home, she swore she could still hear the sound of smashing glass coming from the neighbors' place.

"Something is really wrong with that woman," Lynn muttered as she went down the steps to the car parked in front of the garage. The kids were already inside, rolling the windows down, Mitch in the front passenger seat, of course. As the oldest, he claimed that shotgun was his birthright. Lynn chuckled, opened his door, and dropped the loaded beach bag on his lap.

"I guess you can hold this, then," Lynn said to him, laughing at his slight grunt as he caught the bag. She shut the door and hurried to her own side, the tinkling sound loud enough to be annoying but not quite loud enough for the kids to question it yet. She hoped they didn't because she sure as shit didn't have any explanation for it.

Lynn started the car, started the kids on a round of dad jokes, and backed the car out of the driveway. The park wasn't far away, only a few miles, but today it felt like they were going across country, and Lynn felt her stomach and her jaw both unclench as she put Virginia's place in the rearview.

After a long, sun-filled day at the park, Lynn pulled into the driveway. For once, her stomach didn't immediately hurt seeing their neighbors' junk-filled yard. Old toddler toys of all shapes and sizes filled what had once been a rather sizable pond in Virginia's front yard. Plastic ride-on toys, playhouses, toy kitchens, and several fading green turtle-shaped sandboxes filled the depression in a haphazard manner. The whole atrocious display was flanked by two old carousel horses, badly chipped and fading but still attached to their poles. It was like a bizarre yard sale or circus gone wrong.

She shook her head as she put the car in park and followed the kids up the stairs. A bit of a glint sparkled on the bright green of her lawn, and she smiled as she reached the top of the deck. There must have been a quick rain shower to make the lawn sparkle so brightly in the late sunlight. She loved her front lawn with its thriving trees and colorful flowerbeds. The creek made a pretty picture framed with violets and daisies as the water split the front lawn in two and filtered to their yard below. They took good care of their property, and it showed, unlike whatever travesty Virginia had erected in her front yard.

Lynn let the kids inside, then lingered on the deck, taking in the sunset, and admittedly, the peace and quiet. Her neighbor must not be at home. It was far too quiet over there, but Lynn was not about to question it. She walked over to the grill on the far side of the deck and turned it on, lighting the burners with a few clicks of a button.

Dinner on the deck sounded lovely right now. Burgers, some hot dogs, cut up some fruit, and open a bag of chips. Simple, quick, and three happy kids. It would be a perfect end to what had been a great day.

Lynn vanished inside her house. A happy mom headed to her kitchen to make a simple feast for her brood, happy and content for the first time in weeks. The kids had tossed their things right inside the door, and she sighed. A mother's job was never done. A few terse words to the three heathens piled on the couch and soon shoes and towels were put away, and idle hands were put to work setting the picnic table on the deck while she prepared the food.

Less than an hour later, the kids were full of burgers and chips, skipping around the front yard and chasing fireflies. Lynn stood on the deck, leaning over the railing, watching them. Even Mitch was content for once, helping his brother and sisters catch the lightning bugs rather than scowling at them in disdain. He was in an odd place right now, and Lynn tried to understand.

He was not quite a teen but was the oldest of the kids. He was also a bit of a bully toward them but would terrorize anyone else that dared say an unkind word about them. He was quick to anger, just as quick to hit someone, but quicker still to defend his family. Drew didn't always understand the complex being that Mitch was, but he worshipped him, anyway. Monkey see, monkey do, and all that jazz. Drew was her people pleaser and peacemaker, always the one to calm the raging sea whenever Mitch was set off.

Kasey was just Kasey. The baby of the family, the only girl, and often left out. But she seemed to be just fine on her own, content to play with the boys when they allowed her and didn't cry when they didn't. She preferred the quiet and her books over noise and dirty crawfish from the stream. Lynn sighed, watching them play. It had been a really great day, and she couldn't have asked for a more peaceful night. She turned to go inside the house, wanting to clean the kitchen while the kids were occupied, when a dreadful scream pierced the night air.

She whirled around with her heart pounding in her chest. Fear and panic gripped her in its clutches as she flew down the steps, not pausing to ask what happened. She knew that cry, and it was a sound of pain. Drew was still screaming when she reached his side, dropping down in the grass beside him, wincing as something dug into her flesh and ground against her knees. Drew was wailing, both hands clutched to his face as he thrashed around. Dots of crimson were soaking through his shirt, with more splatters running down his neck and dripping from his arms.

"I didn't do nothing! I swear, Mom. He was running, and he fell. I didn't do it." Mitch was babbling over and over, the fear in his voice coming out as a defiant tremor. "Is he okay?"

"Ssh, baby, what happened?" Lynn tried to soothe Drew, attempting to peel his hands from his face. His wails only grew louder as he rolled side to side on the ground. "Baby, let me see, please. I can't help you if I can't see." Lynn grit her own teeth as tiny rocks dug into her skin where she knelt.

Finally, Drew let her move his hands, and she gasped in horror. His face was a bloody mask of punctures with glittering rocks embedded into the wounds. One nasty shard stuck out of his skin just below his eye socket, and Lynn bent over him, taking hold of the rock and plucking it from his skin as gently as she could. She stared, horrified, at the shard of green glass she held in her fingers. Drew whimpered, snot, tears, and blood coating his face and bottom lip.

Suddenly, it hit her. The pretty glittering on her lawn earlier was not from a rain shower. Virginia had sprinkled that smashed glass all over the yard. Lynn shifted her stance, rising from her knees to a crouch, and verified what she already knew. Bits of green glass were stuck to her knees and shins. Blood seeped and oozed down her own legs as she slid her arms under Drew and lifted him from the ground. Mitch and Kasey were watching wide-eyed behind her as she lifted her son and began walking to the car.

"Mitch, run inside and fetch my purse. Be quick about it. Kasey, go with him and get Momma some clean towels from the bathroom." Lynn calmly gave orders to the kids as she carried Drew down the driveway. "Mitch, lock the door on your way out."

She reached the car and opened the back door, setting Drew gently down on the seat, but as she laid him on his back, he screamed harder. Lynn bit her lip and rolled him to his side, lifting his shirt to see what she feared. Shards of glass littered his skin, ground into his flesh, sticking to his arms, his neck, anyplace that hit the ground while he lay there thrashing and screaming. She ran her fingers down his side and found no wounds there, so she settled him on his side, holding him in place until Kasey came skittering down the steps with her arms full of towels.

Lynn tucked the towels around him, told Kasey to slide in the backseat, then settled Drew's head on his sister's lap, cushioned by a towel.

"Kasey, I need your help, okay?" Lynn said. "Momma's gotta drive. I need you to hold Drew still, just like he is now. There's glass all over his back and his front. We gotta keep him on his side. Can you do that?"

"Yes, Momma," Kasey said in a small voice. Her hands pressed to Drew's shoulder, holding him steady even as he rocked and whimpered in pain. "I got him, Momma," Kasey said again, her eyes wide and full of tears.

"Here's your purse, Mom," Mitch said, appearing at her side, "and the keys." He held the car keys out to her, then settled in the back seat, letting her rest Drew's towel-covered legs across his knees.

"I'll help keep him still, Mom. It'll be okay," Mitch said. "Let's go."

Lynn gave them a weak smile, her own tears still flowing, then quickly got into the driver's seat. A minute later, they were hurtling down the country road toward the nearest hospital, thirty miles away. Drew cried the whole time. So did she, but her tears... those tears were ones of rage.

By the time Lynn had reached the hospital, Drew's wails had turned to painful whimpers. Both Mitch and Kasey were wide-eyed and pale in the backseat, both of them trying to hold their brother still as much as possible. Lynn tried to keep the panic out of her voice when she parked at the emergency room entrance and told the kids to sit still while she got help. She put the car in park, jammed the button for her hazard lights, and damn near tumbled out of her car and dashed inside.

Lynn rushed to the registration desk, skipping the security guard completely. With tears now streaming down her face, she quickly explained what happened and that they needed a stretcher, not a wheelchair, due to Drew's multiple injuries. Hearing her story, the guard flagged down two interns, barked a few orders at them, and guided them to Lynn's car.

There, they gently extracted Drew from the backseat and the clutches of his siblings and hurried him inside. Lynn and the kids followed, blood-stained, teary-eyed, and frantic. The guard waved the kids through, briefly checked Lynn's purse, and offered to park her car for her while she handled the registration. She smiled at him, grateful for the kindness, and handed over her keys.

The gentleman told her that it would be all right, then disappeared outside. Lynn numbly went through the registration process while nurses hovered over Drew in the triage room nearby. Mitch and Kasey stood quietly behind Lynn; Kasey was still crying while

Mitch glared at the team examining Drew, growing angrier with each whimper his brother made.

Lynn saw Mitch and set a gentle hand on his shoulder when she finished with the registration desk and guided him and Kasey to seats in the waiting area.

"You guys wait here. I'm going to check on Drew. I'll be right back."

"They keep hurting him, Mom," Mitch snarled, fists still clenched.

"They're helping him, not hurting him. I'm sure they'll give him something for the pain soon, but right now they need to see how badly he is hurt," Lynn reassured her angry older child, then hurried over to the triage room just a few steps away.

"Ma'am, what happened?" one of the nurses asked as Lynn stepped in the doorway. Three nurses and an orderly were huddled around Drew, each working with tweezers to gently remove the glass shards that were visible.

Blood streamed down Drew's torso, and his face was a mask of blood, snot, and tears. His teeth were clenched, as were his fists at his sides. Whimpers escaped his lips every so often, but he was doing his best to be brave. Lynn's heart broke watching her child try to pretend like he wasn't in agony.

"I'm not really certain," Lynn began. "They were playing outside after dinner, and I heard Drew scream. I ran outside, and he was on the ground, thrashing around and wailing. When I looked him over, he had glass all over him. It was all over the yard, smashed glass scattered all over our yard."

Lynn's voice had grown in pitch, and her stomach rolled inside her. Acid churned and her blood boiled in her veins. Rage was quickly consuming her, and she took a breath, trying to regain control.

"It was my neighbor. I saw her before we went to the park. She was smashing glass on her front steps. Green glass, just like this stuff." Her voice went quiet, almost dreamlike. "Why would anyone do that? Why would you put glass in a yard where children play? What kind of monster does that?"

She asked the nurses that were still working on Drew, but the sound of her voice was still quiet and reflective, almost as if she were talking to herself. They were all looking at her now, hands paused over her son's bloody body. Tears streamed down her face, and her lip quivered. She moved closer to Drew and took his hand.

"You think your neighbor did this?" the first nurse asked her, noting something on a chart.

"I know she did this," Lynn replied. Her tone was quiet, deadly calm. She looked up at the nurse. "I know she did this," Lynn repeated.

"Okay, ma'am. We are going to alert the authorities so they can speak with you. Right now, we are going to move your son to the back for the doctor to see him, and we will need to get x-rays to be sure we didn't miss any glass shards that may be embedded deeper in his tissue."

"But my other two children..." Lynn trailed off, standing to follow the moving gurney.

"Why don't you go check on them? I'll send an orderly over with some drinks and a couple snacks for them. I'll be back to get you just as soon as we get him settled, then you can bring the kids back. It'll give us time to clean him up a bit, too," the nurse said to Lynn.

"That'll be good," Lynn said, gazing at the blood pooled on the floor where the stretcher had been.

She kept her eyes on Drew until they disappeared into the back, then turned toward the waiting room to check on Mitch and Kasey.

Time seemed to stand still while Lynn paced the floor, waiting for the nurse to come get her. Mitch and Kasey were sitting in the corner, staring at the show playing on the television mounted to the wall. Bottles of juice sat beside them, next to crumpled bags of chips and cookies. Lynn glanced at them, a half-smile on her face as she took in the scene. Kids were resilient. Some snacks and a boring show had gotten them calmed down and settled for the moment.

She knew they were still worried; of course they were. Mitch kept kicking at the floor with his hands balling into fists every so often, and Kasey's face was still red from crying. They both had been watching her pace, neither taking their eyes off her for long, even while occasionally laughing at the show.

A state policeman had shown up and taken her statement, all while saying, "You don't say," and "Humph, your neighbor, eh? Is that right?" The man clearly didn't believe her, but she wanted it on record anyway. Now she was waiting for Don to get there and for the nurse to come take her to Drew's room. Her arms itched. Her stomach felt chewed through like rats were eating her from the inside, and her knees ached where the glass had stabbed into her through her jeans when she was tending to Drew. Her jeans had crimson stains on both legs now, from her thighs down to her knees, from her blood and her son's. Her shirt was stained with it, too.

She looked up when she heard the whooshing of the automatic doors that led to the back of the emergency department but frowned when she saw it was only another patient making their way to the exit. She turned and paced the room again, back to the kids, turned and paced back to the hall. The other few people in the waiting area watched her disapprovingly, but she didn't care. She wanted to know what was happening, and she was growing tired of waiting.

Another whoosh, another patient being released. She paced. The kids watched her, then the show, then her. She turned, made another loop. The doors opened again, and this time it was the nurse she recognized.

"Ms. Stone, can you come with me?" the nurse said to her.

"Kids, come on," Lynn said, gesturing to them. They quickly stood up, gathered their trash, and tossed it into the wastebasket on their way to join her in the hallway. Then they followed the nurse down the hallway, the double doors whooshing closed behind them.

Lynn felt cold all of a sudden, like the air had gone out of the room, had gone out of her lungs, like she was walking the green mile rather than going to see her injured son. Dread fell upon her like a shroud, and every possible worst-case scenario she could imagine ran through her mind in the thirty seconds of walking that it took to reach Drew's exam room.

"He's right in here. X-rays were taken, and I'll be sending someone in to give him a tetanus shot. You said he's not had one yet, correct?"

"Yes, that's right. Is he okay?" Lynn asked her, not opening the door yet.

"He's fine, as far as we can tell. The glass seemed to be just superficial, nothing embedded too deep, but the doctor will review the x-rays to be sure. He's going to be sore for a few days, but he's been a trooper." The nurse opened the door and ushered them inside. "I'll be right back in to check his bandages."

Seeing Drew, bandaged but smiling weakly, made the dread vanish, and Lynn smiled back. Mitch and Kasey crowded into the small exam room and stood next to his bed.

"You okay, Drew?" Kasey asked softly.

"Yeah," he said, his voice raspy from his screaming earlier. "It hurts, but I'm okay."

"Mom, is Dad coming?" Drew asked her. His eyes were glassy and red, tears still drying on his cheeks. He looked so pale and weak on the bed that Lynn almost began crying again.

"He's on his way now, honey," she said, patting his leg gently and gesturing for Mitch and Kasey to sit in the chairs along the wall. "Just gotta see what the doctors say, then we can take you home."

"Okay."

Lynn turned when the door opened, and the nurse was back with a rolling tray full of syringes, bandages, and other things.

"What's all that?" Drew asked warily, looking at the cart full of sinister-looking medical tools.

"Well, young man, you need a shot to make sure you don't get any nasty infections from the glass. And there are some fresh bandages here and some ointment that will help the pain. Nothing too scary, okay?"

"Okay," he said.

His voice sounded small to Lynn. She moved closer to him and squeezed his hand, watching him watch the nurse prepare the shot.

"Big sting here, okay, Drew? Take a deep breath and let it out for me," the nurse directed. She watched him do it and slid the needle home as he exhaled. It was over before Drew could take another breath, and he smiled as she gently set a blue Band-Aid over the small puncture.

"All done," she said. "That wasn't so bad, was it?"

"No, it was okay," he said. Drew let his head fall back on the pillow and quietly let the nurse move his gown to the side so she could check the bandages on his back.

Lynn watched as the nurse worked on Drew. Her touch was gentle, and her voice was kind as she explained to them what they were doing and why. How the wounds looked and what Lynn would need to do to care for them at home. As she was finishing the instructions, the door opened, and both Don and the doctor stepped inside.

"It's a bit crowded in here," the nurse said kindly. "How about you kids come back to the waiting room with me for just a few minutes and let your parents speak to the doctor?

"I'll keep an eye on them," she told Lynn.

Lynn nodded and told Mitch and Kasey to behave for a few minutes, and the nurse led them out. Drew had a smile on his face, seeing his dad there. Don was not smiling, but he tried to when he saw Drew's big smile.

"Hey, buddy, how you doing?" he said, stepping closer to the bed.

Lynn turned to the doctor, anxiously watching while he looked over Drew's chart.

"How is he?" she said. "Anything more we need to know?"

"Well, his x-rays look good. We removed all the glass, cleaned out the wounds, and treated them with a numbing ointment for the pain. I'd like to give him a mild sedative now and write him a prescription to last him a week or so. He will be uncomfortable, especially when sleeping, without one. Most of the damage was on the surface, but several shards did go in quite deep. Those wounds will take some time to heal." The doctor finished speaking, then looked at her and Don.

"Any questions for me? Any other concerns?" he asked.

"The shard that went in near his eye. How deep was it?" Lynn asked.

"That one was a close call for sure," the doctor said. "It just barely missed his eye socket, but it should heal fine. It is a deep puncture and may leave a small scar, but there shouldn't be any lasting damage."

"And the other wounds? Will they scar?" Don asked.

"Some will, yes. But in time, they will mostly fade, and by the time Drew is an adult, he will hardly notice them at all if they're even still visible," the doctor said. He tapped a few more notes into the computer he held, then nodded at them.

"If there's nothing else, let me get these printed out and we can get you folks on your way home. How's that sound?" the doctor asked, directing the last question to Drew, who smiled and nodded.

"I'll send the nurse back in with that sedative. It should kick in pretty quickly. You will need to carry him from the car to the house, most likely, once you get home."

Lynn watched him leave, then turned back to Drew and Don. Don stood near the head of the bed, one hand on Drew's shoulder.

"We need to do something..." she began, but Don shook his head.

"Not now," he said, glancing at Drew. "Later tonight, and yes, I know."

Lynn nodded, satisfied with the answer. Getting Drew home was most important right now, getting all the kids to bed. Then she and Don could figure out what to do about their nightmare of a neighbor. She sent Don to go check on Mitch and Kasey while she waited for the discharge papers from the nurse and Drew's medicine. A very long ten minutes later, they were on their way to the car.

A quiet Kasey rode with her, with Drew laying in the backseat. Mitch opted to ride with Don, which was probably a good idea. Lynn could feel the tension rolling off the older boy. He didn't deal with his anger very well, and he was very protective of his brother. Don would know what to say to him.

Lynn didn't have the words for it tonight. She barely had control of her own anger. She drove home, tight-lipped, caging the beast within her until later. But she knew later would come, and when it did, Virginia would be dealt with, once and for all.

The next week passed slowly for Lynn and the kids. She kept them in the house most of the time, only letting them out to play in the side yard, far from Virginia's property. Drew stayed in bed or on the couch most of the time, gingerly moving around when needed. He had grown pale from lack of sleep, and the pain weighed on him. He said it wasn't too bad, but Lynn saw the dullness in his eyes and how he winced when she helped him sit up or change. Drew wasn't used to pain. None of her kids were, nor should they be. Aside from a few scrapes and bumps on the playground or riding their bikes, they had never been severely injured.

Lynn found herself standing on the back stoop more than once late at night glaring at her neighbor's trash can of a house, or rather, what had become a house after they added several ramshackle sections onto their old trailer that sat at the core of the mess. The dark only made the dried-up lake more sinister with its toddler toy graveyard and carousel horses. Junk everywhere, heaps of it, in some lunatic orderly fashion that only Virginia knew. Rusted cars lined their driveway, rotting wood piles nestled up to the rear of the house, and everywhere in between, plastic moldy toddler toys lined up like toy soldiers ready to defeat whatever monster that might creep down from the woods that sat just above the junkyard her neighbor called home.

Lynn would just stand there, seething silently while she stared, feeling the burn in the pit of her stomach, letting her fists clench so hard she drew blood from her palms. Night after night, she tended to Drew's wounds, settled him in bed, then found herself there in the dark, just watching. Don made a comment or two, but the look she had given him could have melted bone, so he retreated to his horror movies and his easy chair.

Lynn let herself cycle through all the odd things that had been happening around their property since they moved in, and slowly the dots began to connect. The random piles of dogshit left in their driveway when they didn't have a dog. The pile of rotting food that had been poured at the base of their mailbox. The bizarre gopher holes that had been dug all through their front and back yard, appearing overnight, dozens of them. Kasey had nearly sprained an ankle falling in one. It had taken her and Don hours to fill them all in. That had happened at least four different times.

All the bizarre things she and Don both had tried to chalk up to just living in the country, dealing with rodents, or bored teens littering or playing pranks. It was neither. All of it had been Virginia. Lynn knew it. Her gut knew it. And now, blood had been drawn and lines had been fully crossed. Rage turned her skin hot, and her vision blurred. Lynn took a breath, visibly shaking with anger.

A sudden laugh spilled into the night air, breaking the silence: Virginia's laugh. "I see you," the neighbor called out, using a child-like sing-song voice. "Every night, watching. I keep you up at night, don't I? Wondering what's next?" The woman cackled again, an old raspy sound like glass in a tin can. "You just wait, dearie. Your boy was just the beginning."

Lynn stared, eyes darting around the black shadows that shrouded Virginia's house until she finally spotted a faint red glow, the cherry of Virginia's Newport as she smoked, leaning against the rickety toolshed that sat right on their property lines. Chills ran up her spine as she watched the cherry fade, then brighten again as the old woman took another drag on it.

"I see you. I see you. I see you," the old woman sang again. The voice slithering through the night straight into Lynn's skull, venom direct from the source. The cackle rang out again as Lynn slipped into the house, her rage dissipating into something new. Fear.

"Don, I am telling you, something is wrong with that woman," Lynn said, setting a plate down in front of him the next morning. "She is threatening us. I don't know why, but I know what I heard. All of this shit that's been happening, it's been her. I know it's her!" Lynn exclaimed, throwing the dish towel down on the counter. Her face was flushed with anger.

Don only shook his head and sipped his coffee. "We can't prove that any of it was her. I talked to that trooper. He said he can go question her, but if we are wrong in our accusation, it will only make us look bad. He also said if we are right, but they can't prove it, it may only make things worse. He said he's seen it before, neighborly disputes gone wrong." Don set his mug down and looked at her. "I know how you feel, but I don't really know what we can do here."

"What do you mean?" Lynn snapped. "We gotta do something. She's hurting our kids, for fuck's sake."

"We can't prove that," he said again. "Which part of this don't you understand?"

"So we do nothing?" She stared at him. Her expression contorted into livid rage, but this time, it was directed at him. "We just let her continue booby-trapping our yard? We wait until she kills one of them?" she snapped, almost screaming now. "What then?"

"I didn't say that," he replied calmly. "We just figure out how to fight back." He sat back in his chair, smiling at her, waiting for the light to click. It did, immediately.

"How?" Lynn said, sitting down across from him, her anger leaving her as swiftly as it had consumed her. He was finally on her side. "What do you mean?"

He shrugged. "Two can play this game. Let's see how she likes it." He picked up his mug, stared at it for a minute, considering his next words, then drank the rest of his coffee before he spoke again.

"So, when I was a child, we had some issues like this with the farmer next door. My father... let's say he knew some things he should not have, knew some things that most others don't, at least not anymore. And let's say that he passed some of those things on to me." He grinned at her, looking like a schoolboy.

Lynn sat back in her chair, her eyes locked onto his intently, waiting for the smirk or the laugh. None came. "I thought that was just a story. Like, things he said to be funny or scare us?"

"Nope, but he knew no one would really take him seriously, not these days, anyway. No one here believes in such things. And no one around us is from the old country, not like he was."

"So what do we do?" Lynn said, her voice almost a whisper, as if the world around them could hear her and bear witness.

"Let me look at some of his journals and refresh myself and we can make a plan. In the meantime, keep the kids in the side yard, ignore her as much as possible. Otherwise, just do as you have been. We will handle this ourselves." Don rose from his seat and kissed her on the top of her head.

"Are you sure we should be doing this?" Lynn asked, looking up at him from her seat.

"She's attacking our kids, our home, disrupting our lives for no apparent reason, and no amount of kindness or talking to her has helped make it stop. Do you have a better idea?" he asked. "I'll only do what you agree to."

"Whatever it takes." Lynn nodded. "She put our son in the hospital." She rose from her seat, feeling that familiar burn in her gut, the rage taking hold. She nodded again and kissed him. "Whatever it takes."

The next few days passed quietly for the small family. Lynn stuck to her routine. Took the kids to school, ran errands, cooked and cleaned and tended to Drew, who was slowly getting better. He was still very wary of going outside, though. That was the worst part of it for Lynn. Seeing her once-active outside boy grow afraid of being outside. Seeing his face grow paler when she took him out to play with Mitch and Kasey, the way he stared at the ground, searching for danger. It broke her heart and renewed her rage. Mitch and Kasey were not spared from the same trauma, either.

The kids loved being outside, but now they were timid and cautious, inspecting every inch of ground they stepped on, skipping the rough play for the tire swing, or just sitting on the porch. It only fueled her rage more, and she hoped Don was closer to a plan they could enact soon. She opted to take the kids to the local park after dinner, allowing them a few hours of worry-free play. She loved how their entire demeanor changed once they got to safe ground, but it again, seeing the change in them, kept her angry and motivated. This woman would not drive them from their home. They had done nothing to her to cause such animosity. But like her husband said, two could play this game.

By the following weekend, Drew's wounds had mostly healed, and Don and Lynn were sitting down at the table to discuss their options. The kids were in bed. Darkness had fallen across the quiet countryside and the two of them sat with coffee in hand and an old journal between them. Lynn gazed at it reverently, running her fingers along the cracked leather binding, inhaling the ancient smell of the parchment pages, listening to Don explain why he knew what he did and why he kept it from her.

As she sat quietly, she listened to her husband's story. The book had belonged to Don's great-grandfather, passed down to the oldest son from the oldest son. The warlock had trained his son well and, as customary, Don had been trained in the ancient knowledge, as had the oldest sons for centuries in his family. As a youth, he had scoffed at it, until his father took him deep into the woods one day and showed him the power of the old ways. It took that moment of truth for Don to understand the world around him was not what he had assumed it to be.

In that one afternoon, he learned that powers exist beyond our control and comprehension. That evil exists and that the universe had provided a way for the good in the world to balance out evil. Warlocks and witches of a certain path were often misunderstood. Don's family worked for the balance of good, rarely causing harm until evil dictated it was necessary. He accepted this knowledge then and embraced what he had been given. While Don rarely had occasion to employ it, every so often he pulled out the old texts to rectify a situation. But this was the first time he would be using it for his own family.

When he finished talking, Don took the book gently from Lynn and opened it to a page marked with a leather bookmark. He showed her the pages, full of handwritten notes and a few symbols that she did not recognize.

"These are the pages we will be using," he said. "It's a reversal of sorts."

"Meaning what exactly?" Lynn said.

"Meaning that anything she tries to do to us, our family, or our home, will result in the outcome being done to her instead," Don said. "While we will be causing this reversal, it will not be anything that she is not bringing upon herself by trying to cause us harm.

"I did go see her yesterday afternoon and made one more effort to warn her to stop," Don said.

"What did she say?"

"She laughed and said she was only getting started," Don admitted. "But I did try. I owed her that, as part of the vow that I took when I was trained, fair warning and forgiveness, but she ignored it. There is just no reasoning with her."

"So what do we do?" Lynn asked after a quiet moment of looking at the words she couldn't read.

"I'll handle it," Don said. "You won't be able to help with the binding. I only wanted you to agree with my plan first."

"Are there other options?" she asked. "Or is this the best one?"

"There are many options, but I felt like this one technically keeps our hands as clean as possible. There is no direct involvement on our part with what will happen. This only ensures that any harm she tries to cause us ends up being done to her instead," he said. "I figured you would be most comfortable with that idea."

Lynn nodded, her lips in a smirk. "Honestly, I'd like to beat her head in, but I can see how that would be wrong."

Don chuckled. "At the very least, the cops may be able to figure out who did it. This way, keeps us out of their line of sight."

"All right, then, that's what we do," Lynn said. "When will you do it?"

"Tomorrow," he said. "I'll gather what I need tonight and do the casting during my hike tomorrow."

Lynn nodded, her eyes drawn to the book again, fascinated. Who knew that things like this actually existed? She felt powerful and small all at the same time. So much sudden knowledge at her hands, while feeling so insignificantly small in the grand scheme of things. Witchcraft was a thing of fairy tales and here was her husband, telling her that he was a warlock of an ancient bloodline.

Her reality had suddenly turned upside down, and she understood the vastness of the responsibility that had been placed on Don's shoulders. To do good or evil? To act for revenge or for protection? To decide when it was necessary and when it was not. He suddenly seemed like a different man altogether, though she felt no fear, only pride.

"I'll handle everything," he told her, squeezing her hand and drawing her out of her reverie.

"I know you will," she said. "You've always protected us."

Don smiled, a smile that spoke volumes, and Lynn went to bed wondering what else he had done for their family that she didn't know. A deeper part of her did not want to know. Her children had been put at risk. She would do whatever it took, whether by her hand or Don's, no longer mattered.

The next few days passed somewhat quietly. Don went on his hike, went to work, spent his evenings with Lynn and kids. A few grumbles from Virginia were all they heard, some screaming, loud cussing, all-out rage at one point as she cussed at her husband.

Don and Lynn just chuckled. Don had found and removed trash from their mailbox. A mangled racoon corpse from their front deck, piles of dogshit left all over their front yard. Minor annoyances, but ones they knew had all somehow made their way to Virginia's home as well. Lynn was wary, though, watching for anything that Virginia might do. Don assured her that she did not need to be afraid anymore. What he had done would not allow them to be harmed, no matter what Virginia tried to do. The harm would go to her, but a tinge of dread hung over Lynn, anyway.

Several days later, while hanging clothes, the pole snapped in half, almost hitting Lynn in the head. The same day, Virginia was clobbered with a branch that fell from a tree as she mowed beneath it. Later that day, Lynn tripped in a small hole in the driveway. She was annoyed but not hurt.

A scream an hour later brought her outside to see Virginia lying on the ground near the toddler toy graveyard. Her ankle twisted in an odd way, also caught in a hole. The words coming from her mouth would have made a sailor blush. She smirked, waited to see Virginia's husband come outside to assist her, then she went back inside, her smirk a full-grown grin. Maybe now the bitch would just stop.

The next morning, Lynn was startled by a pounding on the front door. Don was at work. The kids were at school. A barrage of cursing followed the pounding. Lynn sighed and went to the door, preparing for the worst. When she opened it, Virginia stood there with a crutch under one arm and her ankle in a cast.

"What do you want?" Lynn asked, doing her best to keep her tone in check.

"What do I want? Don't think I don't know what you are doing, you prissy cunt! Putting shit in my mailbox, tossing dead animals at my house! You and those heathen kids you brought up. Trash, all of you! I knew it the moment you moved in!" Virginia screamed, her ever-constant cigarette burning down in one hand. "You mark my words, you uppity bitch, you'll pay for this! You all will! No one fucks with me! No one!" The old woman poked Lynn in the chest. Her bony finger jabbing like marble, ashes dropping to the ground.

Lynn stepped back, out of reach. "Fucks with you?" she asked, her rage boiling over. "Fucks with you?! You put glass in our yard. You put our son in the hospital. You are the one fucking with us for no reason. We have done nothing to you, you old bitch," Lynn said. Her voice was calm, colder than ice, as she glared at the crone on her porch.

"I suggest you get the fuck off my porch and leave us alone before you reap everything you sow. You've been warned. Now fuck off, before I call the cops," Lynn said, then slammed the door in the woman's face, leaving her shrieking more curse words before she finally hobbled away. Lynn stood in the living room, chest heaving, shaking with rage. As the old woman's steps faded away, she forced herself to count to ten. Immediately after that, she hoped like hell that whatever Don had done would have a greater effect soon. She didn't know how much more she could take. She itched to put her hands around the old woman's neck and squeeze until her head popped off.

Two nights later, Lynn woke to the smell of smoke in her

nostrils, faint but there, like fading wood smoke from a campfire. She lay in the dark room for a moment, listening to the house, breathing the smoke and trying to determine if it was real or the remnants of a dream. Don answered the question a moment later, when he sat up beside her.

"Do you smell that?" he asked her, alarm in his voice.

"Yes," she said, sitting up and swinging her legs over the side of the bed. "I thought I was dreaming it, but it's stronger now."

"Go check on the kids," Don said. "I'll go investigate."

As they headed toward the bedroom door, a faint cackle made the hair on the back of Lynn's neck stand up.

"That bitch," she snarled, "I'll kill her."

"No, I'll look. You go check on the kids," he told her. "We are not in harm's way, remember?"

Lynn met his eyes, then nodded, sighing. "Okay, but be quick."

Don hurried down the hall toward the front door while Lynn poked her head into the kids' rooms. First Kasey, then Mitch and Drew; all were still sleeping in their beds, safe and sound. She stepped deeper into the boys' room and drew back the curtain, stifling a gasp at almost the same moment she saw the flames flickering around the base of their front steps.

She saw Don coming down the steps. She waited, terror in her heart, but trusting what he said. As she watched, she scanned their front yard, searching for the culprit. She saw nothing but shadows, but there, just beyond the property line, the bright cherry tip of a glowing ember. Lynn fumed, fury consuming her. She turned her gaze back to Don, watching as he reached the bottom of the steps.

The closer he went, the smaller the flames appeared, then they dwindled to flickering tongues of orange on the ground as he reached the bottom. Lynn exhaled, relief filling her. She turned away, left the room, and headed down the hall to the front door to check on him. As Lynn stepped out onto the front porch, a bright glow filled her peripheral vision. She turned her head to see the front of Virginia's house ablaze. Giant orange flames were already reaching the roof.

She froze in mid-step, staring at the blaze, not even registering Don coming to stand beside her. They watched as a human-shaped flame burst from the house and began to roll on the ground. Lynn gasped. Another shape emerged from the house screaming, but not aglow. This shape belonged to Virginia's husband, Paul. Don took Lynn by the hand and led her inside. Virginia lay on the ground, blazing orange and shrieking loud enough for both Heaven and Hell to hear.

Lynn called the police and fire department while Don checked on the kids, then they waited on the porch like any good but scared neighbor would do. Minutes later, the yard was full of firefighters, police, and ambulances. Paul and Virginia were carted away, but it was too late for the house. By morning, nothing was left of the home but the empty husk of the trailer that sat beneath.

Lynn and the kids played in the front yard that afternoon, free of fear and worry for the first time in years. Don came home to a smiling family for the first time in months. Next door, nothing stood to threaten them but the charred skeletons of the carousel horses and melted globs of toddler toys.

THE HOUSE SPECIAL

REBECCA ROWLAND

I t isn't intended to kill them, not right away.

That's what I tell Kim, Angelique, and Missy as we gather in a feminist huddle, fourth down and ten from our first block party of the season. It's an annual affair, the Memorial Day party, followed by two more during the summer months: one on the Fourth followed by fireworks, one on Labor Day followed by hangovers. Everyone in the neighborhood attends.

We've lived on the same street for nearly a decade: Kim and Brian, Angelique and Amanda, Missy and Erik, me and... me. Kyle has been dead for five years now, and while a few overnight guests have rotated in and out of my bedroom since then, I am determined to remain a solo act. Stop telling me about your single coworker, your Pilates trainer at the gym, your mom's best friend's son. There is a dignity—a glory, really—in being alone, and I intend to embrace it.

They should as well.

Missy scratches at an invisible mosquito bite on her arm. "Won't it be traceable? The poison, I mean." She glances at Kim, then at Angelique. "I wouldn't do well in prison."

"Why are you looking at *me*? I wouldn't do well either," Angelique agrees. "The food alone—"

"I'd thrive," says Kim. "Three squares a day, guaranteed weekends off, and daily gym time?" She takes a swig of her IPA. "Sounds like a better deal than I have now."

"And free health care," adds Angelique. She appears to ponder my proposal.

I uncross and recross my legs. The sun is making them itch, or maybe it's the pollen. I'm so hopped up on Benadryl and Allegra that the gin and tonic I'm sipping makes visual trails as I rest my plastic cup on the picnic table. "No one is going to prison," I assure them. "It is virtually untraceable." I dig deep in my sundress pocket and pull out a tiny baggie containing nine white capsules.

The three women bend forward for a closer look. "What is that? Deadly nightshade?" asks Kim.

"Belladonna is a dark berry," says Angelique. "And the closest place it grows around here is New York State." We all look at her, our eyebrows waiting. "Am I the only former Girl Scout here?" she asks.

"The fuck kind of camping activities was *your* troop doing?" asks Kim.

"I only joined for the cookies," admits Missy.

"No, these caplets contain thallium," I say. "It hasn't been manufactured in the U.S. since the eighties, but you can still find it in toxic waste centers, smelteries, coal power plants."

Angelique takes a long drag off her THC vape. "Smeltery. That's a word you don't hear every day."

"Didn't Kyle work at that coal power plant in New Hampshire? Before you moved here?" Missy asks. "I recall being surprised that anyone in New England was still using coal for power." She wrinkles her nose. "Seems so Loretta Lynn."

"'Don't Come Home a Drinkin',"' says Angelique as she begins to hum a few bars of the tune.

"I still don't understand where you got these," says Kim, pointing to the bag in my hand. "Surely they aren't making thallium pills at the power plant."

"No," I say, shaking my head. "I compounded these myself. It's the powder inside of each cap that you'll use. It's odorless, tasteless, and almost undetectable in blood after twenty-four hours."

Kim holds her hand out, and I shake three pills onto her palm.

Missy makes a face. "Will it be quick?" She glances first at Angelique, then at Kim. "I—I don't want anyone to suffer." Missy takes out her cell phone, and after a few taps of her screen, looks back up at me. "It says the victim's organs shut down one by one, beginning with the digestive and nervous systems."

"They will just feel like they have a bad flu," I say, trying to reassure her. I pause to stifle a sneeze. "Or maybe allergies."

"Allergies that cause you to die," Angelique clarifies, holding out her hand.

I shake three capsules onto it, then turn to Missy. "Didn't you say Erik's student loan debt was crushing you?"

Missy bites her lip. "He just enrolled in a doctoral program. And took out fifteen thousand more. We already owe more to that cunt Sallie Mae than on our house."

"The federal government forgives college debt in full upon death," Kim says.

Missy holds out her hand reluctantly, and as I shake the remaining pills from the bag, I say, "Just mix one capsule's amount into dinner each night, for three nights in a row. The second dose might do the job, but if not, the third is sure to."

Across the street, Brian and Erik stand beside a rose bush, talking excitedly. "Hey, Kim!" her husband yells, turning to look at us. "Grab me a beer!"

Kim points to the cooler only a few feet away from him. "They are right next to you."

Brian shrugs. "So?"

We all stare at Kim, silently shaming her for the acquiescence. She rolls her eyes and points at Angelique. "At least my spouse shows up to shit. Where is Amanda?"

Angelique looks at the ground. She stubs her toe against a small stone half-buried in the lawn. "She wasn't feeling well," she mumbles.

"Funny how that malady always seems to flare when she has to hang around with us," I say, then look from Kim to Missy. "Remember: I made dinner plans with each of you this week. It will be at least a partial alibi."

"Tomorrow at Milano's," Missy pipes up.

"Yeah," Kim says, "and I'll catch you after work on Wednesday."

I look at Angelique. "We said Thursday lunch at The Falls. You want me to come by, and we can walk down? It's supposed to be nice weather."

Angelique stops kicking the rock and looks up. "Nah, I have to do some stuff before. I'll just meet you there."

And with that, Kim walks across the street and over to the cooler. She does not look at us as she hands a cold can to her husband. And Brian does not thank her.

Tuesday, Missy and I sit in our cars in Milano's parking lot, the sun baking us like kneaded dough beneath our windshields. When the restaurant opens promptly at six, we scurry into the air-conditioned restaurant, the only people in town excited to shovel spicy Italian food into our mouths in the ninety-degree heat of the afternoon.

The waitress takes our drink order and places a large basket of rolls between us, tidy squares of butter wrapped in gold foil lying in wait beside them. Before I reach down to grab a piece of bread, I look down at my hands. "I should go wash up," I say.

"Do you know what you want?" Missy asks, picking up the menu. We eat at Milano's every month, and I almost always get the same dish: pasta *putanesca*, my whorish ziti. Something makes me hesitate, however, and I tell Missy I will be ready with my order when I return.

Our drinks are on the table when I do. Missy is a teetotaler and ordered a Diet Coke, but she's holding my cocktail in her hand when I sit down. "I hope you don't mind," she says. "I don't know what came over me: it just looked so good, so I took a tiny sip."

I sit down. "Of course not," I say. "The pistachio martinis are the best here." She hands my glass to me, and I take a hearty swallow. It's cold and sweet, and I'm already happy we are sitting in the booth, the smell of garlic and tomato wafting over us from the kitchen.

The waitress reappears, holding a small notepad and a tiny pen. She lists the soup of the day, the special dessert they've crafted for the beginning of summer, and the new House Special. "It's a penne vodka: caramelized onion and spinach in a creamy tomato sauce with a splash of vodka." My mouth waters and makes the decision for me: the House Special, it is.

I remind Missy to order something to take home for Erik, and she swallows hard. "And the meatball platter with spaghetti," she tells the server.

When we are alone again, I take another sip of martini. "Are you ready to do this?" I ask.

Missy looks at me for a beat longer than is comfortable. Then she takes a deep breath. "Yes," she says. "After you left last night, Angelique, Kim, and I talked for a long time about it." She grabs a roll from the basket and breaks it in two. "We finally realize that some things just need to be done. And, well, you've given us this perfect opportunity..." She looks down at the bread for a beat before opening a butter packet. "We don't want to waste it."

"Smart cookie," I say and swallow the last of the drink.

"Can I ask you something, though?" Missy says. Her eyes are dead serious. "What happened to Kyle," she says, her voice soft, "really?"

I take a sip of my water. "Kyle was..." I begin. I consider my words. "Kyle was a handsome guy." His face appears in my forefront of my mind as I say it, like someone has pulled a photo album off a shelf and opened it to a double-page spread of our decade of marriage. "Yeah, he sure was handsome. Knew it, too. Usually, it's the ones who know it, the ones who have that backbone of self-love who don't need to be told all the time, but Kyle, he was something else."

I back away from the table as the waitress sets our salads in front of us. Before I continue, I take another sip of water. "Kyle needed to be reminded he was handsome. And the only way he could do that was by fucking every woman at the factory." I stab a cherry tomato with my fork. "Every. Woman. He wasn't going to stop. He'd never be faithful to anyone, you know? So," I pop the tomato into my mouth and chew it, "I put him down."

Missy looks like she is going to be sick, right there at the table. She turns away and drinks a few swallows of her soda before turning back to me. "Do you ever feel remorse?" she asks.

I swallow the tomato and stab a spiny lettuce leaf. "No," I say, "and neither will you." My nose begins to tickle, and I put down my fork and grab for the napkin in my lap before I sneeze.

Wednesday, I sit at a table near the back of the Whiskey Barrel, staring at my phone. *Just left work and am hitting all red lights. ETA 5*, reads the text from Kim. A waitress approaches me and asks if I'd like a drink. "I'm expecting a friend, but I'll take a Tito's and soda," I say. "With extra slices of lemon?"

She slaps two plastic-covered menus in front of me and retraces her steps back to the bar. I only glance at the food selections. Milano's penne vodka special must have been sitting around the kitchen for a while: a few hours after eating it, the meal sailed right through me, leaving behind a dull ache in my belly that still remains. I share this with Kim when she arrives, tossing her sunglasses on the table and shaking off her cardigan.

"Well, you know what that means," she replies, picking up a menu. "It didn't have time to stick. A full-proof way to gorge on pasta and gain no weight!"

I raise my eyebrows. "Yeah, a little botulism will do that."

The waitress puts my drink down in front of me and turns to Kim.

"I'll have a peanut butter Old Fashioned and..." she says, her eyes still on the menu, "and the barbecue pork baked potato, and later, I'm going to take home a Philly cheesesteak baked potato."

The waitress makes a note on her pad. "Let me know when you

want me to put that in for you, hon," she says. She looks at me. "And for you?"

I take a big gulp of my drink. The alcohol pokes a sharp knife at my temple, exacerbating the ache there that the food poisoning inspired, a side effect of dehydration. "I'm going to skip food for now," I say, but Kim reaches over the table and stops me from handing in my menu.

"What's your soup of the day?" she asks.

"Pulled pork chili," the waitress says. "House special."

"Chili?" I echo. "You really think that's a good choice?" In response, my stomach makes a loud growling sound, and a sharp pain follows.

"She'll have the chili," Kim says. "Would you make sure it's extra hot? Temperature-wise, not spice."

The waitress disappears again, and I down half of my drink before replacing the glass on the table. My thirst is suddenly overwhelming. "Extra hot?" I ask.

She picks up her glasses and begins to wipe the lenses on her sweater. "To kill any bacteria. You're not getting food poisoning from here. This is our regular place: we can't ruin it!" She smiles then lowers her voice. "Speaking of poisoning, how did... you know, the operation go last night?"

I shrug. "I didn't go home with Missy or anything, but I helped her mix the powder into Erik's take home. They didn't give him a lot of sauce, so it was kind of a pain, but I think everything went okay." I pick up my glass again. "She didn't text me last night. Did you hear anything?"

"No, no," Kim says quickly. The waitress slides a rocks glass containing an amber-colored concoction in front of her. "Thanks. Could she have another of those?" Kim points to my drink, which I am actively draining even as the server stands there.

I put the glass down, condensation still dripping along its sides. "You're right," I say, "I do need to eat something." My vision swirls a bit as a wave of light-headedness washes over me. "Ugh: I'm so sorry to be a drag. Between the pollen and the bad food, I'm feeling pretty bleh."

"What are you taking for the allergies? The tree pollen is bad this season," Kim says, just as a woman who is not our waitress slides a plate with her baked potato in front of her. She then slides a wide bowl of chili in front of me. The steam drifting from the concoction nearly burns my chin, but the aroma instantly kicks my salivary glands into gear.

"Be careful," the food server says. She points at my bowl. "Very hot." Our waitress appears behind her and places another tall, sweaty glass of vodka and soda on the table.

When they are gone, I dip my spoon into the chili hesitantly. My stomach growls. I blow on the tiny mouthful three times before shoving it into my mouth, and instantly, I'm met with a sting akin to a hot poker. "Faaaack," I curse, putting the spoon down. "That really IS hot!" I gulp half of my new drink, but my lower lip still swells with pain. "Did they set it to boiling?!"

"Eat a bite of my potato," Kim says, her mouth half full. She stabs her fork into a small piece and brings it toward me.

I wave it away and quickly swallow the rest of my drink. "I'm going to pee," I tell her. "Blow on my chili while I'm gone?" She nods but picks up her phone to respond to an incoming text message.

In the Whiskey's one-stalled ladies' room, someone has placed a vase of fresh lilacs on the vanity; it half covers the sign insisting that EMPLOYEES MUST WASH HANDS BEFORE RETURNING TO WORK. I bend down to sniff at them, but I can barely sense their fragrance.

When I stand up from the toilet, my feet are prickling with a pins-and-needles sensation, and I become paranoid that I accidentally passed out cold. I scrub my hands thoroughly with soap and water.

"How long was I gone?" I whisper to Kim, who is wrapping up a conversation on her cell phone.

"What?" Kim says. "What do you mean?"

I sit down, shaking each of my legs as I do so, trying to regulate the blood flow that mysteriously stopped and started. "Was I gone for a long time?" I ask. I push my empty glass to the end of the table. "No more liquor for me. I need to eat something."

"You could put an ice cube in there, stir it around?" Kim suggests.

I wave off her suggestion and dig my spoon back into the chili. It isn't steaming anymore, and I cautiously take a bite. "This is pretty good," I say, and Kim gives me a half-hearted smile. I finish more than half the bowl until my stomach lurches, folding itself into a cramp and stapling it there.

"Are you okay?" Kim asks. "Here," she says, sliding over to me a glass of water I don't remember her ordering. I take a few sips, then push my chili away. "No," Kim says. "You're feeling crappy because you drank on an empty stomach. Your lining is irritated from the alcohol; you have to eat a bit more."

I frown. "Spicy chili is the solution for an inflamed stomach lining?" She stares back at me, saying nothing, so I acquiesce. "Okay, okay," I say. "Order Brian's food and I'll keep working on this."

I am scraping the last of the chili from the bowl when the waitress brings a fat brown bag to our table. "Open it up," I say, licking my spoon. "I'll help you mix it in."

"No," she says. "I gotta keep the potato warm. I'll mix it in when I'm in the garage, right before I go inside." She shows me a brown opaque pill bottle, unscrews the top, and shakes out its contents: two of the capsules I gave her two days ago.

"Where's the third one?" I ask. Suddenly, I am exhausted, like the heavy chili is a sedative fogging my brain.

She laughs. "I put it in his food last night," Kim says. "That was the plan; that was YOUR plan, remember?" She wraps her cardigan around her shoulders and places her sunglasses on her head. "I paid the bill while you were in the bathroom," she says. "My treat. It's the least I could do for giving us the pills."

I smile weakly and stand up. "It's a good thing I'm on vacation this week," I say. My voice sounds hollow, like I am speaking through a narrow glass cylinder. "I'm going home and taking a nap."

Thursday, my hand is trembling slightly as I gulp down the double Tito's and diet cola the bartender brings me, flashing a bit of a side-eye since it's almost noon and I can barely keep my eyes open sober. I gave away all of my thallium stash to Kim, Missy, and Angelique, but I wish for two more capsules, if only so that I can hunt down the creator of the Deep House music trend and shove them down his or her throat. The Falls' bar area is thumping with the stuff, even though there is no dance floor and baseball games replay on three different widescreen televisions around the room.

Every table in the bar is a high top, and my barstool has one leg that is slightly shorter than the rest. Even the slightest of movement teeters the chair off balance and makes me overcompensate to keep from falling backward.

My allergies have worsened: I debate texting Angelique and telling her that I am going home. I walked to the restaurant but had to stop twice to rest. It feels as if the muscles in my legs are liquifying, and my head screams with pain. I fold my hands in my lap to keep from scratching my bare thighs beneath my shorts; imaginary bugs crawl under my skin.

I pull out my phone and tap the screen just as Angelique walks through the entrance; I make up my mind to ask her to drive me home. She looks directly at me as she pulls the heavy glass door open, then turns her head to focus on someone behind her.

Amanda.

I frown. What is Angelique's wife doing here? The two of them approach my table and sit across from me without explanation as if this were the plan all along.

"Hi," I say, looking from Angelique to Amanda. The heat in the restaurant is squeezing the room like a vice, and it is still early in the day. I wonder if the bartender will turn on the air conditioning soon. "I'm not feeling great," I say, keeping my eyes on Amanda. "Do you mind if we do this later, or maybe tomorrow?"

Angelique pulls a folded menu from behind the battalion of condiments—ketchup, mustard, hot sauce—and peruses the contents. "What do we usually get when we come here?" she asks, ignoring my request.

"The bacon bleu burger," Amanda says. "It's delicious."

"Will you eat my fries?" Angelique asks me.

I nod, but the motion seems somehow out of synch with my speech, like an image on a television streaming two seconds slower than the audio. "Yeah, sure." I try to focus on the text on the back of the menu Angelique is holding, but it wavers in and out of my comprehension. "I'm really thirsty," I say, wrapping my hands around my sweaty glass. The ice cubes have hardly melted.

Angelique motions to the bartender. "Could we get three of these?" she asks pointing to my drink. To me, she says, "We'll just get a quick drink and take the burger to go."

I rub my eyes. "I'm so sorry, guys. Maybe I caught a summer cold, too, and between the pollen and that, I'm just beat."

The bartender slides the three drinks in front of us, and Amanda places the lunch order to go and gives him a handful of bills. As he walks away, Angelique pats my arm. "Why don't you put your head down for a few minutes? We'll drive you home when the food comes. Sound good?"

I think I nod at this. My head is already halfway down to my arm on the table before the thought is complete. When I open my eyes again, Angelique is stirring my soda with a big plastic straw. "Drink this," she commands. When I don't lift my head right away, she pushes on my arm. Hard. "Hey. Sit up and drink at least half of this. Your face is really pink. You probably have heat exhaustion."

I sit upright again. The black Formica next to the crook of my arm is slick with sweat. I gulp down every drop of liquid in the glass, but it's too fast, and before I can stop myself, my stomach tightens into a stiff cramp and a mouthful of the drink, dotted with digestive acid, sails back up my esophagus and splashes onto Angelique's shirt. "Oh, god..." I begin. "I'm so sorry, I—"

Without a word, Amanda slides off of her stool and walks around to help me off of mine. She steadies me as we walk slowly toward the door, Amanda's arm wrapped stiffly around my shoulder. My legs are wobbly, and my knees knock together like a marionette's. "Thanks so much," Angelique calls to the bartender as she grabs her to-go bag from the host stand. "She's a little under the weather. We're going to get her home."

When we are in the parking lot, Amanda ducks down and heaves me over her shoulder, firefighter-style. She tosses me onto the back seat of their Honda Pilot. The cloth seat is soft against my face, but the air around me grows more oppressive, even hotter than it was in the restaurant. Angelique rummages through my purse, pulls out my cell phone, and turns it off before squatting down and placing it outside, on the pavement. The way she angles her arm, it almost appears as if she is putting it under the car's back tire.

"I think I'm really sick," I say. "Can you bring me..." My vision goes black for a terrifying instant, and there is a tightness in my chest I hadn't felt previously. "Bring me to the hospital," I gasp, my voice coming out so softly, I wonder if I am speaking at all.

I feel the rumble of the car's engine beneath me and the car lurch forward. There is a faint crunch as my cell phone is crushed under the wheel. Angelique puts the car in reverse, runs over the phone again, then shifts the car into drive.

"The second dose didn't do the job, apparently, but the third is sure to," she says, her voice even. She glances at me into the rearview mirror before pulling into traffic and stepping on the accelerator. "Knocking off Kyle was one thing. None of us were fond of him. But our spouses—" She looks over at Amanda, who pats her arm knowingly. "Our spouses, well, they aren't perfect, but they aren't so bad either.

"You, on the other hand," she says as she brakes at a stop sign and turns around to look at me. The image of her flickers and jumps, an 8mm film playing a hair too slow, and the searing pain leaping from my chest lights my abdominal cavity on fire. "You're one evil fucking neighbor."

THE ONLY GOOD GUY IN YOUR LIFE

GAGE GREENWOOD

Violet and Ethan grew up together. Their parents were best friends, and between their houses, there was a strip of grass perfect for two children to meet up and play actions figures. And that's what they did for years. Action figures on "the island," as they called it. Day in and day out, Violet's Ninja Turtles went to war with Ethan's G.I. Joes. Pew Pew. Snick. Snick.

During the summers, they broke up the action figure monotony with swims in Ethan's above-ground pool or runs through the sprinkler in Violet's yard. Meanwhile, Ethan's mom Tess and Violet's mother Lisa would stand about twenty feet away, smoking cigarettes and talking shit about every other person in the neighborhood.

As Violet and Ethan got a little older, their hobbies expanded. Violet grew to love drawing, while Ethan dove headfirst into comic books. That worked out well, because Violet learned The Marvel Method of drawing so she could make books for Ethan. Boom! She had an audience.

After Ethan would flip through her pages of work, eyes wide and mouth practically drooling, he'd rant and rave about how much he loved her stories, then he'd run down the stairs, pages crumpling in his closed fist, and he'd show their moms, who were usually sitting together in the kitchen, smoking cigarettes and talking shit about every other person in the neighborhood.

Tess and Lisa would pretend to love the art, or maybe they really did, but Violet had trouble believing she was any good. Her art was raw and unpolished, although she thought she had some potential. Where she knew she sucked was in the writing, which was fine by her. That wasn't her passion anyway. Most of her comics were stories copied right from Ethan's graphic novels. One time she nearly word for word plagiarized *World War Hulk*, except the main character was called Bulk. She wasn't proud of that one.

When Violet and Ethan reached middle school, they stayed friends, although they otherwise branched off into different groups. Violet continued her pursuits in the arts and found friends who also enjoyed those endeavors, while Ethan found a liking, and a natural talent, for sports. He ran track, played as a shooting guard for the Tanner's Switch Signalman basketball team, and sat on the bench in soccer.

Even with their busy schedules, Violet and Ethan found time for one another. He'd come over, and Lisa would let him in, eager to ask him about his sporting victories before sending him up to Violet's room, where he and Violet would talk, watch television, and eat snacks. He still loved to see her art and always fawned over any of her drawings or paintings. While *he* still obsessed over comic books, Violet had long since abandoned creating art within panels. Instead, her budding interest in horror films reflected heavily on her work, where her style veered toward the gothic, weird, and sometimes grotesque.

On Fridays or Saturdays, if Ethan had a game, Violet usually sat on the bleachers cheering him on and doodling in her wire-bound sketch pad. Sometimes she'd miss a big play while she shaded a misty cobblestoned street or an elongated face in a puff of smoke, but she'd jump up and cheer when the crowd around her led the way.

In their final year of middle school, Ethan nervously asked Violet to the eighth-grade dance, just as friends, and she agreed. A few days later, Clay Williams from her artist's circle asked her, too. Despite her crush on him, she kept her obligations to Ethan and didn't regret it. She and Ethan had a blast. They danced, cracked jokes, and laughed the night away. If she had gone with Clay, she would have spent the night warring with a ball of nerves, trying too hard to impress him, or at the very least not make a fool of herself.

She *did* get to dance with Clay, though, when he asked for her hand during "Wonderful Tonight" by Eric Clapton. Ethan didn't seem to mind and spent the song hanging and goofing with his basketball teammates. By the end of the song, Violet had agreed to a date with Clay on Saturday, assuming her mom would drop her off at Warwick Mall, so the two could hang out at the food court before crossing the parking lot to the movie theaters. Sounded great to her.

After the dance, Violet's mom drove her and Ethan home. They both changed out of their dress clothes and met back in front of Violet's house to hang on the front stone wall and chat about their night. They did this often, meeting at "the wall" and catching up on their day, although they rarely did it when they'd spent that time together. But, hey, it *was* both of their first times at a school dance, so it felt like they had a lot to process.

They laughed about Mallery O'Connor's dancing style, and how it resembled someone holding a fork in an electrical socket. Tadd Denson's blue tux and bowtie also garnered some chuckles.

Her stomach twisted when she told him about the potential future date with Clay, having suspected Ethan might harbor a small crush on her. For a sliver of a second, his face sunk, but then all he said was, "That's awesome. I hope you have fun."

As it turned out, her concerns were backward. She and Clay dated for about six months, and during that time, Clay ended up the jealous one, constantly throwing sideways remarks about Ethan and telling Violet she shouldn't hang out with her best friend. He minced his words, avoiding outright accusations, keeping himself from looking bad. *I just don't trust that guy. I trust YOU. It's him I don't trust. He obviously wants you.*

He accompanied her whenever she sat in the stands at Ethan's games and looked for excuses to get them out the door early, knowing she and Ethan would usually hang out and talk afterward.

She never stopped finding time for Ethan, though. "The wall" housed their butts many nights, where they'd stay and chat for hours, while Lisa had to endure the constant ringing of the house phone from Clay's nervous "checking ins."

Eventually, Clay's jealousy grew, his accusations ceased being subtle, and Violet would end up in a rip-roaring fight with him. The day he finally said what he always meant and demanded she make a choice was the day she did, and Clay found himself single again.

She cried to Ethan on the wall, and her best friend hugged her until the moon came out.

High school moved fast. Ethan continued to play basketball, first on the freshmen team, and then right to Varsity, and he broke some records in cross country. He didn't even try to make the soccer team. Violet continued her art training, studying in school and after with a few various local classes, even though most of the time she proved more skilled than her teachers.

Some of her pieces made it into small art shows, and Ethan showed up to every single one. He took her out to dinner to celebrate when she won a spot on the cover of *Horror Craft Magazine* with her piece *Poe's Requiem.*

They went to their senior prom with different people. Ethan went with his girlfriend Shelly, who Violet thought looked breathtaking in her purple sequin dress. Violet went with her boyfriend, Brian, who won prom king. Violet did not win queen, but she wasn't upset about it. In fact, the idea of it hadn't even been on her radar, and she was astounded to find out later that she'd received the third most votes, something she assumed only happened because she walked the halls side-by-side with Brian. Neither Violet's nor Ethan's relationship survived the summer.

On graduation night, Violet and Ethan ended up at the same party, and they spent a lot of time drinking and reminiscing about their life-long friendship, the variety of bad dates they'd each experienced, and a mishmash of other random memories.

Both continued to live with their moms during college. Violet went to the Rhode Island School of Design in Providence, while Ethan attended the University of Rhode Island, where he sat on the bench for their basketball team. He confessed to Violet that he never had any aspirations for playing in the NBA, well aware he was too short for it, but he'd hoped to have a little more standing in the college realm.

At the same time Violet refined her craft at college, Instagram blew up in popularity, and she used it to develop a fandom around her work. By the time she graduated, she had over fifteen million followers and no shortage of commissions.

Ethan attended her graduation, and she his. After both, Lisa and Tess bought pizzas, and they all celebrated together.

Their friendship saw its finale when they were in their mid-thirties, just after April 30, 2023, a date that would be easy for both of them to remember, because it was the day an overworked truck driver fell asleep at the wheel and crashed into Lisa's Toyota Camry, killing both Lisa and Tess instantly as the two women headed home from a day at the casino in Connecticut.

After the funeral, Violet collapsed onto her couch, curling into a fetal position and clutching a pillow. She cried loudly and violently, and at some point, when all the tears had drained, she fell asleep.

The phone buzzing on her coffee table woke her up sometime after midnight.

I don't like being in this house without her here. Want to sit on the wall and have some drinks?

She sat up and stared at the text for a few minutes, trying to decide if she wanted to get up or not. She sighed, responded, fumbled her way to the bathroom, peed, and headed for the front door. On the way, she noticed an open pack of her mom's cigarettes sitting on the hallway bench next to a blue lighter. She grabbed them on her way out the door.

Ethan sat on the wall with a six-pack of Blue Moons. She sat next to him, and for a few minutes, they both looked across the street, but not really at anything, just avoiding conversation. Violet spun the pack of cigarettes in her hands, and Ethan noticed.

"Are those your mom's?"

She nodded. "You know, I have never tried a cigarette in my life. Not even one inhale." The pack flipped open, and she slid one out. "But tonight, I think I will."

"I tried them a few times in college but never took to it. If you want to give one away, I'd also have one tonight."

She put a cigarette to her lips and lit it, keeping the smoke in her mouth instead of inhaling, knowing full well the coughing fit she'd have if she dove right in. As the smoke slithered out of her mouth, she handed one to Ethan.

He took it and said, "To Tess and Lisa," before putting it in his mouth and lighting it, which he did with much more confidence than Violet had, resulting in an immediate hacking fit.

They kept up with the cigarettes, Tess inhaling a little more smoke each time, warming her throat up for it. Because of this, she never coughed, although she did get quite light-headed. Ethan, on the other hand, brute forced it, coughing and coughing until he finally got used to it. In the meantime, they each nursed a beer.

"How are we ever going to manage living on this street without them here?" he said.

"At least now we aren't losers still living with their parents in their thirties."

The hard sadness in his face washed away, and he fell into a laugh. "Wow. I did not expect that."

She inhaled another drag. "If you can't laugh—"

Trying to keep the momentum, he said, "How will we ever know if Mr. Walsh is still stealing everyone's admail so he can clip the coupons without Tess and Lisa's gossip?"

"I guess we'll just have to carry on the tradition. The torch is passed, and we must keep track of our neighbors now. I think Miss Donato wears the same bloomers every day."

He doubled over cracking up and fell into another coughing session. And then, suddenly, he stopped and said, "I love you, Violet."

Something inside her hit the brakes, and her heart slammed to a stop. She had no idea what kind of face she made in response, but whatever it was, he noticed it.

"Oh, don't look surprised. You had to have known. I've loved you since we were kids. One time, your mom let me in to go see you, and she whispered to me, 'I hope she figures it out, because you two are perfect for each other.' Everyone knew."

Violet tossed her cigarette into the street and climbed up the wall, back toward her front door. "I have to go. Have a good night."

He stood up. "Wait. Don't do that."

She turned back to him. "Our moms just died. I can't have this conversation right now. You're dealing with a lot of shit, and I'm dealing with a lot of shit. I'm not mad. I just can't talk about this tonight. I'll call you tomorrow."

He made no further objection, but she gave him one last glance as she opened the front door, and he stood in the same place, staring as if shocked and nursing a deep wound neither of them could fully process.

In the morning, she had four missed calls from him, and a text, which just read: **Sorry. Bad timing. Maybe I was cigarette drunk.**

She ate oatmeal while scrolling through her Instagram messages and then worked on a commission for an indie author's book cover. Eyes floating above an island. They always wanted creepy eyes floating above something or a hand on something. A bloody handprint on a wall. A hand coming through a shower curtain. Handprints on the windshield. Fucking hands and eyes.

She finished up and took a shower before heading out to meet with a festival director who'd hired her for promotional materials for their Halloween event. On her way out the door, she checked her phone again to see six more missed calls from Ethan, and another text.

Please don't ignore me. Not now. I'm sorry I said anything. But I need you right now. We need each other.

The last line gave her a shiver. She knew what he meant. They both suffered a major loss, and they'd always been each other's support during tough times, but she hesitated at the concept of people needing each other. Violet wanted to move on, to keep busy. She loved her mother, but sitting around thinking about the tragedy would destroy her. Moving. That's what she *needed.* Having another human to rely on was great, but she would continue to live no matter what.

Still, she understood Ethan hurt and probably felt very alone, and she was his best friend. She wanted to be there for him, and would be, but she didn't know how to proceed. Just ignore the confession? Pretend it never happened? She couldn't figure it out just yet, but she also didn't want him to spend the day suffering thinking she'd never speak to him again. So she sent a quick text.

Not ignoring you. Just super busy this morning. I have a meeting in Narragansett. I'll message you when I get home.

He responded with: **Okay.**

Her meeting with the festival director went well. He gave her a list of tasks: designing art for ads and promos, a logo for the event, and sending all of it as JPEGs, PDFs, and PNGs, but he also wanted her to resize all of it to fit everything from stickers to Facebook banners and a million things in between. If the director approved the initial designs, the work was easy. Just resizing and changing file types. And the pay was fantastic.

She had other projects to finish first but had a few ideas for the festival and wanted to get right on them while the iron was hot. She remembered she'd promised Ethan a message when she got back, but creativity called, and it took precedence.

An hour into sketching a few ideas, she heard the doorbell through the music blasting in her earbuds. She sighed and put the pad down.

"Fuck. I don't want to do this right now."

She opened the door to Ethan's smiling face.

"Thought you were going to message," he said.

When did he become this way? He'd never been like this. She got it, their mothers had just died, but that didn't mean she forfeited her right to peace. What made Ethan and Violet's friendship last was the knowledge they each had their own lives to live, and there was no pressure to be around each other all the time. Space is the best gift a human can offer another. The more space they'd given each other, the more they'd worked hard to make time for their friendship. That's how it had always functioned.

She tried to put herself in his shoes. He just wanted to recover from embarrassment during what was already the hardest point in his life. But she just operated differently. Comfortable in her own mistakes and faux pas. When she fucked up with something, or embarrassed herself, she just did what she always did. Kept moving.

"Sorry. I have a big project." She lifted her arm to show the pencil ink covering the underbelly of her left hand.

His eyes widened. "Can I see the work in progress?"

She hung on the door, not wanting to break the seal. "Not yet. I just want to finish getting these concepts down."

He stepped back. "Okay. Do you want to meet on the wall later? Give me a chance to make up for last night's error?"

She brushed some hair out of her eyes. "Yeah, maybe. I know you think it's about you, but I'm honestly just swamped and dealing with my mom in my own way. It has nothing to do with last night. I promise."

He filled his cheeks with air and motorboated it all out of his lips. "Fair enough. Tell you what, I'm going to sit on the wall at eight. I hope you'll join me, but if not, no worries. No pressure."

She agreed, and they said goodbye. As she got back to work, she felt her mother's judgmental eyes on her. "I know, Mom," she said. "I know."

Ethan had said, "No pressure," but it felt like there was. If this had all been about their mother's deaths, she'd be out there. She wouldn't be working. But it felt more like she needed to help him lick his wounds, and that made her resentful. She grieved, too. And she had a life to continue if she hoped to take over her mother's mortgage and bills. She didn't have time to make Ethan feel better about his lifelong crush on her, and he was shitty to have dropped that on her and then expect her to jump hoops to make him feel better about it. Where did the line exist between being his friend and getting stomped by another fragile ego?

She ran circles in her own mind trying to consider his feelings, but who considered hers? Growing frustrated, she put her work away, unable to concentrate. She sat there, counting down the clock until eight, for the first time in her life, truly angry with her friend, and even more startling, nervous.

She stepped outside at two past, and he stood in front of the wall, rocking on the balls of his feet. He'd brought the four leftover bottles of Blue Moon. "I knew you'd come out."

"Did you?" she said and hopped off the wall. "Because I didn't."

He cracked open a beer and handed it to her, she shook her head, and he took a swig for himself instead. "We've always come through for each other."

She pulled her mom's pack of cigarettes from her pocket and lit one.

"Really taking to those, huh?"

A stream of smoke left her lips. "I know it sounds stupid, but they make me feel connected to her."

Ethan sat next to her. "That doesn't sound stupid. It sounds like grief."

Violet's shoulders relaxed. Maybe her friend was back, and last night could be forgotten.

"Wanna hear the dumb things I've been doing at home?"

She looked up at him, eyes watering. "Kind of." To keep it light, she added a giggle.

He sat down next to her. "Well, she had a stack of laundry by the washer, and I moved it upstairs, because I don't want to wash her clothes. Feels like I'm scrubbing away a piece of Mom or something." He laughed. "I know it's crazy, but I just can't wash them, or remove them, or anything other than keep them in the living room. On top of that, whenever I walk by her room, I talk to her. Not in some cute kind of 'miss you, Mom' sort of way, but like a compulsive need to let her know I'm still alive. Barely. But I am."

The lightheadedness came back to Violet. "Fuck. I'm sorry."

He shook his head. "Not even the dumbest thing I've done, though. I also told my best friend I loved her."

She put her head down, embarrassed by the whole situation. "Please, it's fine. We're both just messed up right now."

He leaned into her, touching her shoulder with his. "I'm not messed up, Violet. I mean, I am, but I meant what I said. It's not like losing my mother made me say something crazy. Sure, it made me come out with it at the worst time possible, but what I said was true."

She looked at him, a second wave of sadness hitting her. "I don't know what to say to that."

He scoffed and turned away from her. "Bullshit."

"What?"

When he returned his eyes toward her, they contained flames. "I've wanted to say that to you since we were kids. And it always felt like the wrong time. When's the right time, Violet? When would have been the appropriate time to tell you?"

She stood up and snuffed the butt on the same stone she'd sat on. "I guess never, Ethan. I don't know what you want me to say."

He stood up too and raised his voice to match. "I want you to tell me you love me too, because I know you do."

"I don't. I'm sorry. And I'm not doing this right now."

She hopped the wall toward her door, but this time he followed her. "I think I deserve for you to stick around and finish the conversation. I've earned that, Violet. Don't walk away again."

She opened the door, but he put his hand out to stop it. "Ethan, back the fuck up. I'm going inside."

"Back the fuck up? Really? That's where we are now?"

She pushed herself through the opening. "Apparently," she said as she slammed herself inside and twisted the lock.

By morning, she'd finished off the last few cigarettes in her mother's pack. She couldn't sleep, tossed and turned when she tried. Anger, frustration, sadness, hurt, confusion, it all flowed through her.

When the sun came out, she decided she couldn't stay in the house, so she called an artist friend, Ryan, and asked if she could work in his studio for the day. Ryan was a painter, and a very successful one. He rented out a large studio in a converted mill, and sometimes Violet came by and worked on her commissions while shooting the shit with him. It usually involved a lunch where both ended up in tears laughing, and she needed a good distraction.

When she arrived at his space, he immediately put down his brush and came to her, draping her in a heavy hug. "I'm so sorry about your mom," he whispered in her ear.

Her hands gripped the back of his shirt, and a loud moan left her throat as the flood gates opened wide. He squeezed her tighter and rocked back and forth. "It's okay," he said.

She pulled away. "I know you're busy, but can I talk to you? I just need to vent."

He grabbed two chairs and slid them next to each other. "Have a seat. You've come to Therapist Ryan's. If I wasn't an artist, I would one hundred percent be a shrink. Just ask any of my friends."

She smiled. His happy personality already chipped away at all of her stress. She told him about Ethan's confession, and all of these emotions she had from it.

"So why are you so angry about it?"

She scrunched her brow. "What do you mean? Don't you think it was an inappropriate time to confess that to me?"

He smirked. "I do. But I don't think that's why it upset you so much. The night Remy and I got married, my old friend John told me he'd always wished we'd end up together. He'd been drinking and he apologized the next day, but I still haven't really forgiven him. At first, I thought it was just because he decided to tell me on my wedding night, that it was a cruel and classless time for such a confession, but over time, when I thought about it more, I realized it was something else entirely."

Violet leaned forward. "What?"

He raised one eyebrow like The Rock. "I don't want to influence your feelings. But I think if you really take a deep breath and think about it, you'll have the same ones."

She bit her lip, feeling antsy. So many different emotions ran through her, and she couldn't settle on the underlying source, that thing in the middle of it all, spinning and creating the whirlpool in her guts. "I'm hurt. I think that's it. I'm not sure why, but I'm really hurt."

He pointed at her. "You're getting there, but I'm not sure you hit the mark just right."

"Disappointed? No, although there's that. I also feel kind of bad, because if he's been harboring all these feelings all this time, always hoping we'd end up together, and he's finally seeing my reaction, it's like mourning all over again. He has a new thing to grieve over. But part of me doesn't give a shit, because I'm hurting too, and he's not worried about it in the least. I know he's not. I don't know. I don't." Then she gasped. "I feel fucking betrayed."

Ryan slapped the side of his chair. "There it is. You feel betrayed because you were betrayed. The second he decided he loved you, and he chose not to tell you for whatever reason, then anything after was a ruse, a trick, manipulation. And look, if it happened when he was a kid, maybe those years are forgivable. But you're how old now?"

"Thirty-four."

"Thirty-four! That's a whole lot of adult years he chose to keep his secret. And every single one of those years was a lie. He wasn't being a friend in good faith. He wanted something from it. He was after something. And worse, he's going to pretend he's the victim now. But think of all those times you came to him, believing you had something special, a person you could go to simply because they cared about you as a friend, and the whole time, he was think-ing, 'How will this end in us being a couple?'"

She felt it now, the pin in the center of the problem, and she wanted to pluck it, let all the air out of the tire. "Yes! It's like every single moment I spent with him isn't what I thought it was, like when you find a twist in the end of the book, and you need to go back and reread it all to experience it with that hidden layer. But in this case, I don't want to revisit it. It spoiled all of it. I remember sitting in my bedroom as a teenager, watching movies with him, and thinking I'd never feel so comfortable around another person, and now I know the entire time, he was looking at me in a totally different way." She sighed, letting out a gust of frustration. "Maybe I was stupid to think a man and a woman can just be friends." Then she looked up. "Present company not included, obviously."

He shook his head. "Don't do that. First, it's insulting to me as a gay man for you to act like I'm only safe because I'm gay. Who I choose to love is not the reason I can be a well-adjusted adult that can separate friends from people I love. Good humans can do that. And there are plenty of straight men worth being friends with, plenty within our circle of friends who would care about you and take care of you like a friend should without ever assuming or wanting anything else. You know that."

She put her head down in shame. "I know. You're right. I just feel so burned right now."

"You were burned. But don't make it change you. I would, however, avoid the fuck out of him right now."

She scanned the room, just now taking the time to see all of his new work. He had a way of mixing bright, intense colors like Matisse and other Fauves with the dark and isolating themes of Francisco Goya's Black Paintings. They were haunting yet inviting like a lullaby from a demon. A bright green-and-red fish getting crushed to death by a neon orange boot. Rainbow-colored grapes entering the mouth of a crudely shaped witch. The Enchantress's elongated mouth and fiery eyes contradicted the welcoming, warm blues of her cape and flailing hair.

"I probably will for the sake of not dealing with it, but why do you say so?" she asked while still appreciating his work.

"Because dudes like that can't move away from it. Once they've confessed their feelings, it's out forever, and they can't accept an outcome that doesn't coincide with their dreams. Every single day he yearned for you and hadn't spoken up is another day where his belief that he owned you grew bigger, that you were destined to be together."

She stood up and shook, literally shivered considering it. "I don't think so. He's still Ethan. He's not an evil person."

Ryan followed her suit and stood up too. "Just be careful, okay?"

She nodded. "I will."

"Good. Now that we've managed to get zero work done, I think it's time for lunch. What do you say?"

When she returned home that evening, she half expected to see Ethan sitting on her wall or on his own walkway waiting for her to return, but the lawns were clear. Still, she rushed from the car to the house, hoping to avoid any possibility of him confronting her.

When she entered the front hall, she clicked the lights on and nearly screamed. All of her artwork hung on the walls, the doorways, the banister leading to the second floor. It covered the hallway and continued into the kitchen in front of her. Pictures hung on the fridge and the door to the basement. It wasn't her newer work either, but the paintings and drawings that had sat in dusty boxes in the basement, placed there by Lisa who refused to consider any of it trash. There were old comic book panels, school assignments showing horizons and landscapes, painted fruits, poorly shaded faces. There were remnants from her anime phase, and from the time she drew nothing but farmhouses.

Something covered the kitchen table too, but she couldn't make it out, and she sure as fuck wasn't moving in for a closer look.

Someone (and she had a pretty good idea who) had broken into her house, had invaded her privacy, had unearthed her crude artistic past, showcasing them in an embarrassing display no different than waving around photos from a person's childhood without their approval.

She knew Ethan had done it, but she didn't know how. And worse, she didn't know if he was still in the house or waiting for her outside, leaving her statuesque at the front door, fingers wrapped around the handle, ready to twist and run, or hurry and lock.

Then footsteps came from the other side of the fridge, where a doorway led to the living room. Ethan came into view.

"What the fuck are you doing?" she asked him.

He smiled and waved his hands toward the lines of artwork decorating the house. "This is our life. I wanted to show you."

"Ethan, how did you get in my house?"

He looked surprised by the question. "Tess and Lisa exchanged spares in case they locked themselves out."

"I didn't give you permission to come into my house when I'm not here."

He stared at one of the pictures taped to the fridge and plucked it off. She couldn't see what the picture consisted of from her angle. "You talk to me like I'm some crazed psychopath, and not the guy you always ran to when you needed someone." He turned the picture around. It was an unfinished sketch she made in college of a woman climbing a mountain of skulls. "You remember this one?"

She nodded. Her muscles tensed, and the air in her lungs refused to escape.

"You made this one when you were with... I think his name was Chris? Christian? Something like that. When he broke up with you, you cried on my shoulder. Remember that?" He didn't wait for an answer. "How many men did I have to endure? Each one worse than the last. One fuck up after the next. And you'd cry to me and ask me when you'd finally get to meet the right one. Can you imagine how insulting that was to me?"

"Ethan, I need you to leave my house now. I'll call the police." She pulled her phone out of her pocket, but she couldn't mask the trembling in her fingers.

He showed no worry over her threat, stepping forward. She panicked, unsure if he was taking her orders or coming toward her for some other reason.

"All this just because I said I love you. Do you not see how crazy you're acting?"

She slid away from the door, giving him room to leave, but she kept her free hand on the handle, in case she needed to run. "Says the guy who broke into my house to tape up pictures I made when I was nine."

As he left the kitchen and entered the hall, he brushed one finger along the hung artwork, creating a wave in the bottom of the drawings. "It was a romantic gesture, Violet. Not a threatening one. These pictures represent our lives together. I can tell you the story behind each one." He pointed toward a drawing of a weeping flower. "You made that one from the bleachers while I played in the playoffs against Cranston West."

He ripped another off the wall. While Violet held no sentimentality toward her drawings and told her mother on numerous occasions they were worth tossing, seeing Ethan callously pull them from their corners hurt her deep within her bones.

"This one you made during summer vacation in between sixth and seventh grade. I went to basketball camp at Providence College, and you ran to show it to me when I got off the bus. I remember all of these, Violet. Every story behind them. Every moment with you."

Tears formed in her eyes, not from sadness, but from fear. Her chest caved in. The world did, too. How would she ever feel safe again? "I said you need to leave, Ethan."

He reached into his pocket and pulled something out. Violet's heart leaped into her throat until she saw what he held. The house key. He placed it on the hallway bench. "We belong together, Violet.

One day you'll see that. It's hard to see the fear in your eyes. I haven't changed into a monster. I'm still me."

He brushed by her, opened the door, and left. As soon as the door closed, she bent over and heaved out the air she'd held in so tightly. Her arms shook so hard, she dropped her cell phone. When she stood back up, the room spun. She ignored the dizziness and ran through the hallway, ripping every page from its tape. Screaming, she tore some to shreds, stomping on the remnants after they fluttered to the floor.

"Oh, God. What the fuck?" She grabbed her phone and, with trembling fingers, dialed Ryan.

"What's up?" he said. "Everything okay?"

She sniffled. "He was here. In my fucking house. He taped up all my artwork in this big display." She tried to continue ranting, but Ryan interrupted her.

"Call the police. Right now."

She shook her head, staring down at the crumbled, ripped, and fragmented pieces of her life's work, now poisoned by Ethan's touch. "What do I say? He had a spare key. And he didn't rob me or attack me. All he did was hang up my artwork and tell me he loved me again. When I told him to leave, he did. I mean, he looked threatening, and he definitely wanted to intimidate me, but like, he didn't actually do anything. He even returned his key before he left."

"Listen to me, Violet. Call the police. Tell them exactly the truth. They won't arrest him, but it creates a timeline. You're making it clear you didn't want him there, and you want no further contact. They will go tell him that, and anything he tries to do from that point forward will be considered harassment."

She nodded. "Okay. Okay."

As soon as she hung up, she dialed the police and explained everything that happened. It didn't take long for two officers to arrive in separate cars. The female officer was short and muscular, her hair pulled back in a tight ponytail. The male officer was tall and lanky. He had kind eyes surrounded by tired wrinkles.

The woman extended her hand. "Hello. Violet?"

Violet nodded.

"I'm Officer Mendez, and this is Officer Pruitt."

Pruitt nodded and shook her hand. "So what's going on, Violet?" he asked.

She explained it all again, feeling the terror mount with each retelling.

"Do you mind if we see what he did?" Mendez said, staring at the front door.

"Um, yeah. Come on in." She glanced next door to see if Ethan noticed the police presence.

When the officers entered the hallway, they stopped dead in their tracks.

Mendez said, "Did he do this?"

Violet scratched her arm. "Oh, no. He had taped them all up on the walls. I ripped them off in frustration when he left. I know it sounds stupid, but it felt dirty keeping them where he put them, like it physically hurt seeing them there."

"Can we all sit at the table? I don't want to step on your drawings," Mendez said.

"Yeah. No. Don't worry about it. Just step on them. I'm going to toss them anyway."

As they walked to the kitchen table, Pruitt said, "Do you have a Ring camera or anything we could view?"

For the first time, she noticed what was on the kitchen table. Ethan had set up all of her old action figures from when she was a kid. When they were children, one of them would usually get to the island before the other, and while the first arrival waited for the other, they'd set up all of their action figures in various poses, ready for war. When the second person showed up, they'd get theirs all set up, and they'd have little fights with all the figures until one was standing. Then they'd both set them all up again before another round of war. When they grew up, they'd laugh remembering it, because they often spent more time posing the figures than actually warring with them.

Now, as she looked at all of her old figures, from Michaelangelo to her Barnyard Commandos to Cobra Commander and his crew, all posed along the table, she felt the crushing weight in her chest again. He had the toys all posed and ready for battle. This was a message. He was saying, "Let's play. Your move. Let the war begin." Worse, he did it with *her* figures.

She could never explain all of this to the officers, just like she couldn't explain what was so wrong about him confessing his feelings.

"No, I don't have a Ring camera," she said.

The two officers sat at the table. Mendez said, "Did he do this too?"

Violet couldn't stop staring at the figures. It must have taken hours for him to get the figures set up and tape all of her artwork to the walls. "He did. We used to play with these when we were kids. He was trying to make some kind of point."

Keeping things on topic, Pruitt said, "I highly recommend you get a Ring camera and have your locks changed. Just because he gave you back the key doesn't mean he hasn't made copies."

She hadn't even considered that, but now that the idea was in the universe, she knew she'd never sleep until the locks were changed. "Okay."

He leaned back in his chair. Both of their walkie-talkies blipped at the same time, and it made Violet flinch. Pruitt said, "Here's what we can do. We'll go next door and give him what we call a CTW, which is a criminal trespass warning. It lets him know you no longer want him on your property, and if he steps on it, he will go directly to jail for trespassing. I'd also advise you to go to the Richmond Court House and apply for an order of protection."

She eyed both of them back and forth. She honestly hadn't expected this much help. "Will they grant it? I thought it was extra impossible to get those things. I've heard horror stories."

Mendez leaned forward, knocking a transformer over. "Those horror stories are all true. It can be difficult, but it's gotten better. Still not perfect, but it's not like it used to be. You can explain to the judge you were advised by us. We'll give our names and badge numbers. For now, you'll get a temporary one. You said the key was given to his mother. Not him. Even with a key, he can't just come into your home without your permission, and we can see the proof all around here that he wasn't trying to help you out with something. Pardon my language, but this shit is crazy."

Ten pounds of stress rolled off Violet's back. "Thank you! I thought I was crazy for being so upset about it. But this is crazy, right?"

"It's insane. And guys like this know what they're doing. He wanted you to feel like you were the crazy one. We'll go talk to him now."

Violet walked them to the front door and then quickly grabbed her cigarettes. She'd bought her own pack at this point. She wasn't addicted yet but didn't care if she ever got there. She liked them. They meant something to her now. Although she'd given herself a headache a few times from smoking too many too fast, and she'd also met those hacking fits she so easily avoided on her first one.

Like her mother, she went to the back patio to smoke it. A nearly full moon crouched behind the woods. Crickets and cicadas sang. Violet went to the side of the patio closest to Ethan's house, hoping to hear the conversation between the officers and Ethan, wondering if he'd try to defend himself.

It didn't take long before the officers were back at her door. She ran to let them in.

"How'd it go?" She nibbled on the skin around her fingernail.

"Went fine. He didn't put up any kind of argument. So that's that," Pruitt said.

"Yeah, except I feel like I shouldn't stay here until I get those locks changed."

Mendez said, "Do you have somewhere you could stay tonight? It might not be a bad idea until you get the locks swapped out. He seemed pretty subdued, but he also seemed like a smarmy prick."

"Yeah, I'll call my friend Ryan and see if I can crash in his studio."

Pruitt said, "Don't hesitate to call us again, even if you aren't sure if it's a big deal. If something is bothering you, call us."

She thanked them again and went inside. Her own house felt dangerous. All the dark corners grew teeth. She couldn't settle her pulse. But something else was happening, too, something opposing the anxiety. Her eyelids grew heavy. Then her arms and legs. She stared at her cellphone, knowing she needed to call Ryan, to get out of the house, but she couldn't muster the energy to reach for it. Something was wrong. And then all went black.

The birds chirped when she woke up. Her mouth was dry, along with her throat. She coughed hard. For a while, she laid there on the couch, just looking at the ceiling, trying to remember why she was there. Slowly her night pieced together, and she sat up, looking around as if Ethan might be standing there staring at her. He wasn't.

She slowly checked every room of the house to be sure of it. She was wobbly at first, and her limbs felt heavy as they sometimes did after a night of deep sleep. But how did she sleep so deeply, when she spent the evening in terror?

It made no sense. She would have worried Ethan drugged her somehow, but she hadn't had anything to drink or eat after she'd returned home to find him in her kitchen.

Unable to wipe away the grogginess, she plopped at the kitchen table and ate a yogurt, completely lacking the mental capacity to look at her social media or check her email like she normally did at breakfast.

Everything she touched felt cold. Maybe a cigarette would help wake her up. Her mother always smoked one in the morning.

She grabbed the pack from the bench and swiped her cellphone at the same time. The back patio chair rocked as she flopped into it. As she lit her cigarette, she clicked on Instagram. It opened to a sign-in page, which was weird, but she thought nothing of it, letting the iPhone do its thing to sign her in. As soon as it did, a popup came on that said, "Your account has been disabled for violating our terms. Learn how you may be able to restore your account." She hurriedly clicked the "LEARN MORE" button.

And instantly, another message appeared. "You can't request a review. The decision to disable your account can't be reviewed. This is because we already reviewed it and decided it can't be reversed or because thirty days have passed since your account was disabled."

Tears formed. She couldn't breathe. What the fuck was happening? She'd heard horror stories of bots accidentally deleting accounts because bots were fucking stupid, but usually there was an appeal process.

She went to Facebook, and the same message came up. "What the fuck?"

She felt tired again. Too tired.

She went to email. The first one was from a friend, Jill.

"Jesus, Violet. What is happening? Did you drink last night? They kicked you off Insta! I'm assuming someone hacked you."

She clicked out of the email and called Jill. Before the girl had a moment to speak, Violet said, "What happened? What are you talking about?"

"Oh no. You don't know? Violet, you posted like fifty pictures in a row last night."

"What are you talking about? What pictures?" She felt like she could collapse.

Jill hesitated. "I'm sorry. They were nudes. Like really racy pictures of you."

She hung up. She had naked pictures of herself on her phone, hanging in the iPhone cloud, pictures she took for her last boyfriend. She still communicated with him and knew he wouldn't ever post them anywhere, nor was he smart enough to hack into anyone's account.

She went back to her email because she'd seen another one had come from the festival. She opened it. It was an outraged message telling her the contract was voided. She scrolled up to see her last sent message and clicked on the attachment. It was a photo of her naked with black paint streaked down her body. In the photo, she was curling her lip and flipping the camera off. She never imagined anyone would ever see that picture outside of Tom, who she'd sent it to.

She felt exposed, cold, and naked anew. It had to be Ethan. But how? She didn't share passwords with him, and she had her phone on her when she'd left the house. He never would have figured out her password to get into her computer.

She stood up and ran inside, dropping her cigarette into an empty bottle she'd left out there.

Fuck. Her tablet. She ran to her desk where she always left it. It was gone.

"Oh shit. Oh fuck. This isn't real. This can't be happening." The stages of grief passed by her in a flash. Denial, anger, bargaining, depression. The only one she couldn't land on was acceptance.

Her eyes felt heavy again. Her limbs too. Wooziness came over her. The room spun as her knees buckled. And then it clicked. He *had* drugged her. The cigarettes. Everything turned black and the last thing she felt was the side of her head slamming into the floor.

When she came to, she was lying in bed. Again, she stared at the ceiling, trying to remember how she'd gotten there. Movement in her peripheral made her jolt, but her hands and legs both met resistance, and something dug into her wrists and ankles.

"Whazgoinon?"

"Take a few minutes to get your faculties back, huh?"

He was blurry, but Violet saw Ethan's outlines. Boom. It all flooded back. She yanked her arms forward and heard the chains snap taut as they stopped her from moving farther.

"You're cuffed to the headboard, and your ankles to the legs of the frame. Don't scream or I'll have to duct tape your mouth shut, and then we can't talk this all out, and I'll get even more angry than I am. We don't want that."

"What the fuck are you thinking, Ethan? This isn't you. This is crazy."

He jumped forward and shook his fists. "YOU did this. You made me crazy." He took an exaggerated breath. "I wasn't even going to do this. When I came in here yesterday, I just wanted to show you our life together, but I saw your cigarettes sitting on the bench. I'd once read an article about something called fry cigarettes where men drug women by giving them a cigarette laced with embalming fluid shit. But when I looked into it, it apparently makes the women giddy and more open to sexual activity. It doesn't knock them out like a roofie, so, I, being the scientist that I am, had to tinker with it. I didn't know if it would work.

"I laced your cigarettes with my own little mixture but planned to keep the cigarettes on me. I thought you'd figure you lost them somewhere and would replace them. I'd keep mine around in case of an emergency. Just something to hold onto if I ever grew desperate. But the coldness you had when you kicked me out. That fucking look on your face."

He wiped the corners of his mouth. "You didn't even see me replace the cigarettes on the bench when I put the key there. By the way, I have like five copies of that key. Also, you should do a better job searching your house. I've been here since last night. I've been here so many nights."

Violet wiggled her hands around, trying to find some leeway to escape the cuffs. They were too tight. She had no hope.

Ethan sat on the end of the bed. "I didn't know if my concoction would work. But when I snuck in last night while you were sleeping, you didn't move an inch." He put his hand on her knee. "Not even when I slid my hand up your leg." He closed his eyes and made a face filled with ecstasy.

Her stomach lurched. Had he raped her? She would have known. Of course she would have. No. He couldn't have.

"I could feel your warmth. God, I can't tell you the number of times I've thought about being inside you. Every single time I've ever had sex, I pictured it was with you. Every night when I masturbated, it was your face looking back at me when I closed my eyes."

She squirmed, wanting to throw up.

He slid his hand up her leg, stopping around mid-thigh. "See the look on your fucking face right now?" His jaw clenched. "I pictured us having sex, Violet. Making love. I'm not a rapist. Jesus Christ. You think I'd rape you?"

Did he not realize that drugging her, tying her up, and sliding his hand on her body when she didn't want it was sexual assault too? In the moment, she wasn't even mad at *him*. She hated herself. How could she have been so close to a monster? How had she not seen this in him all these years?

"I could have fucked you all night last night, and you wouldn't have done a thing to stop it. But I'm not the villain you're trying to make me out as. I'm your best fucking friend. We were meant to be together. I wish you could see that."

Tears dripped down her cheeks. "Well, I don't. And I never will. So what now?"

He stood up and walked away. She jerked her arms, hoping to break the thin wood ornamentation the cuffs latched to on the headboard. Bang. Bang. Bang. She pulled forward until the cuffs ripped into her flesh, rushed them back and then slammed forward. Over and over. She heard the cracking of wood, but it stayed in place.

Ethan walked back in and sat back on the bed. She didn't stop, though, didn't care if he saw her trying to escape. This couldn't end well, and she knew it. Her only chance was in breaking free.

"I thought about this so much. What do I do now? I mean, not now now. I mean now as in since I told you I loved you. I didn't have many options. I could just move on, right?" He giggled. "Yeah, right. It's been too much. I couldn't possibly endure seeing you date one more shithead while you ignored the only good guy in your life. I just can't do it anymore."

He leaned over and pulled her arms back hard, slamming them into the headboard. With his face right in front of hers, he said, "And you've made it just about clear you're never going to be with me. You're never going to see how good I would be for you." He released his grip on her and moved back.

With one hand behind him, he stood up. "There's only one way I can make us be together forever."

She realized too late what he planned to do. "Wait!" Before she could say anything else, the gun was aimed at her head and a loud boom stole the world.

She woke up in a daze, melodic beeping at her side. Her face felt weighted, as if buried in cloth.

Beep. Beep. Beep. Beep. Beep.

She came to again, this time for a longer period. A doctor came in and explained what had happened. A bullet entered her skull. She struggled to understand some of the terminology. Lodged in the right occipital region.

The doctor called it a miracle. He explained how there was minimal damage to the brain, and the trajectory of the bullet worked in her favor. But he mentioned the potential for long-term difficulties with mobility, especially on her left side. Her drawing hand. Ethan had killed her in more ways than one.

She asked what happened to him, but the doctor said he'd send someone else in to give her that information, and it took days for that to happen.

Her prayers were answered by a kindly older police officer who came to talk to her and ask her some questions now that she was awake. Ethan turned the gun on himself right after he shot her, and unlike her, he didn't survive.

She hated him for that, too. He didn't deserve the easy way out.

She answered some questions, and then the officer told her the real kicker. Above the porch roof of her house, they found a small chunk of wall carved out and boarded up with a swinging door. It led to a small crawl space behind a chest in her mother's sewing room.

They believe Ethan had created an entrance into their home a long time ago and snuck in as he pleased.

When? she wondered. *At what age?*

And what did he do with it? Sneak in and watch her sleep? Why, if he had a key? As much as she shouldn't, she believed him when he claimed he would never rape her, at least in the traditional sense of the word. Obviously, he had no trouble raping her at all in many other ways. But she didn't think he'd sneak in and take her sexually.

She'd never know exactly what he did with his secret entrance, and it added on to the pile of assaults. She'd never know peace again.

She spent months in hospitals and rehabilitation clinics. Eventually, out of boredom, she made a new Facebook profile and used it to scroll through an endless sea of inanity.

One day, a few months after she created her profile, she received a friend request from her old middle school crush, Clay. She accepted, and within a few seconds, he messaged her.

"I saw what happened to you on the news. Crazy! I always knew that guy was crazy. Remember, I told you that I never trusted him!"

She turned her phone off and cried. Clay was just another Ethan. Gather them up. They'll pose and go to war.

AGORAPHOBIA

MIKE SALT

It wasn't like he enjoyed this part of the night.

The idea of walking around his small apartment, checking the locks on every window, double checking the multiple deadbolts on the door, checking the locks on his small delivery door, using a mirror to peek between the floor and the door, verifying the duct tape around the edges of the door was undisturbed, double checking the painters tape he had over the vents, none of it made him feel safe, but all of it made him feel crazy.

Maybe he was?

Dexter wondered that as he stood on top of a stool, layering on some fresh tape over a vent. Maybe this was all in his head? No one was coming to get him. No one was watching him.

Satisfied with his work, he climbed down and moved on to the next part of the night, checking his email.

The computer hummed to life, casting an uncomfortable glow on a room that was permeated in darkness. He had painted over the windows years ago, and when that didn't seem to be enough, he stapled tinfoil to the windowsill. The only opening to the outside world was the small window beside him at the computer desk. It was nailed slightly open, barely half an inch; the opening was sealed from the left to the center and right to the center, leaving just a four-inch gap between them. The gap was covered with a shoebox that had been duct taped to the tinfoil and wall. Every couple nights Dexter would check the box, making sure it was still empty.

Dexter waited as he clicked the email icon on his screen, allowing his mind to wander, just for a moment. He remembered his life before he moved into this apartment. His nights out with friends, coworkers, and family. Hosting game nights and bottles of wine and fresh boards of cheese and crackers. His brother would bring over his kids, although it'd been so long that Dexter could barely remember their faces. In fact, it'd been a long time since he'd seen the face of anyone he loved. Every picture of his life before had been burned to ashes in his bathtub over a year ago. The handwritten letters from his grandma, torn to shreds and disposed of. The box of keepsakes and memories he collected since his youth, blacked out and lost someplace in the mess of his home. All evidence of anyone he loved was removed from his life. He had spent countless hours making sure there were no clues to the connections he had to the outside world. It was safer that way.

Finally, the display came to life and his inbox illuminated the screen.

A single unread message in an otherwise empty email inbox.

Dexter felt his heart racing as his mouse slowly inched toward the icon.

The message header was nothing but squares and circles, both outlines and fully solid. The header wavered as his mouse moved closer.

Thu-tunk!

The sound made Dexter jump from his seat as he turned to the box attached to his window.

"Who are you?!" Dexter screamed at his window as he heard the unmistakable sound of someone running down the fire escape. "What's your REAL name?! Help me!"

Dexter pounded his fist against the frame of the window, careful not to hit the glass, afraid of what would happen if he broke it.

Finally, the sound of the person fleeing was long gone. His heart slowed down, and he could concentrate on his breathing.

With trembling fingers, Dexter carefully opened the bottom of the box, allowing the contents inside to fall out.

He picked up a small white letter, sealed, with no writing or labeling on the outside. The same type of letter that started this entire experience all those years ago.

Dexter opened the letter and carefully laid it out on the desk beside him.

In the same handwriting as always, it read, "Don't believe them."

And as usual it was signed by *Cabela*.

Dexter leaned back in his chair and looked over every inch of the page. Looking for anything else. There was nothing. Not that there ever was, but that didn't stop him from inspecting the paper every time one came in.

With a long sigh, Dexter leaned back into his desk chair. He rubbed his eyes and yawned deeply. He remembered what he was doing before the letter's arrival interrupted him, so he turned back to the computer.

Nothing.

The inbox was empty.

No new message.

He had missed it.

This was the part that always pissed him off. Dexter spent hours waiting for something, anything. However, if he wasn't fast enough, he would miss it. And sadly, that happened more often than he liked to admit.

Frustrated, he decided to call it a night. There was nothing more he could do.

Sleep came easy. He felt it happen all at once, but at the same time, limb-by-limb. Dexter could feel his legs losing movement, then a few minutes later his arms became heavy, his head felt like it was in the clouds, and a few minutes after that, he was asleep.

It happened at least once a month. Dexter wasn't stupid… it was them. Was it gas? Something slipped into his drink? Food? Really, it could be anything.

Still, he woke up when his phone told him it was time. The alarm blasted a chime, and with it his eyes shot open. He rolled over in his bed and looked out toward the open door of his bedroom.

Dexter was immediately alert.

He never left his bedroom door open. Period. Yet there it was.

Dexter sprinted out of bed, almost tripping as his legs were tied up inside his sheets.

As he stumbled, he used a hand to balance himself and brought his body upright. He moved into the small living room of his apartment and began to search.

Searching for two things he knew would have transpired:

One: something would be missing.

Two: it would be replaced with something else.

Sure, there were times that he couldn't figure out what was missing and what was replaced. He would search his entire apartment, hoping for something to click, but would come up empty handed. He knew in his bones it was happening, but sometimes he was not meant to find it. However, sometimes the thing that was missing was the same thing that was replaced. One time Dexter noticed his favorite coffee mug missing. A white mug that had a logo from his favorite author on it. On the same side of the logo, on the bottom, was a small chip. He knocked it against the counter literally the first time he used it. That particular time, the replacement mug had no chip.

It was the kind of thing that made Dexter feel crazy. He knew how it sounded. The mug of a very obscure author that no one had really heard of was replaced with an identical mug in the middle of the night. However, Dexter knew it wasn't the same mug.

Now he was searching his apartment for the next thing.

He started by combing his desk area. Was his pencil holder always red? Was it? How about his stapler? Was it always navy?

Dexter shook it off and moved on to the kitchen. He might as well get some food in his belly as he looked.

He looked over the magnets on the fridge as he placed a hand on the handle. A jackalope, a cactus in a desert with the words "Dude Sexy," a frog wearing sunglasses, and an assortment of black magnets that all looked correct. He opened the fridge and reached in for his morning meal: two hard-boiled eggs and the milk to pour on a bowl of off-brand Wheaties cereal. He closed the door and turned to his table, about to investigate the collection of odds and ends, when something clicked in his brain.

The picture.

He turned back to the fridge and reached for the picture that was pinned to the door by the frog magnet, pulling it to his face.

This was it.

The picture was different.

He looked at it, was an image from the old days. The days before he won the state lottery. When he still worked dead-end jobs and actually left his dwelling. The picture showed Dexter sitting on a bench next to a statue of a man who was reading the newspaper. Dexter remembered that day; the picture was burned into his brain. He looked at it several times a day. He was always on the left side of the statue; now he was on the right. Small change. Something insignificant. Something he might have missed if it was any other picture.

"Not today," Dexter said to himself as he took the picture with him and sat down to eat his breakfast.

He smiled as he poured a good splash of milk into his bowl.

Sixteen days had passed since he found the picture.

No new emails.

No new letters.

No changes in his apartment.

Just a lot of days alone.

Dexter used to read books daily, by the handful. However, he unfortunately ran out of them fairly soon into the days of isolating himself. He used to pay his brother to swing by the library and swap out some of his books; however, as everyone else had in his life, his brother cut him out. And with that, he stopped getting new books to read.

He spent a lot of his days journaling. He had accidentally ordered a bulk order of notebooks a couple years ago, around the same time he canceled his orders through Amazon. He was annoyed at first but was now grateful for the mistake. Dexter spent all his spare time theorizing what was going on with him. Who were the people messing with him? Why him? Was it all about his money? Dexter used to think that. However, no one had ever touched his account. He left out crisp hundred dollar bills to tempt them, but they were never missing.

No, it wasn't about money.

A government experiment? Maybe.

A stalker? Dexter doubted it, but couldn't rule it out.

A person that was bored and just loved the challenge that Dexter presented them? Why the fuck not?

Lizard people.

People from a neighboring multiversity that slip into his dimension to check in.

Time travelers.

Dexter had thousands of theories. None of them carried more water than any other.

However, one thing that Dexter was making grounds on were the letters from Cabela. It was definitely a girl. Her name was definitely not Cabela. She was trying to help. In fact, she was the only person trying to help.

Dexter closed his current journal and threw it on the stack of countless other journals that were stacked beside him.

He leaned back in his chair and waited to feel the satisfying pop of his spine.

Dexter was going to figure it out. It was only a matter of time.

Thu-thunk!

Dexter nearly fell out of his chair as he heard the letter land in the box beside him. He rolled over and braced himself on the ledge of the desk, swinging wildly over to the windowsill, and fumbled to recover the letter.

Again, he heard the scattering of feet as the person who dropped the letter ran down the fire escape.

Dexter tried to yell something, but his voice came out scratchy and painful. He then realized that it'd been weeks since he'd said anything out loud.

Instead, he turned to the box and removed the letter, making sure to keep it sealed around the window.

Same type of letter. Small white envelope, sealed, with no writing or labeling on the outside.

He carefully opened it up and laid it flat on the desk. *Be ready.* Dexter read the letter to himself in a whisper. He flipped the paper over and inspected it inch by inch, looking for anything else. Of course, there was nothing else besides the signature of *Cabela*.

He spent the next hour looking over the letter before placing it back inside the envelope, dating the top, and placing it on a stack of other similar white envelopes.

Cabela's letters were always warnings. They were never about catching up nor were they inquisitive in nature. They were always about *them*. Whoever *them* were still managed to escape him.

Three hours later, a knock came at his door. This didn't shock Dexter since he placed the order for grocery drop-off for exactly this time.

The instructions on the app were clear that the delivery person was to knock on the door, wait for Dexter to open the custom doggie-type door, slide the box of groceries in, and leave. Sometimes the delivery drivers would have a hard time grasping it, but for the most part it was easy.

Dexter unlocked the small door inside the main door and opened it. It was latched with a padlock that gave Dexter the extra feeling of security. He didn't want anyone coming in that didn't need to be, and after years of being alone, this system was the easiest, even if it was the most obscure. With the delivery door open, the box slid in, and Dexter pulled it all the way in and immediately closed and latched the small delivery door.

He picked up the box and moved it to the kitchen table, ready to unpack the two weeks of groceries a single man would need. He opened the box and froze. His eyes grew large as he looked at what was inside.

The room was dark as the men entered Dexter's apartment.

Their black attire was all the same shade, with hoods pulled tight around the gas masks on their faces. Even the small booties they wore around their boots were black. They would leave no evidence they were even there... except for the exchange.

As the men opened the door to the living room, the man in front looked back to the two men with him, then pointed toward the computer. They knew their job. Copy the available files and data, information that Dexter assumed was safe. They'd pull out a portable scanner, scan any new pages he'd added to his journals, and remove and replace the single item. This time they were going to swap out Dexter's old radio with a completely different old radio.

The other men nodded and moved toward the living room.

The man in front had his own task. He needed to take a blood sample and check Dexter's vitals. The blood was pulled from a different place every time; they weren't even sure if Dexter was aware it was happening. This time he'd get the sample from a vein in Dexter's foot. Easy peasy.

The man approached Dexter and placed his bag on the bed. He opened it and recovered a pad of paper and pen, a manual blood pressure cuff, a wrapped kit for the blood sample, and a flashlight.

Dexter had been exposed to the gas for over three hours this time around. He would be out as long as the gasses were still being pumped in through the small lines that Dexter had never noticed, even after all these years he spent trapped inside his apartment. The lines fed up through his floorboard, through a hollowed-out leg of his bed, and blended in with the black pattern of his bedframe. The canister fit perfectly inside the bedframe and would never be discovered, unless Dexter ever moved his bed or messed around with the frame... then he'd surely discover it. However, Dexter was a creature of habit and not only never thought of moving the bed but couldn't imagine a scenario he would want to.

The man opened the hidden latch in the bedframe and swapped out the canister with a larger canister. It would last long enough for them to finish their work, then he'd place a full canister inside the frame, make sure it was able to operate when the time came for them to do a check-in, and leave. After a few hours, the gas would clear out enough that Dexter would wake up from his slumber, not knowing how it happened again.

The man then moved to his pad of paper and pen and began to work, placing the date in the corner of the paper and then pulling the sheets off Dexter to begin his work. As the sheets flung in the air, it took a moment for the man to register the blade that slipped into his throat.

Dexter wasn't a fool.

He knew this wasn't all in his head.

When he opened up the delivery box, expecting a restock of his usual purchases, and found a white envelope and a gas mask, he didn't have to ask any questions.

The letter had one simple word on it: *Tonight.*

He recognized the handwriting. It was Cabela. Dexter tucked the gas mask beneath his shirt. Hoping his suspicions of cameras hiding in his house was just in his head, he reached to the butcher block and recovered a knife, and beelined it straight to bed.

Dexter felt the spray of warm blood hit his skin and splash over the visor of the mask. He sat up more in the bed as the sheet floated back down on top of him, pressing the knife deeper into the man's throat. Dexter grabbed the man by the back of his head and pushed it into the knife until he felt the tip of the blade slip into the spinal cord. The man stopped moving and dropped to the bed, his blood spraying all over the mattress.

Dexter quickly grabbed the man and checked him for anything relevant. He had nothing. No identification, no money, no wallet. The man's pockets were empty. Hell, even the bag was empty besides the few items he had taken from it.

Dexter saw the movement of a flashlight through the bedroom door and into the living room. He adjusted his mask and wiped the blood from his knife on his bed sheet.

Slowly, he moved through the room, careful not to make a peep.

He slid into the living room and peered his head around the corner, spying two men at his desk. One behind the computer and another taking his journals and scanning the pages. Both of them had their backs turned to Dexter.

Dexter didn't consider himself a quick person. He ran out of energy fast, gasping for air if he had to go up more than a couple flights of stairs. However, since he locked himself away from society, he made sure that working out was part of his daily routine. Pushups, sit-ups, yoga, CrossFit, anything he could do to get his heartbeat moving. He even used some empty milk jugs and filled them with water and used them as weights to lift. Even after all that, Dexter had never had to use any of these newfound strengths.

However, there was always a part of him that wondered if he could fight off whoever was intruding into his apartment.

Now was that moment.

Dexter slipped up to the man scanning, assuming that taking him out first would at least give him a second to attack before the man behind the computer realized what was happening. By then Dexter hoped to be prepared to defend himself. He plunged the knife into the back of the man's neck and thrust it all the way through as violently as he could, feeling the spray of warm blood spread from the wound. The man released the journal he was holding and threw his hands to his throat. Dexter yanked the knife back and turned to face the other man as he looked at his partner and then up to Dexter.

Dexter raised his arm, pointing the knife down at him. He stepped forward.

And slipped on the blood beneath his feet.

Dexter felt his body dangle in the air for a moment as the shock of the situation finally took over. The adrenaline he was running off of was now wasted as he tumbled to the ground.

Dexter looked to find the knife had skid across the room, and before he could reach for it, the other man had stood from the desk chair.

Dexter kicked out a leg, connecting with the man's knee, which buckled backward. The man fell to the ground, grabbing at his knee. A horrible shrieking sound exploded from his mouth as the pain overwhelmed him.

The room seemed to spin for a minute, and Dexter began to blink harder than he intended. He was tired. He could feel the blanket of sleep slipping over him.

He reached up to his mask and realized that during the encounter it had slipped partially off of his face. The gasses that filled the room were now filling his lungs, and if Dexter hadn't realized it as soon as he did, he would have passed out. Instead, he pulled the elastic band at the back of the mask, sucking it back to his face.

Dexter quickly found himself on his back again, the man with the collapsed knee on top of him. Dexter felt blow after blow strike his face. His mask cracked and broke on the man's fist, chunks of black plastic poking out of his flesh as he continued to strike Dexter.

After several blows to the face, Dexter turned his head and the fist flew by him. Dexter wrapped an arm around it and tucked it to his body and rolled with it and the man. Now Dexter was on top. Dexter wasn't interested in punching the man in the face; he wore a mask that Dexter knew would block the majority of the punches he threw. Instead, Dexter made his hand flat and chopped the man in the throat as hard as he could. The man reached for his throat as Dexter rolled off him to recover the knife.

Dexter turned back at him with the knife. The man was holding a single hand to his throat as he used the other hand to leverage himself off the floor with the desk chair. He lunged again at Dexter, who shoved the knife into the man's belly. With no hesitation, Dexter drove the knife forward and up, carving his belly like it was a pumpkin in the fall. Dexter removed the knife and crawled backward a couple steps. The man put pressure on the wound, trying desperately to keep his insides from slipping out with the rush of red that flowed over his waist.

Dexter stood and calculated his movement. He could feel the heavy weight of the gas taking effect again; his arms were now like cement slabs, and his legs were like pudding. He didn't have much of a choice... he needed to get that mask from the man's face onto his own.

With as much force as he could, feeling like he was moving in slow motion, Dexter dove at the man, missing his torso and connecting with his knees. The second knee collapsed, and the man now had two knees that were struck out at a ninety-degree angle, one off to the left and one to the right. The man released his hands from his stomach and the gush of blood and guts flowed like a raging river. Dexter closed his eyes, trying not to let the fluid breach them, which helped, but also made him even more tired. Dexter felt a blow to his shoulder. The man's fist connected and broke his clavicle.

Dexter didn't have a choice: he had to push through the pain. He forced his eyes open and shot through the flowing blood and up, connecting his fist under the man's jaw.

The man stumbled backward and crashed into the computer desk. Pages and journals flew through the air as the man fell over, dead.

Dexter felt his legs go numb. His vision began to blur and the taste of nickel overwhelmed his taste buds as the red liquid on him ran down his face and into his mouth. He army crawled on his stomach toward the lifeless body in front of him. Inch by inch.

The room was rolling now. He could feel the sleep taking over him. Dexter shook his head and continued to crawl. He reached an arm forward and pulled his body with it, then again with the other arm, and again, and again, creeping forward slowly.

Finally, as his eyesight disappeared in the darkness, he felt his hand wrap against the man's ankle. With a sudden burst of energy, Dexter squeezed and pulled the man toward him. Blindly, Dexter fumbled for the mask on the man's face, ripped it off, and struggled to get it on his own face.

Darkness.

Dexter had no idea how long he was out.

He opened his eyes and felt his lungs breathing in fresh oxygen, thanks to the mask.

He rolled over and saw the dead man in front of him.

The blood and guts spilling from the body were still pooling; the sludge still looked warm.

He hadn't been out too long. He had just made it.

Dexter slowly pushed his body to sit up straight. He took a moment to gather himself before feeling beside his leg for the knife.

With the knife in his hand, he stood to his feet and paused.

He looked around his apartment, which was now a giant crime scene. Blood splattered all over his living room. Bloody handprints pressed on to the floorboard and walls. Sprays of blood misted the wall like some kind of painting that Dexter never understood the value of. Not to mention the mess in his bedroom.

Three dead bodies.

And he was still standing.

Dexter needed to find out what to do next.

He reached out to find his landline, picking it up before putting it back down.

If these men had set up gas lines in his apartment, there was zero chance they left his phone lines untapped.

Dexter walked over to his door, which was usually locked in several different ways. Now it was slightly ajar.

He peered through it into a hallway that he hadn't seen in years.

However, before he could see anything, he recognized a shadow walking in front of him. Another man in a black outfit and gas mask.

Dexter peeled himself away from the door before he could be seen.

It wasn't just his apartment; it was the entire complex.

Dexter knew he had to get out, but the door wasn't going to be his passage.

Instead, he turned toward the window beside the desk.

He needed to climb out and get someone's attention. Hopefully someone not dressed in black with a gas mask.

He stepped over the dead body on the floor, being careful not to slip on the blood again. However, something stopped him.

The face of the man.

It was wrong.

It was swollen and purulent. Boils, large and small, spread across his face. The skin, a toad-ly shade of green. His hair was stringy and greasy.

What in the fuck? Dexter thought before realizing that he was currently wearing a mask that had been on this man's face, and he needed to rip it off his own face as soon as possible. Which meant he needed to get outside that window as soon as possible.

Dexter fought the urge to rip the mask off forcefully and dive out the window, fearing that would be too loud. Even though he had just fought for his life in the living room and that ruckus didn't bring any unwanted attention his way, there was no reason to risk it.

Painstakingly, Dexter peeled the duct tape off from the corners of the window and removed it with the tinfoil and shoebox. He had forgotten he had nailed the window shut, but that wasn't going to stop him. He moved to the junk drawer and recovered the hammer, using it to rip the nails from the frame of the window. He tucked the hammer in his waistline and gripped the knife in his hand.

The window slid open, the screeching betraying his intended stealth. Dexter didn't know how much time he had, but he didn't care. He needed to get out onto the fire escape and out of his apartment.

He went out the window with one foot, straddled the frame, and then wrangled the other out. His two feet planted on the cold metal of the fire escape, blanketed by the complete darkness of night.

Dexter tried to look down, to see the street below him, but it too was too dark to see. It had been a while since Dexter had been outside, but he knew that there should be cars and streetlights below.

Something was wrong.

Dexter was on the fifth floor of the complex, which meant that he had to be cautious that no one heard him as he descended the levels.

He reached out for the rail and used it to guide him in the dark.

Dexter found the railing that led down the ladder and yanked the mask from his face as he maneuvered his body down the ladder.

What Dexter expected to feel beneath his feet were the next series of rungs on the ladder and eventually another metal landing. Instead, Dexter felt the purchase of concrete on bare feet.

He looked over and stepped forward in the darkness.

Dexter was confused.

He couldn't wrap his brain around what was happening.

He tried to look around, hoping to see anything that could explain what was going on. This felt like a dream, a nightmare rather, and Dexter had no idea how to wake up.

Movement came from his right, from the open window in his apartment.

A man in a gas mask looked out at him. Dexter knew the man saw him. There was no way he didn't. The man slowly raised a handheld radio to his mask.

Dexter didn't move. He didn't know where he would move if he did. Instead, he held still like a deer in headlights.

Slowly, one by one, windows appeared. First, one across from Dexter. The second one appeared to be thirty or forty feet away from Dexter's apartment. Another one, directly above it. Soon it was happening fast. Window after window was being revealed, and each one had a man in a black outfit and gas mask holding a radio to his ear.

It took a moment for it to register with Dexter, but he realized what he was looking at. Hundreds of identical apartments, each of them with boarded or sealed windows. Each of them with a group of gas-masked men invading them as the people inside slept. As window after window released light out into the dark void in front of Dexter, he realized that they weren't even actually apartment complexes, but solid blocks stacked on each other. Each one had a single metal "fire escape" that ran a straight line all the way across, connecting each box to the other. They weren't as much fire escapes as they were another way for them to be observed through.

The same man in Dexter's apartment brought the radio back up to his face.

As quick as a snap of a finger, the men throughout his view, in each open and available window, began to reattach their own respective covers to their windows.

Dexter took a step back. Unsure of what to do next.

He felt a grip around his wrist, causing him to spin around and raise a fist.

A female stood in front of him.

She smiled at him.

"Dexter," she said softly. Dexter knew immediately who it was.

"Cabela," he answered.

She nodded and pulled on his wrist, beckoning him to move with her. She reached her hand out toward Dexter's knife.

Dexter looked down at it and reluctantly gave it to her.

"Follow me," she said as she guided him away. "I can give you all the answers you need."

Dexter turned and watched as the eyes of the man in Dexter's apartment followed him and Cabela as they walked away.

Cabela guided them to a door that was almost impossible to see in the pitch-black room.

She pushed it forward, and a brilliant white light shot through.

Dexter shielded his eyes as he tried to blink through it and waited for his pupils to adjust.

"Follow me," she said as she walked out in front of him. The hallway was wide and long. Each inch of it was covered in white. The walls, white. The ceiling, white. The floor, white. Every inch of the area in front of him was white for as far as the eye could see.

Dexter thought about the choices in front of him, but there didn't appear to be any. He couldn't run; he had no idea where he would be running to. He had trusted Cabela this far. She was the one, after all, that left him the gas mask. She was helping him. Right?

Dexter stepped after Cabela as she moved past white door after white door.

"Where are we?" Dexter asked.

"All will be explained in a moment," Cabela said as she walked up to a random door and opened it. She held it open for Dexter to enter.

Hesitantly, Dexter paused before entering the room.

A man approached from outside. She handed him the knife and he left.

"Sit," she said as she pointed to a single silver chair beside a silver table. Monitors covered every square inch of the walls, all of which were powered off. The room wasn't white like it was outside. The ceiling, the floor, the walls, all of them were black.

Dexter sat and turned to Cabela.

"What is all this?" Dexter asked. "A government experiment? A shadow government? Lizard people?"

Cabela chuckled. "No." She walked over to the wall and pressed a button on a control panel that Dexter hadn't noticed before. The monitors beamed to life.

Each monitor was a different apartment. They all looked similar to Dexter's own apartment. However, none of them were.

"You are part of an experiment, though," she said.

Dexter watched the monitors as he saw groups of men in other people's apartments, cataloging, scanning, taking vital signs of the sleeping residents.

"Each one of you has a severe case of agoraphobia. Which makes you perfect for these tests. Slowly, we fed into that fear, sending cryptic emails, the swapping of items in your living quarters so you knew someone must have been there, dropping off letters from Cabela..." She let that last sentence float in the air.

Dexter turned to her. "There is no Cabela, is there?"

She shook her head. "No, I am sorry. These are tests, each one of them unique and set up differently to see how the human race reacts. In your particular case, Cabela was not only your lifeline outside, but she was going to help you, save you from them."

Dexter lowered his head.

The woman took a step forward.

"She was used to see how you would react. You have been busier than most, journaling, charting, trying to solve this on your own. All of these test subjects," she said as she waved a hand toward the other monitors, "none of them ticked the way you did. None of them have been as interesting. The human race is very fascinating, and we are anxious to see what it is that made you different."

"So..." Dexter said softly, his head down, looking between his legs. Defeated. "...I guess that's that, then?"

The woman chuckled as she approached the table and placed both hands down. "Don't act that way. It's not like that. It isn't personal."

In the blink of an eye, Dexter reached into his waistband, flung his arm in an arch, and thrust down with the claw of the hammer, into the skull of the woman. She blinked as blood slid down her forehead and into her eyes.

"Sorry, that *was* personal," Dexter said as he ripped the hammer out of her skull.

Dexter walked over to the monitors and the control panel on the wall. He sighed in relief when the buttons were in English.

He hovered over the button that said *WAKE*.

A smile stretched across his face. "Okay, let's get this party going."

He pressed the button down and stepped back to the monitors.

He watched the corner of each screen as each room's oxygen level climbed and replaced the gasses inside.

Slowly, screen by screen, the people began to wake.

In some monitors, the people were alone in the room, their vitals already reported.

In others, the person woke up, and even though they were startled to see a gas-masked person in front of them, they were able to spring to action.

He watched monitor after monitor as the majority of the people trapped inside their rooms were fighting off the invaders.

After all, they had spent years of their lives preparing for this moment.

And Dexter couldn't smile any larger as he watched it all collapsing in front of him.

COME TO THE SHED

NICK ROBERTS

M onsters exist, but they don't have sharp claws and pointy teeth. They live next door to you. They wave at you when you check the mail and they're cutting the grass. They bring packages to your doorstep that were delivered to them by mistake. They unload their groceries, wash their cars, and walk their dogs. They welcome new people to the neighborhood with Tupperware full of cookies. They pass out candy to your kids on Halloween.

They dress like you and work regular jobs. They attend church and youth sporting events and frequent the city pool. They believe in this facade as long as they're able to hold it together. But when something threatens to expose them—to tug at the loose strand of flesh on their skin suit of human decency—their true natures come out. If you're around during this unveiling, you won't realize it until it's too late. This is why you always hear the neighbors on the news say, "He seemed like such a nice fella," after the fact.

The following events occurred two years ago. I will do my best to describe what happened as accurately as one who was so emotionally involved in the situation is capable of. My only hope is that it prevents someone out there from going through what we did that summer. If my testimony helps at least one person take an extra second to spot that neighbor wheeling the garbage bin to the curb with that fixed grin and mechanical wave, then it'll be worth it.

Yes, monsters are very much real, and sometimes they're just guys named Phil.

Night 1: Friday, April 14, 2022

Nothing disorients your reality like being woken up by a child in the middle of the night. I felt a pressure on my cheek and flicked my eyes open to see my eight-year-old son, Trevor, standing beside the bed with his finger tapping my face. He looked like a little gremlin standing there in the dark, silhouetted by the moonlit window behind him. I sat up like he just told me the house was on fire.

"What? What is it?" I said as my heartrate returned to normal.

"Daddy, there's someone in my room."

I fell back against my pillow and sighed. Sadie, my wife of ten years, stirred beside me. She looked so beautiful, still sleeping with one arm at her side and the other draped around her head.

"Daddy."

"Shh. I heard you." I stepped out of bed and stretched.

"I also peed the bed."

I already knew that. He'd been having issues with wetting the bed for the last year. We couldn't determine the cause. He'd go months on a dry spell and then regress.

"Let's go," I whispered and held his hand as we walked into the hall. I shut the door behind me and turned on the hallway light. The smell of urine hit me as soon as I stepped foot in his bedroom. I didn't bother to turn on the light.

"You know there's no one in your room, right?"

Trevor didn't say anything as I felt his comforter for wet spots. It was wet, which meant an extra load of laundry. I yanked his sheets off the bed and balled them up, leaving the mattress protector in place.

"He's in the closet, Daddy."

I closed my eyes and sighed, wondering if it would ever end.

"No, he's not. There's no 'he,' buddy. I promise. There never is."

I opened one of the two bifold closet doors. As usual, nothing inhabited the space other than too many shirts hanging on the bar. Eliminating the clothes he outgrew was always the last item on my to-do list. I brushed the hanging horde to the right side, revealing nothing but the white wall behind it and a pile of toys that he played with once or twice and then downgraded to the confines of the closet.

"See?"

Trevor had his hands on my lower back as he peeked around my side. He took one cautious step forward, examining it in the same way Sadie did when she needed me to kill a spider. I patted his head and slid the door shut, folding it flat.

"Let's get you some new sheets."

After we redressed his bed—he helped by tucking in the sheet in that hard-to-reach corner against the wall—I tucked him in and kissed his forehead. He rolled over as I approached the door.

"Want me to crack it?"

He looked back over his shoulder and nodded his head.

"You got it. Love you."

"Love you, Daddy."

I took the blanket and the ball of soiled sheets downstairs and threw them in the washer. The clock on the microwave displayed 4:47 a.m.

Thank God it's the weekend, I thought. Those late-night episodes made a drag out of the following workday. As I made my way upstairs, I thought I heard footsteps.

Great, I woke up Sadie.

I paused, waited, and listened, but no more sounds came. After I turned off the hallway light, I quietly opened my bedroom door. Sadie was still sound asleep. I managed to slide into bed without waking her. As I listened to the soothing rhythm of her breathing, my mind quieted, and I fell into a dreamless slumber.

Day 1: Saturday, April 15, 2022

Sadie woke me up the next morning. I looked at the clock and saw that it was almost eleven a.m.

"You going to sleep all day?"

I rubbed my eyes and sat up. My head pounded from sleeping on it weird. She opened the blackout curtains, and the sunlight punched me in the face. I recoiled, knowing that my monthly migraine had shown up. My headache had nothing to do with the way I'd slept.

"Shut the curtains."

I squinted at her, and she understood, closing them immediately.

"Migraine?"

I nodded my head, and she handed me the water beside the bed.

"Well, there goes our plan," she said.

Her voice pulsated behind my right eyeball.

"What plan?"

"You said last week that you'd get the shed and clean out the garage today."

The sigh escaped me before I could catch it.

"Never mind," she said.

"No, no. I'll still do it." I got up and walked to the bathroom sink and brushed my teeth. Each bristle stroke clawed the inside of my skull.

"You really don't have to."

When I finished, I opened the medicine cabinet and took two of the prescription painkillers that sometimes worked and sometimes didn't.

"I'll be fine."

"It's pretty bright out there."

I kissed her forehead.

"I'll wear my sunglasses."

The two-car garage still managed to fit her Telluride and my Mazda, but only barely. Totes of holiday decorations, bicycles, tools, her gardening supplies, the lawn mower and weed eater, and boxes of old clothes that should've been taken to Goodwill months ago all bordered the vehicles. It had reached the point where we were sliding out of our partially opened doors.

I reached in my car and grabbed my sunglasses, pressing the garage door opener attached to the visor before shutting the car door. The slam felt like a mallet to the temple, but the meds began to kick in. I quickly put on the shades as sunlight inched its way toward me with the rising door.

Good God, it's bright out.

My dad never taught me much in the way of construction, and my mind was about as mechanically inclined as a potato, so the task of building a shed seemed monumental at the time. I had one picked out at Lowe's. It was just one of those little aluminum ones that I could fit the bikes and tools in, but it would do the job. Plus, it looked relatively easy to assemble.

As I made my way around the side of the house, I realized the biggest hurdle was the terrain of our back yard. We lived on a gradual slope with only one semi-flat spot in the back. A chain-link fence stretched up the hill on both sides and met at the top. Beyond that, stood the illusion of a forest when, in actuality, the people who developed this neighborhood had just planted a few rows of trees between houses. I could walk a hundred paces and hit someone else's property.

I opened the fence door near the side of the house and closed it behind me. The metal-on-metal sound was grating but muffled by the meds. Before I was halfway up the hill, I smelled cigarette smoke. I looked to my right and saw my neighbor, Phil, sitting on his open porch with his legs dangling off the edge, shoes swiping the grass as he nervously swung them back and forth. Phil didn't smoke, though. At least, I thought he didn't.

As introverted as I was, I'd never really engaged the older man in conversation. Beyond a few head nods and quick waves, we didn't communicate much. Each time we did, he'd been the one to engage me. Through these exchanges, I gathered a few facts. I knew he lived with his wife, but I couldn't tell you her name. (It was Suzette.) The only time I saw her leave the house with him was on Sundays for church. Phil told me he was an electrician, and she did some sort of customer service gig from home. They were in their early fifties and had one son who had grown and moved out before we bought our house. You knew the kid was in town when he parked his truck in their driveway. This only happened on major holidays.

Phil stared at the grass but wasn't really looking at it. The ash on the Marlboro hanging from his lip was about to break any minute like a snow-covered branch. If he'd noticed me, he hadn't acknowledged it. He just sat there with his wiry build, save for his pot belly, wearing his white T-shirt and gym shorts.

"Phil?"

He turned his head, knocking the ash loose to fall on his exposed kneecap, but he didn't notice.

"You okay over there?" I asked.

"Oh, yeah. I suppose." He stood up, barefoot in his yard, and took a puff from his smoke.

"You sure?"

We both took our time approaching the shared fence. The closer I got, the more I could tell that something was definitely not okay with him. His thinning hair looked matted like he'd been sweating and hadn't taken a shower yet. He had dark crescent moons under his bloodshot eyes. I remember wondering if he'd been crying. When we were about five feet apart, separated only by the metal barrier, the smell of whiskey wafted with the wind like it was seeping through his pores.

"Ah, what the hell?" he said and took a drag. "What are neighbors for if not for an occasional vent session?"

Before I could probe any further, he said, "Suzette's cheating on me."

My social awkwardness paralyzed me.

"I, uh, I'm sorry, man. That sucks."

I was no psychologist.

"Yeah, well, it is what it is. At least, that's what they tell ya in AA."

"You go to AA?" I regretted asking as soon as the question left my mouth.

"Been a friend of Bill W. for over a decade. That's gone to shit now, though, if you can't tell."

"How'd you find out? About your wife, I mean."

"She came clean. Just unloaded on me. Said she'd met a man who looks at her the way I used to. What does that even mean? She packed her stuff and went to stay with a friend."

"Damn. That's rough."

"I begged her to stay. Can you believe that? I begged her, betrayal and all. She said she might come by tomorrow to talk."

Another painfully awkward silence ensued. I knew he was waiting on me to say something, and that's precisely when my brain doesn't want to work. It's like it goes on strike when confronted with the prospect of human interaction.

"Is there anything I can do for you?" I said, an empty gesture if one ever existed.

"Like what?"

The question caught me off guard. He'd seen through my bullshit.

"I don't know. Just felt like the neighborly thing to say. I'm sorry."

He smiled and dropped his cigarette, stomping it out with his bare feet.

"I appreciate the gesture," he said.

I needed to get out of this conversation as soon as possible.

"I have to assess the land up here. I'm putting a shed down. I'm probably going to have to mow and clean up the area."

"Do you need a hand?"

"Huh?"

"Do you need help putting it together?"

I thought about it and realized his help was exactly what I needed.

"No, that's okay. I can't ask you to—"

He waved me off.

"Please. It'll keep my mind occupied. I promise I won't reek of booze when you need me."

"Are you sure? You really don't have to."

"You'd be doing me a favor," he said with a desperate smile.

"All right then. I've got a wicked migraine, so I'm just prepping the area today. I'll go pick it up from Lowe's in a little bit and plan on assembling it tomorrow morning."

"Sounds like a plan."

Phil went back to his stoop as I walked up the hill and cleared some sticks and rocks. It didn't take very long, but it was enough to work up a sweat. When I went back inside, I headed for the laundry room. I took off my shirt and dropped it in the open washer and remembered Trevor's blanket and sheets were still in the dryer from the previous night. But when I opened the door, it was empty. I figured Sadie took them and put them back in the closet, leaving the clean sheets I put on the bed.

Chopping sounds came from the kitchen. When I walked by, I saw her going to town on a celery stalk with a butcher knife. My stomach growled at the thought of her chicken and noodles she was preparing for dinner. She turned around and did a double-take at me wearing my sunglasses.

"How's your migraine?"

"Tolerable. I'm going to take a shower. Do you think you can make me something to eat?"

"What do you want?"

"Anything. I don't care."

"Sandwich it is."

I thought about telling her what Phil had just unloaded on me but decided to wait until later. The hot water beckoned me.

"Thanks," I said and walked upstairs.

As I passed Trevor's room, a hint of piss lingered in the air. I scrunched up my face. It'd never been that bad. Normally, the smell would go away after changing the sheets and giving the kid a bath. I grabbed the Febreze from the hallway closet and gave his room a quick spritz and then retreated to my bedroom for more meds and a hot shower.

Night 2: Saturday, April 15, 2022

I remember being in the middle of a bizarre dream about my parents not taking me to the zoo when I was younger, which was odd because we lived nowhere near a zoo growing up, and I never had a desire to go to one. They just seemed depressing to me, even as a kid. The dream abruptly shifted into a memory of my first handjob in junior high. I was at a friend's house, and we snuck out to go to his girlfriend's house because she had friends over. This girl, Amber, sat next to me as we all watched a movie under a shared blanket. About twenty minutes in, she forced her hand down the front of my pants until she grabbed ahold of what she was searching for.

Just as she started to squeeze, she let go, and the memory faded away. I woke up, confused and a bit disappointed, but definitely sporting a full hard-on. My hands were tucked behind my head, so I hadn't done it to myself in my sleep. I wondered if Sadie had stroked me awake. It wouldn't have been a first for her, but it certainly hadn't happened like that in a long time. She moved closer to me in bed. I reached over and slid my hand under her shirt and cupped her breast. She moaned and scooted even closer. I knew it was her at that point. I kissed her neck, and she grabbed my dick and pulled it out of my boxers. My blood started pumping. It'd been too long since we'd had sex.

Our bedroom door swung open, and Trevor came marching in. Sadie immediately let go and rolled away.

Fuck!

This shit kept happening, and it was getting old. I remember being so angry. God, I was such an asshole.

"What do you want, Trevor?" I said with zero patience.

"I think there's still a man in my closet. I never saw him come out last night."

"No, there's not!"

"Don't yell at him, Billy."

"There's no man. Did you pee the bed?"

After a long pause, he said, "Uh huh."

"Shit."

Sadie smacked me in the chest.

"What?"

She sat up and got out of bed.

"Come on, honey. I'll show you there's no one in your closet," she said, putting her arm around him.

"Just one kid-free night…" I mumbled, not meaning for her to hear it, but she did.

She shot me a look that made me realize how out of line I was acting and then escorted Trevor into the hallway. I stayed in bed, still pissed but redirecting the anger toward myself for being so selfish. The thought of her coming back after she took care of him and us picking up where we left off gave me hope. The hallway light flicked on. I closed my eyes and listened to her open the closet door in Trevor's room and go through the same motions I did the night before. She shut it back. I heard the squeak of his bed as they put new sheets on it.

As I listened to them, there was a faint creak from inside our room. I let my eyes wander straight ahead to the source of the sound: our own doorless, walk-in closet. The light from the hallway illuminated part of the carpeted floor, but not all of it. I did that thing where I stared into the darkness until shapes began to form.

My stomach turned in on itself when I noticed the tips of a pair of boots pointing toward me. Whoever inhabited those boots was completely concealed by the darkness. I was two seconds away from swallowing the fear and leaping out of bed to grab this intruder, but I realized that those were my boots. Relief washed over me. If me, a grown man, could get freaked out by my closet, I had no room to be irritated by my son's fear. I felt like an even bigger prick.

A minute passed, and Sadie shut Trevor's door, turned off the hallway light, and entered our room.

"All good?" I asked.

She just looked at me and got back in bed. Before I could reach over to touch her, she rolled on her side and turned her back to me.

"Really?"

"Yes, really. You acted like an asshole. Good night."

I threw the covers off me and stood up, taking a pillow with me.

"Where are you going?"

"Downstairs."

"Why?"

"To jerk off and sleep on the couch."

"You're unbelievable."

I shut the door on my way out and went to the living room and did exactly that.

Day 2: Sunday, April 16, 2022

When the sun rose, I remembered why I hated sleeping on the couch. There were no blinds on the windows, only drapes that I'd neglected to close. My migraine disappeared overnight, but it left a tolerable bit of nausea in its wake. Thoughts of my actions from the previous night invaded my mind. A cloud of shame hung over me.

Selfish prick.

I looked at my phone. It was six fifteen a.m. As badly as I wanted to shut the curtains and go back to sleep, my conscience wouldn't let me. The only way to remedy the situation wasn't with a half-assed apology. I needed to show that I was sorry. Sadie wanted a shed, and I refused to waste any more time getting it for her. Lowe's didn't open for a couple of hours, so I decided making breakfast in bed for her would be a good start.

As the bacon sizzled on the skillet, I heard little footsteps descending the staircase. Trevor entered the kitchen, rubbing his eyes. I took a sip of coffee and stirred the eggs around before they could burn.

"Morning, buddy. You hungry?"

He yawned and shook his head.

"No? Not even for bacon and eggs?"

"I want biscuits and gravy."

"Oh, well, I guess it's good I've got those cooking in the oven then," I said and gave him a wink.

He smiled, opened the refrigerator, grabbed a juice box, and turned to leave.

"Don't forget your vitamins."

Trevor turned back around and grabbed the little container off the counter. He put the two gummies that I'd left out for him in his mouth and put it back.

"Thank you."

I listened as the TV turned on and some YouTube jackass started raving about an overpriced toy his sponsor had given him.

I fucking hated YouTube. Still do. But on restless nights when the dreams turn down a dark path, I'll find those old videos and watch that obnoxious jackass and cry.

When the biscuits were nearly finished, I whipped up some instant breakfast gravy and made Trevor's plate and then Sadie's. I put the biscuits and gravy on his favorite Paw Patrol plate and took it in there to him.

"Here you go." I set it on the coffee table and made sure he had everything he needed. "Don't spill that on the rug or your mom will kill me."

"I won't."

"I love you, buddy."

He looked up at me as if to see where this was coming from.

"I'm sorry that I was grumpy last night. I'll do better."

"Okay," he said and turned back to the jackass YouTuber.

The bedroom door squeaked when I opened it, stirring Sadie from her slumber. I crept to her side of the bed and placed the tray holding the plate on the nightstand. She opened her eyes and looked at me.

"What's wrong?" she asked, quickly sitting up.

"Nothing." I chuckled. "It's morning. Everything's okay."

It took a few seconds to fully settle into reality. I could tell by the abrupt change on her face that she remembered our little tiff last night.

"I hope you got everything out of your system," she said.

"I'm sorry," I said, looking her in the eyes. I forced a grin. "I made you breakfast."

She looked to her left and saw the as-fancy-as-it-gets-in-our-house presentation of a five-star hotel breakfast in bed: eggs, bacon, biscuits, gravy, and sausage patties with a glass of orange juice and a cup of coffee on the side. She smiled.

"Thank you."

I sat at the foot of the bed.

"I'm going to take a shower and go get the shed."

"You sure you can do that by yourself?" she asked, biting into a crisp strip of bacon.

"Phil's going to help me."

"Our neighbor?"

"Yeah. He was outside yesterday, and I told him what I was doing, and he offered to help. Seems like a handy enough guy. Might keep me from killing myself."

"Let me know if you need anything."

"Will do," I said, standing up.

As I gathered my clothes and put them on the dresser, I realized something about the closet that I had to double-check. I poked my head back, and just like I thought, my boots were missing. Panic surged through my system.

"Have you seen my boots?"

"No. Why?"

I didn't want to freak her out, so I kept my answer to a minimum.

"I just thought they were in the closet, and they're not."

After searching the entire house from top to bottom, I still couldn't find them. On my way back to our bedroom, I passed Trevor's room, and the piss smell damn near clotheslined me.

Did she not clean it up very good last night?

But then I remembered that even after I changed the sheets the night before last, the odor lingered. It was just more pronounced now. Sadie finished her food as I came back in.

"I think we need to buy him a new mattress. Did you change his sheets again?"

"Yes. Does it smell as bad as it did yesterday?"

"Worse."

"Great."

"All right, I'm getting in the shower."

"Hey," she said like she just remembered something. "Did you check the back deck for your boots?"

As soon as she said it, I remembered it clearly. The migraine meds messed with my short-term memory, but I could recall things with an assist. A couple of days ago, I'd gotten them muddy, sprayed them with the hose, and left them on the back porch to dry. My face went pale at what that implied.

"What is it?" she asked.

"Last night, when you were in Trevor's room, I laid here and thought I saw someone in the closet. I almost flipped shit, but then I realized it was just my boots on the floor. It looked like a person standing there in the dark."

"You sound like Trevor."

I thought about that. The immediate dismissal irritated me, but I let it go. She must've seen the torrid waters under the surface because she said, "I'm just saying, what's more probable: a stranger standing in our closet and then somehow disappearing without us knowing, or your eyes just playing tricks on you in the dark?"

I knew what I saw, and it freaked me out. I told myself that maybe the migraine or the meds had aided in the illusion, and eventually that narrative stuck.

"You're right," I said and headed toward the shower.

I walked out the back door into a balmy, overcast day. The gray sky didn't look pretty, but it made me grateful I didn't have to build this shitty little shed in direct sunlight. As soon as I stepped off the porch, I smelled cigarette smoke.

Phil sat in that same position with his legs hanging off the wooden porch, swinging his bare feet back and forth while the cigarette dangled from his lips. He looked even worse than the day before. His hair was greasier, and I could see the weariness in his eyes from across the yard. At least he'd managed to change clothes.

"Morning, Phil," I said with a wave.

Once again, he came back from whatever dimension he was in, looking around like he didn't know how he'd gotten outside. His eyes found mine, and his demeanor shifted from alien to human.

"Oh, good morning. It's a muggy one today, isn't it?"

I stepped onto the grass and approached the fence, prompting him to do the same.

"How are things really going, man?"

The laugh lines around his eyes flattened as he released his forced smile. He nodded his head, and I saw the storm brewing behind his eyes.

"Not so good."

"Suzette?"

"Yeah. She's not coming to talk today."

"Sorry, man. What happened?"

"She snuck in last night while I was asleep. *Passed out* would be a better description, I suppose. Drank myself to sleep even though I sat here yesterday and told you I wouldn't."

I tried to interrupt to tell him it didn't matter, but he pressed on.

"She left this on my nightstand," he said and pulled her wedding band out of his pocket, holding it in the palm of his hand. I stared at it like Gollum from *Lord of the Rings*, thinking one day that might be what would happen to me if I kept on my current trajectory. "I can't get ahold of her. She's turned the service off for her phone."

"Maybe it's for the best," I said without thinking.

He shot me a quizzical look.

"Or not, what the hell do I know?"

He half smiled and shook his head as if to tell me not to worry about it.

"Hey, aren't we building a shed today?" he asked.

"Indeed. I'm headed to the store now."

"Good. Good. I'm going to go splash some water on my face. I'll be here when you get back."

"See you in a little bit."

I took the SUV to Lowe's and had to fold the rear seats down to fit the boxed shed inside. Even then, the kid in the lawn and garden section had to help me tie it down with bungee cords because we couldn't get the trunk to shut all the way. It didn't matter. I only had three miles to go.

When I pulled into our driveway, I parked just shy of the open garage. I needed all the room I could get in there to empty it once we built the shed. Phil was probably on his back porch waiting on me, but I wanted to grab a quick bite and had to use the bathroom. I carefully dragged the heavy box from the back of the car and leaned it against the side of the house.

Sadie sat on the living room floor with Trevor. The two of them were following along to one of those YouTube drawing tutorials that guides kids step-by-step. I looked at each of their zebra illustrations.

"Oh, very nice," I said.

"Whose do you like more?" Trevor asked.

Sadie held up hers, and he followed suit.

"Hmm," I said, looking back and forth, pretending to be judging artistic merit. I stopped on Trevor's. "That one."

"Really?" he said. "Mommy's lines are straighter."

"Yeah, but yours is more fun. Look at his funny eyes." I held my hand to the side of my mouth like I was shielding my next statement from his mom. "Mommy's looks boring."

"What?" she said, flipping her drawing around to examine it.

She then glanced at the googly eyes and happy-go-lucky legs prancing at unnatural angles. "Fine. His is better."

I made a motion for her to come with me and walked to the kitchen. She followed me as I placed my wallet and keys on the counter.

"What's up?" she asked.

"Phil from next door is going to help me put up the shed."

"Okay..."

"His wife left him. Cheated on him and told him about it."

"Oh no."

"Left her ring on the nightstand and everything."

"That's harsh."

"He said helping me with the shed would take his mind off of it."

"And you could use the help."

"I'm aware," I said. "Thanks for the vote of confidence."

She smiled and gave me a kiss.

"I think I'll take Trevor to the park and stop and get lunch while you all are doing that."

"Okay."

I opened the refrigerator and grabbed two bottled waters.

"Wish us luck," I said and walked out the back door.

"Good luck. I'll see you later. Love you."

"Love you, too."

As soon as I stepped onto my porch, Phil got up from his, freshly showered and shaved and wearing clean clothes. He even had a toolbox in hand. I smiled, knowing I'd bought the shed that came with every tool needed for assembly for a mechanical ignoramus like me.

"Ready to knock it out?" he said, approaching the fence.

"Yes, sir. Here, I'll take that."

He handed me the toolbox, and before I could set it on the ground, he leaped over the chain-link fence in one swift motion like he'd done it a hundred times. I remember thinking he must be deceptively fit to pull off a move like that.

I looked at him, and he returned my gaze with a sly grin.

"You ready to get to work?" he asked.

"Yeah. It's around the side of the house."

"Okay then. Lead the way. Let's get to it."

We tightened the final screw just as Sadie pulled her car up the driveway.

"I think your wife's home," Phil said, wiping sweat from his brow. "Perfect timing."

"Right?"

I took a step back to admire our handiwork and thought it looked pretty damn good for what it was. It wouldn't survive a tornado, but it would store a few bikes and a lawnmower, enough to make Sadie happy.

She opened the gate to the front yard with Trevor following behind her. They each had milkshakes. Phil put his hands on his waist and looked at Trevor.

"Where's my milkshake?" he asked.

Trevor shrugged his shoulders with a grin.

"Hi, Phil," Sadie said.

"Afternoon, ma'am."

I prayed she wouldn't bring up anything about Suzette, and luckily she didn't.

"I just wanted to thank you for helping Billy with the shed."

"Oh, it was my pleasure. I enjoy manual labor. Idle hands don't suit a fella like me."

She smiled and looked at me.

"You all must be famished. Let me get him situated, and I'll whip you up something to eat."

"Don't trouble yourself, ma'am. I've got leftovers next door calling my name."

I knew it was bullshit. He just didn't want to intrude, or appear that way, at least.

"Plus," he continued, "I'm going to need a shower. You don't want me anywhere within smelling distance at the moment."

"Okay, suit yourself," she said and then looked at me.

"You know I can eat," I said.

Phil closed his toolbox and picked it up. I waited for him to hop the fence again, but he headed to the gate that led to the side of the house.

"It looks great, Phil. Thanks again," Sadie said.

"Yeah, I couldn't have done it without you," I echoed.

"Bullsnot," he said, eliciting a snort from Trevor. "You did most of the work. You all have a pleasant evening."

He winked and then left through the gate.

"It really does look good," she said.

"Thanks. I just need to move the stuff from the garage in here, and I'll be finished."

Trevor ran into the empty shed and zipped around in circles, hooting like an owl as it echoed in the empty metal enclosure.

"Come on out, Trevor. Let Daddy finish."

The two of them went inside, and I began phase two of the job: emptying the garage. By the time I finished, the sun had set, and I was losing daylight. I used my shirt to wipe my face and gave everything a good once-over. The garage did look better with all that stuff out of it, and the shed didn't look crowded at all. Sadie's idea definitely paid off.

I turned around and jumped when I saw Sadie watching me from right outside the building.

"Your dinner is ready," she said and brushed by me to look inside. "Wow! You did such an amazing job. Thank you."

Out of nowhere, she turned and put her hands around my neck, pulling me in for a series of deep kisses. I pulled back.

"What's Trevor doing?"

"He already ate and is currently glued to the TV, eating ice cream and watching a movie," she said and resumed kissing me, this time sliding her tongue in my mouth.

I pulled back once again, this time feeling a bit self-conscious.

"I smell horrible," I said.

"Billy, I don't give a fuck."

She started rubbing and massaging my crotch until I was rock hard. My entire body was on fire. My heart thumped against the inside of my chest. I grabbed the sides of her shorts and pulled them down and saw she wasn't wearing underwear. My hands automatically caressed the back of her thighs as they made their way up. I squeezed her ass and lifted her onto the empty tool bench. She spread her legs and pulled me closer, taking out my dick and sliding it into herself.

A moan escaped me. I'd been thinking about this since we got interrupted the night before. Animal instinct took over, and I forgot about everything else in the world and focused on her, sliding inside and out, slowly at first and then as hard and fast as I could until I felt her body spasm, and she moaned. Her orgasm sent me over the edge, and I finally let loose. The heavens couldn't have orchestrated a more perfect release.

We both held onto each other, panting as we came down from the high. She laughed, and I did, too. We kissed and cleaned up.

"Phew, I needed that," she said.

"Not as bad as me."

"That's what you think."

"You think Trevor is still occupied?"

She looked at me like I was the ultimate buzzkill.

"How about we see if we can get another one in?"

I grinned and took a step toward her when I heard a door shut.

"And there he is," she said.

We giggled like teenagers getting caught smoking pot as we exited the shed. But as I looked at our back door and the absence of Trevor, I realized ours wasn't the one that closed. My eyes immediately shot to Phil's door. Sure enough, the blinds on the inside were swinging.

"Did Phil just shut his door?" Sadie asked.

"God, I hope not. Guy's wife just left him, and then he has to listen to his neighbors screwing in the shed he just built."

I couldn't help but laugh, and that made her start giggling uncontrollably.

"Come on," she said, taking me by the hand and leading me back inside. Right before entering the house, I gave Phil's yard the side eye. I wasn't sure at the time, but it looked like he was standing in his dark kitchen, looking through the window blinds.

Night 3: Sunday, April 16, 2022

I woke up to the sound of the back door slamming shut. My eyes shot open, and the first thing I noticed was that Sadie wasn't sleeping beside me. I sat up and looked around the dark, empty room. Without waiting any longer, I climbed off the bed and walked down the hall. Trevor's door was shut like I left it.

The light above the stove was on as usual. I had a habit of sneaking down for midnight snacks then, not so much anymore. A white piece of paper lay on the kitchen counter. The words were written in black Sharpie and so big that I could read it as I approached the note. Four words: "COME TO THE SHED," followed by a little heart and "XOXO."

Come to the shed?

And then it hit me. My pulse quickened at the thought of repeating our little quickie from earlier. I was so charged up that I didn't think twice about why she would want me to go to the shed and not just initiate sex in our bed. I opened the door and peered through the darkness at the black aluminum building that could only be seen from the reflective moonlight. A soft white light glowed from the cracks around the flimsy door. I smiled and crept across the lawn, immediately regretting not at least putting on sandals or something as I ascended the hill with the occasional rock or root.

"Sadie?" I whispered.

She didn't say anything.

I felt for the handle and pulled the door open, baffled at what I saw. A cell phone with the brightness turned all the way up was perched on Sadie's bicycle seat. I stepped inside and picked it up. The excitement I felt on my way there quickly turned to worry as I had no idea whose phone this belonged to. Once my eyes adjusted to the blinding glow, I noticed that the phone was on its home display, and there was only one app: PHOTOS. My trembling finger pressed the icon.

A grid of thumbnail images populated the screen, most of them too dark to see anything going on in the picture. Every instinct railed against the idea of playing the first video, fearing what unknown horrors possibly awaited, but I had to know.

The video started with shaky, grainy footage. It took me a minute to figure out that the cameraperson wore a GoPro type of device with night vision. My heart sank when I realized the camera was pointed at my house, but the person recording stood in Phil's yard because the fence was in front of him. He fumbled with the lens to get a clear shot of my house and then moved forward, leaping over the chain link exactly like Phil had done. He moved across the yard with the stealthy grace of a seasoned sleuth.

Two gloved hands entered the frame when he reached my porch and climbed onto the railing and then the porch roof. I found it difficult to swallow as I watched him sneak to the second-floor bathroom window and pry it open so quietly that I couldn't even hear a sound on the recording, only his raspy breathing like I was watching the beginning of *Halloween*. Once he was inside, he crept through the house, looking in all directions like it was the first time he'd done it. And since this was the first video on the phone I held, I assumed they were in chronological order.

My stomach turned to cold knots as the gloved hand opened our bedroom door and the camera peeked in at me and Sadie sound asleep. His breathing intensified, and then he closed the door, effortlessly silent. He snuck across the hall to Trevor's room and did the same thing—stood at the doorway and watched. After he'd gotten a good ten seconds of footage of my sleeping child, he crept out of the house the same way he'd come in and turned the video off when he stepped out the bathroom window.

I'd never been so scared in my life. I just played video after video. Each one started and ended the same, but he became more brazen with each break-in. Sometimes he'd stand right at the foot of our bed and stare for fifteen minutes, just breathing. Other times, he'd randomly move items around the house or take souvenirs. The hardest one to watch was when he entered Trevor's room and just kept the camera focused on the innocent boy. But merely watching wasn't good enough for him anymore, and he reached out and caressed my son's cheek. He even took off his glove to do it.

I neared the end of the videos. Even though I was on the verge of vomiting, I played the next one. This one was different. He breathed harder like he struggled to walk. That's when something appeared in the bottom left corner of the shot. It looked like a bedsheet wrapped around something that hung over his shoulder. I realized he must be carrying something heavy and long, and then a foot slid out of the sheet. He quickly covered it back up.

He's carrying a body. He's carrying a fucking body wrapped in a sheet into my house.

Somehow, he managed to ascend the same side of the porch and heave the heavy load onto the roof. He climbed up and opened the bathroom window—his usual method of entry—and reached outside to drag the body in. The sheet caught on the roof and peeled back, revealing Suzette's face. Phil's wife, who'd supposedly cheated on him and left, laid there in the moonlight with welts and a horrified expression frozen on her face. He reached out and wrapped her tighter and pulled her inside.

The camera shook as he heaved her back on his shoulder. Even though terror collapsed my lungs, I couldn't help but notice how quiet this invader was. He moved gracefully down the hall and into Trevor's room. My eyes widened when I realized what he was doing. He opened my son's closet door, rearranged the mess on the floor, and propped her body in the far corner. She looked like a small rug leaning against the wall. Once he moved the toys around her bottom half and concealed her with the mess of hanging clothes, she had disappeared.

The door squeaked when he shut it. Trevor gasped from behind him. The camera whipped around, and I watched in horror as he stared at my terrified kid who was sitting up in bed. A gloved finger entered the frame, and the invader whispered, "*Shhhhh.*" Surprisingly, Trevor flung the covers off him and jumped off the bed.

"Daddy," he said, barely above a whisper.

My eyes teared up. I wasn't there for him.

"Daddy," he said, louder this time.

It must've spooked the intruder because the camera turned back around to show him open the closet and step inside. He moved clothes around and wedged himself in the corner with Suzette's bundled corpse.

Trevor bolted out of the room. The cameraman's breathing intensified as he peered through the slats in the door. I could barely hear voices off screen. Another heartbreak struck as I watched the hallway light turn on and saw myself enter his room.

Holy shit. This was the other night.

I saw myself open the closet doors and look all around, but I knew I wouldn't see the boogeyman hiding in there. Trevor couldn't see him either, so I guess that he thought he fled as soon as he woke me up. I watched as I told Trevor there was no one in the closet and removed his soiled linens. The kid wet the bed because he was scared to death, and there I was treating him like shit. I hated myself in that moment.

After I tucked Trevor back in, the camera stayed focused on him until he snored. Then the intruder managed to sneak into the hallway without making a sound. He walked downstairs and retrieved the sheets and blanket that I put in the washer and left through the back door.

That's where the sheets went. And that smell... It wasn't a pee-stained mattress or dirty sheets; it was Suzette's body releasing its natural gases as she began the process of decomposition.

Standing in the dark shed, I couldn't see myself, but I knew my complexion had paled. There was one more video to go. I didn't think twice before playing it. I didn't think about how stupid it was for me to just stand there watching these videos that had clearly been left for me to do just that. But I know now that I was in a state of shock. The chemicals in my body had paralyzed me as I watched the final recording.

Again, the intruder broke into our house, and he entered our bedroom and slowly walked around the bed to my side. His gloved hand rose into view, and he slowly pulled it off. His breathing quieted as he got closer to me, sound asleep on my back with my mouth half-open. I watched him lift the comforter and slide his hand under it. The camera switched from my sleeping face to the hand under the covers bobbing up and down as he jerked me off. As I started to moan and wake up, he released me and backed into our walk-in closet.

He recorded me initiate sex with Sadie, just like he planned. I knew what came next. Trevor walked into our bedroom and said the man was still in his closet and that he peed the bed. I acted like a cockblocked asshole, and she left to go calm him down and clean him up. That was also the point where I spotted the man in my closet, well, his boots, at least. I watched myself stare in the direction of the camera, not seeing the full picture.

The intruder's arm rose into frame. He'd put his glove back on and now held a black pistol in his hand, pointing it directly at me. The footage looked like something from a shoot-'em-up video game. I had no idea how close I was to getting killed.

Somedays, I wish I had been.

Sadie came back in the room, and we had our little fight. Watching it made me want to punch myself right in the face. I got up and stormed out of the bedroom to go downstairs and jerk off like the asshole that I was. The camera stayed focused on Sadie as she huffed and puffed before settling into sleep. He snuck down the hallway and left the same way he came in. The video ended.

Just as I realized how long I'd been standing there, the shed door slammed shut and locked. I darted over to it and shook the handle, but it wouldn't budge. I grabbed the sledgehammer that I'd placed in the corner earlier that day and was about to pound my way out when the phone rang. It startled me so badly that I nearly dropped the handle. I picked up the phone and saw that it was a FaceTime call from Sadie's number.

"What the hell?"

I answered it, but it wasn't a person I saw on the screen. A static shot of the shed I was trapped inside of populated the screen, coupled with the same breathing from the videos. I pounded my fist into the flimsy corner of the door and watched it buckle from the outside on the phone. Whoever had Sadie's phone was standing in my back yard recording me.

"Hey!" I screamed. "Let me out!"

The person recording slowly backed away from the building and turned around to reveal two more bodies wrapped in sheets. One was longer than the other. I gasped at the sight of Trevor's treasured, blood-soaked blanket covering his small body. I remember thinking that I was having a nightmare. There was no way this was happening.

I dropped the phone and assaulted the door with the sledgehammer until I busted it enough to squeeze through. Still gripping the tool that was now my weapon, I stormed the yard, screaming like a maniac. There was no cameraman or any wrapped bodies in the grass. For a moment, I stood there questioning my sanity. I looked up and saw Phil's truck pulling out of his driveway.

"No!"

I sped across the yard and opened the fence, running after the vehicle as it peeled out and squealed down the road. The last image I saw of my wife and son were their sheets flapping in the truck bed as they disappeared into the night.

It's been two years, and Phil has yet to be apprehended. After he drove off that night, I ran inside and called the police. They put out an all-call for his truck and searched the surrounding area, but like I said, they didn't find anything. I kind of knew they never would.

I gave them the phone that had lured me into the shed and told them about Suzette's body that was probably in my son's closet.

They searched both of our houses, uncovering horrors in each one. I found out later that when they unwrapped Suzette, they found a note stapled to her forehead that had the following message: "She found my videos."

The officers in Phil's house found a stockpile of mementos from his crimes tucked away in the basement. Under the stairs, a section of the drywall had been cut to be removed and put back as needed. This was Phil's secret stash. They found VHS tapes, DVDs, and external hard drives full of nothing but videos of Phil through the ages breaking into different houses and recording the families while they slept.

Apparently, he'd been doing it for quite some time. He'd get more comfortable and start moving items around or even taking stuff for his memento cabinet. The groping came next, but the police said it was never about sex for him. He got off on the power, the control. When night fell, he turned into the master puppeteer. There were never any murders, though. Not until my house, at least.

Based on the blood in the basement and the still-open door to his life of perversion, they surmised that Suzette had somehow found the tapes and confronted him. He panicked and killed her by first bludgeoning her with a croquet mallet from the set in the basement and then strangling her. The sloppiness of the assault and subsequent neglect to clean up the crime suggested that this all caught him off-guard.

The FBI psychologists told me that they think the only reason he hung around those last few days was to finish the cycle of breaking into our home. He stashed Suzette's body in our house out of both guilt and to add an extra layer of excitement to his sick game. Once he killed her, he had a new drive. And because he knew he'd be fleeing anyway, he wanted to experiment on two more people: my wife and son.

This seemingly normal man lived a life of secrets and, when forced to face them, embraced his darker nature. God help whoever finds this monster lurking in their bedroom one random night. I shudder to think how his new videos end, now that he's acquired a taste for blood. And make no mistake about it; he's still out there, still doing his thing, and he could live next door and you'd never know it. If you're fortunate, you'd be the one on the news saying, "I can't believe it. He was so normal."

I still live in the same house. Our house. I refuse to let Phil take that away from us. I also pray that he comes back, if only to tie up loose ends. I spend my nights staring at the closet. Sometimes I think I see him, other times not, but I don't care either way. I leave my front door unlocked more and more as time passes, not because I feel safe, but because I want it to end...

One way or another.

UNDER FLOORBOARDS

JEREMY MEGARGEE

I want to burn this house down to cinders, and I want to burn with it, twisting and boiling and screaming. I want to suck down smoke and writhe until the flames shrink me down into a little nothing doll, because that's all I am to those I meet already, a little nothing doll. Long red hair, inferno-colored hair, and blue ocean eyes that have seen too much and wish to see no more. I'm pretty, and there are so many expectations when you're pretty. People expect you to be confident, self-assured, and capable of gliding along the pathways of life with relative ease.

They don't see what's inside, and in my experience, they do not care. But I'm going to tell you what's inside. Enough childhood trauma to fill up every chamber of the *Titanic*. Crippling anxiety, threadbare self-esteem, and this loathsome desire to be loved by all the wrong people. When you are loved wrong so many times, it creates a complex in your brain. You attract the bad ones, you are attracted to the bad ones, and it's a cycle of self-sabotage. It's like a nail that juts out of your skull, and with each failed or aborted relationship, the head of a hammer taps that nail in an inch deeper. It never stops. The tap-tap-tap of that constant reminder. You are not lovable. You are not worthy. You are a soft, pliable thing to be touched and used, and it is so easy to throw you away when the using is done.

And you think and you hope, in that desperate deer part of your brain, the doe-eyed shameful part of yourself, that if you show extra compassion, more kindness, more parts of yourself, if you give and give until your guts are raw and your heart is obliterated, then at long last, they will see your *worth*. Spoiler alert, they never do. They take what they like, and they leave the rest. They splay me out like gristle on the highway, and even though I'm still twitching and alive, they piss on all the parts of me that could have been something. I go both ways, so I've gotten it from both sides. Unmerciful men, unmerciful women, and if I'm always chasing the rotten ones, surely that must mean that I'm rotten too?

I think about that a lot. I think about it during the weeks when I self-isolate in my room in this rancid fucking hoarder house. I keep my room clean and nice, a pocket dimension in comparison to the filth of the rest of the place. There are vines of ivy affixed to my walls and warm string lights, a typical room for a girl, but it feels like a false sanctuary. My girlhood is tainted. I am in an environment that smothers, and I do not thrive. Are there others in the world that relate? Do you ever feel like a worm on a hook? I see those memes all the time now when I doomscroll social media, "Would you still love your girlfriend if she was a worm?"

Only a hook would love me. A hook that likes to puncture and tear and impale. I think maybe that's all I'm good for. I'm afraid to show people what my brain looks like, because it's so horrible up there. I think things that I wish I didn't think. It is the great, pulsing adversary in my skull, and if I could scoop it out and press it down deep into the garbage disposal, I would do so without hesitation. I'd fill up the empty space with thrifted trinkets and scraps of silk, a little rat's nest, and surely that would keep the ugly thoughts away from me forever.

If you're ugly on the inside, I guess it doesn't really matter what you look like on the outside. I've covered all my windows with blankets and trash bags and sweaters that I don't wear, the cloth all nailed together to keep even a small glimmer of sunlight from shining in. There is nothing to see out those windows. Just corn, and sky, and a Nebraska that never fucking ends.

Is there some tutorial out there on how to be a person? I'd read it over and over. I'd study it until my eyeballs lost all their moisture. Maybe there would be some level of guidance there that I missed out on when I was a kid. Maybe it would teach me how to be a wife, how to sleep properly, how to eat what is good for me, how to not flay my own emotions every single hour of the day until nothing is left within me but quivering meat.

I don't remember who lives in this house with me. It might be toxic parents, but perhaps they're dead already. It might be roommates, addicts that I almost never see because I almost never leave the room. I know there are cats and rats, because they have their quarrels ceaselessly, and I hear them at all hours. There's never any sun, I don't allow the sun, so I rarely care when it is day or night. I don't work, too mentally ill for that, so someone has to pay the bills here. I'm not lucid enough to know.

In my heart and my soul, I am overwhelmingly alone, but I don't think I'm fully alone in this house. There's this paranoia about someone or something that lives alongside me. It might be nothing but old house sounds and intrusive thoughts. But I don't think it's only that. You know that feeling of betrayal when you find a tick on your skin? You never even knew it was there. Just a painless wound and this bloated insect attached to you, supping on your blood, making you weak, making you anemic, and if you don't see it, you'd never even know it was with you.

I have that feeling all the time now.

I want so badly to find it, to stomp it, to watch it explode with all the blood it dared to take from me. Maybe I'll leave my room and hunt for it. Tie back my hair, smear war paint beneath my eyes, and seek out a kamikaze end.

It wants to leave me broken. Everything I've ever made the mistake of trusting has wanted to leave me broken. More shattered than before.

Tell me, am I not shattered enough for you?

She sleeps a lot. She is a beautiful little sloth of a girl, and she is blanketed in layers of depression. I see her in those moments when she feels good, which are rare, and I watch her attentively in those moments when she feels very bad, darkly bad, and those times are far more frequent. She has lost weight recently, and I wish I could appear before her and spoon feed soup into her pouting mouth. But that is a dream within a dream for me, and it can never be so. If she were to see me, this jarring thing that I am to look upon, surely she'd scream until the blood vessels popped in her eyes. I don't want that. Her eyes are tide pools, flecks of coral there, and it would be wrong to pollute such soulful bodies of water.

I spend long hours listening to her cry. There's something so heartfelt about her blubbering. When you live as I do, when you languish in the pits that I've languished in, you forget what it means to be human. I was born human, but I don't feel human anymore. Those parts of me are in the past, and I have left them in the land of half-formed memory. But she is human. She is everything flawed and harmed and cast aside, and is there anything more human than that? It's often painful to see her. My eyes are crusted over with what feels like a thousand styes, but that is nothing, because the emotional turmoil of looking at her is so much worse.

I only allow myself glimpses, and it is more than I deserve. I see her through grimy floorboards, through slits in the wall, through mouse holes in the ceiling. I'm a voyeur, you see. I used to feel such shame about that. Such a foul rolling sensation in my belly, that deep-seated desire to *watch*. But with time, I accepted my role in this world. I am meant only to watch, only to look, only to yearn and sniff and peep and imagine. She is my pet even though she has no knowledge of this. Maybe she is a pet only in my own mind. I am meant only for breadcrumbs of pleasure, and I am grateful for every nibble I am afforded when it comes to her.

I'm used to lying prone and quiet for hours on end in confined spaces. I've done this before. She isn't my first. I have watched many since I chose to become a watcher. I've watched them from suffocating summer attics, cobweb-strewn cubbies behind drywall, and in coffin-shaped apertures that exist under loose floorboards. I am proficient at wiggling as worms do in blackened spaces, and the dark has become a welcome gift. Years in the dark. Years letting the dark define me. I resent the light because it does not want me, and even a thing that used to be a person can feel the sting of rejection.

I collect small parts of her. These are intimate bits that she no longer needs, and into the jar they go. Eyelashes that slip between the floorboards. Dandruff crumbs that tumble down to where I am. Toenails she clips and discards. These little lost pieces of womanhood, and I take them, because in my heart I am a scavenger. If I cannot possess her in the way that a man wants to possess a woman, then I will indulge in my totems and talismans.

Six years ago in the dead of winter, I shared an experience with her that I'll never forget. She was lying on the floor, high on opiates, lost and sad, arms pin wheeling as though she was dying to create a snow angel. No snow, only her, only my sweet empty angel.

She fell into something like a fitful sleep, and I could feel her warmth baking down. I breathed in the full scent of her, and I felt a stiffening in that forbidden root that I once tried to cut off with a box cutter. Let us not talk of that. This is the story of her, not the story of my private mutilations.

I listened to her breathe for a while. Her chest sounded wet and wounded, full of things meant to haunt. But nothing like me. Nothing that haunts her as lovingly as I do. I could see the nape of her neck through that slit in the floorboards. Just a narrow portal, a portal to pretty, and I couldn't help myself. There were soft feminine hairs on that nape of neck. I pressed myself up, the weak atrophied parts of myself, and I made of my tongue a serpent. I sent it moist and seeking through that crack, and I let it run along the length of her neck like a paintbrush.

Shall I tell you how she tasted? How I dribbled and mewled with delight, trying so desperately to silence myself. She tasted like nostalgia. Her flavor was like a dream where I could have been something more than what I am now. Sweat, dirt clogged into pores, and the hysteria of a broken spirit in a broken place in a broken universe.

It took all of my will to hold back. I had to beg myself not to smash my long fingernails up through the floor and take hold of her warmth. I wanted to consume her, to cannibalize her, to take all of her into me. If she were to be all eaten up, it would cure my lonesome ache. But I practiced restraint.

I allowed myself only that single midnight lick.

I think of it often, and the thought nourishes me.

Won't she be mine? Won't she be mine?

Won't she be my neighbor?

I want to eat something. I have to go scouting and scurrying if I want something solid in my stomach. I'm just a rat girl in her room, and it feels like ages since I've left these four walls even for a moment. I look in the mirror, and I see smudged winged eyeliner, chapped lips, and a void inside of me that swirls and swirls. Why do I care how I look? I'm just going to rummage around the house to feed myself. There is no one to impress.

There's no one here, right? Or is there someone here? Is there *something* that just lurks and fucks with me and blooms like a corpse flower in my heart? I think I should be honest. It's important to let the vulnerability out sometimes. I have a drug problem. I don't discriminate, but the painkillers and the psychedelics are my favorite. I just need to fucking escape sometimes. This body is a prison, this mind is a prison, and this soul is a rusted-out asylum where shit drips down from faulty sewage lines.

It's enough to make a madwoman of me, and if I can make myself sweet and soft and blurry for a while, barely tethered to the fringes of reality, then I have some semblance of peace. It doesn't last. I'll awaken sweaty and shaking, craving more of something I shouldn't. Maybe that's why I've been so scattered about anything and everything here. I barely have any awareness of what goes on in this house aside from my room. When I'm high, I never care.

I know it's wrong. I'm pouring acid on wounds, and those wounds just gape wider, become bigger, and before it's all said and done, I will be nothing but a wound in the shape of a girl. Maybe I already am. God knows I bleed on all the things I make the mistake of touching and holding too close.

I crack open the door, and I stumble through the hall, past the cardboard boxes, the dusty paintings, and that old upstairs furnace that hasn't felt a fire inside of it for at least a hundred years. I hear scratching and rustling from the walls, like when I go anywhere, there are millions of insects following me. It's gotta be imagination, or paranoia, or some haze of drugs still in my system. If an exterminator were to come here, his solution would probably be to burn the whole house down to stinking ash.

I cling to the banister and I descend the stairs, hollow step after hollow step, and I should remember how to reach the kitchen. Why does it all feel so unfamiliar? Everything is dim, so dim, and I can't tell if it's day or night. The windows are all covered, just like the one in my room, but I don't remember doing that.

Everything is shadow, and there's a never-ending buzzing in both of my ears. I've stumbled into a massive cloud of flies, and I've interrupted them from a long banquet. I feel their fat little bloat bodies bumping against my face and arms as they attempt to fly to safety. It's all compound eyes and glimmering wings, and when I open my mouth to suck in breath, I swallow down a few of them inadvertently. I'm choking on the flies, the living flies, and how I wish to drop to my knees and beg Beelzebub to call his familiars back from whence they came.

I swat my hands back and forth, seeking sight, and once it comes, I wish for my eyes to be taken from me. The smell is putrid. It is rot still fresh, and the death aroma refuses to leave my nostrils.

I am looking at parents that are not parents anymore. They are just congealed flesh puppets sitting jaws agape in their chairs, hands on the tabletop, fingers black like sausage gone bad. No eyes, just flies. Crawling hungry things where their eyes used to be. They twitch a little, because their clothing is full of flies, and the skin left to them is puckered and feasted upon. There are knives deep in them too. Knives in their heads, chests, and necks. The knives were just lazily jammed in and left there.

I've lost so much time, and they've rotted so much. The knives tell the story. Something did this to them. Something *is* here with me. I'm standing here and crying, and the flies get stuck in my tears and drown on my cheeks.

I want to hide and die and rot.

I want to curl up in the fetal position on this floor and just let the maggots eat me up, all my fears, all my doubts, all my constant fuck-ups. No one expects anything from a smear of gore that's decomposing on the tiles. I can just be nothing. I have always aspired to be nothing.

But maybe I can do something else.

I know that it is in the walls. I sense this overwhelming negative presence that seems to get off on staring at me. It is afraid to show itself. It is shy and deranged, but if I bring it out howling into the light, it may wither.

I rarely feel that I can accomplish anything. I don't believe in myself like that, and I never truly have. But I resent the intrusion. I like my privacy. Let me spiral and be a damaged doll all on my own.

What are you, and where are you? How long have you been in this house?

I understand now, and I'll find you.

There are eyeholes in the walls, long slits in the floor, and so many lost crevices in this house for an invader to contort into. I never noticed them before. Too strung out, or maybe I just didn't bother to look. But now I'm forced to see. There is no more looking away, no more pretending, and I am forced to confront this.

I've left the flies to their dinner, and I am hunting. I almost think that I can smell him, or her, or *it*. It's a musk, bordering on animal, but also the spice of some faded perfume. I'm following my nose, and I wish my nostrils weren't so damaged from coke, because I'd be a better bloodhound than I am now.

The chosen she is determined to see. I can be incognito no longer. She wanders now from her enclosure, and I am afraid of what is to come. I am self-conscious. I have always been on the outside looking in, but now change comes roaring to the forefront.

It's been so long since I've had a mirror. Ages since I've seen myself reflected in the shining orbs of human eyes. Will she hack me to pieces? Will I feel the warmth of her hands as she strangles me, and all the while I'm spitting out whispers of worship?

I hope she does not resent me carving those devils that brought her into the world. They were no good. They were intent to shape her into something bad and sad, and I couldn't be a bystander to that. I want her to see what she truly is.

Glorious.

The lone gemstone in a picked-over riverbed. I gave them over to the flies so that she could understand her own nature. The weight of her potential. It is there, and it is bright.

I hear great cracks, stomps, and the precursor to wreckage. I breathe deeply, and the splinters baptize me.

A god has come.

The sweat pours from my brow as I rip up the floorboards, and nails fly out behind my shoulders. The aroma is strong here, and once the dust settles, I see the watcher for the first time. His eyes glimmer like fox eyes from the edge of a deep, dark wood. I didn't know what I'd expect, but not this.

I had thought it would be some monster or hideous freak, the stuff of nightmares. Instead I find myself looking down at an emaciated young man with wild locks of chestnut hair and a beard that hasn't seen a razor in a very long time. He looks like some mountain hermit, clearly disheveled and coated in grime, but I'm shocked to find him somewhat appealing to the eyes. He has a nice bone structure, and even though the eyes seem demented and out of touch, the soft brown of the irises calls to me. There is kindness buried there, but life has covered it over with soil and sadness.

But despite the shock of appearances, he is still a killer. I take up a ragged board with crooked nails jutting from it, and I lift it high overhead, holding it there aloft while I study him.

"How long have you been in this house? How long have you been *watching* me?"

"Longer than either of us can remember. It feels like I've always been here."

His voice is a hollow croak, the voice of a person that is relearning how to speak after a period of dormancy.

"You hide in the walls and the floor. How do you eat or use the bathroom? What the hell kind of life has that been?"

"A lonely one. I have my places for things like that, and there are critters down here to eat. Not nice things, but I make do. It is a sacrifice. But I'd sacrifice anything to be closer to you."

I stand over him, my face surging with emotion. I don't know how to feel. He speaks with such warmth and conviction. I should feel repelled. I should want to bash his brains into paste. But I hesitate.

"You killed my folks."

"They were dead inside already. I slid the knives into them, yes, but it was for you. They were unkind. They gave you the wrong kind of childhood. I knew from the very beginning what they did. I knew when I saw how much *hurt* they left you with. I want you to know that you never deserved that hurt."

The watcher pauses, his eyes drifting up to flit across the splinters.

"I've known hurt like that. They earned the knives."

I want to call him a liar. I want to tell him that he's wrong about that. But he's not. I repressed it, I buried it, and I never wanted to think about it, but my parents were awful. They did unspeakable things. Somewhere along the way, it broke my brain, and I let so many parts of myself drift away.

"You could smash that board down into my face. It would be divinity to meet an end at your hands. I'd never blame you for it, and I'd never fight. I am a friend. Just a nobody beneath the floor, a *neighbor* you never knew you had. You could give my body to the flies and nail the floorboards back. Or..."

I cock my head while staring down at him.

"Or?"

"Or you could come down here and be with me. It's quiet in these dark spaces. Nothing but the whisper of spider legs and the soft touch of dust. There are no expectations. You don't really have to be a person. You can just *be*. The world up there is full of fangs and poison. It bites and bites until nothing good is left. It's different here."

I'm crying, and my lips are quivering. My muscles feel weak, and I'm so tired. Even my bones are tired. My soul is this exhausted rag that has been twisted so much, and I fear what another twist will bring.

"A place to rest. A place to watch. I'll hold you until time unspools and the world ends. Someone else will buy the house. We will see their lives through floorboards and ratholes. And we will take solace in the fact that we'll never have to be like them. Come down with me."

His eyes implore, painfully vulnerable. It's clear that something in life has gutted this man.

"A home for the haunted ones."

I allow the board to slip from my fingers and clatter to the side. Before I realize what is happening, I am lowering myself down into that coffin-sized aperture in the floor. I embrace the man, clinging to fragile ribcage, and I hear the beating of a tender heart.

I nuzzle close, and soon we are crawling much deeper into the dark. I realize that I was meant for it.

How wonderful it is to watch.

WHAT'S YOUR NAME?

R.E. SARGENT

The U-Haul truck backed into the driveway next door caught Spike's attention when he turned the corner into the cul-de-sac. He slowed down and tried to spot the people that had shown up in it. There were two vehicles parked haphazardly in front of the house as well, one a lifted GMC truck that was bigger than a truck really ever needed to be—Spike felt his eyeballs rolling already—and one of those foreign cars with the huge tailpipe and the tall wing connected to the trunk lid, which was as tall as the car itself. The truck was parked halfway on the front lawn, and the ass end of it was jutting out in the street. Spike's stomach churned at the thought of the extra noise that was sure to come with their arrival. The new neighbors were douchebags; he already knew it with every fiber of his being.

Spike continued to creep down the street, and when he was in front of his house, he turned into his driveway and parked. Curious as to what they looked like, he sat for a couple more minutes and finally shut off the engine to his Toyota Corolla, got out, and headed toward his front door.

"Looks like we have a new neighbor."

Spike jumped at the voice. Looking over, he saw Jeff, his next-door neighbor on the other side, who held a watering wand and was hydrating all of the beautiful flowers that dotted his front yard landscape.

"Oh hey, Jeff. I didn't see you there. Yeah, it looks like my new set of neighbors is complete!"

It was an inside joke between the two of them. Jeff Lewis had only moved in a couple of months before, snatching up the beautiful home the first day it went on the market. Several weeks after Jeff moved in, the house on the other side of him had gone up for sale. Spike and Jeff had joked that he was running off all the old neighbors and was working on getting a new set.

Spike had immediately liked Jeff the day he met him. Jeff lived alone, but he was friendly, polite, and quiet. Spike liked that Jeff minded his own business but was always there to lend a hand if needed, and he always said hi when he saw Spike. He was the perfect neighbor.

Spike was hoping he'd luck out and hit the jackpot with the new neighbors on the other side, but he wasn't feeling good about it from the cars they drove or the way they parked. That and there was trash all over the front lawn, surrounding the front of the truck. Sure, they were just moving in, and he understood the chaos, but it seemed to him that they could pile their trash elsewhere... like in the corner of the garage or something. Although he already had his concerns, he decided to keep them from Jeff. At least for now.

He hadn't particularly liked his last neighbors, and he tried to avoid them at all costs. Needless to say, it was a surprise when Jeff moved in and he was actually a pleasure to talk to. He and Jeff were close to the same age—mid-thirties—but Jeff wasn't one of those immature macho men. He was just a regular guy who seemed responsible and took great care of his home. His front yard was immaculate.

"Yeah, two new neighbors in two months. I'd say so," Jeff said. "Guy looks like a douchebag though."

Spike laughed loudly. "Oh my god, I was just thinking the same thing. I mean, I haven't seen him or anything, but jeez, just look at the front of the house. It paints a pretty vivid picture."

"Yup. Glad you are living next to them and not me," Jeff said, smiling.

"That's helpful," Spike said, laughing.

"Glad I could help. Let me know if you actually do need help dealing with them though. I have my garden soaker here—I could do some real damage."

Spike smiled. "The neighbors should all be skeered! Anyway, I guess we will see what happens. I'm going to pop inside and see what Steph is up to and if I can help her with dinner."

"See ya later, Spike. Tell her I said hi."

"Will do. Later, Jeff."

Spike used his phone app to unlock the front door and stepped inside.

Spike Creamer and Steph Kneeland had purchased the home a few years prior after their dating relationship had turned serious. Rather than one of them moving into the other's apartment, they decided to give both apartments up and do the grown-up thing and get saddled to a mortgage. They loved living there for the most part. The house was great, but Spike one day wanted to buy a house on some acreage, so he didn't have to put up with the bullshit that living in a regular neighborhood created. Case in point: the new assholes moving in next door.

Spike found Steph in the kitchen.

"Hey, babe. How was your day?"

Steph turned around and walked over and gave Spike a kiss on the lips. He wrapped his arms around her waist, pulled her in tighter, and gave her another kiss, grabbing her ass in the process.

"Perv!" she said, tapping him on the chest with the back of her hand like one might swat a fly. Steph smiled. "My day was good. Lots of clients on the table today. Just got home like fifteen minutes ago."

"Any requests for happy endings today?" Spike winked.

Giggling, Steph said, "Not today, but the week isn't over yet."

"There's always that one guy."

"One per week, maybe."

"Fuckin' creeps!" Spike said.

"It's always the gross ones, too. Obviously, the ones that can't get laid."

"Sure you don't want to change careers? Move away from being an LMT?"

"I'm good, hun. I like what I do. I'm not going to let the assholes ruin it for me. I simply end their massage and tell the front desk to never schedule them again."

"At least you don't have to see them again. That's good. But, speaking of assholes, did you see we got new neighbors?"

"Oh yeah, I'm so thrilled," she said, her voice dripping with sarcasm.

"Yeah, me too. Did you actually see them?"

"No. You?"

"Nope."

"I saw the clusterfuck in the front yard though."

"Same."

As if choreographed, both let out a sigh at the same time.

Spike felt something on his leg and looked down and saw their cat Kody rubbing against it. Spike reached down and petted Kody for a minute and then turned his attention back to Steph.

"What should we make for dinner?" Spike asked.

"I took some chicken out of the freezer this morning. Want to make some chicken fettuccine alfredo?"

"Sounds amazing. If you cook the chicken, I'll work on the noodles, sauce, and some veggies."

"Want me to make some garlic bread too?" Steph asked.

"Now that you mention it."

Together they cooked, making small talk about their day, until the sound interrupted them.

"What is that?" Steph asked, her forehead wrinkled.

"I dunno. But whatever it is, it's loud as fuck!"

They stopped talking and stood still, listening. The distinct sound of heavy bass vibrated the items on the counter. Spike went to the back door and opened the slider, stepping out onto the back patio and into the yard, careful to avoid the pool. Steph was at his heels.

They couldn't see into the neighbors' back yard, because of the six-foot wooden fence separating the properties, but it was clear where the sound—some bass-heavy screaming music—was coming from. The new neighbors.

"Un-fucking-believable!" Steph said.

"First fucking day, too!"

"I mean, we love loud music as much as the next guy, but at least we are considerate about it. Did you see the bass was vibrating the dishes on the counter in our kitchen?"

"I saw."

Spike went back inside and motioned for Steph to follow him. Back in the kitchen, they dished out the food.

"What should we do, Spike?"

"Not sure what we *can* do."

"Call the police?"

"We could. But maybe we should wait and see if it stops, or someone else calls. I hate to start out on the wrong foot with them on the very first day."

"Seems like they don't share the same sentiment."

"No kidding."

They ate dinner, trying to ignore the vibrations, however it was impossible to do. After dinner, they tried to watch television, but neither could concentrate.

"Why haven't the cops come yet?" Steph said.

"You'd think someone would have called them."

"You'd think. But maybe everyone else is also afraid to make waves."

"Maybe. I'm just going to put in my earbuds and read."

"I guess I can try the same, but..."

"But?"

"If this is day one, what is the rest of our time here going to be like?"

Spike looked down at the bed, contemplating. "You're right. This is bullshit."

Spike grabbed his cellphone off the side table and called the non-emergency number. After he told the story, he hung up.

"What did they say?" Steph asked.

"They are sending someone out."

"Thank god! I'm not sure how much more I can take."

Half an hour later, the music stopped. Spike went to the front door and stepped out on the porch, peering around the side to get a view of the property next door. There were two police cars sitting in front, their lights off. Two officers stood at the front door, talking to somebody. Spike tried to get a better look and saw a man, maybe six-five, tall, broad shoulders. He wore a black tank top and his head was shaved. He looked irritated.

Just as Spike was going to retreat back into the house, the man looked over and spotted him, nodding toward him.

"Well, howdy, neighbor!" he yelled, slurring a little. "So sorry about the music."

Spike felt dread in his stomach, the man's words heavy, drenched with malice. Without saying a word, Spike backed up around the corner of the house and went inside.

"Are the cops there?" Steph asked.

"Yes, and the guy saw me. And I think he knows I called."

"What's he look like?"

"Tall, broad, bald."

"Of course he is. You're not worried about him, are you?"

"Just annoyed by him. Hopefully he got the message now."

"Hopefully."

"Now maybe we can get some sleep before work tomorrow."

"Maybe."

Spike picked up his book, the newest Malerman. "I'm going to read for an hour or so before bed though."

"I think I might do the same."

Eventually, they got lost in their stories and the events of the evening slipped away.

"What did he say?" Spike asked, a scowl on his face.

"He said I had a nice ass."

"What??"

Steph beat Spike home again the next day, and as she was getting out of her car, the new neighbor approached her.

"Let me start at the beginning."

"Please."

"So, when I pulled up in our driveway, I noticed the U-Haul and the riceburner were gone."

"Okay."

"But that truck was parked on the grass still. Not sure why the idiot can't use the driveway like everyone else."

"Was he outside?"

"No. I didn't see him, but when I got out of my car, he was standing beside it... I never saw him approach."

Spike took a deep breath. "What did he say?"

"He asked me my name."

"Just like that? Nothing else?"

"Just like that. I was startled when I saw him, and I tried to recover and be courteous, so I told him, 'Hi,' and then he said, 'What's your name?'"

"Did you tell him?"

"I did. I wasn't sure what else to do."

"I get it. But that's creepy. Just appearing out of nowhere and shit. What happened next?"

"He told me it was nice to meet me. I replied in kind to try and not be rude and then told him I had to get dinner started. He said he'd see me later. I walked toward the door, and he said, 'Pretty fine ass you've got there.'"

"I'm gonna kill him."

"You're going to do no such thing, Spike. I don't need you to be in jail. Besides, wouldn't you agree that I have a fine ass?"

"No argument there. But it's mine, not his, and what the fuck is he even doing on our property?"

"Is someone a little jealous?" Steph said, laughing.

"More irritated than anything. But that's what you get for wearing scrubs. Your ass definitely looks nice in them." Spike paused for a minute, then his face changed as he remembered something. "Not to change the subject, but speaking of things on our property, did you see someone's dog shit on our front lawn?"

"No, but figures."

"Grass has shit on it, shithead standing in our driveway... lots of shit out front."

"No kidding. I'll go pick it up. Fucking dog owners."

"I'll go with you just in case *he* gets any bright ideas to come harass you again."

Steph grabbed a plastic grocery bag from under the sink and headed to the front door, Spike following closely. Steph walked out to the grass and looked around. Spike pointed at the turd that sat there proudly, standing partially vertical at about a forty-five degree angle, as if it were flipping them off. Steph turned the bag inside out and put her hand in it, ready to pick up the poop, using the bag as a glove. She paused.

"Um, Spike?"

"Yeah?"

"I don't think that's dog shit."

"Why do you say that?"

"Look closely. Corn."

Spike leaned closer. "Mother fucker."

"Do you think..."

"Yes, I think. It's gotta be that asshole. I knew calling the cops was a bad idea."

"Not like we had a choice."

"There is always a choice."

Steph wrinkled up her nose and reached down with the bag and picked up the log of corn-laced crap, wrapped the bag up, and walked over to their outside trash can and dumped it inside.

"Let's go back inside, Spike. It feels like we're being watched."

Spike looked at the house next door, shuddered, and started toward the front door, with Steph in tow.

"Spike, have you seen Kody?"

It was Saturday, and Spike was sitting in the living room reading a book when Steph approached him.

"Not this morning. He was sleeping on my head last night for most of the night. I'm sure he's just hiding like he always does. Did you check under the bed?"

"Yes, I looked everywhere."

"You probably just missed him. He has to be somewhere. No way for him to get outside."

"One way to find out. If the can opener doesn't do the job, I don't know what will."

Steph went to the pantry and pulled out a can of cat food and clamped the electric can opener down on it. The motor started, and the can spun as the lid was cut. Kody always came running when he heard it no matter what was being opened. Except this time, he didn't.

"Spike?" she called, alarm edging her voice.

Spike got up from the couch and walked into the kitchen.

"This doesn't make sense. Did we leave the door open at all this morning?"

"Not open. I might have left it unlocked when I went for a run this morning."

"Oh no."

"There's no way he could have gotten out."

"I'm thinking someone let him out... or fucking stole him."

"Oh shit. You don't think—"

"I do," Spike said. "That guy is bad news."

"Let's go outside and look for him."

Spike went to the front door and opened it, walked out onto the front grass, and started calling for Kody. Steph joined him.

"Kody kitty, where are you?" Steph called.

Spike glared over at the neighbor's house but saw no movement behind the windows.

"What's going on?"

Both Spike and Steph jumped before looking over and seeing Jeff at the edge of their lawn.

"Hi, Jeff, have you seen a cat roaming around out here anywhere?"

Concern crept into Jeff's face.

"I haven't. Is your kitty missing?"

"We can't find him anywhere," Steph told him, her voice cracking.

"Do you think he got out?" Jeff asked. "I can help you look for him."

"We aren't sure," Spike told him. "We can't find him in the house anywhere, though."

"Is he an outdoor cat?" Jeff asked.

"Strictly indoor," Steph said.

"So how would he have gotten out?" Jeff asked.

"Great question," Spike said. "Right now, we're just grasping at straws."

"You don't think…" Jeff started, his head nodding toward the new neighbor's house as his voice trailed off.

"The thought crossed our mind," Steph said.

Spike's forehead wrinkled up. "I just thought of something. Do you guys remember seeing a flyer taped to the side of the mailbox cluster a couple of months ago? Someone lost their cat?"

"I remember that," Steph said. "I guess pets get lost all the time, but that's definitely coincidental."

"Probably not related," Jeff said, but it definitely looks weird.

"Well, and thinking about it, the neighbors didn't live here then, so if they are responsible for Kody, they wouldn't have been involved with that other cat," Steph said.

"Do you think he really opened our door while I was sleeping and stole our cat?" Spike said.

"I don't know," Steph admitted. "But think about it, they've only lived there a few days and it's been a shitshow."

"There goes the neighborhood," Jeff said.

"What should we do, Spike? Call the police?"

"And tell them what? Our cat is missing?"

"We can't just let him get away with this."

"Let's be real. As much as we want to believe that this guy is fucking with us by stealing our cat, just because he's a douchebag doesn't mean he walked into our house and stole our cat."

"It doesn't mean he didn't, either."

"I'm really sorry, guys. I will keep my eyes open for your cat... What did you say his name was?"

"Kody," Steph said.

"I'll keep an eye out for Kody and will holler if I see him. In the meantime, please let me know if there is anything I can do to help. I'm sorry you two are having to deal with this."

"Thanks, Jeff. Really appreciate it," Spike said.

They said their goodbyes and went back inside. In the kitchen, Steph grabbed two beers out of the fridge, opened them, and handed one to Spike.

"I think we could use these."

"And more. This is some bullshit."

"So what should we do?" Steph asked.

"Maybe leave the back door open as much as possible in case he comes back?"

"I like that idea. Also, how about a flyer like the last family?"

"Nothing to lose, I suppose," Spike said.

With the loss of their boy weighing heavy in the air, the mood in the house was solemn the rest of the weekend as they trudged through the things that had to be done, but no joy could be found in the midst of things.

The next Saturday, Spike surprised Steph by announcing he was taking her out for the day. After a nice breakfast, they went to a small nearby lake and rented a paddleboat for a couple of hours, working their way across the lake and back. Afterward, they grabbed lunch at the lake café and general store and walked it off by hitting some of the local trails along the water. By late afternoon, worn out from their day, they drove the hour home.

Parked safely in the driveway, Steph leaned over and gave Spike a kiss.

"Thanks for the best day ever. We haven't gone out and done something fun like that for a long time."

"Yeah, it was extremely overdue."

"I almost feel like I could take a nap. I'm so tired."

"Do that and you might not get back up," Spike said, laughing.

"I'd probably wake up around bedtime."

"That's the way it works!" Spike said.

Steph opened the lock, and they went inside, Spike plopping on the couch with Steph joining him a minute later after using the bathroom.

Spike kicked off his shoes and turned on the television.

As he started flipping channels, Steph grabbed his arm and whispered, "Mute it."

He did.

"Hear that?" she asked.

Spike listened to the silence, unsure about what Steph was talking about, and then he heard it too.

"Is that coming from the pool?"

"I think so," Steph said.

Spike got up and walked to the vertical blinds that covered the slider leading to the back yard. He parted one of the slats and peeked out.

"Holy... shit!"

"What?" Steph asked.

"You aren't going to believe this."

Steph walked to join Spike at the door. Spike stepped aside while still parting the blinds and let Steph look out.

"Are those... uh... tits? In our back yard?"

"Rather large ones."

"What the fuck?" Steph asked, watching the woman wearing only a bikini bottom jump into their pool.

"Great question."

"Do you know her?" Steph asked.

"No. Do you?"

"Never seen her before."

"What the hell is she doing in our pool?"

"Inquiring minds want to know."

"Wait, is there someone in the pool with her?"

Spike went back to the blinds and peered out again.

"Shit!"

"What?"

"It's the dickhead from next door. The woman must be with him."

"What huge fucking balls," Steph said.

"You can see his balls?" Spike joked, trying to lighten the situation, even though he was seething inside.

"No, but obviously you got a good eyeful of her 'rather large' tits," she retorted.

"That I did, but don't blame me. They came with the meal!"

Steph smiled for a second before it faded.

"Do something, Spike."

Spike twisted open the blinds and pulled the cord to slide them back against the wall. When he unlocked the slider and pulled it open, both sets of eyes turned in their direction, the woman with her mouth hanging open.

"Oh my god! You said no one would be home for a long time," she yelled as her right arm covered up her bosom and she crawled out of the pool and ran down the walkway on the side of the house, leaving her wet footprints along the path.

The man had a different sense of urgency, which equated to none at all.

"What's up, neighbors?" he asked as he nonchalantly walked toward the steps and then out of the pool.

As he moved toward the gate, without turning around, he said, "Have a nice day." And then his voice lowered a notch, but he said the next part loud enough for Spike and Steph to still hear.

"...but not as nice as her ass."

Frozen in place at the scene unravelling before him, the last comment spurred Spike into action. He ran toward the gate after the guy.

"Stay the hell off my property and especially stay away from my fiancé."

The guy kept walking out the gate and across the grassy strip between their houses, toward his own, where Spike assumed the woman had already gone.

"Did you hear me?" Spike called out after him. The man still didn't answer.

Finally, when the guy reached his front door, Spike yelled after him one last time.

"What's your name?" Spike yelled.

The man finally turned around and faced Spike.

"What?" he yelled back.

Spike yelled louder. "WHAT'S YOUR NAME?"

The man paused for a minute and deciding there was no harm in answering, replied, "TONY."

"FUUUUCK YOU, TONY!" Spike yelled before heading to the back of the house and pulling Steph inside.

"What was that about?" Steph asked.

"I have no idea. The balls on that guy."

"No, I mean you."

"Me?"

"Yeah, you know... the 'fuck you, Tony' thing. Don't you think you might be poking the bear?"

"I really don't care. He's provoking me. And he better stay away from you."

"I think I like you jealous."

"It's not jealousy, really. I can't sit back and watch him disrespect you."

"My prince in shining armor!"

"Something like that. But seriously, I feel like this is all a bad dream. How could everything change so quickly?"

"I've been wondering the same thing. We don't really know the other neighbors, but Jeff's been great. Living here was great. And then everything went to shit when dickhead moved in."

"I almost feel we should call the police. He was trespassing on our property."

"What's that going to accomplish, Spike?"

"I don't know. But at least it will send a message that we won't be harassed without taking action."

"Something tells me it won't help... He'll probably just get worse."

"Any suggestions then, Steph?"

"Maybe we should go introduce ourselves. Try to start over. It's evident we started off on the wrong foot."

"It makes a lot of sense. It really does. The biggest problem I have with it is that we didn't do anything wrong to start off poorly. Yes, we called them names behind their back, but they don't know that."

"Well, we *did* call the cops on them."

"True, but *they* don't know that."

"It doesn't matter what the facts are, it's what they believe to be true, and I strongly feel that he believes we called the cops. Plus, if we call them about the pool incident, then they will definitely know."

"He's an asshole."

"Agreed, but that doesn't change anything," Steph said.

"So we are back to what we should do."

"I gave you *my* suggestion."

"And I'm not discounting it. I just feel like his hatred toward us has nothing to do with us calling the cops. He's got a hardon for us, and nothing will change that."

"Then I guess we do nothing."

"Let's just think on it. I certainly don't want to live like this." Spike rubbed the back of his head. "I certainly don't want to move again either."

"We shouldn't have to."

"No, we shouldn't."

Steph walked over to the fridge and grabbed a couple of beers, popping open one and handing it to Spike.

"Thanks, babe. I needed this."

"There isn't enough alcohol on the planet right now."

"No truer words were ever spoken."

"Want to watch a movie?" Steph asked.

"Yeah, maybe a comedy... something to lighten the mood."

In the living room, they settled in on the couch, dimmed the lights, and started a movie. For the next hour and a half, their neighbor problems didn't exist.

Things were quiet for a couple days, and Spike and Steph both dared to hope that things had settled down. They quickly learned their thoughts were foolish. If anything, the fuckery ramped up.

Tuesday, Spike noticed the pool cleaner—which they referred to as the "Pool Monster"—seemed to be stuck in one spot on the bottom of the pool. It definitely wasn't doing its job as dirt was starting to accumulate on the plaster. Upon further inspection, Spike found that it had sucked up two small rocks. Where they came from was anyone's guess, but Spike had his suspicions. Further inspection revealed ten more rocks of similar size lounging at the bottom of the water.

Thursday, Steph came home to the mailbox looking like it had been visited by the Unibomber. It was bent to shit.

Friday, all four tires on Spike's car were deflated. They were surprised to find a small slit in all four sidewalls. A major and expensive inconvenience, but nothing compared to what came next.

Sunday, the neighborhood was shook when reports of a murder hit the airwaves and the barrage of official vehicles and hundreds of yards of yellow-and-black crime scene tape took over the streets eight houses down at the end of the block. The reports indicated that the eighteen-year-old house sitter that was watching the house while the owners were on vacation was found in the house, nude, bruised, and bloody. At least most of her was. Her head was missing, and they never found it.

She had been raped and strangled, or possibly the reverse... The autopsy would provide more information. Home from college for the summer, Sophie Collins had taken the job to make extra money, an endeavor that her father had lined up for her when one of his coworkers had been asking around about someone to watch their house while they took a month to travel extensively through Europe.

When Sophie's parents hadn't heard from her for a few days, and their calls went unanswered, they called the police. While Sophie's parents were utterly wrecked, to make matters worse, the owners of the home were unreachable and would probably arrive home in a week to find a young girl—their house sitter—had been killed in their bedroom.

Spike turned off the television and turned to Steph, his face ashen. They hadn't talked during the news report and had turned to the television when they had come home from a late breakfast and saw the flurry of activity and flashing lights at the end of the street.

"Holy fuck!" Spike yelled out.

"No kidding." Steph's eyes were wide with concern.

"This is getting out of hand. This guy is unhinged!"

"You think he'd really do something like that? So far, most of his bullshit has been minor in comparison."

"I wouldn't put anything past him."

"Spike, I'm scared."

Spike went over and wrapped his arms around Steph, her purple locks hanging over his shoulders.

"It'll be okay, Steph. If he did this, and he had a problem with us, we'd probably already be dead."

"Speak for yourself. It's my ass he wants."

"Maybe, but this happened down the street. Probably coincidental. We're just on edge because of all of the other stuff."

"I really don't feel safe here anymore, Spike. I want to put the house up for sale."

Spike said nothing, his head hung low.

"Please?" she begged.

"I was hoping it wouldn't come to that, but deep down inside, I knew it probably would."

"I can't live like this anymore—always wondering what's next. Always feeling like I'm being watched."

"It definitely is creepy. I've felt it too."

"Spike?" She looked at him, hoping he would see just how much everything was affecting her.

He looked her in the eyes, saw her soul laid bare.

"I'll call our agent tomorrow."

Steph let out a breath. "Thank you."

"Don't thank me... It's what's best."

"God knows where we're going to live if this place sells."

"Maybe it's time we get a house on a little land. You know... no evil fucking neighbors close by?"

"Can we afford that?"

"I don't think we can afford not to."

The anxiety in the house hung in the air like a thick fog. Both Spike and Steph tried to read but couldn't concentrate. Steph turned on a crime show and they zoned out watching it. Finally, Steph got up.

Spike gave her a look as if to ask where she was going.

"I can't do this. Sitting here trying to concentrate with my thoughts running a mile a minute. I'm just gonna go to bed."

"Okay, babe, I'll be in soon."

Steph gave Spike a kiss on the forehead and headed toward the bedroom. Spike changed the channel and put on a scary movie. The dark, ominous music filled the living room as the inky black from behind the panes loomed motionless, watching, waiting.

Spike could hear the shower going in the master bathroom. The girl in the movie had also been showering, and she stepped out on the mat, toweling herself off with a bright white terry towel. Spike thought about how the blood that was about to be spilled would contrast nicely with the stark white of the towel. The shower stopped in their bathroom, and Spike's mind slipped to thoughts of Steph toweling off her own body, and Spike felt himself swelling. The man with the knife showed up as if on cue, stabbing in wide arches, and Spike watched as the towel turned crimson red, screams coming out of the girl in loud wails, the towel falling to the floor, followed by the girl, a crumpled heap of sliced flesh.

Spike waited for the screaming to stop—surely she must be dead by now—when he realized it was coming from the bedroom.

"STEPH!!"

Spike was up off the couch as fast as his feet were able to push him upright, and he bolted to the bedroom, all caution abandoned. If Steph was being attacked, he would either intervene or die trying.

When he rounded the corner into the bedroom, he stopped short. Steph stood by her side of the bed in a nightgown, wailing, tears flowing down her cheeks.

"Babe? What's the matter?"

Steph wailed louder, simply staring at the bed.

Spike made his way to her side, his hand sliding onto her back to comfort her. That was when he saw it.

"Kody????"

Steph nodded.

"What the fucking shit?" Spike yelled.

He walked closer to the pillow. Kody was curled up on the pillow, looking a little worse for the wear, unmoving.

Spike reached over to touch him and see if he was alive. His hand immediately retracted, and Steph bawled louder.

"He feels like a block of ice," Spike whispered.

Steph had a coughing fit as she tried to get her crying under control.

"Where did he come from?" Spike asked.

"He... he was right... right here when I came out of the bathroom."

"That motherfucker was in our house," Spike said, a snarl on his lips.

"That motherfucker was in our bedroom, while I was naked in the shower with the bathroom door open!"

Spike paused, his eyes wide, his chin trembling.

"Are you sure? Sure that Kody wasn't here when you came into the bedroom?"

"I'm positive, Spike. I would have noticed."

Spike rushed out of the bedroom, and Steph heard the front door open. She ran to the bathroom and grabbed a robe and followed him.

"TONY!! YOU WANNA DANCE, MOTHERFUCKER?"

Steph was outside on the lawn beside Spike.

"Spike, stop, NOW. Come inside."

"I'm gonna kick his fucking ass!" Spike yelled.

"Please, Spike!" Steph pleaded through gritted teeth.

Both of them flinched when the yard was lit up by the front porch lights from the house next door.

"Are you guys okay?" Jeff's face was etched with concern.

"Shaken," Spike said, and Steph nodded. "The thing with Kody, an intruder in our bedroom, and the murdered girl. And don't get me wrong, we feel terrible for the girl's family, but this hits too close to home. I mean, what if that had been Steph?"

Steph looked at Spike, her mouth hanging open.

"Let me get you something to drink, guys," Jeff said.

Jeff had heard the commotion out on Spike and Steph's front yard and quickly intervened, bringing them back to his house for support.

"Got any whiskey?" Spike asked.

"I certainly could use some," Steph said.

"I do."

Jeff left the comfortable living room and retrieved a bottle from elsewhere in the house and came back with three glasses.

"Knob Hill! Nice!" Spike said.

"I keep this bottle especially for when I have company," Jeff said. He poured them all a generous glass of the bourbon and handed Steph and Spike a glass.

Steph noticed the bottle was almost full and wondered if Jeff got lonely. Company was obviously a rare commodity.

"Who would do such a thing to a defenseless cat?" Jeff asked, scratching his head.

"I'm so fucking sick over this," Steph said, taking a substantial pull off her glass.

"It's hard to believe someone could be so evil. And it's all too coincidental to be random," Spike said, also taking a sip of his.

"You really don't think..." Jeff's voice trailed off.

"Yes," Spike said. "I do think. It's gotta be that asshole, Tony."

"Tony?" Jeff asked. "Is that our new neighbor?"

"Yeah. There's no other explanation. He just moved in and all this shit's happening now," Spike said.

"You really think he'd kill a cat? AND a person? All in his own neighborhood?" Jeff asked.

Spike shrugged.

Jeff looked over at Steph, noticing she was staring off into space.

"Are you okay, Steph?" he asked.

"Yeah," she said, turning her attention back to Jeff. She looked at his face, full of concern and kindness. They had lucked out getting him as a neighbor. Unfortunately, that luck hadn't held out when their other neighbor had sold their house.

"Have you had any problems here since you've moved in?" Spike asked.

Jeff searched his memory for a moment. "You know, I don't think I have."

"I wonder why *we* got so lucky," Spike said sarcastically.

"Fucking rotten luck," Steph said, almost lethargically.

"Did you call the police?" Jeff asked.

"Not yet," Spike said. "We had to get out of the house. Someone was in there. And it had to be while *we* were in there. Steph was taking a shower in the bathroom with the door open. They were in our bedroom, putting our dead cat on the pillow. I'm sure they saw her naked. Watched her even."

Steph's entire body shook as a shiver ran up her spine. Tears sprung to her eyes as she let out an involuntary groan.

Spike got up off the recliner he was sitting on and went and sat next to her, rubbing her back.

"I'm sorry, baby," he said.

"I don't want to go back," she said, her voice pleading. "I'm so scared. So tired."

"We have to, Steph. That's our home. We won't be run out of our home. Plus we need to call the cops. Get them involved."

"Please, babe. I'm not ready. Not yet. Can we go for a drive? Find a parking lot and take a nap? Get a hotel room even? I'm freaking the fuck out."

"Steph—"

Jeff cut Spike off. "Sorry to interject, but why don't you guys lay down here and get some rest? There is safety in numbers, and I have an extra bedroom."

Spike stopped speaking and looked at Steph. Her eyes pleaded with him. Finally, he relented.

"Okay, you go lay down. I'll go back to the house and deal with the police."

"NO! Please. Stay here."

Spike sighed. "Okay, I'll stay out here with Jeff. But in an hour or so, we need to go back. As much as it sucks, we have to deal with what's waiting for us."

"I'll show you the bedroom," Jeff said. "The sheets are clean if you want to climb in, or there are some blankets at the foot of the bed if you just want to cover up."

Steph laid her hand on Jeff's shoulder and whispered a thank-you as she kicked off her shoes and crawled onto the pillow-top mattress and pulled the blanket over her that was at the foot of the bed. Jeff pulled the door shut and joined Spike back in the living room. Spike jerked his head and snorted, then shook his head to clear it.

"Did you just fall asleep?" Jeff asked.

"I think so," Spike admitted. "This shit has me exhausted. Steph had the right idea."

"It's all good," Jeff said. "Feel free to fall asleep if you want. I can wake you in a couple hours. Why don't you kick back in the recliner?"

Feeling weak, Spike got up on wobbly knees and made his way back to the chair, slipped in, and reclined it back, bringing up the foot-rest in the process. He was asleep before he even realized it.

Spike fought to open his eyes, unsure of how long he had been asleep. He blinked several times, trying to clear the blurriness from his vision in the dim light. Only the light from the television cast a glow in the room. He saw a shape standing over him.

"Jeff?"

"Get your ass up now," the voice growled lowly.

Spike blinked again in rapid succession trying to make out the face. He had never heard Jeff talk like that before.

"Come with me, now!" the voice ordered.

Spike focused, and the face came into view. The sight scared him. The other next-door neighbor, Tony, stood over him, menacingly.

"Get up!" Douchebag demanded.

It was then Spike noticed a gun in his right hand. While it wasn't pointed at Spike, that didn't mean anything to him.

Spike reacted and kicked both of his feet out rapidly, connecting with the bigger man's balls. Spike heard a heavy grunt, and the man went down like a sack of potatoes. Spike took that moment to spring out of the recliner. Spotting the lamp on the side table, Spike brought it down on the man's head.

"I'll say it again... Fuck you, Tony!" Spike yelled as he hammered the man several times with the lamp until the base fell apart.

Winded, Spike called out, "Jeff? Steph? We have to get out of here!"

Spike ran to the bedroom to get Steph. His heart sank into the pit of his stomach when he pushed the door open. The covers were messed up, but the bed was empty. Spike switched on the light switch, and the shadows retreated. The room was empty except the furniture. Spike checked the closet. No luck.

Spike exited the room.

"STEPH??? JEFF???"

There was no answer. Spike went room by room, looking for them. They were gone. As Spike headed toward the sliding glass door that led to the backyard to see if they were out there, he saw light creeping through a crack at the bottom of a door that was almost indistinguishable, set into the wall in the corner of the living room.

Spike made his way to the door and pushed, and it popped open, although it provided resistance, as if the hinges were spring loaded and trying to slam the door shut in his face. The landing beyond the door served a set of stairs that descended to some sort of basement under the house.

"STEPH? JEFF? You guys down there?"

"Oh, thank goodness, Spike. So glad you are here. We need you down here... Steph is hurt."

Spike started down the stairs at a rapid pace. "Fuuuuuuck, is she okay??? Was it the neighbor douchebag?? Fucker's got a gun."

At the bottom of the stairs, Spike turned the corner and ran down the narrow hallway to the only door that existed. Beyond the doorway, the light burned bright.

"I'm coming, baby!!" Spike yelled, and then he turned the corner and entered the room.

Spike stopped in his tracks, and the door closed by itself, making a CLANK sound. It took him several seconds to take in the room, then the air left his lungs like he had been punched in the gut.

"WHAT THE—"

The actual punch to the gut that Jeff delivered was so much more damaging than Spike would have ever imagined. He sank to the floor, a chuckle emanating through Jeff's maniacal grin.

"Looks like you found her!" Jeff said, chuckling more.

Spike took in the view from his new position on the floor. Steph was laying on her back on a twin bed. Naked. The sheets were crisp white, almost perfection, except for the splattering of blood around her head and shoulders. Steph's neck—her perfect neck that he loved to brush his lips over when he made love to her—was opened, her lifeblood flowing around her.

Spike tried to suck air into his lungs, which was further complicated by the huge sobs that tried to escape his body simultaneously. He tried to call her name, then to crawl to her. Jeff delivered another kick to Spike's gut, hard enough to knock him over on his back. He struggled to flip over like a cockroach that had somehow ended wrong-side-up. From his point of view, he noticed the shelf running along the top of the wall, all the way around the room. The shelves on three walls were empty. The fourth shelf contained seven polycarbonate cubes about eighteen inches square. Spike immediately lurched the contents of his stomach, which drenched Jeff's feet and the floor around him. The cubes contained human heads, floating in some sort of liquid. *Human. Fucking. Heads.* He looked at each one for a few seconds until his eyes landed on the last one. The girl from the news. The house sitter from down the street.

"Jeff?" he whispered.

"Hey, neighbor," Jeff said. "You getting it all figured out now?"

Spike knew it was too late to help Steph, and he was dying inside. He wanted to join her.

"Take me, too," Spike whispered.

"In time!" Jeff said. "I thought you might like to see what else I have planned for her though, first."

"Don't... you dare... touch her," Spike warned, his breathing slowly returning to as normal a state as he could possibly hope for under the circumstances.

"Oh, too late," Jeff said, smiling.

A sound came from the door. Spike looked over and saw the large metal barrier move ever so slightly, but it didn't open. Banging ensued.

"Open the fuck up!"

Fan-fucking-tastic. Caught in a nightmare with fucking psycho neighbors living on both sides of me.

The door took a couple of kicks and the metal bulged out slightly.

Spike took the opportunity to run to Steph's side, taking her wrist to feel for a pulse, calling her name at the same time.

Jeff pulled his attention from the door and ran to Spike.

The door took another heavy kick.

Spike jerked his elbow back and caught Jeff's nose, breaking it. Blood sprayed out and joined the spew on Jeff's shoes.

Jeff's hands went to his nose, and the kicking at the door

increased in frequency, urgency. The metal door bulged in more and more, and each kick rattled it in its frame.

"I'm going to kill you!" Jeff screamed, his bloody hands outstretched as he charged toward Spike again. Jeff landed on Spike and knocked him to the floor, and they rolled a couple times before Jeff came out on top, his big hands wrapped tight around Spike's throat, squeezing. Blood dripped rapidly from Jeff's nose and landed on Spike's face, like a Chinese blood torture, if such a thing existed.

Spike tried to pry the vice-like grip from his neck, his face red, eyes bulging, but the lack of air hindered his strength. He bucked his body like a bronco and tried to throw Jeff off, the bucks keeping time with the kicking at the door, but Jeff held tight, trying to finish the job.

Spike's mind momentarily turned to the threat at the door. The psycho neighbor with the gun. Die by choking, or die by bullet. Some choice. As his world started to turn gray, Spike wished for the bullet. At least Jeff would take a bullet as well.

And then everything happened so quickly that Spike felt he hallucinated it. There was a loud splintering as the door gave way, and part of the wall ripped away with it, the door clattering to the ground. Jeff letting go of his throat and springing to his feet. The cool air rushing down his fiery throat and into his starved lungs. The shouts from the door. Jeff running toward the door, attack mode accelerated. The 9mm pistol coming into view. The freestyle dance of the recipient being riddled with lead. The flash of the muzzle. The smoke from the barrel permeating the air. Jeff's body hitting the floor. The psycho neighbor Tony turning toward Spike. The blood starting to crust on Tony's face from the lamp attack. The gun tracking as he turned. The look of rage on Tony's face.

This is it. Be careful what you wish for, Spike thought.

Spike heard Tony yelling but couldn't understand what he was saying. Spike instinctually covered his head with his arms, a silly move that would never stop a bullet, and then when nothing happened, he removed his hands and looked around the room.

Tony was on one knee, taking Steph's pulse.

"She's alive!" he yelled, and for the first time, Spike dared to hope.

Tony reached to his belt and pulled something from it. Confused, Spike watched as his nemesis spoke into it.

"Dispatch... shots fired. Undercover officer involved. Undercover is wearing a black t-shirt and jeans. Additional victim on scene with severe injury to the neck. Start ambo and additional units with supervisor. Suspect is 10-7. 2520 Emerson St."

Tony inspected Steph's neck closely.

"You're a fucking cop?"

"It looks like the cut on her neck is superficial. It did damage, but he didn't hit anything major. Probably part of the show. Not sure what else is wrong with her though. The ambulance should be here soon."

"What the hell is going on here?" Spike scrunched up his face.

Tony pulled off a flannel shirt he was wearing over a t-shirt and draped it over the top half of Steph's naked body.

"I think he might have drugged us. I barely touched my drink, but I still got extremely tired. Steph downed her entire bourbon."

"He had plans for both of you."

"Do you really think he's a serial killer?"

"You see the heads, don't you?"

"Yeah. But... but what about you?"

"Had to get close. We couldn't get anything solid on him, but we knew."

"So you were here for *him*?"

"Yeah. We didn't really buy the house next door. The department rented it until we got what we needed."

"But... all the... Why? Why did you do all that shit to me and Steph?"

"Don't go blaming me for all that shit. We played loud music. Swam in your pool. I hit on your wife. Typical unacceptable behavior. He had to think he was safe. That he could move freely and someone else would get blamed. We made it easy for him to fuck up."

"So you... you're not really a douchebag?"

Tony smiled. "You'd have to ask my wife. Opinions vary."

Spike felt a weak smile form on his face as he sank to the floor next to the bed, Steph's hand in his. In the distance, he heard the sirens.

THE CHALLENGE

NIKKI NOIR

"Turn the car around," Lawrence's friend Pete demanded over the Bluetooth speakers. "You and Susan broke up for a reason."

"And then we got back together." Lawrence accelerated the Dodge Challenger Hellcat around the winding upstate roads. "Everybody cheats, everybody breaks up, and everybody gets back together. That's the natural order of things."

And Susan knows it too.

Deep down, she knew she didn't belong to anyone but

Lawrence. Though it took her time to come to terms with the idea. Several months, in fact. She'd gone silent after declaring their previous breakup was their last... It never was.

"Didn't you say you were sick of Susan and her beefy vagina? That Lisa had much better—"

"I wasn't the one who texted last week that we should hang out. She clearly wants me back. Why should I say no?"

"Because you're a dick. A horrible guy to date." Pete's voice crackled in the reception as the Hellcat went around another curve in the mountain.

"Thanks a lot, asshole."

"You're my best friend, and I got your back, but let this one go. She's a nice girl. Seriously—besides choosing you. Do not make her just another notch in your belt."

"She's not going to be just a notch anymore. Her parents died shortly after we split. Do you know how loaded they were? Man, the shit I would do to never work again. Can you imagine? I could be retired by thirty."

"Dude, no."

"How do you think she's able to afford this fucking cabin in the woods?" It was hardly a cabin. The pictures he saw online of the Crownwood Community were nothing short of sprawling mountainous estates. "It was a downgrade for her to live with me. Hell, maybe if she'd bought this place for us rather than cramming all her stuff into my tiny pad, I wouldn't have been annoyed enough to go out drinking that night."

"Don't act like you need an excuse to cheat. You do it all the time." The Bluetooth went out briefly, and Lawrence hoped it wouldn't return. "You're my best friend and I got your back." Pete paused. "But her parents just died and you want her money? Bro, come on. This is shitty."

"To show that it's not all about dollars and cents, let me just say Susan gives the best head ever." Lawrence navigated the Hellcat into the left lane to pass a minivan. "I crave variety as much as the next guy, but you can't give up on a girl who sucks dick like that."

"Don't be an asshole."

"What's that?" Lawrence blew air at the speaker, pretending the forest had overtaken his signal again prematurely. "Sorry bro, gotta let you go."

Trees and foliage flew by in a blur, and highway hypnosis stole Lawrence's attention, bringing him fond memories of Susan—her bashful eye contact when his cock was in her mouth, the way her nipples got hard at the mere sight of him, and the way she squinted through ropes of cum after he unloaded on her face.

One more chance at that type of sex was worth the drive alone. The chance of marrying into the type of money her parents left her was just the cherry on top. No more than a mile later, he slowed to turn down a dirt road leading farther into the wilderness. The muscle car wasn't made for off-roading, but the terrain was stable enough; so long as he took it slow, rocks wouldn't scratch the custom paint job.

His new, slower pace gave him a chance to reflect on Susan's words from their last fight. Pete was his friend and concerned by the manipulative games he played, but Susan had straight up called him a sex addict. *As if there was such a thing.*

Not a single guy thought he was an addict. They thought he was a god. Pete called him an asshole, but that was just because he couldn't pull pussy the way Lawrence could. People hated what they couldn't attain themselves.

He smiled, thinking of Susan's plump lips around his dick while he struggled to identify the turn he needed to take.

The back roads of Crownwood didn't register on the car's GPS. House numbers were impossible to see from the road and the turn offs weren't marked. Based on the mileage, he guessed the next turn off was Susan's. He veered down it and navigated between the overgrown brush on either side.

He stepped out of the car and gave the paint job a once-over for scratches. Satisfied, he slicked back his hair in the reflective surface, and he headed to the front door of the sprawling estate.

He rang the bell and waited. When the door unlocked, he fixed his signature smile and prepped his greeting speech. When the door opened, the hottest piece of ass he had ever laid eyes on stood in the doorway.

"You're not Susan."

"And you're not the large sausage I ordered."

Oh God, I could be though, he thought, pulling out his phone and reading Susan's text.

"Is this 1441 Needle Street?"

"Oh, you're looking for our new neighbor," the sexy blonde said as she twisted a lock of her hair. "She's about a quarter mile down the road."

"Thank you."

"She just moved in, didn't she? You friends?" the woman asked with a hint of curiosity.

"Yep, we're..." His mind raced, running through potential scenarios. Would Susan know if he fucked this woman? He thought quickly. "High school friends. Couple of us are going over to Susan's new place."

"Oh yes, Susan. That's her name. I told her she will just love it here. So peaceful. You'll love visiting." The woman pressed her hips against the doorframe with a bitchy confidence he couldn't ignore.

"I'm sure I will." Without letting more than a second slip by, he asked, "You live here long?" Anything to prolong the amount of time he could bask in her rocking body.

"All my life. My grandaddy raised me. Passed it on to me. It's over one hundred years old." She stomped on the floor. "Good bones."

He glanced at her left hand. No ring.

"You live in this big place all alone?"

"Aren't you a curious cat?"

"Well, you really talked up these bones. I wouldn't mind giving them a closer examination."

"What about Susan and your old friends?" She stepped backward into the house, offering him a view of the inside.

"It's important to make new friends," he said, stepping inside. "They'll hardly know I'm gone. Besides, how long could a tour take?"

"You're right. We'll make it a quickie." She closed the door and brought him to an oversized red couch.

Emily's hand squeezed the unrelenting bulge in his jeans. She rubbed her fingertips across it gently, caressing it while she leaned her face in close to Lawrence's. The teasing seemed to drive her crazy, as she pulled her face away with a smile every time he went in for a kiss. Her hands, however, didn't pull away. Instead, they unbuttoned and unzipped his jeans, allowing his junk to spring forth like a jack-in-the-box ready to pop into an unsuspecting bitch's face.

Here he was on the way to smooth things over with his ex after cheating, and he was about to fuck the neighbor girl on his way there. The idea of nailing both Emily and Susan back-to-back strengthened his boner. It might be a record, even.

One fuck after the next in such rapid succession was not a common occurrence for him, especially when neither woman was aware of the other, or a willing participant in his sex-based challenges, which ran the gambit from timing of lays to number of sexual acts performed, to number of successive cumshots and how many holes he could make drip with his seed.

Lawrence imagined Susan watching as Emily went down on him. Susan's delicate brow pressing into that sad, sexy face she made when her heart had been ripped from her chest. Something about the way Susan looked when she was miserable really got him going. Wet tears would build around her eyes, loosening the black liner before running down her cheeks.

With newfound vigor, he grabbed a hold of Emily's head and shoved her face down on his cock, bottoming out against the back of her throat before adjusting his position and the angle of her head, to start working his way down her throat. Emily gagged, choking on a mix of pre-cum and saliva that exploded from her lips and gathered around the base of his dick. Releasing Emily's head, he reveled in the sight of her gasping for air as she pulled her head back, a long string of sticky fluid still linking her mouth with the tip of his cock.

Before she could catch her breath fully, he stood, grabbed the back of her head, and fucked her face until she forced herself off. Rather than be put off by his display, Emily loved it. She ripped off her shirt and pulled her pants down, revealing that her wet pussy had already soaked through her panties. She laid down on the couch, placing one foot on the floor and draping the other over the head of the couch, leaving her pussy wide open for him to fill.

There was a creak upstairs, possibly footsteps.

Lawrence pulled away. "Is someone here?"

"No." Emily held her cunt apart, waiting for him to enter.

He paused, denying her taint while he strained to identify the sound.

"Don't worry, we're alone." She tugged on his penis.

"And the sausage pizza delivery...?"

"It was a joke." She licked her fingers and sunk them into her pink pussy. "Now get that sausage inside me."

He stood over her tight body and slapped the head of his dick on her smooth cunt, watching his pre-cum and her discharge gather and slop. With a thick glob of body fluids, he inserted just the tip into her cunt. Then he brought his face to hover over Emily's and locked eyes with her. He didn't know if it was the color of her irises or their sparkle, but he knew seeing those eyes in pain was everything he needed. He shoved the full length of his erect cock inside her, splitting her at the seam. She screamed and wrapped her legs around him, forcing him deeper inside.

It was time to try out a fancier position with this woman, as testing a new and uncommon move on a stranger was a recent sex benchmark Lawrence had set for himself. He pulled out, flipped Emily over, then dragged her legs away from the couch so she was suspended in the air, with only her arms left to support her on the couch. Then he railed into her from behind, fucking her wheelbarrow style, feeling all the blood rush to his dick, making it more engorged and harder than he could remember in recent history.

He held back his orgasm, letting it build up inside of him, then slowing his pace just enough to keep from cumming until he regained his control. Emily, meanwhile, got the benefit of cumming hard on his dick, coating him in lubricant that kept his motivation strong. He imagined again Susan watching him as he fucked the shit out of this helpless girl, watching in tears as he made Emily cum time after time. The pressure built up too much. Lawrence couldn't hold it back anymore. He exploded into Emily's tight cunt, pumping hard through each successive pulse of his orgasm until her pussy was filled to the brim and overflowing onto the floor beneath them.

Lawrence jumped back into his Hellcat and revved the engine with the vigor that only winning could provide. He waved goodbye to his latest conquest and sped a quarter mile down the road to the next turn in.

Surely, this must be the one, he thought. *It better be.* As ridiculous and fortunate as it would be to run into another hot neighbor, he didn't think he had three loads in him. Emily had emptied him so completely, he worried how long he would have before performing for Susan.

And there would be a performance. You don't text your ex to come to your new place without expecting some action. At the very least, he was going home with one of her world-famous blowjobs and a record for back-to-back loads.

He parked in front of the next sprawling colonial and cut the engine, repeating his process of checking the car for dings and slicking his hair back into place. This time, however, he sniffed his fingers as they passed by his face, ensuring the musky scent of vagina lingered on them no longer. Then he walked up to the door and gave the bell a ring.

Susan opened the door a minute later, grinning from ear to ear. "I can't believe how long it's been since—"

"Too long," Lawrence said as he wrapped his hands around her waist and went in for a kiss.

Susan was quick to stifle his effort with a small peck before grabbing his hand and leading him inside for a tour of the house. The place was massive, even more impressive than he had imagined, and he knew Susan's parents had been loaded before they croaked. This was definitely a place he could hang his hat.

As Susan took Lawrence from room to room, he imagined all the places he would fuck her, and the exact positions he would accomplish in each place. At once, the house became a blueprint of fucks to come, a whole new set of sexual challenges for him to accomplish. There were nooks where he could fuck Susan against the wall, a massive dining room table he could fuck her on top of, and, of course, the walk-in shower and three-person tub which sat alongside it. Oh, the things he could do in that fucking tub, in this fucking house.

"It's incredible," Lawrence said. "This is really something."

"I know, right?" Susan smiled as she rubbed her hands on the purple drapes adorning the master bedroom window. "Can you believe how pretty these drapes are?"

"I prefer your pink drapes." He snickered.

Susan rolled her eyes, walked past him, and continued the tour until they were back where they started, beneath the grand entryway ceilings where there was a couch, coffee table, and television set up. Lawrence was dismayed to see that this was where Susan intended to spend their time together. Of course, he'd made a sex plan for both the couch and coffee table, but Susan was less inclined to rekindle their relationship, getting split like a protractor over a coffee table than a traditional missionary pounding on the bed. The crazy stuff could come after he was back in her good graces.

Unfortunately for Lawrence, Susan seemed intent on making him work for forgiveness. She started in with a card game that tested his knowledge of her as a couple. Sweat started to bead on his brows as he continued to get answers wrong. How could she expect anything else, he wondered, considering they hadn't fucked for months? Besides, did anyone know their partner's favorite color?

"You're going to need to up your game," Susan said. "To prepare you for later."

Lawrence's ear perked up like a dog in heat. "What happens later?" he asked with a wink.

"I invited my neighbors over for dinner and board games. If we're going to win, then you need to dust off these cobwebs to get your game on."

Lawrence clenched the arms of the couch, keeping his voice steady. "Did you say, neighbors?"

"Sure did." Susan beamed. "They are such a cute couple, always together. I want to find a marriage like theirs someday..."

"Someday," Lawrence breathed a sigh of release.

Thinking back to his previous encounter, Emily wasn't wearing a ring, and there was certainly no husband nearby while he was busy destroying her cunt.

"Lawrence, I need something from you." Susan took Lawrence's hand and made that fuckable face she made when she was being serious. "If we're going to make this work, then I need to know that you can act normal and behave yourself around other people. I know you're a sex addict, but I need you to be a partner first, someone I can spend time with and not be afraid to introduce to people."

"That's what I want too," Lawrence said through clenched teeth.

For the next hour, he tried to keep his dick in his pants and his jokes to himself. Even his infamous "that's what she said" jokes, which were exceptionally difficult to contain while Susan was preparing dinner and saying things like, "Great, it splashed right in my face!"

Finally, dinner was prepared, and the doorbell rang. He only had a meal and a few board games to make it through, then he could bang one out with Susan. Given how late it would be after every-thing was said and done, he was hopeful he could parlay intercourse into spending the night, seeing as these were dark and unfamiliar woods he would need to drive through if she cast him out. Then he could get some of that freaky, protractor sex on the coffee table he had on his mind. Yeah, everything was going well until Susan answered the door.

Emily was standing on the other side of the door. "Hey, girl," she said, wrapping her arms around Susan and casting a devious glare over Susan's shoulder at Lawrence.

Lawrence tensed. "Uh..." he stammered, before spouting the words, "nice to meet you."

Please, god, let her be discreet.

"You too." Emily winked, an indication that she was willing to play along.

Lawrence breathed a sigh of relief as he turned to Susan. "I thought you were inviting a couple over to play games with."

"Chuck's just grabbing some games from the truck," Emily said as she brushed her hair behind her ear, flashing a wedding ring that hadn't been there earlier.

Not that a ring would have stopped Lawrence, but it would have been nice to know what he was getting into. This Emily chick was a freak, and he hadn't been careful with her. A fucking like the one she just received at the mercy of his wang would have left swelling and bruising, not to mention the normal collection of scratches and marks that went along with an ample fucking.

Chuck walked up behind Emily, carrying a large case slung over his massive shoulder.

"You don't mess around with your games," Lawrence said.

Chuck snorted, walking past Lawrence to the couch, his biceps bulging as he lowered the overstuffed bag of games to the floor. There were few things Lawrence feared in this world, but a man the size of Chuck whose wife he had just used as fuck meat was on the list right next to shark attacks and atomic bombs.

They all sat down to dinner first, roast beef with a side of potatoes and greens. Chuck offered to cut the meat, taking his time to sharpen Susan's carving knife like a crime boss getting ready to cut someone's pinky finger off.

Lawrence swallowed hard as Chuck dug the blade into the roast beef, watching the precision with which Chuck cut. Soon the serving tray was filled with thin sliced cuts of pink and red beef, resembling the state in which Lawrence had left Emily's pussy earlier.

"You like it a little raw, don't cha?" Chuck asked as he lifted an exceptionally red piece of beef off the serving tray between the carving knife and fork.

Lawrence nodded and held his plate out, though his body slunk back as the blade neared his face.

Chuck dropped the meat onto Lawrence's plate, then served the girls and finally himself before settling down into his chair. "So, Lawrence, what do you do?"

"Computer stuff. Like password resets and troubleshooting."

"Lots of fires to put out, then?" Chuck snickered.

"Oh stop." Emily rubbed Chuck's back and turned to Lawrence. "He's a big, strong firefighter. Can't help bragging about it everywhere we go."

Lawrence swallowed hard. "So what games are we playing first?"

"That's a surprise, Lawrence." Chuck took another bite of his food, chewing and swallowing it, building the suspense before continuing. "I guarantee you this, though. It's gonna be nuts."

Once dinner concluded, the four of them headed back to the couch, bringing two chairs along with them so the teams could be sitting on separate sides of the coffee table. For the purposes of their first game, couples would need to be directly across from each other, leaving Lawrence to squirm on the couch beside Emily.

"Get comfy," Susan said as she headed back to the kitchen. "I just need to put away the dishes and I'll be right there."

Lawrence sat still, looking back and forth between Emily and Chuck. Emily eyed him back, too flirtatiously for someone whose husband was across the table, and Chuck didn't look like the type to mess around. Lawrence tried to break the ice with a joke, but before he could finish, a dish shattered in the kitchen.

"Fuck," Susan called out. She appeared in the doorway with a dish rag wrapped around her hand. The fabric was quickly turning red.

"Oh my god." Lawrence stood up.

So did Emily and Chuck.

"Do firefighters know how to stitch a split palm?"

"Absolutely." Chuck jumped past a shocked Lawrence. "Head upstairs. I have my first aid kit in the truck. We'll get you stitched up." He left the house, and the doors of the truck in the driveway sounded.

"Sorry," Susan said. "Didn't mean to spoil the party."

"It'll be fine." Lawrence kissed her lips, and then she headed to the upstairs bathroom.

Chuck returned with the kit and called up the stairs, "I'll be right there." He stared at Lawrence for a moment. "Shouldn't take too long," he said. "But every stitch job is different."

"Don't worry," Emily said to Lawrence. "Chuck is trained for this. You should stay here and keep me company."

Lawrence agreed, returning to the couch.

The minute Chuck was off the stairs, Emily's hands were on his crotch. "Ready for round two?"

"Are you nuts?" He laughed.

"What? You don't think I can get you off in ten minutes?" She worked his jeans' button.

"Your husband is less than a hundred feet away." He stopped her hands but didn't push them away.

"Doesn't that make it even better?"

Cheating was one thing, but doing it in the same house as the girl he was trying to get back with, risking life and limb... this was something else altogether.

You are an asshole, he heard Pete's voice.

No, I'm a god.

And this was another record. Soon he would be a legend.

"Challenge accepted." He unzipped his jeans and helped her whip out his cock so she could taste herself from earlier.

Emily got to work, bobbing up and down on his cock while he kept an ear out for any stirring from upstairs. Lawrence straightened when he heard a whimper. Susan cried out briefly. Then he looked at Emily, who smiled around his meat and shrugged. "No anesthetic."

He laughed and let her continue. It felt so good, but he couldn't help hearing every movement above. Instead of turning him on, it was freaking him out.

This is the kind of shit men get trophies for. Did you think it would be easy?

"All done." This time, he heard Chuck's voice loud and clear.

"Get up," he told Emily. "They're coming back."

"Finish then." She jerked his cock using spit for lube.

"I can't." He tried to pull her from her knees, but she resisted. "Get up."

"I want to taste your seed. I've got like five minutes left to win the challenge."

"This isn't a fucking challenge." Footsteps creaked across the floor above them. "They're going to catch us."

The footsteps moved to the stairs, but Emily increased her grip and sucked harder.

"Cum," she mumbled with a mouthful of cock.

"Bitch." He slapped her, and Emily recoiled, giving Lawrence just enough time to jump to his feet and close his jean zipper.

"Ahhhh," he groaned as the sensitive flesh of his penis caught in the zipper teeth. Blood gushed just beneath the head. He looked frantically for something to cover himself with, settling on a pillow from the sofa, which he set into place just as Chuck and Susan walked back into the room.

"What's going on?" Chuck asked, eyeing the pillow covering Lawrence's dick.

"I spilled my coffee, and my dick is burning!"

"That pillow is going to stop your dick burn?" Chuck approached Lawrence. "I should have a look."

"No." Lawrence shuffled from Chuck, each movement twisting his poor penis skin further beneath the pillow. "I don't want you looking at my dick."

Susan took note of the blood dripping from behind the pillow, spilling out onto the floor. "Lawrence Wittinger, remove that pillow from your penis this instant!"

Lawrence froze. More than her demand, he feared that he may ruin his dick. He felt so queasy from the pain, he was about to let another dude peep his schlong.

"Please," he said, moving the pillow. "Just help me. Please."

"I plan to do just that." And Chuck punched him in the face, knocking him out cold.

When Lawrence regained consciousness, his hands were bound behind his back. Meanwhile, his eyes were met with a confusing scene. Susan, Emily, and Chuck were standing over him, and Chuck's overstuffed bag of board games had made its way onto the coffee table for some reason. For more than a minute, Lawrence sat bewildered, unable to formulate a response to what had transpired, until at last he muttered an accusation.

"Emily came on to me."

Susan stepped forward and slapped Lawrence across the face. "From what I've heard, you came *into* her."

Lawrence cast a fearful glance at Chuck, who turned around and unzipped his bag. What Lawrence had thought was a bag of board games turned out to be a bag of equipment fit for a medieval dentist. There were rusted pliers, scalpels, and crude hammers, and that was just the beginning. Soon Chuck was unloading whips, chains, and hedge trimmers, of all things.

"What the fuck is going on here?" Lawrence asked.

"What's going on here?" Susan repeated. "You broke my fucking heart. I trusted you, loved you, gave you every piece of me, and all you did was cheat on me. Time after time I took you back, believed you when you said you would change. Shit. I felt bad for you. Tried to explain that you have an addiction and you need professional help. But you never tried to stop. You didn't want to change. You only wanted to use me."

"I am addicted. I see that now. Why else would I do this so stupidly, so blatantly? Please help me change. I'm ready now."

"You're beyond help." Susan eyed the hedge clippers. "I was almost beyond help, but there's some amazing support groups for women like me, who suffer at the hands of toxic men. That's where I found Chuck and Emily."

Lawrence looked at Emily. Terror spread throughout his chest. "You were in on this?"

Emily smiled. "It's been my pleasure."

Chuck's eyes widened; his stomach twisted with the sting of betrayal.

How could her lust for me have been anything but real?

"Everyone needs something," Chuck said. "Emily and I have our own... addictions. But we use ours for good."

"For teaching lessons." Emily picked up the hedge trimmers that had caught Susan's eye. "We own both houses, you know. Susan hired us to present you with one more chance. All you had to do was show up, and not treat her like garbage, and you could be living happily ever after with all her parents' money. Instead, you stumbled upon me first. Everything after that was just for fun. You managed to seal your fate before ever setting foot in here."

"Your hand..." He gawked at Susan's still wrapped hand with the bloody cloth.

"Acting." She dropped the dishrag, and her skin was smooth and pristine.

Emily passed the hedge clippers to Susan. She opened the sharp edges, positioning them against Lawrence's sack, then began to press them closed. Not tightly enough to sever the testicles, but forceful enough to break the skin. Blood cascaded through each sack wrinkle, pooling in the crevasses until they were saturated. Then the blood ran the length of each curly pube before dripping to the floor like dew from a leaf.

"Please don't do it," he sobbed, shaking uncontrollably but struggling to stay still against the thick steel.

"What causes men to act like this?" she asked. "What's compelling your toxic masculinity? Is it these dangling fuckers?" She pressed harder on the hedge trimmers, causing more blood to flow from his sack. "I think it's these little fuckers."

Lawrence tried to cry out but failed. He didn't have enough breath in his body; he was choking and woozy from the massive loss of blood.

"You want another chance?" Susan asked. "To keep these fuckers?"

Lawrence nodded, whimpering with a distinct sense of release at her willingness to spare his manhood.

"Too bad!" Susan squeezed the hedge trimmers shut, severing his sack.

Her eyes were filled with satisfaction as she watched his sack fall to the ground. His balls rolled out of the severed end like a spilled bag of marbles. And just to make sure they couldn't hurt anyone, ever again, Susan stomped on them, pulverizing them to the ground like bugs. Then she lifted her foot, pulling the remnants of his severed organs from the sole of her shoe and forcing them into his mouth.

It was finally over, the nightmare of their relationship and the countless people Lawrence had fucked and fucked over. He'd spend the rest of his life, however long it be, treated like the piece of shit he was.

BLEEDING FROM THE INSIDE

JOHN DURGIN

J enny Ellis peered out her bedroom window as the moving truck pulled away next door. For the first time since she'd inherited the house from her mother, she was about to have neighbors. She watched as a sturdy man, likely in his mid-forties, opened the hatchback to his black SUV and grabbed a suitcase. At first, Jenny thought maybe he was moving in alone and that *maybe* this attractive man might be single and be someone worth pursuing. But then, the passenger door opened on the SUV, and a frail yet beautiful woman stepped outside. She had the appearance of someone that aged far too quickly, with dark circles below her eyes and wrinkles around her mouth frozen in a frown, masking much of the beauty beneath.

Jenny knew that look.

She had been in an abusive relationship herself before she moved into her home, and the look on this woman's face mirrored that of a victim. The momentary attractiveness she had for the man a second ago quickly vanished. He moved with efficiency, grabbing what he could and forcing his female companion toward the door. Jenny could only imagine he was trying to hide her from the outside world, afraid to let anyone see his handy work.

When they disappeared from view, Jenny promptly moved to the next room to get a better view into the neighbor's house. The spare bedroom she stood in was mostly empty but contained the last few packed boxes of her mother's stuff. Jenny tried avoiding the room whenever she could, but the excitement of learning more about the people next door pulled her in without thinking. From this window, she had a direct line of sight to the kitchen and dining room next door. With no curtains up yet, it was pretty easy to see inside the house and locate the new couple.

While she could see in, all she really made out was someone walking by the window here and there as they moved boxes. With the sun setting, it was shining against the side of the house, making it difficult to know who was passing by. Part of her wanted to introduce herself, maybe pick up on the abusive asshole vibes she smelled from a mile away. She decided to hold off for now and allow the couple the chance to settle in. Tomorrow, she would bring over a housewarming gift as an excuse to be nosey.

Later that night, Jenny ordered a pizza and had the intention of staying up late to watch a movie. It wasn't the ideal weekend plans she would have hoped for, but all her friends were currently in relationships and rarely made time for one-on-one hangouts these days. And Jenny had no desire to play third wheel and feel even worse about herself. Most of her friends didn't even know the true reason she broke up with Chase. On the surface, he seemed like a great guy. Charming, handsome, and he had a well-paying job on top of it all. They didn't see the other side of him. What he was like when the door shut and the curtains closed. If he wasn't verbally degrading her, he was often physical with her, regularly getting jealous over even the most minor things.

So, while staying in alone on a Saturday night wasn't much fun, it was far better than getting slapped around and called names. The memories of Chase reminded Jenny of her new neighbors, who she hadn't spied on in a few hours. She got up from the couch after calling the pizza in and went to the kitchen, turning the light off to make herself less visible if someone was outside looking in. To her disappointment, the neighbors had already installed curtains on the visible side of their house.

It sure seems like he tried to get them up pretty quick to me, she thought.

Jenny knew it in her bones. This man was up to no good, and she wanted to get to the bottom of it. She moved to the next room, hoping to get a better vantage point and locate him. She scanned each window in the other house, only seeing dark rooms behind them all, like giant obsidian eyes staring back at her. As she was getting ready to give up, one of the curtains moved. Jenny stifled a scream and dropped to the floor beneath the window frame. Her heart thrummed in her chest as she tried to regain composure.

"They can't see in here, it's dark. It's okay. It's okay..." she whispered, taking deep breaths.

Slowly, Jenny sat up to look out again. A figure stood in the window directly across from her. It was the man, and while she couldn't see enough detail to know if he was looking at her, she knew it. She *felt* it. The hair on the back of her neck stood on end. This time, she slowly backed away from the window, hoping the deliberate movements disguised her in the darkness. She didn't take her eyes off the window until she was far enough back so that she could no longer see out.

Jenny loathed herself for allowing her imagination to get to her. She hadn't even talked to these people yet, and here she was creating some make-believe backstory for them. If the man saw her spying, *she* could be the one to get in trouble with the authorities.

I read too many thrillers...

She closed her eyes and sighed, determined to leave this family alone.

The doorbell blasted from downstairs.

"Fuck!" Jenny yelled, almost jumping out of her skin.

She froze in place, unsure if she should get the door or pretend to be asleep. But then the doorbell rang again, almost scaring her as much as the first time. She swallowed a mouthful of dry air and tiptoed out of the spare room to the top of the stairs. The outline of a man stood on the other side of the stained-glass window on the door, highlighted by the porch light.

"Shit, shit, shit."

When the doorbell rang a third time, she realized he wasn't going away until she answered, so she sped down the stairs, looking for anything to defend herself with. She spotted her old field hockey stick leaning against the wall and grabbed it, gripping it tight as she unlocked the door with her other hand. The first sign of any ill intentions and she would club the fucker in the head. She opened the door...

...and stared back at a terrified teen holding a medium cheese pizza.

"Oh my god, I'm so sorry."

"I, um, did you order a pizza?"

"Yes. This is what I get for staying home alone and watching scary movies. Here, I don't need change," she said, handing him a twenty-dollar tip.

"Hey, thanks. Sorry to scare ya," he said with a smirk.

Jenny forced a smile and shut the door, setting the pizza on the kitchen counter. She needed to stop being so careless if she was going to learn about her neighbors. The spare room was calling to her, so she went back upstairs to get a look. She didn't bother pulling back the curtain this time; instead she leaned close and peeked through the tiny slit.

The figure across the way was gone.

Jenny woke to sounds of screaming. She opened her eyes and immediately realized it was morning, the sun trying to force its way through her light-cancelling blinds. It took her a second to figure out where the cries were coming from. It was the new neighbor's house. She jumped out of bed and ran to the spare room. This time, she didn't care if she was caught as she aggressively slid the curtain aside. She had just enough time to see a flash of movement in their window, the man speeding by as he moved from room to room. He was advancing through the house in a hurry as the screams continued to roar from within.

Jenny lost track of where he went, but as soon as he was out of sight, the screaming stopped. Was his wife trying to escape, and he subdued her somehow? Hit her, or put her to sleep with some poisonous needle? Jenny had heard enough. She grabbed her cell and stuck it in her back pocket, then stormed down the stairs ready to confront this monster. Had she not been triggered by past events, she probably would have called the police first, but it felt personal. She had defeated one abusive asshole already; why not add a second to her tally?

Jenny burst through her front door and marched across her front lawn to the neighbor's home. As she reached the top step of their porch, she had a momentary pause, but it quickly vanished as she heard something thumping around inside the house. She slammed her fist into the door as hard as she could, ignoring the jolt of pain shooting through her knuckles. When nobody came, she did it again, then followed that up by ringing the doorbell incessantly.

When the front door flew open, Jenny thought maybe she'd made a mistake. Maybe she let the adrenaline win out over logic, and she was about to feel this guy's wrath. But when she saw his face, the mood shifted. He looked *sad*.

"Yeah? How can I help?" he asked, panting.

All the confidence Jenny felt on the way over vanished. She stared at the man and suddenly felt bad for him but didn't know why.

"I-I'm sorry. I heard screaming and thought something was wrong. Is everything okay?"

He closed his eyes and sighed, then stepped out onto the porch and shut the door behind him. Standing this close to him, Jenny couldn't help but admire his attractiveness. He was well built, with a chiseled jawline and wavy blond hair.

"Yeah... I'm sorry about that. It's... it's just my wife. She's sick. Terminally. She's in a great deal of pain, and sometimes it gets so bad that she starts screaming. It's a side effect of the meds they have her on. Sometimes she thinks she's—well, like she's being held against her will. I'm sorry if it scared you."

Jenny was at a loss for words. Here she was thinking this man was a monster, and instead he was just a sad husband who was taking care of his sick wife. She felt terrible. While he could always be lying, the pain in his eyes said otherwise. She believed him.

"Oh my. I'm so sorry to hear that. Is there anything I can do to help?" she asked, then realized she hadn't even introduced herself yet. "My name's Jenny Ellis."

He held his hand out and shook hers.

"Martin. Nice to meet you, given the circumstances," he said with a forced smirk. "I appreciate you offering to help, but there's not much you could do. She has stage four ovarian cancer. All I can do is be there for her, give her the meds she's prescribed, and hope that she won't have one of her episodes like this morning."

"I lost my mother to cancer recently, which is why I'm living alone in this house now. It used to be hers," Jenny said, immediately chastising herself for bringing death into the conversation.

"Well, you must be pretty tough then. I lay in bed at night with my eyes open, trying not to think about the inevitable. Stage four isn't exactly something to get my hopes up over. Just feels like we're counting down, you know?"

Jenny nodded, fighting back tears. She felt like such a jerk for immediately throwing this poor guy into abusive asshole territory. He was so vulnerable yet open to her, as if he knew she had been through something similar. She knew more than anyone what he was going through right now.

"I'm sorry you're dealing with this. And I'm sorry for your wife as well. If you guys ever want to have dinner, a drink, or anything, let me know. I'd love to meet her sometime. She must be a strong woman."

Martin's expression changed at the mention of meeting his wife, but he tried to cover it up with a fake cough. Jenny wasn't sure why but assumed he was embarrassed for someone to be around her in her current state.

"We'll see. I don't think that's a great idea at the moment. But I appreciate the offer. Maybe we can have a beer out here sometime while she's resting. She isn't exactly in the mood for guests these days."

"I understand. Well, I won't hold you up. It was nice to meet you. Where did you move from?"

"We lived near Boston. Prices got too much to handle with all her medical bills and treatments. Moving up here to New Hampshire cut those costs down significantly."

"It's nice to have you in the neighborhood. Talk to you later," Jenny said, then awkwardly headed back toward her house as he waved goodbye and went back inside.

The thought of her mom brought back the sadness that had controlled her existence for the last few months. She went inside and straight to the cabinet of liquor, ready to drink her sorrows away. And that's just what she did. After countless chugs from the bottle of vodka, the pain numbed, just slightly. Jenny began to fade, sitting on the couch as her vision blurred. She knew she was shit-faced drunk, but she didn't care. She had the day off, with no commitment to anything. As she had done countless times since her mom's illness became serious, she passed out on the couch, sleeping away the pain.

When Jenny awoke, her living room was dark. She had slept the day away and now had a killer headache in return.

"Fuck me..."

She sat up, blasted with a bout of nausea. After allowing herself a moment to adjust, she stood from the couch and went to the kitchen for a glass of water and some Advil. As she steadied herself over the sink, fighting against the bile trying to force its way up, she heard a sound from outside. She pulled back the kitchen curtain and noticed whatever room was directly across from her in Martin's house had the light on. But then she caught a flash of movement from their driveway. It was Martin, grabbing something out of the back of his SUV. He stood and looked around, apparently making sure nobody was watching him, then lightly shut the hatchback. For a brief second, Jenny thought he looked directly at her.

He lifted whatever it was he'd grabbed from the vehicle and walked toward his porch. In the faint moonlight, Jenny had trouble picking up what was in his hand at first, but it appeared to be a large trash bag. Martin struggled to carry it inside, so it had to be heavy. When he reached the front door, he set the bag on the porch and grabbed his keys. Jenny remained fixated on the trash bag, wondering what was inside.

And then the bag moved.

She jolted back and suppressed a scream. Her eyes had to be playing a trick on her, the space too dark. The bag wasn't big enough or strong enough to hold a person.

You don't know that. It could be a kid…

"Why? Why would he have a kid in a trash bag, you idiot?" she asked herself, disgusted that her mind would even go there.

There was no logic to it. She didn't have any reason to let her thoughts go so dark, so why did they? Too many nights alone with *Dateline* and wine. She inched closer to the window again, and when she peered out, Martin was gone, and so was the bag. The light behind the curtain was also off now. Martin seemed like a nice guy, full of heartbreak and love for his sick wife.

Yeah, well Ted Bundy was a charismatic hunk too. That means nothing.

When she calmed herself enough to leave the kitchen, she grabbed a tall glass of water and went back to her bedroom. She tried to go back to sleep, but she'd slept so much of the day that her body rejected the thought of any more. So she grabbed her cellphone off the nightstand and scrolled aimlessly through social media, envying all of her friends and their happy lives. But then she had an idea.

Jenny thought back to the conversation with Martin, trying to remember if he said his last name. She didn't recall him providing it, which put a damper on her idea to search for details on the husband and wife. She considered ways to investigate with only a first name. The first thing she searched was the listing of the home for sale, but all that indicated was "sold." It didn't provide details of the buyers. Then she attempted to do reverse searches for the name Martin in the towns surrounding Boston after remembering where he had come from. Still, all searches led to a dead end. Without a last name, it was like trying to identify a specific snowflake in a blizzard. She wouldn't be able to learn more about his past.

She jumped out of bed and slipped on her sandals which sat next to the door. Martin had only lived in the home a few days, but maybe there would be some mail in the mailbox already. Her mailbox was right next to his, so if for some reason anyone questioned why she was outside in the middle of the night, she could at least say it was her own mailbox she was interested in. When she made it to the porch, the neighborhood was silent, outside of the nightly crickets in the distance. She double-checked to make sure nobody was watching her from Martin's house, then beelined for the mailboxes.

As she went to grab the handle to open Martin's mailbox, a scream erupted from his house. It sounded exactly like the one Jenny heard earlier. But then she heard something else, something she didn't notice from inside her house earlier. It was Martin, yelling between the screams. The home was too much of a barrier to hear what he was shouting, but he didn't sound happy.

"LET ME GO! You cocksucker!"

The voice was still muffled, but his wife yelled it loud enough to hear exactly what she said. It was followed once again by Martin saying something. Almost as if he was chanting, not shouting in anger. Jenny forgot all about the mailbox and retreated toward her house. She didn't take her eyes off the neighbor's home the entire way.

The next morning, Jenny sat stoically in bed, rehashing everything that happened the night before. She knew for sure that Martin was chanting something. That something was alive in that trash bag he pulled from the vehicle. She needed to hold it together long enough to have another conversation with Martin. There was no point calling the police on speculation. Hell, they would look at her record—all the police reports from public fights with her ex, drunken scenes, her DWI—and think it was just another episode in the life of "Crazy Jenny." Until she saw something concrete, there wasn't much she could do about it.

There was also the part of her that thought maybe she *was* crazy. Bored after weeks of being alone and drinking herself to sleep most nights. She needed to get back in and see her therapist as soon as possible. But first, she wanted to confront Martin.

She waited until she heard him exiting his house and timed it perfectly to check her mail when he arrived in the driveway. He gave a slight nod and smile and went to get into his vehicle.

"Morning, Jenny. How you doing?"

"Oh, fine, I suppose. You?"

You're doing real swell, Jenny. You think your neighbor is a serial killer, she thought.

"Another tough night last night. I hope she wasn't too loud again," he said, nodding toward the window on the second floor.

"No, of course not. How's she doing? I mean, today. Is she any better?"

Martin shrugged. "As good as she can be. I'm off to get her some meds right now. How about that beer tonight? I could use it after these last few days."

His proposal caught her off guard. Still, she wanted to play it cool. If he thought she was trying to pry information from him, he would likely balk at her questions. Maybe a few drinks would loosen him up.

"Sounds good. Talk to you later, Martin."

He got in his SUV and backed out of the driveway, waving as he pulled away. Jenny watched the vehicle shrink in the distance, then grabbed her mail. She remembered wanting to check Martin's mailbox the night before and looked around to see if anyone was watching. When she felt it was safe, she opened his mailbox and was relieved to see an envelope sitting inside. With her luck, it would be the previous owners' mail that was delivered before they changed their address.

She was relieved to see his name. Martin Lebbon. At least it wasn't Smith or Thomas—something that would have a million results pop up in a search online. Jenny tossed the letter back in the mailbox and shut the lid, again looking around to make sure she wasn't being watched. Then her eyes landed on the second-floor window of Martin's house.

His wife stared down at her, as still as a mannequin, sending a chill down Jenny's spine.

Even from this distance, Jenny spotted the dark circles beneath her eyes, begging for the nutrients needed to vanish back into obscurity. Her hair was wiry and greasy, hiding most of the features on her face.

Jenny pretended not to notice the woman and returned to her porch, out of sight from above. Hopefully she just assumed Jenny was grabbing her own mail and not snooping through their mailbox. It seemed farfetched, but she clung to the small ounce of hope and went back inside.

The first thing she did once back in her living room was grab her cell and search "Martin Lebbon, Massachusetts" in her browser.

A list of results popped up, the typical ads that had nothing to do with the original search, plenty of partial results of people named Martin or having the last name Lebbon, but there were only a few that contained everything she wanted. The headline that grabbed her attention most said, **"Somerville Resident Martin Lebbon Demands Answers on Wife Nancy's Pregnancy Clinical Trials."**

Jenny read the entire article, which was pretty vague overall but detailed enough for her to get the gist. Martin's wife had gone through all of the standard steps to fight the cancer, eventually leaving them with nothing left to try. She was on borrowed time, and they were counting down the days until she died. Then a once-in-a-lifetime trial came along, and she was a candidate to get approved. The article went on to talk about her side effects, most of which were not included in the warnings on the paperwork she had to sign. While the article didn't get into specifics of the side effects, it was clear that things didn't go according to plan.

Every time Jenny had a reason to distrust Martin, something proved her wrong. She was allowing her past relationship to dictate how she viewed others, and it wasn't healthy. Apparently, she'd spent a lot more time searching the web than she realized, as the sound of an approaching vehicle parking next door brought her out of her daze. She looked at the clock and noticed it had been a few hours.

A couple minutes later, there was a knock at the door. Jenny could tell by the outline of the figure behind the glass that it was Martin. She opened the door and put on her best smile, which wasn't hard when she noticed the twelve-pack of Sam Adams in Martin's hand.

"Care for that drink?" he asked.

She nodded and met him on the porch, then sat on her wicker

couch. He handed her a cold beer, the perspiration sliding down the glass bottle as she grabbed it. They sat in silence for a moment, taking sips of their beer. She couldn't bring up the information she discovered but hoped it would come out organically.

"What's your wife's name? You never said."

"Oh, really? Sorry. It's Nancy. We met back in college and fell deeply in love. Tried having kids, but never made it that far. They told her she couldn't get pregnant. We were heartbroken but managed to go on living our lives."

"You're pretty open about things considering we just met," Jenny said, hoping he took it as a joke and not as an insult.

"Ha! Yeah, well, life is too short to worry about what people think, right? I find it's easier to accept things if I talk through them. Otherwise, it gets bottled up inside, and that's never a good thing."

"Wise words," Jenny said, taking another sip of her beer.

Maybe you should live by those words too, she told herself.

"I don't know how wise they are, but I live by them. We tried everything to get pregnant, and eventually it got to the point where we were meeting some shady people who said they had unapproved methods to get her pregnant. We were desperate. To this day, I'm positive that is what gave her the cancer..." He trailed off, lost in his thoughts.

"You can't blame yourself for that. Anyone would have done the same given the circumstances."

"I don't know about that, but thanks. So what's your story? Why you living alone?"

Jenny debated how much to tell him. She decided to take a play from his book and be honest. Maybe it would feel good. And maybe it would get him to open up even more. She wanted to know what was going on in the house at night.

"I mentioned that my mom died and left the house to me. That's all true. But I didn't move in until I went through a tough breakup.

He... he was abusive. It was a godsend that I had this place waiting for me to escape to, like it was my mom's last act of protecting me."

"Jesus. Sorry you dealt with that. Is he out of your life now?"

"Fuck yes. I won't go near that asshole again."

"Good. Look at us, a couple of broken-down sob stories. We'd be the life of the party, huh?"

Jenny laughed and found it easy to talk with Martin. It didn't change her plans, but it was obvious there was some good buried inside this man, even if he was a monster when the lights went out.

"I don't want to get too personal, but I have to ask. What were you yelling last night? I swear I wasn't trying to be nosey (*yeah you were*), but I couldn't help but hear stuff. What were you saying while she was screaming?"

Martin shifted his attention toward his home, staring up toward the second floor, then cleared his throat. "Sometimes she likes it when I pray while she's going through an episode. It helps calm her down if I'm there to say those things."

The reasoning made sense, but it didn't explain the trash bag. She couldn't bring herself to ask about that yet, if ever. They continued to drink over the next few hours, and Jenny found the conversation very cathartic. It was just what she needed.

"Well, I better get back to Nancy. She'll wake from her nap soon, and I hate not being there when she wakes up in pain. Let's do this again sometime, yeah?" Martin said.

"Sounds like a plan. Good chat, Martin."

After he was gone, Jenny went back inside, unsure what her next step should be.

Long after the sun set, Jenny heard the front door to Martin's house slam shut. She got up from the couch, where once again she had passed out drunk, and ran to the kitchen window. He was backing out of the driveway, and she got a quick glimpse of his facial expression. He appeared agitated as he sped off down the road. Jenny instinctively switched her focus to the second-story window next door, noticing a faint glow behind the curtain. She assumed Nancy must be watching television in bed.

A scream ripped through the night, startling Jenny.

It was as if the home itself was hurt, bleeding from the inside. But she knew it wasn't the house; it was Nancy. Martin wasn't home to help his wife, and she sounded like she was in a great deal of pain. Jenny considered her options, wishing that she got Martin's cell number so she could text or call him. Considering he just left a moment ago, the odds of him returning home soon were slim. Jenny decided she had to help. Hell, if Martin really was doing anything strange with his wife, now was as good a time as any to save the poor woman.

Jenny tossed her sandals on and grabbed her phone as she exited her house. She sprinted across the lawn, the screams now amplified in the open space. She'd kill for another neighbor to hear and tag along to help, but the house on the other side of Martin and Nancy was an elderly couple that probably didn't even hear the screams, and the house across the street was vacant. Jenny was the only one suitable enough to assist.

She climbed the porch and tried the door, unsurprised to find it locked.

Damn it. Now you're about to get arrested for breaking and entering, might as well add it to your tally, she thought.

She went around the side of the house, entering the back lawn, which wasn't visible from any of her windows. She had never seen the space behind the home, which was bigger than she imagined. As she prepared to check the back door, she spotted a dirt hole dug in the lawn. She ignored the screams for a second and approached the mound of dirt. As she got closer, she realized there wasn't just one hole, but *dozens*. Some were freshly filled, while others were still open with piles of dirt next to them.

"What the fuck…"

They couldn't be more than a few feet in each direction. What the hell would Martin be doing back here? Planting vegetables? She didn't exactly have a green thumb, but she was pretty sure this wasn't your typical garden setup. She turned on her phone light and aimed it at the first hole, displaying a freshly dug space, empty of any vegetables or flowers. She moved down to the next to find it filled, packed dirt covering the space.

A smell permeated the air, and Jenny couldn't help but inhale as she attempted to recognize it. She gagged when the scent of rotten meat stung her nostrils. Like week-old roadkill. With trepidation, she moved down the line, finding what looked to be the most recently filled space. A shovel leaned against the privacy fence. Before she could stop herself, Jenny had the shovel in her grip and began digging. The metal tip stuck on something a few inches down.

What are you doing, Jenny? Get the fuck out of here now!

Instead, she dropped to her knees and began digging with her hands. She did so with precision, burrowing like a rabid dog until she felt something beneath the dirt. She picked her phone up and aimed the light at the hole.

A small finger poked out of the dirt like a nightcrawler coming up for air. Jenny fell to her backside, dropping her phone and crab-walked away from the hole. The *grave*. It was a human fucking finger. She crawled back to the hole, needing to know if she was seeing things. But what she saw forced bile to the back of her throat.

Two blank eyes caked with dirt—tiny yet so big in their own way —stared up at the night sky. But it wasn't the baby's eyes that made her sick. Beneath the eyes, the nose separated down the center, spreading to form a giant mouth that was open wide. There were no nostrils on the sides of the nose. Jenny remained locked in place, unable to take her eyes off the deformed baby, until something moved inside the mouth. A bug, mouse, she had no idea without her phone light, but she quickly backed away.

"Oh god. Oh god..."

She fumbled for her phone, ready to call 9-1-1. But then the screaming started back up, sending Jenny's heart into her throat. With all her attention on the lawn, she hadn't realized the screaming had even stopped. Nancy was in danger, and Jenny couldn't wait for Martin to get back and cause more harm. She had to save his wife. She ran to the back door and tried the knob. It was locked as well.

"God damn it!"

She had to find another way in, even if it meant breaking a window. There wasn't anything close by to break the glass with, and she wasn't about to use her bare hand and cut an artery. *The shovel.* Jenny turned to head back and grab it... and came face to face with Martin.

"What are you doing back here, Jenny?"

"I..."

He charged at her and grabbed her by the hair before she even had time to react. Then he slammed the back of her head against the house, sending flashing lights through her field of vision.

"I wish you hadn't done this. I really liked you," he said, almost calmly. She was losing consciousness as he drove her head into the side paneling once again. Her legs turned to rubber, the fight leaving her body. And then he drove her head back one more time with a disturbing crunch, sending everything to darkness.

Jenny tried to open her eyes but was met with a searing pain in the back of her head. She blinked away at some of the pain, attempting to take in her surroundings. The first thing she noticed was that she was tied at the hands and feet with thick rope. She was no longer outside, and she wasn't in her own home. Martin must have dragged her inside in an effort to hide her from the neighborhood. Not that he needed to do that, the damn place was a ghost town when you needed someone most.

As her eyes adjusted to the dim light in the room, she determined she must be in the basement. She chastised herself for not going with her gut. Letting Martin's smooth talk woo her into believing he was a good guy was the exact thing she told herself would never happen again. Yet here she was, bound in the basement of a psychopath who buried dead bodies in his backyard.

Why was that hand so small?

She couldn't and *wouldn't* allow her mind to go there. Not yet. First, she needed to put all her focus into trying to get out of here. The earthy smell of the damp space made her think of the graves out back, and she wondered if they too were tied up down here before Martin eventually had his way with them.

It was a kid. A fucking baby in that hole. You know it was.

Jenny pulled at the rope, but all that did was press the rough material into her skin and send jolts of pain through her wrists.

"God damn it!"

Her voice triggered movement overhead. Footsteps creaked along the floorboards above, heading in a direction she assumed led to the basement door. And then a handle jiggled as the door opened and sent a dim beam of light spilling onto the stairs. At the top, Martin's outline stared down.

"Jenny, Jenny, Jenny. I didn't want this. I didn't plan this with you, I swear. Now we're going to have to move again, and I wanted peace and quiet," he said, taking the steps slowly until he reached the bottom. His expression conveyed anything *but* a monster. He appeared genuinely sorry.

He flicked a light switch, blasting the room with a yellowish tint. Jenny squinted, her headache not agreeing with the newfound illumination. She scanned the room, and with each passing item she sat her eyes on, a sense of defeat pushed away any hope she had. The unfinished basement was set up like a makeshift lab, full of medical instruments and tools. Jars full of a hazy fluid lined the walls on rickety shelves.

"Why are you doing this to me? What is this place?" she asked, trying to sound stronger than she felt.

"Everything I've told you is true. Please know that. Nancy really is sick, and I truly do feel it was caused by the trials to get her pregnant. But there are certain parts I couldn't tell you. It would scare you, probably even make you think I'm crazy."

"Probably? You have me fucking tied up in your basement. You have dead bodies buried in your back yard. What the hell is that, Martin?" she snapped.

"Those... those are my children. *Our* children," he said, wiping away tears. He saw the confusion in Jenny's eyes and continued. "After all of the procedures, all of the trials, tests, and medications, we were desperate. When the cancer came, I went after the hospital for answers. A woman named Stella Yvonne saw our story on the news and reached out to me. She was an old lady with a thick accent, from some European country. She told us she could help us get pregnant. That if we met her at her home, she would cure Nancy's fertility issues and get rid of her cancer. It sounds ridiculous, I know. But it *worked.* All we had to do was agree to take on a burden, and she would change our lives. We agreed. So we showed up at the address she provided—a small mobile home with windchimes dangling from every imaginable spot—and she brought us in her home. We almost left after seeing the display she'd prepared for us ahead of time. She set up a séance on her living room floor, laying out some aged rug that looked haunted, covering it in small candles that lit the dark space. After she was done chanting something in her foreign language, we went home.

"A few months later, Nancy got pregnant. We were the happiest we'd ever been. Then there were... complications. The baby came early, and not only was it stillborn, it was deformed. Like some mutant created in a lab. We were heartbroken, didn't know what to do. I had no idea how to track down Stella again, because she left the address shortly after we went to see her. But then one night she showed up on our doorstep with a smile that even the vilest killer couldn't produce."

Martin stopped talking for a moment as he walked along the shelves, looking at the jars and tools. Jenny wasn't sure where he was going with this story, but she was starting to put the pieces together.

"I told her she lied to us. That she created this monster that came out of my wife. All she did was laugh in my face. She cursed my wife, filled her with something that needs to consume. Like some human wendigo whose hunger never goes away. When we sacrifice to this thing inside her, it allows her to get pregnant. Only we've tried many times, and the babies always come out deformed and dead on arrival. It's taken its toll on my wife, and I'm not sure she can go through with it again."

"What do you mean sacrifice? What the fuck are you doing, Martin?" Jenny asked, thinking back to the moving trash bag he carried into the house.

"We give it something, and in return we *get* something. Except, all this time, I don't think we've been giving it enough. Stella told us the reason our pregnancies were failing wasn't because she broke her word, but because the thing—this curse—inside my wife wanted more. I didn't know what she meant. We tried giving it animals. Small at first. When mice, hamsters, and rabbits didn't work, I tried bigger. I can't tell you the pain it brought me to look a dog in the eyes before feeding it to that thing. With each sacrifice, she got pregnant. But as you see out back, there have been many failures."

Martin grabbed something from one of the shelves, but Jenny couldn't see what it was from her position on the floor. Everything he was telling her seemed so farfetched that she struggled to believe it. But everything leading up to this backed up what he was saying. Still, a curse? Was this some fucking evil fairytale?

"This is such bullshit, and you know it. Why not try adopting? And you told me she had cancer, made me believe that was why she was sick. Why should I believe a word you say?"

"Because she DID have cancer! And for all I know, she still does. But it's overshadowed by this monster inside her, eating away at her soul. I... I can't go on like this. There's only one other thing to try."

He stepped forward, revealing a needle in his hand. Jenny wanted to throw up. What was his plan here? She had to break free.

"What are you doing? Think this through, Martin. Don't make a mistake that you'll regret the rest of your life. *Please.*"

"I'm full of regret. This is the last thing I can try. It has to work," he said with tears now glossing over his eyes and sliding down his cheeks. He stepped closer to Jenny as he checked the syringe. She had no idea what was inside, but she didn't plan to find out.

"I can help you find a better way. It doesn't have to be this way..."

"Yeah... yeah it does. I'm sorry," he said, then kneeled to grab hold of her arm.

Jenny swung her bound hands at his face, connecting with the side of his head. Martin fell back, slamming into the nearest shelf.

Glass jars fell to the floor, shattering on impact. Her feet were tied to a metal cross beam that traveled along the floor. She tried to pull on the rope, hoping it would eventually slide off saw metal and free her, but she found no such luck. Martin stood upright and came back at her, this time prepared. Jenny tried to shimmy her way back, pulling as far as the rope would allow, but Martin was on her. He backhanded her face, forcing her head to jerk back against the wall behind her. The impact reinvigorated the pain in her brain from earlier.

"Please... don't fight this. I don't want to hurt you," he said.

She found it hard to believe considering what he just did. Before she could swing again, she felt the warm prick of the needle jabbing into her neck. Within seconds, her vision blurred, her body numbed. And then she was out cold once again.

"Nancy... I brought a sacrifice."

Jenny heard the statement that sounded far off in the distance, but in reality, Martin was standing right over her. She couldn't move. Whatever he drugged her with paralyzed her body and left her at his disposal. He must have noticed her move slightly, because he kneeled by her side.

"I'm so sorry, Jenny. We have to try this. If we don't... I don't even know. It's not like this was the plan. We should've never listened to that monster."

He was talking to himself as much as Jenny, attempting to convince himself this was the right choice. Jenny tried to open her eyes. It was like navigating under water, everything beyond a few feet a complete blur. She could see the outline of a bed in the corner, and she wasn't certain, but she thought she saw movement on the bed. Martin said he fed the thing inside his wife. Was he about to throw her on the bed like an afternoon snack?

"*St-stoppp. Peeasse,*" Jenny mumbled. Her mouth felt as if it was injected with a lethal dose of Novocain when she tried to speak. Her lips like two thick sausages blocking her vocal cords. Martin didn't listen; instead he lifted her off the floor and dragged her closer to the bed, then dropped her dead weight next to the right side.

"Martin, is it worth it? Can we do this and live with ourselves?"

Jenny didn't recognize the voice but knew it had to be his wife, lying on top of the bed like she was awaiting him to climb on top of her.

"No. I can't live with myself. But I can't if I don't do it either. I need to know if this can save you, Nancy." His voice trembled as he said it.

Nancy didn't respond, but then the bed shook, so much that the bedframe scraped along the floor a few inches.

"Nancy?" Martin whispered.

"Feed me the fucking cunt! Feed her to me!"

Jenny shook her head, fighting the grogginess. That voice—it wasn't human. Whatever was controlling Nancy, it wanted to consume Jenny.

"Will this work? Will it get us what we want?" Martin asked.

"There's only one way to find out, pretty boy. Give me her fucking flesh! Give it to me!"

Nancy's voice rumbled through Jenny's head, adding to her headache. She was about to die and couldn't control her body enough to even fight it. She tried to force her body to move, to crawl away and get the hell out of this house before it was too late. But then Martin grabbed her by the hair and lifted her to her feet. If he let go of her, she'd drop to the floor like a deflated bouncy house, but he held her up. His grip was so tight that her hair started to rip from her scalp. Jenny found it impossible to take her focus from the bed, and now that she was this close, she got her first glimpse of Nancy.

Martin's wife was on the bed with her legs spread. She wore a white satin gown that rode up high enough to reveal her silk panties. Her skin was clammy, glistening in sweat. Jenny brought her attention to Nancy's face and instinctively tried to back up, unable to do so as Martin held her steady. Nancy looked beyond sick —she looked deathly. The dark circles beneath her eyes had sunken in so much that her bottom eyelids sagged. Black lines webbed out from her pupils, spreading across the whites of her eyes. She licked her lips, revealing a tongue that was caked in white bacteria and dead cells.

"Yes. She will do. Give her to me," Nancy said, her cracked lips turning upward into a hideous smile.

Martin threw Jenny onto the bed, and she landed face first across the lap of Nancy's bony body. Martin backed away from them, as if even being close would infect him. He began to chant something, the words masked behind his trembling voice. Before Jenny could move, Nancy's brittle fingers clamped around her wrist and pulled the arm close. Jenny had no idea what the crazy woman was about to do, but she didn't have to wait long to find out. Nancy bit down into the meat of her forearm, tearing flesh from the bone. Jenny screamed as an intense pain rocketed through her entire arm. Her vision still wasn't clear, but she could hear everything. Martin crying in the corner, watching it all unfold. Nancy chewing the muscle that she had stuck between her yellow teeth.

Nancy pulled Jenny's arm close to her mouth again, this time severing her pinky finger, her teeth cutting through the bone like it was nothing. A guttural squeal escaped Jenny's lungs as she fought to stay conscious. There was no possible way this frail, sick woman should have this much strength. As Nancy groaned with satisfaction, she brought the arm closer once more. This time, Jenny was prepared, flipping over to her back. She hauled back and kicked

Nancy in the mouth, feeling her teeth crunch beneath the weight of her shoe. Martin hollered and ran toward them, but Jenny rolled out of the way and fell off the other side of the bed. She hit the floor hard, but quickly got to her feet, feeling light-headed.

"No! Get back here! We must finish the act!" Martin screamed. The genuine softness behind his voice had vanished, replaced with a grief-stricken panic.

Jenny clutched her wounded hand and stared back at him on the other side of the bed. Nancy writhed on top of the comforter, holding her bloody mouth.

"You people are fucking crazy! How the hell would eating me help you get pregnant? Think about that, Martin!"

"You have no idea what this thing is. Now that it's tasted human flesh, it won't stop. It's too late for you," he said.

Jenny ran for the door, and Martin was hot on her trail. She turned just as he was grabbing her hair and kicked him in the knee, then clawed his face, feeling his skin cake beneath her nails. He bellowed in pain and fell back, giving her enough time to exit the room. She bolted down the stairs, unfamiliar with the layout of the house but keeping her eyes open for the front door. She spotted it around the corner and ran to it, grabbing the knob. It was locked, but not just a regular lock, the door was padlocked. She'd need a key to open it. Martin slammed through his bedroom door, spotting her at the bottom of the stairs.

She ran down the narrow hall, feeling through the darkness in front of her. When she reached the back door, her heart sank when she saw the same level of security trapping her inside.

The basement.

Jenny recalled the door she spotted when Martin had her tied up. It didn't have padlocks. If she could get down there, she could go for help.

"Jenny! Don't make this harder than it needs to be! Come back."

Martin wasn't far behind her, she needed to get moving. Unsure of which door led to the basement, she tried the first she came to, revealing a pantry. The second door opened to a set of stairs heading down into the darkness. She descended, holding the railing with her good hand. The earthy smell welcomed her back with open arms. The room felt much smaller with the lights off, but she didn't think to look for the light switch on the way down. She pulled out her phone and turned the light on, locating the door. Before she went anywhere, she needed to call for help. She dialed 9-1-1 and hit **<CALL>**. The operator picked up, asking for her emergency.

"I'm being attacked, they're trying to kill—"

Martin jumped from the fourth step and landed on her back. The phone flew from Jenny's hand and slid across the dirt floor out of reach. The faint light from the device lit up the floor around her, and she spotted some of the shattered glass from earlier. The muffled voice of the operator continued to talk on the other end of the phone. Martin fought to get hold of her, and she reached out for a piece of glass as he grunted from behind, grabbing at her hair. She turned and swung blindly, feeling the glass slide across his throat. A shower of crimson splashed on her face and continued to pump out of the newly produced gash. Martin clutched his throat, desperate to stop the blood from flowing out. His eyes widened, the realization hitting him that he was about to die.

"Nu-n-no..." he mumbled, his sentence cut short as his hands filled with blood.

He collapsed to the floor next to her. Jenny didn't move for a moment, regaining her breath. But then she heard the voice on the phone again and pushed away from Martin's limp body. She picked up the phone and was relieved to hear the operator still there.

"I... I killed him. He was attacking me when I called you," she panted.

"Ma'am, stay calm. Who attacked you?"

"My neighbor. Martin Lebbon."

The operator told her to go outside and stay on the line, so she did just that. It wasn't until a police officer did a sweep of the house that she remembered Nancy upstairs. They found her, covered in blood. She had apparently slit her own throat, trying to end her own life before they got her. But she was still breathing. EMTs brought her out on a stretcher, and she spotted Jenny sitting on the curb and flashed a smile. Jenny got to her feet, unable to control the anger festering inside, and charged at the stretcher.

"Ma'am, that's not a good idea. Please stay back," the EMT helping her said.

Jenny ignored the plea and came face to face with Nancy.

"It... It's passed on," Nancy said, struggling to get the words out.

"What the fuck are you talking about?"

"The... c-curse. It's with you now. I'm sorry..."

Jenny stood numbly as the stretcher was wheeled away toward the ambulance. How could the curse be passed on to her? She wasn't part of some ritual, some agreement like the Lebbons made with Stella. She looked down at her wounded arm, a fresh bandage now covering the bite mark. Her hand was wrapped in gauze, hiding her missing finger.

It wasn't until one of the responding officers was questioning her about the events leading up to Martin's death that she felt a hunger building inside. She caught her reflection on the side of the ambulance window, spotting dark circles sunken well into her cheekbones. Jenny knew in that moment—whatever had been inside Nancy Lebbon, whatever had haunted their family and led to the monstrosities in their backyard, it was now living inside her.

SOLITARY

MEGAN STOCKTON

Chet slid the end of the plastic toothbrush in and out of the screw hole in the bunk bed: rotating it, and angling it, so that it had the sharpest possible point without sacrificing integrity. Every motion he made created a squeak in the ancient springs of the mattress, but he gritted his teeth and continued his work.

A frustrated voice came from the bunk above him: "Can you *please* for the love of all things holy... One day. Can you not start *one fucking day* without jacking off?"

Chet started working faster and played along, voice breathy, "Almost done. Almost done."

He pulled the toothbrush back, blowing the dust particles off of it before testing the end with his fingertip. It was sharp... It was really, really sharp. He wrapped a torn piece of bedsheet around the brush end, fashioning a crude, cushioned handle. He stuffed it into his shoe, jagged tip digging into the flesh of his ankle. He swung his legs off the mattress as he heard the guards coming down the block, dragging their batons along the bars for a wakeup call.

His bunkmate, Hector, started to get down from his place on the top bed, and Chet offered him a hand.

Hector recoiled. "Don't touch me with that. You nasty."

Chet smiled as the shorter inmate jumped to the floor and stood in front of the door. Both men put their hands behind their heads, fingers laced. This was one of the most poorly run prisons in the state: crumbling infrastructure, nonexistent compliance, zero safety parameters, shitty employees, and careless management. Some saw this as a negative aspect. Chet saw it as an opportunity.

Multiple men had escaped the prison at Fallen Church Penitentiary, and they all had one thing in common: they had been placed in solitary confinement. The warden tried to keep it hush-hush, but the guards talked plenty. There were two cells in solitary, side-by-side, and one of them had been occupied by the same guy for ages... but the lucky sons of bitches that got into the second cell were finding ways to get out.

He guessed that they assumed anyone who *did* escape would die before he got far enough out to actually get away; there was nothing but rugged and unforgiving terrain for miles and miles. They also had dogs, and the rumor was they starved them so they had bloodlust for days. He wasn't afraid of dogs, or of the wilderness outside these walls... He would handle all of that, if he could *just* get out.

Hector and Chet walked in the line of inmates to the mess hall, and while all of the other men had their eyes on the slop they called food, Chet was looking for Steven Amory. Steve was in for involuntary manslaughter and was probably going to get released early for good behavior. He was the ideal inmate, and he sucked up to (and probably sucked off) guards on the regular. Chet had nothing personal against Steve... He was just the easiest target.

Hector had already moved toward the line and hesitated when he saw that Chet hadn't moved from the doorway where other inmates were pouring in around him.

"You all right?" Hector asked.

Chet saw Steve across the room, already seated and eating with his back to the entrance.

He smiled at Hector and responded, "Been great knowing you, brother."

Hector set his jaw in surprise, and Chet headed across the room. He knew that every inmate that saw him knew what he was about to do, but no one moved to stop him. He stopped behind Steve, lifting his foot up to rest it on the bench beside him, and then retrieved the shiv.

"Hey, Stevie."

He had a white-knuckled grip on the makeshift weapon. Steve looked back and smiled, tipping his head back to look up at him like a girl in a romance movie. Chet hesitated as he stared down at the boyish face, but he knew that if he waited too long they'd stop him. He'd lose his outdoor privileges, and they'd take his toiletries... but he wouldn't go to solitary.

He gritted his teeth as he jammed the tip of the knife into Steve's neck, surprised when it went straight through: piercing the bumpy cartilage and shoving it through the opposite side. He had to use his knee to pull the shiv free like a stubborn sword, watching as Steve fell backward off the bench and hit the floor with a thud followed by an echoing wail. The entire mess hall fell silent, and then bodies were in motion. Guards and inmates were rushing in equal time toward him, and so Chet fell atop of Steve and used both hands to stab Steve's puppy brown eyes out.

The right burst, fluid squirting onto Chet's gritted teeth as he dug at the eye like it had offended him. He could hear the scrape of the sharp handle across the interior of Steve's skull. He wasn't even fighting him off; he gasped and floundered like a suffocating fish beneath him.

Chet felt hands grab him from behind, ripping him away. He sighed a breath of relief, closing his eyes and leaving the shiv embedded in Steve's skull. He took another long inhale and opened his eyes as the guards hoisted him as though he were weightless. He let them drag him away, watching as the inmates gathered around Steve's body and a guard fell to his knees to attempt to provide aid. Hector sat on the table beside Steve's tray and started eating his mandarin oranges with his fingers. He sucked the juice from his fingertips and nodded once at Chet in approval.

They wasted no time taking Chet straight down the hall to solitary. As they entered the unfamiliar wing, he cleared his throat.

"Don't I see the warden?"

No response.

One of the guard's dropped his grip on Chet to move to unlock one of two doors in the hall. Chet noted how the door to the opposite cell looked like it hadn't been opened in ages: corroded with green neglect. There was a tray door at the bottom.

"You just throw people down here, I guess? Don't want to hear my side of the story? I don't get some kind of chance to explain myself?"

Still no response, they didn't even acknowledge that he was speaking at all. Of course, Chet *wanted* to be here, but he didn't want them to know that. They opened the door and shoved him inside, closing it behind him before he could gather his bearings. He heard the lock turn, and then the footsteps fade down the hall. He stood up slowly, taking in his surroundings with intense attention to every detail.

"Where are you?" he muttered, starting in one corner and walking the perimeter as he looked for any sign of weakness or manipulation. Whatever they were using for escape would have to be easily covered once used so that it wasn't being repaired or taken care of in between inmates.

He paused, hair creeping erect along his neck as he heard the quietest voice. Somehow it felt like it was right behind him, but at the same time so distant. He noticed the eerie calm and quiet that followed the sound, and he froze as he strained to hear it again.

There it was.

He dropped to his knees, holding his breath as he followed the sound to the wall adjacent to the other cell.

"*Silatrom... idul arret atarg.*" It sounded like two voices saying the exact same phrase: one guttural, and one quiet and of a higher pitch. The words didn't make any sense to him, but he didn't speak any languages other than English either.

He scooted the bed away from the wall and noticed a piece of brown paper stuck to the stone wall with a strand of peeling tape: more lint than adhesive. There was a crudely drawn upside down triangle in the center of the paper in what could have been blood. Chet's short fingernails picked the tape's corner until it peeled away, revealing a hole about three inches across. He had to press himself against the floor to look into it, but there was no light on the other side. He couldn't tell if it went far enough to be open on the other side or not but there was a coolness that emanated, and the smell of something damp and animal-like. He suddenly remembered the way his childhood dog often smelled after he had been outdoors: that distinctly "outside" odor that clung to his coat.

"Hello?" The voice came again, but in a drawling moan with the tone of a metal drum. The way the "o" echoed down the length of the hole made Chet somehow feel sick to his stomach, but he found himself returning the greeting.

"Hey. You're the guy in the other cell, I guess?"

Who was he, Mr. Obvious?

"I'm your neighbor," the voice responded.

"How long you been over there?"

"Forever."

Chet laughed. He was sure it did feel that way in a room like this. Stone walls, stone floor. And *so damn quiet.*

"You won't be here long," the neighbor said.

"Yeah, speaking of... you know how the other guys are getting out of here? Have they told you?"

There was an uncomfortable silence, something that bordered on a deafening reverb of buzzing that was maybe just an octave too loud for the human ear to detect: a loudness that could come crashing down if it dropped only a half-step.

"I know where they go."

"Yeah?"

"Do you want to go too?"

"Yes," Chet hissed. "Yes. That's why I came here, man. Look I know it is probably lonely as fuck here, and I know you probably hate seeing everyone else get out while you're stuck, but I *have* to get out of here."

"Why are you covered in blood?"

"I—"

Chet looked down at his blood-stained hands. He had already forgotten about Steve, who probably bled out on the floor of the cafeteria. His fingers were numb, a creeping tingling of a million needles, as he recalled how he had more or less lobotomized him with a toothbrush.

"I can smell your fear," the voice cooed, and Chet would have sworn it was just beside him.

A sudden bang on the door caused him to lurch upward, and as the door unlocked and opened, he quickly shoved the bed back in front of the hole.

The guards from earlier stood outside the door, and between them was a woman of no more than five and a quarter feet. She had her chestnut hair pulled back in a tight ponytail, girl-next-door vibes if not for the pantsuit.

"Chester Joyce?" she asked, voice quizzical as though she really wasn't sure if that's who she was talking to or not.

"Guilty as charged... oh, too soon?"

There wasn't an *ounce* of amusement on the trio's features. People on the outside would always say that Chet couldn't read a room, but in reality he just didn't care.

"I would like to apologize that I wasn't able to see you yesterday after your incident at breakfast. I felt that you deserved, at minimum, to see me personally so I could explain why you're here. You know by now that anyone who exhibits violence has to spend time in solitary confinement. Your unprovoked attack on Mr. Amory has left us shaken and surprised. I have instructed that you spend no less than two weeks here."

"Let's back up a second. I scooped Stevie's peepers out this morning."

She exchanged glances with the guards and then said, "Being in solitary can be disorienting. Time can dilate, or pass by very quickly. It sounds like you are experiencing the preferable option. Now, get a good night's rest, Mr. Joyce... or nap for a few days. You have nothing but time."

The guards shut the door in his face, and Chet sat heavily on the edge of the bed. They were fucking with him. He hadn't been in here staring at the ceiling or sleeping for hours on end. He had explored the corners of the room and then found the hole where he talked to the creepy fucking neighbor.

He *was* tired though, he realized. His entire body ached, he suspected from being dragged by his arms and from the stress and force of stabbing Steven Amory so passionately. He laid down and curled into the fetal position, knees tucked against his chest. There was no pillow, not even a top sheet for him to put over himself. He heard something rattle in the dimness, and he opened his eyes long enough to see a small air conditioning unit, or a fan, in the left corner near the ceiling. It didn't appear to be working, but he noted that the face looked crooked. Maybe, just maybe, the unit could be knocked out and you could climb through. He would get a good night's rest and check it in the morning.

Chet dozed off as soon as he allowed himself to let go, tumbling through dreams that were mostly warped memories of killing Steve. The way he had walked up behind him, and Steve had tipped his head back to look at him, brown hair falling away from his face. In the nightmare, his head continued to fall backward, neck elongating, until it became a fleshy serpent with the youthful face at the end. It pursued Chet through the halls of the prison endlessly.

He woke up in a puddle of sweat, but his flesh felt so chilled that he would not have been surprised to have rubbed frost from his arms as he used friction to warm himself. As he swung his legs over the side of the bed, he felt a cool draft, and he scooted the bed away again to observe the hole there. It seemed larger than he had remembered it, smooth edges widened to the size of a saucer. The smell was more significant, as was the cold air that came from within. He still could not see to the other side, and he put the tips of his fingers just inside to prove to himself that it wasn't just a clever painting.

Chet felt like the longer he gazed in, the darker his peripheral vision became. Spots burst across his vision like ink into water, his ears filled with the distant hum of a dead television channel. He heard another distant sound, like banging on a drum.

"Are you there?" Chet called into the hole.

His voice didn't echo but was absorbed by the darkness somehow.

Returned in a voice that, at first, sounded nearly identical to his own before it took on the mournful tone, was the simple response: "Yes. I am here."

Now what? Chet didn't know what possessed him to speak in the first place, to call for the neighboring inmate in solitary confinement. No one talked much about who it was that was down here. All Chet knew was that he had been in solitary for as long as he'd been inside, and he must have been a really, really bad guy.

"So... what are you in here for?"

"Pain."

"Pain?" Chet repeated.

"Yes. So much pain."

"So... you hurt people?"

"Yes."

"Killed people?"

Silence.

So likely murder. It would explain the weirdness. Chet had found that all murderers fit into three categories here: brains and charm, weird as fuck, or no brains all beef. His neighbor was definitely the weird-as-fuck type.

Chet cleared his throat. "So the guys who have escaped from this room... do they get out of the vent for the air conditioner?"

"No."

"Then how? Is there a loose tile somewhere?"

"No."

"Come on, man. You've got to give me something."

"Do you want to go where they go?"

Chet rolled his eyes, burying his head in his hands. "Yes. Yes, I want to go, however it is they go."

"All you have to do is ask."

The distant drumming grew louder, echoing in his skull like he was hearing it from underwater. He stood up suddenly, reaching up to grab his head in his hands.

"What is that fucking *noise*?"

The sound clarified around him, and he realized that it was someone banging on the door. Chet walked over, legs aching and heavy. He leaned into the door as a slot at eye level slid open, revealing the upper half of one of the guard's faces.

"Just checking for signs of life," the guard stated.

"If I didn't answer, were you just going to keep on banging until I came back to life?"

"Worked, didn't it?"

Chet could've reached through the slit in the door to jam his fingers into the guard's eyes, but he resisted.

"Can a guy get some food down here or do we starve until we can slide under the door like a sheet of fucking paper?"

The guard huffed. "You eat what you're offered. This ain't a Burger King. You can't have it your way."

The slot slammed shut, and Chet kicked the bottom of the door, effectively stubbing his toe. He jerked the foot upward, clinging to the throbbing toe as he stumbled away. His heel struck something, and it clattered across the floor behind him; he turned and looked down to find a pile of trays.

The plastic trays of different colors were piled in a corner, and the smell of rotting food reached his nostrils. These hadn't been here this morning when he'd woken up. It was several meals, all in various states of decay other than a single tray of macaroni and a dry-as-bone hamburger patty.

"What the fuck is going on?" he wheezed, heart pounding in his throat. "I have got to get out of here."

He moved back to the bed as fast as he could force his weak legs. It was like walking through tar, dragging his lead-laden feet through a thick and relentless mire. He dragged the mattress onto the floor and then took the frame of the bed to the wall under the air conditioner. He wedged the base beside the toilet, propping it up to use the slats like a ladder. Then he started up it.

It took every ounce of strength he had to pull himself to the top. Some broken element inside the unit rattled still, and although it put out no air, the metal face was cool to the touch. Chet steadied himself, holding his own elbow as he rammed his shoulder into the unit. It groaned, scraping against the stone wall that held it fast, but it didn't give way.

"C'mon, you piece of shit," he muttered, leaning away to ram into the unit again. The force caused the bed frame to shift and, when it did, the toilet dislodged from the floor and the bed collapsed beneath him.

Chet flailed in the air, arms windmilling for what felt like ages as he fell to the concrete floor.

Sleep, or in this case unconsciousness, seemed to exist in the same moment as awareness. Chet had no sooner hit the floor when he found himself opening his eyes. Blood was crusted to his scalp; he could feel the throb of pain from where he'd struck the ground. Straight across the room from where he lay, he saw the hole in the wall now stretched large enough that it could be crawled through.

"Hello, neighbor." The voice droned from inside, louder than it had been before.

Chet crawled to his feet, unsteady and wavering.

"What is this?" he asked from a dry throat, voice husky and tongue like cotton.

"All you have to do is ask."

"Ask for what?"

"To leave this place."

Chet took a hesitant step forward, and he felt a pull. It was a magnetic sliding against his will, like he had been put onto a conveyor. He dug in his heels, gritting his teeth. The pull pulsed and then stopped.

"Do you want to leave?"

"Is this where the other inmates went?"

"This is the way. *The* way. *The only way.*"

He took another step, this one more confident. The hole in the wall seemed to yawn, pulling in a deep breath as it stretched upward against the possibility of physics. Somehow, Chet fell into it, tumbling forward, but then forward became up, or maybe it was down. He felt like he was falling into the sky, but there was nothing but black around him.

"I'm so glad you came to me," the neighbor cooed, voice around and inside Chet's ears. "You fascinating, terrible little creature."

"Who are you?" Chet screamed, grappling for purchase on the ground or wall or *anything*.

The neighbor didn't respond.

"Where am I?"

Chet was suspended in the air, spinning slowly as the neighbor examined him. He couldn't see its face, not in the traditional sense, but he could feel its eyes upon him. It squeezed him gently, forcing the air out of his lungs. He couldn't breathe but somehow wasn't suffocating. The pain of his tightening chest never subsided, and he was never given a release. His eyes moved away from the presence of the neighbor, and he saw that the ceiling stretched into infinite darkness above them. The bodies of the inmates who had "escaped" from solitary before floated there: orbiting above, bodies folded into shapes of stars. Their faces were contorted into frozen visages of terror and pain, their chests barely fluttering with breath. Their flesh was bruised and swollen, some torn by splintered, ivory bone. They looked like effigies, but Chet had a feeling it was much more mundane than that.

They were just playthings, crafts.

The neighbor leaned in, the essence both powerful and soft. Its touch felt like a prickle of electricity, causing gentle spasms as it crawled across his flesh. He could feel it climbing up his arms and across his chest, then onto his face where it paused around his mouth. The lingering touch was unbearable.

"I want to feel every vile fiber of your soul," it said, and fingers of static pushed past his lips, clicking against his teeth and tongue like Pop Rocks. More tendrils still pressed into his nostrils, filling his turbinates with a hurt that was unfathomable. Smaller even strands erupted from his tear ducts, pulling through like threads of lightning from his eyes. His perception briefly flatlined from the noxious stimulation and for a fleeting moment he felt nothing at all: gazing up at the constellations of broken, naked men.

The neighbor spoke again, and Chet was pulled back into his torment. It washed over him in a wave that started from his core and spiraled outward.

"Isn't it so beautiful?... This," something pressed deep inside Chet, against a part of him that he didn't know existed, "fragile little spark."

Chet's mouth opened involuntarily and a darkness poured from inside him, emerging like a serpent. His throat expanded and his jaw cracked open to its limit. He felt the hinge give way and separate, mandible sagging. The darkness came from his nose, deviating his septum. The shadow arm finally left his mouth and at the very end, in a sort of hand, it withdrew a ball of the brightest light. The neighbor drew the thing close to itself and then Chet's vision grew dim, bursting with pink and black as the image of the otherworldly being burned his retinas like ruined film. He was not meant to look upon its face; no man was.

In the darkness that followed, Chet heard the sound of his limbs shattering, being broken and folded into his own cosmic formation. He felt every manipulation, every fracture.

The neighbor exhaled, moaning quietly as it cradled his soul in its arms and watched it die.

"Isn't it so beautiful?"

THERE GOES THE NEIGHBORHOOD

BRIAN ASMAN

D oug Renner began to suspect his new neighbor Randall might be a serial killer the night he spotted him digging a very large backyard hole at three in the morning.

Since entering his forties, Doug found his bladder to be more foe than friend, frequently awakening him in the middle of the night. And that fateful night was no different. He awoke, hurried to the bathroom, and while waiting for the stream to come—his bladder could be quite demanding, but also gun-shy—he peered out the small window next to the toilet, which just so happened to look out onto Randall's backyard.

What he saw made his urethra clench.

Randall, the amiable, square-jawed man about Doug's own age who lived next door, was digging a rather ominously shaped hole. Klieg lights ringed the excavation, giving Doug a perfect view of his neighbor, knee-deep in the hole, sweat plastering his brown hair to his forehead, piling shovelfuls of dirt beside him.

Doug blinked, rubbed his face, wondering if perhaps this was a dream. But no, Randall was still digging. And he himself still stood over his toilet, the open seat like a laughing mouth, mocking him, his shortcomings, his failures.

Still he watched, despite himself. Realizing how creepy it might be, surreptitiously spying on his neighbor. Especially with his dick in his hand.

Doug shook out of habit, despite the fact a single drop of piss had yet to escape his sounding hole, and tucked his penis back into his boxers. He knew he should go back to bed, but he couldn't. The hole got deeper. The dirt pile grew taller. Randall got sweatier.

The hole got so deep Randall disappeared, the top of his head dipping below the earth, then his shovel sailed out of the hole and Randall climbed out. He stood, brushed himself off, then loped across the yard, out of range of the lights.

After a moment, Randall reappeared, dragging something behind him. A sack of some sort. Heavy, too. Randall must've been exhausted from all that digging, and now he was dragging something that looked like it weighed a hundred pounds or more. (Lisa Marie Whitman, age thirty-four, one hundred and forty-three pounds to be precise, but Doug Renner had no way of knowing that at the time.)

With great effort, Randall manhandled Lisa to the edge of his nocturnal excavation and, using his dirty, scuffed boots, toed her over the edge.

Doug gaped at the sight. Either his new neighbor had a strange trash disposal method, or—and perhaps this was simply the product of a weary mind roused from sleep at such an ungodly hour—the unfailingly amiable Randall had murdered someone and was now in the final stages of burying them in his backyard.

As if in answer to Doug's musings, Randall picked up the shovel and, spade by spade, began to fill the hole in.

Doug watched, frozen at the bathroom window. Eventually the hole was filled. Randall tamped dirt down with the shovel blade. He speared it into the earth, leaned back, and wiped his forehead with a shirtsleeve.

And then looked directly at Doug.

Coincidentally, at that moment, Doug's bladder finally let go.

After changing his boxers, Doug spent a sleepless night wondering what exactly he'd seen. He thought about calling the police but worried he might be mistaken. Perhaps Randall was merely doing a bit of late night gardening, however unorthodox it might've appeared. Chances were they'd think him a crank, or a busybody, and send his report directly to the circular file. Even if they took him semi-seriously, would his own observations be enough for a warrant? And if Randall was indeed a killer, planting bodies in the backyard like begonias, and was somehow not arrested, wouldn't he assume his next door neighbor was the one who ratted him out? Especially when, Doug feared, they had made *eye contact*?

Doug stared at the ceiling, feeling the walls close in upon him. None of his options seemed remotely palatable.

Then, aswirl in bizarre, insomniac musings, he started to think his other neighbors, the McGills, were also serial killers, when he realized they—Wendy and Everett—were constantly bringing home teenage runaways, dirty and wild-eyed little things, both male and female, who went into their two-story Spanish-style house with the immaculate landscaping and never came out again.

But that wasn't all. There was old Mr. Rooker at the end of the street, who worked as a birthday clown despite his bad back and standoffish personality; a nameless man who never once said hello to Doug and owned a primer-gray panel van; a friendlier-yet-also-nameless woman next door to the van driver, a vivacious blond beauty who waved animatedly to Doug whenever she saw him and had been married five times in the three months he lived on Fairvale Lane; and an older nurse named Nancy at whose hospital senior citizens experienced a mortality rate eight times higher than average.

A mother/son duo, Jennica and Harold Bloch, rounded out his immediate neighbors. Jennica was in her eighties, a shuffling figure with wild cat lady hair and a cat hair-covered shawl, while Harold was probably mid-fifties, nearly six foot six, with a boyish face and a round, egglike body. Sometimes Doug saw Harold in the yard, sitting cross-legged and picking dandelions, and as he passed, his neighbor would look up and meet his eyes while tearing a dandelion petal and blowing it off his finger in Doug's direction.

Less than twenty-four hours after witnessing Randall's nocturnal excavation, Doug became convinced he was surrounded by a cadre of bloodthirsty sociopaths.

He was not wrong.

The McGills, for example, had a crawlspace stuffed with the mummified remains of hitchhikers and runaways. Mr. Rooker *did* in fact use his birthday clown guise to ingratiate himself to families with young children and then, months later, sneak back into their houses to murder everyone with a device of his own invention he called the "Whack-a-Doodler" (taking a page from *The Walking Dead's* playbook, said Whack-a-Doodler was not a baseball bat but an oversized clown mallet wrapped in barbed wire). Nurse Nancy, the severe and alliterative neighbor to his left, really was an Angel of Death, fiddling with doses of crucial medications to ensure her geriatric patients checked into Our Lady of Aldergrove but did not check out. The blond woman—Phaedra Wayne Curtis—had killed more husbands and fiancés than she could count, and the man with the primer-gray van was currently standing before a full-length mirror in his bedroom, wearing the face of a youth pastor he'd met in a truck stop bathroom.

In fact, the only person on Fairvale Lane who was *not* an active serial killer was Doug.

One might wonder how so many sociopaths ended up living right next to each other in a bland suburban tract built in the late '90s. One might also wonder how mild-mannered Doug Renner ended up purchasing a home amongst such monsters.

One could also shut the fuck up.

Randall Magree began to suspect his new neighbor Doug might *not* be a serial killer the night he caught Doug watching him dig a backyard grave for Lisa, Randall's latest LoveStalker match, and didn't fucking offer to help.

It was common courtesy, really. Everyone on Fairvale Lane looked out for each other. Like the time one of the McGills' houseguests, a punky chick with spiky red hair and a denim vest covered in band patches, broke out a basement window and ran to Randall's for help. Within seconds he had her tased, trussed up, and tossed over his shoulder like a sack of potatoes, carrying her right back into the waiting clutches of his neighbors.

Or the time Phaedra ran out of strychnine on a wedding night and rushed over to Nurse Nancy's to borrow some, leaving her latest husband bound to their marital bed with fuzzy pink handcuffs.

Hell, Randall himself had depended on the kindness of his neighbors on more than one occasion. They looked out for each other; that's what a community *was*. And what kind of a neighbor watches a man dig a hole at three in the morning and *not* offer to help?

"Did you ask Stan Harvey about it?" Jennica asked him the next morning while they sipped lemonade on her front porch and watched her son Harold dig up earthworms.

Stan Harvey was the realtor who'd handled Fairvale Lane properties since its inception. While not a serial killer himself, he was—like most successful real estate agents—a clinical sociopath, something of a fellow traveler, and strived to ensure no *undesirable elements* like cops or clergy bought properties in the area.

"On vacation," Randall replied. "His secretary told me they vetted Douglas Renner, though. Said he's the Tonguenapper."

"The *Tonguenapper*?" Jennica replied incredulously. "That's *Daniel Renfield.*"

"Shit."

"Mmhmm. *And* they caught him."

Randall's omnipresent smile threatened to falter, but he caught it, hoisting the corners of his mouth back up like sails in a gale wind. "So he's a normie. What do you think we should do?"

The old woman sipped her lemonade, face twisting like she'd skimped on the sugar. "Pay Stan a visit when he gets back from vacation, that's for sure."

"About Doug."

"Call an HOA meeting. I don't want anybody going off half-cocked. Especially old what's-his-name. The van guy."

Nobody, even the other serial killers, knew what the van guy's name was. Didn't know what his face looked like, either, on account of the fact he was always wearing someone else's, which prompted

Phaedra to refer to him as "Face Face." The fact he was quiet and kept to himself didn't bother Randall. Not everybody could be a social butterfly like him.

"If we have an HOA meeting, technically we have to invite Doug."

Jennica nodded. "Well, of course. Be against the rules not to. But if everybody else happens to show up early, we can talk it over. Figure out what we want to do. We can have it here. I don't get around as well as I used to. And I'll make that buffalo chicken dip you like."

Randall watched Harold dangle a wriggling earthworm over his mouth and pull it away at the last second, like he was fishing for himself. "We haven't had a good old-fashioned get-together in a while."

"Too long. Everybody's so busy these days. But we can't forget what's really important," Jennica said, patting his wrist.

Randall finished his lemonade, melted ice cubes clinking together at the bottom. Rising, he gave his neighbor a smile. "No, we cannot." He stepped off the porch, glancing again at Harold, who was reburying his earthworms.

"We still on for book club next week?" Harold asked.

Randall shot him dual finger-guns. "You know it, brother!"

Harold fired back. "Pow, pow, pow!"

From the porch, Jennica waved. Randall waved back, then headed home, a bounce in his step.

The only thing he loved more than murder was a party.

Doug sat in his La-Z-Boy, living room blinds drawn, staring at a soundless TV. Some shopping network show, pitchwomen fawning over incredibly shitty jewelry that totally wouldn't leave a green ring around their necks. Doug had zero interest in necklaces or shopping in general, but he couldn't follow any of his usual shows, which were mostly of the true-crime variety. Desperate, he even cued up an old episode of *Seinfeld.*

He literally screamed when a crazy clown began stalking Jerry.

Thus, the Home Shopping Network, or perhaps some off-brand equivalent, in case the previous paragraph's remarks about the quality of their jewelry reach their legal department. His mind raced a mile-a-minute, stray thoughts careening off each other and forming a smoking, crumpled impasse in his brain. Doug was sure *something* weird was happening on Fairvale Lane. Something downright nefarious.

He just couldn't figure out what to do about it.

That morning he'd called his twin sister, Kathleen, hoping for a second opinion, but he could barely get a word in over her three screaming triplets, the dog barking, her therapist husband begging everyone to quiet down so he could finish a telehealth session with a suicidal patient.

"So your neighbor was gardening, so what?"

"In the middle of the night? It's weird."

"Or maybe you're the weird one. Paranoid much, Dougie?" She only called him that to remind him she was three minutes older. "Look, do you want to talk to Martin? Technically he can't treat you, but if you're working through some stuff, he's still your brother-in-law—"

A muffled *thump* on Kathleen's end, then the triplet screaming turned to triplet sobbing.

"I gotta go," Kathleen said quickly. "Text me if you want to chat with Martin, bye!"

And so he spent another sleepless night, feeling powerless and afraid and stupid, all at the same time. Wondering if Kat was right. If he was going crazy.

Now, he felt all those things again, but ratcheted up to eleven from lack of sleep. He got up from his chair. Walked over to the front window. Peeked through the blinds.

Fairvale Lane was quiet. Too quiet.

The doorbell rang.

Doug almost had a heart attack. Then a panic attack. Then nearly pissed his pants, *again*.

Stop it, you're being crazy.

Doug angled his gaze to the front porch. Randall stood on the stoop, a huge smile plastered on his face.

Oh god, what if he knows? Doug thought. But then Kathleen's voice chimed in: *Don't be silly, he's just your neighbor.*

Doug took a deep breath and opened the door a few inches. Enough he could slam it if need be. "Randall."

"My man! You got a minute?"

Doug couldn't think of an excuse quickly enough, so he just said, "Yeah?"

"Great, mind if I come in?"

Doug cast a dubious look behind him. He didn't really want Randall in his house. Or any of his neighbors, for that matter.

"Bad time?" Randall asked, his smile never dimming a single lumen. "No worries. Just came by to give you this." He pressed an envelope into Doug's hand.

Doug looked at it like it might contain anthrax.

"It's an invitation. Party at Jennica and Harold's Friday night. Okay, technically it's an HOA meeting, but it's also a party. Her buffalo chicken dip is to die for." Randall headed down the front walk, then spun on his heel and shot finger-guns at Doug. "I'm serious, man, you better be there! Don't make me come looking for you!"

Doug watched him walk down the sidewalk and head up the walk to his own front door. He looked down at the invitation, a sinking feeling forming in his stomach. Doug was a confirmed introvert on the best of occasions. But this kind of party? With *these* kinds of people?

Then again, Randall might've been serious about coming to look for him.

Doug shut the door, sinking to the floor, the invitation unopened in his lap. He hung his head.

What the hell was he going to do?

"We're talking an awful lot about your neighbor," Martin said over Zoom, his voice NPR-soft and be-lisped. He wore box glasses and sported a Van Dyke mustache. "What does that say about you?"

"Huh?"

Martin pursed his lips. "Have you ever heard the term *paranoid schizophrenia*?"

"Yes, Martin. I'm a human living in 2024. Of course I've heard the term."

"Aggressive." Martin scribbled a note on an unseen notepad. "Seems like you're projecting."

"Projecting?"

"Mm. You see, if you're worried your neighbor might be a killer, perhaps that means you actually feel those impulses yourself?"

Doug's face reddened. "Martin, what the hell?"

Another scribbled note. "I'm just trying to help."

"Why are you taking notes?"

Martin blinked. "Notes?"

"This isn't supposed to be a *session*, okay? Just two guys talking."

"There's that paranoia again. What do you think's happening?"

Doug resisted the urge to scream. He should've known this was a mistake. His brother-in-law couldn't switch out of therapy mode to save his life. And from what he was seeing, there was a reason Martin's practice had a three-star average on Yelp.

"Look, Martin. It's been great chatting, but I should really—"

"Really *what,* Doug? Are you getting urges you can't explain? Hearing voices? Are they telling you to kill—"

Doug slammed the laptop shut. Complete waste of time. He hadn't even had a chance to discuss the weird party invitation. He glanced uneasily at the front door, knowing Randall and the rest were out there, somewhere.

His phone rang—Kat. He let it go to voicemail. A moment later, she texted, *Did you seriously just hang up on Martin? He's only trying to help.*

Doug pushed the phone away. It rang again. Kathleen refusing to let it go, a dog with a bone. Typical.

Phone. Again. She'd just keep calling, so he picked up. "Look, Kat, I—"

"Kat? Who's Kat?" a male voice asked.

"Huh?"

"It's Randall. You there, buddy?"

Doug held the phone away like it was smeared with something unpleasant. Kicked himself for not looking at the caller ID again.

When you assume, you make an ass out of you and me, an invisible Kat sing-songed in his head.

"Doug?" Randall's tinny voice chirped through the speakers. "Think we've got a bad connection. I'll come over—"

"I'm here, I'm here," Doug said quickly. "What, uh, what can I do you for?"

"Just checking in, chief. You're still coming to the party tomorrow?"

Doug's hand shook. "Yeah, think so."

"Think so? Think harder, buddy! Everybody's dying to hang out with you."

Doug winced at the choice of words. "Okay."

"I realized I forgot to put it on the invitation. It's BYOB. And no dress code or anything. Come as you are."

"Come as I am," Doug echoed.

"Bingo! Hasta manana." Randall clicked off.

Doug groaned, shut his eyes, and willed himself to think of a plan. Maybe he should just call the cops. They might believe him. Or think him crazy enough to warrant a straitjacket and a rubber room, and at least then he'd be safe.

Then he pictured Kat on visiting day, spooning him Jell-O while the straitjacket chafed his arms, clucking about how she knew he'd always end up like this.

"Fuck this," Doug said, shooting to his feet. There was only one way to figure this out.

He was going to have to dig up Randall's backyard.

No one on Fairvale Lane slept that night.

Wendy and Everett McGill were entertaining a houseguest in *Party Central,* as they called it, a dank cement room accessible via a moving bookcase Everett built himself (he taught woodworking at the community college part-time). Their houseguest, a boy of about nineteen with track marks on his arms and a fuzzy orange beard, was strapped to a metal table where Wendy, wearing a leather squirrel costume, sliced four-inch cuts in his torso with a butcher knife and then gently pressed acorns inside. "It's going to be a cold winter!" she exclaimed, *brr-ing* and pretending to shiver, while the boy writhed in pain and Everett jacked off in the corner.

Jennica and Harold, the mother/son duo, had a guest of their own, this one a transient they'd snatched from outside a gas station. The aged Jennica currently rode piggyback atop her hulking son—a configuration that turned them into a single entity they referred to as the MotherFucker—while their hobbled houseguest crawled across the living room floor, his legs pulverized by repeated smashes from the MotherFucker's sledgehammer.

Nurse Nancy worked the night shift at Our Lady of Aldergrove, administering medications in disproportionate amounts while fudging the paperwork so they'd never trace back to her. Perpetual widow Phaedra held court at TGI Fridays, sipping mudslides and flirting with men so recently divorced they still had wedding-ring tans. The nameless man with the colorless van cruised the streets, like a shark weaving through a coral reef. And Mr. Rooker, dressed in clown makeup, spun the Whack-a-Doodler jauntily as he crept through the backyard of a family he'd recently entertained at a birthday party, noting the flattened grass where a bouncy-castle stood not three weeks before.

Doug mostly hung by the bathroom window, casting furtive glances at Randall's lawn. The party seemed like his best chance— perhaps he could tell Randall he was running late, dig up his yard, and then call the cops? It seemed idiotic, but maybe it was just stupid enough to work.

Decision made, Doug headed to his bedroom, where he intended to barricade himself inside and have what could possibly be his final night's sleep on Earth, since he figured he would almost certainly get caught by one of the many, many serial killers residing on Fairvale Lane and meet an exceedingly gruesome demise, more or less like the ones I've just described, but infinitely more horrible for Doug because it would be happening to *him*.

Then he heard the sound of Randall's garage door rattling up.

Heart pounding, Doug rushed to his window. Randall backed his silver Cybertruck down his driveway and drove off.

Doug's pulse beat faster. Maybe this was his chance. Or maybe Randall was just running a quick errand. How to be sure? Doug wished Kathleen were there. She always knew what to do. That was their whole dynamic, Kathleen the dynamo, Doug happy to trail along in her wake.

Except Kathleen wasn't here. And if Doug had really stumbled onto a secret community of serial killers, it was his sacred duty to put aside his fears and ensure justice was done.

Maybe then his fucking bladder would calm the fuck down and stop being such a dick.

Doug went down to his front porch, snagged the Ring camera from its place by the porchlight, then hurried over to Randall's. He duct-taped the camera to a gutter next to Randall's garage, pointing right at the driveway. If his neighbor came home, the built-in motion detector would alert him.

Next, he grabbed a shovel from his garage, went out the sliding glass door to the backyard, then jumped the fence, ripping his shirt in the process. He glanced down at the shorn fabric, stifling a knee-jerk whine—*but I just bought thaaaat*—and instead proclaimed, "You can't make an omelet without breaking a few eggs."

The cliche gave him strength. He started digging.

Randall Magree wrestled with a horrible conflict. Any decision seemed like the wrong one. Normally self-assured, he actually felt *anxious*. He took a few deep breaths, trying to center his chi, then bit into his Costco hot dog. The bold, reasonably priced flavor ignited his taste buds, gave him clarity.

"Fuck it. Cool Ranch Doritos it is." He threw two bags of chips, each the size of a Midwestern toddler, into his cart, and kept moving down the aisle.

Even though Jennica was hosting their party, he volunteered for the grocery run. He would've loved to host himself, show off his

Man Cave—a self-dug aperture beneath his house containing the corpses of an entire chapter of the Nu Sigma Epsilon fraternity—but given that Jennica was getting on in years, he was more than happy to defer to her wishes.

Randall checked his list. Chips, salsa, cocktail wieners, duct tape, Morton's salt, pliers, Cheese Whiz, crackers, paper plates, bleach, plasticware. Pretty standard. He headed over to the grocery aisle and eyed the hummus. Then eyed a woman in her thirties in a tight top advertising a local yoga studio, imagining how great she'd look with her limbs hacked off and nailed to his bedroom wall. Then back to the hummus.

"Have you tried this?" he asked her, holding up a tub of roasted red pepper and garlic.

She held up her left hand, a diamond gleaming under the fluorescent lights. "My fiancé loves that shit."

"Sorry. Honest question." Randall threw the hummus in his cart and hurried away. He hadn't been hitting on her; he just wanted a second opinion on his hummus selection. He felt kind of bad for her. That sort of paranoid thinking wasn't good for anyone.

Randall pulled his cart up in front of the cheese section, losing himself in an entirely new dilemma.

Then his phone rang.

"Go for Randall," he said, cradling his phone between chin and shoulder while he weighed the merits of apricot or blueberry goat cheese.

"Harold saw someone poking around in your backyard."

"Let me talk to him!" Harold shouted in the background. "I'm neighborhood watch captain."

"No, *I'm* talking to Randall, *you're* finishing your Hamburger Helper."

There was a brief commotion on the other end. Randall chose the blueberry goat cheese and went in search of an appropriate cracker.

"Randall," Harold said breathlessly. "I think there's somebody in your yard."

Randall parsed the cracker selection, trying to remember if Phaedra was still gluten-free. "What makes you say that, buddy?"

"Somebody hopped your fence. He had a shovel."

"Give me the phone back," Jennica shrieked.

Randall checked his smartwatch. His resting pulse rate was up to 87 BPM; he was practically hyperventilating. "A shovel, you say?"

"And he was wearing black. Might've been a ninja."

"You never know," Randall said. "Good looking out, I knew we elected you neighborhood watch captain for a reason."

"Thanks, Randall. You want me to go over there?"

"Nah, you finish that Hamburger Helper, chief. I'm on my way." He hung up, eyeing his full cart. He hated to leave all this stuff for some poor employee to put back. But this was an emergency.

Randall Magree power-walked out of Costco, then broke into a sprint once he reached the parking lot. He couldn't know exactly who was messing around in his yard.

But he had a pretty good fucking idea.

Chunk!

Doug speared his shovel into the ground once more. He'd made pitiful progress. Maybe two feet. His arms burned. Despite the cool night air, he was sweating his balls off. He'd doffed his T-shirt, tying it around his head to keep the perspiration out of his eyes, which made him look like a low-rent Rambo or maybe an even lower-rent extra from *Rambo III*. His pale, baby-bird chest glistened in the moonlight. He wasn't sure if he'd ever been this tired.

Still, he kept digging. He hoped Randall wasn't on his way home.

The jerry-rigged security camera would give him enough time to hop the fence again, but not enough to fill the hole in. Randall would know someone had been in his yard.

All he could do was dig and pray he hit pay dirt before his neighbor returned.

Doug tossed another shovelful of dirt aside, then stopped to catch his breath.

Then completely forgot about breathing.

Lights were on in his living room. A shadow moved across the room, then disappeared.

"Fuck me."

Someone was in *his* house.

Randall?

Panic welled up inside of him. His bladder felt intensely full. Doug looked around the yard, but luckily he was still alone. He hopped out of the pathetic hole he'd dug and quickly pushed dirt back in. To both his elation and chagrin, he managed to refill his forty-five minute hole in less than five, all the while keeping one eye on his house. The lights were still on. He thought about calling the cops but wasn't sure what to tell them. How to explain an apparent prowler he'd seen while prowling himself?

Just tell them everything, he thought. But it was too late for that. Without a body, they'd write Doug off as a loon. He was covered in dirt and sweat and wearing a sodden T-shirt wrapped around his head, for Chrissakes.

Doug tamped the soil down as best he could, then hopped the fence back into his yard, heart hammering. He clutched the shovel tightly, advancing across the grass. A new plan took shape. If he could catch Randall off-guard, he could brain him. Tie him up. Doug wasn't really sure what he'd do from there. Maybe torture him. With music. Really bad music. Play "It's a Small World" until Randall admitted to his crimes.

And *then* he could go to the police. Probably.

Doug approached the sliding glass door to his family room. The TV was on and someone was sitting in his easy chair.

Maybe he could catch him unaware.

Doug snuck around the side of the house and slowly opened the side door to the garage. No one inside. He still felt nervous, but this was *his* house. He had every right to be here, and because he was an American he had every right to bash anyone he found inside with a shovel. He—

Caught his elbow on a spray paint can, knocking it off the metal shelf where he kept assorted garagey crap. The can hit the concrete floor with a *ding,* spinning off under his Volvo.

Uh oh.

Doug froze, turning to the door into the kitchen. He cocked back the shovel, ready to swing on anyone who came through.

After the longest thirty seconds of his life, he felt reasonably certain the man in the living room had not heard him. Doug took a deep breath and reached for the door. Once inside, he could circle around the kitchen island and into the family room, guaranteeing him a blind angle on the man in his chair.

Centimeter by centimeter, he turned the doorknob until he felt the latch bolt retract, then opened the door. Immediately he heard the TV, news anchors arguing indistinctly, a low drone that provided perfect cover noise. Doug padded across the tile, shovel at the ready. He rounded the island, the man in his easy chair coming into view. All he could see was the back of the man's head. Brown hair.

Randall.

Doug lunged forward, cocking back the shovel—

The hall toilet flushed.

Doug froze, mid-swing. The bathroom door opened, and Kathleen came out.

"Dougie? What are you doing?"

The man in the easy chair turned.

It was Martin.

Doug stood stock still, in the middle of his family room, feeling like a complete fucking idiot. Then his phone chimed.

Randall was home.

Randall parked a few doors down from his house. He grabbed a .38 from his glove compartment and hoofed it, slinking around the side of his house. He wasn't sure how all this was going to play out, but he was extremely irritated. Mostly at Stan Harvey, for failing to adequately vet his new neighbor. Because of that idiotic slip-up, everything was devolving. A goddamn *normie* had moved into their community, their sanctuary, and had apparently taken it upon himself to dig up Randall's "garden."

"This used to be a nice neighborhood," Randall muttered, then eased the gate open.

Nothing.

Randall scanned the bushes, the shadows, looking for a nosy interloper with a shovel. Nobody was there. He sighed and shoved the .38 in his waistband, then walked into the backyard. He glanced at Harold and Jennica's house. The big man was peering out a window. He caught Randall's gaze and gave him a thumbs-up.

Randall returned it, then paced the yard.

Just as he'd feared, the dirt over Lisa Marie Whitman's grave had been disturbed. He bent down, ran a hand over it. Unbelievable. He tried so hard to be a good neighbor, to support everyone. To lend a hand whenever it was needed. And *this* was how the universe chose to repay him?

Randall stood, sniffing the night air, slowly turning in a circle until his gaze fixed upon Doug Renner's house. Lights were on inside. Had Doug discovered his secret? If so, he should really be grabbing his go-bag and hitting the road. Randall wasn't stupid; he knew his compulsion for burying his playmates close by would eventually catch up to him. A man with his compunctions would be an idiot to think the FBI would never come sniffing around his door. He just never thought he'd get screwed over by one of his own *neighbors.*

And yet.

If Doug found the body, he would've called the cops. Sirens would be filling the air, cop cars and maybe a tac unit descending on Fairvale Lane. But the night was quiet.

The ground was obviously disturbed. But Doug had filled it in. What could that mean?

Maybe he's one of us after all, Randall thought. *Maybe he's playing a game.*

All Randall knew for sure was at that moment, Douglas Renner was the most dangerous man on Fairvale Lane.

"Dougie, really?" Kathleen said, pointing at the shovel. "What's going on with you?"

Martin rose from the chair, adjusting his glasses and running a hand down his Van Dyke. "What are you feeling right now?"

"Cut the shit, Martin," Kathleen snapped. "My brother almost brained you with a shovel. Who gives a fuck what he's feeling? What are you *thinking,* Doug?"

Doug dropped the shovel. It clattered to the ground. He looked from Kat to Martin and back again. "What are you doing here?"

Kathleen marched right up to him. "You weren't answering your phone. We were worried about you."

"You could've texted instead of breaking into my house."

"Right. Those things you weren't answering? Where were you?"

"Oh." Doug looked down at himself. Covered in filth. "Doing some gardening?"

"You look like shit. Your shirt's torn."

"Hey, let's not get too judgmental," Martin said, holding up his hands. "Appearances can be deceiving. Doug, why don't you sit down?"

Doug sighed, shoulders slumping, and made his way to the couch. He sat, realized he was probably smearing dirt everywhere, then decided it didn't matter. Nothing mattered.

Kathleen came over and sat next to him. "Seriously, what's going on? We're worried about you."

"We just want to make sure you're living your best life," Martin said. "Authentically."

"What the fuck does that— Oh, never mind." Kathleen put a hand over his shoulders. "Come on, Doug. I'm your sister. You can tell me anything."

"I tried to, the other day—"

"Yeah, having triplets is a bitch, I'm sorry. But I'm here now."

Doug forced himself to look into her eyes. She had a point. They'd always shared everything. All his suspicions about his neighbors felt like an iron weight around his neck. Kat could share the burden, just like she'd always done.

Couldn't she?

"I think my neighbor's a serial killer," Doug blurted out.

Kathleen and Martin shared a wary glance. Silence hung heavy in the family room.

"What, uh," Martin finally managed, "what makes you say that?"

Those few, halting words opened the floodgates. Doug told them everything, starting with the moment he'd glimpsed Randall Magree burying what looked like a body in his backyard. All his observations of his other neighbors, from the chronic widow

Phaedra to the McGills and their houseguests to creepy Mr. Rooker and Harold and Jennica and even the mysterious man with the gray van.

When he was done, he slumped forward on the couch, then cautiously looked at his sister.

"Okay," Kathleen said.

Martin sat down beside him, putting a hand on his knee. "Doug, I respect your truth. But it's important to remember everyone has their own truth. And yours might not match up with your neighbors'. The good news is that's one of the fun things about being human. When our truths don't sync up. Because that's when we can listen, learn, and grow."

Doug gaped at his brother-in-law. "Martin, what the fuck are you talking about?"

"I think he means," Kathleen interjected, "that you're overthinking things. You've been single way too long. When was the last time you had a conversation with someone who wasn't us?"

"You don't get it," Doug said. "These people are *weird*. This place is *weird*. You haven't seen what I've seen."

"Doug, serial killers aren't real," Martin said. "They're just a media creation."

"Hun, I know this is your field, but serial killers are one thousand percent real," Kathleen corrected.

"They're all up to something," Doug said. "There's something off. And don't you think it's odd none of these people have kids?"

"*You* don't have kids."

Martin drew a face. "Fertility issues are a very sensitive subject. You shouldn't bring them up so cavalierly."

"Hun. Stop."

"Sorry," Martin said, patting Doug on the shoulder. "Hard to switch it off sometimes. I'm honestly just here as your brother-in-law. And, I'd like to think, your friend."

Doug eyed Martin's hand until the other man removed it.

"Dougie, why don't you stay with us for a few days? The kids would love to see you."

Doug thought about it. It would be nice to get away from Fairvale Lane. Get some clarity, a little peace of—

The doorbell rang.

Martin stood. "I'll get it."

"Don't answer it!" Doug yelled, then kicked himself for yelling.

Martin blinked at him. "Huh? Why?"

"Weren't you listening to the entire story I just told you?"

"What does that have to do with anything?"

Doug stifled the urge to scream, instead bunching up his fists. Martin meant well, but he could be so utterly maddening sometimes. He opened his mouth to say something.

And realized Kathleen was no longer in the living room.

"You're Doug's *sister*?" a playful, incredulous voice echoed down the hallway. "Nah, you've got to be his niece, right?"

Doug's blood ran cold. A second later, Kathleen entered the room with Randall in tow. His sister was tittering like a schoolgirl and lightly touching Randall's arm.

"Doug, you never told me your neighbor is so charming."

Randall strolled in like he owned the place, face lighting up when he saw Martin. He pulled him in for a bro-hug. "Man, it is *so* nice to meet you guys!"

Martin pulled away awkwardly. "*You guys* is—"

Randall turned to Doug. "I got to say, I'm a little put out."

"What?"

Randall gestured at Martin and Kathleen. "Well, you're having people over for the first time since you moved in and you didn't invite me? Ouch."

"I'm not—"

"I know the party's not till tomorrow," Randall said, "but since you've got company, we might as well get it started now." He crossed the room to the small wooden hutch where Doug kept a small, mostly untouched assortment of booze. "Don't mind if I raid your liquor cabinet?"

"What the hey," Martin said. "White wine spritzer, if you could."

Doug caught Kathleen's gaze, mouthed, *Call the cops.*

She shook her head. Replied, *Calm down.*

He's a fucking serial killer.

Stop.

"You mind if I open this?" Randall said, spinning around with a bottle of Glenfiddich. "Of course you don't. Glasses, glasses, where would I be if I were a cocktail glass?" Randall bent down to look under the hutch. "Aha!"

Doug's mind raced, trying to come up with some way to convince Kathleen of the seriousness of their situation. Randall had barged into his house for a reason, likely because he'd discovered Doug's pathetic attempt at playing detective. Now he was using his sparkling personality to mesmerize Kathleen and Martin, which could only mean he was planning something vile. Like murdering the three of them. And since Kat wouldn't listen, there was almost nothing Doug could do to stop it.

Almost.

The shovel leaned against the kitchen counter, where he'd left it in lieu of returning it to the garage.

"I'll grab some ice!" Doug said, hurrying to the kitchen.

He was almost there when Randall's hand clamped onto his arm. "I like mine neat. How about you guys?" He nodded at Kathleen and Martin.

"Neat's fine," Kathleen said.

"I was really hoping for that white wine spritzer."

Doug shook loose from Randall's grip. "I think I've got some chardonnay in the fridge."

"You don't," Randall said. He passed Kathleen a rocks glass, then gave one to Martin, who held it up to the light and sniffed uncertainly.

Randall pressed a third drink into Doug's hand, then grabbed one for himself, raising it to the ceiling. "How about a toast? To neighbors, to family, to the bonds that unite us."

"What a beautiful speech," Kathleen said, beaming.

She lifted the glass to her lips.

"Don't drink that!" Doug screamed, knocking the glass from her hands. It fell to the carpet, spilling but not breaking.

"Dougie, what the hell?" Kathleen said, glowering at him and her empty hand.

Martin froze mid-sip. "Yeah, that's not okay."

"It's poisoned!" Doug cried. He pushed Martin and Kathleen away, then turned to face Randall, bravely putting himself between his family and the man he strongly suspected was a serial killer.

Randall looked confused. "Chief? Did I say something wrong?"

"You put something in it, didn't—"

"You could've just said you didn't want me opening the good stuff," Randall said evenly, the smile never leaving his face. "Look, I'll just go, okay?"

"Don't be ridiculous," Kathleen said quickly, pushing Doug aside. She took Randall's hand. "I'm *so* sorry about my brother. He's been a little off lately."

"I keep saying he needs to be in treatment," Martin added. "Erratic behavior and all."

"I'm not *erratic*," Doug protested. Then remembered his filthy clothing and realized how dumb that sounded.

Randall took a long swill from his glass, then set it down on the hutch. "I shouldn't have barged in like this. I'll get out of your hair."

"No, don't go," Kathleen said, disappointment evident in her face. "Like I said, I'm so sorry about all this."

Martin glanced at his watch. "*Actually,* we should be getting back soon. Told the babysitter we'd be home before ten."

"Probably best we call it a night," Randall said. "I'll see you at the party tomorrow, Doug." He headed off down the hallway, calling over his shoulder, "And take a shower, man. No offense, but you smell like death."

Randall watched Doug's sister and her husband leave from his upstairs window, chatting quietly with each other on their way to the Prius. Before getting into the car, Kathleen turned and yelled something. Then they drove off.

Given how the night started, Randall couldn't have been happier with the result. His patented charm had disarmed Doug's family completely. For his part, Doug had come off like a crazy person, playing right into Randall's plan.

Okay, maybe it hadn't been a plan, then. Randall had been winging it. But *now* a plan was forming in his head. A brilliantly diabolical plan. He felt sort of bad about it; he genuinely liked Doug, the same way he genuinely liked everyone he met, even if he ended up killing them, because at his core, Randall Magree was a people person.

But Doug had brought this fate upon himself.

After a quick text pow-wow with the other owners, a sort of impromptu virtual HOA meeting, Doug called Harold, who picked up on the third ring. "Neighborhood watch."

"Hey, buddy, it's me. Got a sec?"

"Sure."

"I need a favor."

Doug Renner stood in the mirror, adjusting his tie. Randall had said the party didn't have a dress code, but he wanted to show up looking his best—or as good as he could look under the circumstances, with the heavy bags under his eyes and sallow complexion—as a kind of apology for his behavior the previous night.

At first, after everyone left, it hadn't occurred to him how badly he'd gone off the rails. He locked his doors, took a sharp knife from the kitchen drawer, and prowled the top floor anxiously, peeking out the windows, alert to any activity. But Fairvale Lane was quiet. Except for Kat's last words ringing in his ears—*keep this shit up, you'll die alone.*

Eventually, he got in the shower. The hot stream washed away Randall's dirt and, surprisingly, a good bit of anxiety, leaving in its wake a terrible feeling Doug was all too familiar with:

Shame.

When Doug tried to look at the situation from an outsider's point of view—Kathleen, for example, who since leaving for home had inundated his phone with several variations on the same theme, i.e. *what is wrong with you*—he began to see things differently. What did he really have to go on? Foibles and idiosyncrasies? His pathetic, aborted attempt to find actual evidence to back up the batshittery failed. Maybe his sister and brother-in-law were right. He'd been single too long, shut up with his own thoughts, allowing paranoia to bloom. What if he fixated on Randall because he was so friendly, and Doug's low self-esteem interpreted any interest in boring old him as a red flag?

If Randall really wanted to kill him, he could've done so already. Kathleen and Martin too. And yet he'd stood there, accepting Doug's accusation with a smile on his face, and didn't even walk away angry, nor did he rescind Doug's invitation to the party, which would've tracked, considering the scene Doug made.

Maybe Doug had been wrong about everything. Like usual.

Doug stepped out of the shower, dried off, and put himself to bed.

Now, tie straightened, he went downstairs and grabbed the bottle of chardonnay he'd bought for the occasion. He actually felt slightly confident. He'd even talked with Kat earlier, who pointed out he might feel better if he formally met his other neighbors and gave them a chance to get to know him.

"Nothing's scarier than the unknown," she said.

He left his house, walking past Randall's to Harold and Jennica's next door. Their home was decorated for the occasion: brightly colored balloons and tinsel draped the front porch. He looked up at the house, feeling silly. If they were planning to murder him, why would they *decorate*?

"Oh, Doug," he said, chuckling softly. "You're going to be the death of me."

Then he snapped a proof-of-life selfie and texted it and Jennica and Harold's address to Kathleen, just in case.

She shot back a thumbs-up. *You can do this!*

The porch creaked when Doug put his weight on it. Not ominously, more like a friendly, cartoon-rodent squeak. He laughed again, shaking his head. What in the world had he been thinking?

Taking a deep breath, Doug knocked on the front door.

Footsteps echoed from inside the house. Doug grappled with the urge to turn tail and run but stifled it. Everything was fine. This would be *fun.*

Randall opened the door, wearing a striped blue shirt, untucked over jeans, and holding a martini glass. He lit up—as much as it was possible, considering his perpetually sunny demeanor—when he saw Doug, clapping him on the shoulder so hard gin spilled over the lip of his martini glass.

"Good to see you, man. I was worried you weren't coming after last night."

Doug smiled sheepishly. "Sorry about that. I don't know what got into me."

"It's my fault for barging in like that. Totally rude. Won't happen again, okay?"

"Okay."

"Well, don't just stand here, come on in!"

Randall led Doug into the living room, where the other residents of Fairvale Lane waited. The McGills, dressed casually and sipping craft beers. Phaedra, sporting an expensive new engagement ring. The man with the gray van wore several facemasks—Doug could appreciate his Covid cautiousness, seemed sensible. Mr. Rooker stood in a corner next to a helium tank, making balloon animals. Jennica was dressed in a vintage black evening gown and elbow-length gloves, holding court in a leather La-Z-Boy by the unlit fireplace.

"I have that same chair," Doug muttered.

"Friends and neighbors! May I present Mr. Douglas Renner?" Randall called in his best village crier voice, topping it off with a bow.

A chorus of greetings came from the other residents. Phaedra patted an empty spot next to her on the couch. "Come join me, Doug."

"Okay."

He sat down, somebody took his wine, somebody else gave him a glass, and the evening commenced, a whirlwind of conversation and music and a rousing game of charades, which the McGills dominated. Jennica regaled the assemblage with stories from her hippy days, thankfully never once mentioning the Manson family or quoting "Helter Skelter." Randall cleared the furniture from the middle of the room, put on some Black Eyed Peas, and proceeded to pop and lock, causing his audience to erupt in *oohs, aahs,* and sporadic applause. Mr. Rooker pressed a balloon into Doug's hands that, he had to admit, was a stunningly good likeness of himself given the medium.

They ate cheese and crackers and buffalo chicken dip. Phaedra dabbed at the corner of Doug's mouth when he got a little dip stuck to his lip, giggling flirtatiously. Booze flowed like a speakeasy. Doug, the occasional drinker, caught quite a buzz and was even persuaded by Randall to join him on the impromptu dance floor for the "Chicken Dance."

All in all, it was a damn good time.

At one point, Doug realized someone was missing. "Where's Harold?" he asked Jennica, having to shout to be heard over the latest hip hop anthem Randall queued up on Spotify.

"He's a little under the weather," Jennica replied.

"Oh. Should we be quiet?"

"Nah, he can't hear us. He's out."

And that was the only wrinkle, mild as it was, in what was easily the best night of Doug's forties, and possibly his thirties too. Maybe it was the booze, but he felt a deep kinship with these people he'd mostly only met hours before. Everything grew deliciously fuzzy.

He ended the night in the middle of Jennica's living room, arm slung around Randall, repeating feverishly, over and over and over again:

"I love you guys."

Doug awoke, groggy, mouth dry and head pounding. His bed felt hard. Cool to the touch. He opened his eyes and didn't recognize the ceiling for a moment.

Then he realized he was lying in his bathtub, fully clothed.

"Oh, man." He rubbed his eyes.

"Hey, there he is."

Doug yelped and bolted upright. Randall was sitting on the toilet, seat down, thankfully also fully clothed. Light streamed in from the bathroom window.

"What're you doing here?"

Randall passed him a glass of water from the bathroom counter. "Here, drink some of this."

Doug did. He pounded the entire glass. "Ow."

"Yeah, you really tied one on last night. It was epic."

"I didn't do anything too embarrassing, did I?"

Randall waved dismissively. "You were a huge hit. Everybody loved you. Hopefully I won't have to twist your arm to get you out next time."

"Huh." Doug stood, his legs wobbly beneath him, and leaned against the shower tile. "Guess I should thank you. For making sure I got home."

Randall laughed. "You would've made it. But you definitely did try to take a shower with all your clothes on. I tried to get you to go to bed, but you passed out right there. Figured I should hang around. You know you can drown in six inches of water?"

"Oh." Doug's face turned crimson. "Sorry."

"Don't worry about it. What're neighbors for, right?"

Doug stepped out of the bathtub. His head spun for a second, then stopped. He took a few breaths. He actually didn't feel too bad. A little rough around the edges, sure, but the thrill of the night before was still with him. The excitement.

"Well, I appreciate it. But I think I'm going to get cleaned up and then maybe take a nap."

Randall rose, cracked his knuckles. "Heard that. I'll be out of your hair in a second. Just need to show you something first."

"What's that?" Doug hoped it would be brunch-related.

Randall went over to the window. "Out here."

"Okay." Doug crossed the room to stand next to him, blinking in the morning light. "What am I looking at?"

"Check out your yard."

Doug pressed his face against the window. "What the heck?"

Someone had re-sodded his entire backyard while he was passed out.

"Yeah, just a little surprise for you," Randall said. "Can you believe Harold did it all himself?"

"I thought he was sick."

"Nah, that was a fib. We wanted to keep you busy so we could surprise you with this. A little housewarming gift."

Doug's head spun again, and not from the lingering booze. None of this made sense. Why would Harold skip his own party to landscape his neighbor's yard? Granted, it looked nice, Doug had been thinking about tearing up the half-dead grass and maybe putting in a zeroscape, but it also felt weirdly invasive.

"It looks great," Doug said, which was true, "but it's a little... much."

Randall clapped him on the shoulder. "Nothing's too good for my pal Doug." He turned Doug away from the window, a conspiratorial glint in his eye. "But there *is* something else."

Doug swallowed, his mouth suddenly dry again. "What?"

"See, you sort of put me in a bind. Not your fault, this is squarely on that jackass realtor." Randall cleared his throat. "Let's get real with each other for a second. Like *really* real. Can you do that for me, chief?"

"What're you talking about?"

"Doug, I know you think I'm a serial killer. Or thought, before last night. Kathleen told me."

"Kat? Why would she—"

"We traded numbers. She asked me to keep an eye on you. But you've been keeping an eye on me, Doug. Haven't you?"

"I don't—"

"Come on, buddy. I saw you watching me the other night. Everybody else, too. You think we're a bunch of murderers. And," he leaned in closer to Doug, so close Doug gagged on his Cool Water cologne, "you were right."

The words ping-ponged around in Doug's skull. *You were right. You were right. You were—*

Doug tried to run for the door. But he was wearing socks, he slipped on the tile, the ceiling cartwheeling through his vision.

Randall caught him, hands under his armpits, lowered him down to the floor, and stood over him.

Doug raised his hands, awkwardly trying to fend off any murder attempts. "Leave me alone!"

Randall raised his hands too, taking a step back. "Easy there, chief. I'm not going to hurt you."

"Why should I believe you? You just admitted to being a, a—"

"Serial killer. Like I said, you were right on the money. I've got a, well, I used to consider it a problem, but that sounds so negative. I prefer to think of it as a *feature*. I've got this compulsion. Everybody else does too. Harold, Jennica, the McGills. Hell, you had to wonder why Phaedra gets married every other week and then her husband disappears, right?"

Doug nodded slowly. Mostly because he was terrified any sudden movement might cause him to piss himself.

"It's just who we are. And it's who you were supposed to be, too. But our realtor fucked up. Sold you, a perfectly normal—and might I add pretty fucking rad—guy a house on our block. He really jammed us up, Doug."

"You're all serial killers," Doug said robotically, his brain still trying to catch up to this new reality.

Randall nodded. "Yep. Or *murder enjoyers*, like the kids say." He grinned. "Learned that from Mr. Rooker. Dude's always up on the new slang."

Doug tried to scooch away, but the toilet stopped him. "You're monsters."

"What's the old saying? One man's freedom fighter is another's terrorist? Morality's relative, Doug. And sure, maybe killing people isn't *ideal.* But we're not monsters. We look out for each other. We have fun. Like last night, pretty good time, right? And nobody got murdered. I think." Randall stooped to a knee, coming down to Doug's level. "Look, being a neighbor's about learning to coexist. To care about people because of your differences, not despite them. I was serious when I said I wasn't going to hurt you, Doug. What would that accomplish?"

"You wouldn't have to worry about me calling the police." Doug shook his head as soon as he said the words. Was he really arguing in *favor* of his own murder? What would Martin have to say about that?

Randall smiled gently. "Okay, two things. One, I don't *want* to murder you. Nobody does. I think I've been pretty clear on that point. And two, if we killed you, your relatives would just inherit the house, and eventually we'd have a whole new neighbor to deal with. So we've got to learn to live together. But," he held up a finger, "we can't have you talking to the cops, either. Or your sister. Even though she's pretty cool. So we found another way."

"What do you mean?"

"While you were busy doing the 'Chicken Dance,' Harold was digging up a bunch of bodies from all over the neighborhood and burying them in *your* backyard. Hence the sod."

Doug's stomach practically dropped out of his asshole. "WHAT?"

"Yep," Randall said, rising again. "A whole bunch of bodies. Like an obscene amount. And they're all. Down. There." He cocked his chin at the window.

Doug's body went cold. Freezing. He was shaking. "No, no, no."

Randall headed for the door. "You could try to get rid of them yourself. But like I said, there's a *lot*. And if you start digging up your yard, well?" He pantomimed holding a cell phone to his ear. "Hello, police? I'd like to report a murder. Er, murders."

"You wouldn't."

"I like you, Doug. But I like not being in prison more. So enjoy your new yard, try not to think about what's buried under the soil, and make the best of it. Live and let live, right?"

He gave Doug a wink and walked out of the bathroom.

Doug lay there, head resting on the toilet seat, completely in shock. Listening to Randall tramp down the stairs, whistling a tune. The front door opened and closed. He stared at the ceiling, the light from the window no longer cheery but oppressive. Like it was filled with ghosts.

"Fuck my life," Doug muttered.

To his credit, he didn't piss himself.

Stan Harvey was furious. His trip to the Bahamas had been a bust, between food poisoning from the shrimp buffet and an allergic reaction to the massage oil his masseuse used, which ensured his endings were anything but happy. On top of that, his flight had been delayed, causing him to miss his connection. He'd gotten stuck in Dallas/Fort Worth for six hours.

Now, he was finally home, but Stan wasn't the kind of guy to let things go. Once he got inside and poured himself a scotch, he'd go out to the garage and pound the heavy bag. Maybe call up a few suicide hotlines and tell the operators to kill themselves, he wasn't sure yet. He just wanted to kick off his shoes and act like a huge fucking dick in the privacy of his own home.

Stan entered, dropping his bags at the door. He had a maid

service scheduled the next day; they could get that shit. He ambled through the foyer, cracking his neck, then into the den, flipping the light on.

Randall Magree reclined in his easy chair. "Stanno, my man."

Stan blanched. "What the fuck are you doing in my house?"

"What, I can't pay a visit to my favorite realtor?"

"You could call the office like a normal human being."

"Oh, Stan," Randall said, mock-sadly shaking his head. "You know I'm anything but."

On cue, the other residents of Fairvale Lane entered the room: Nurse Nancy, in scrubs, carrying a syringe. Phaedra, cocktail-chic as always. The McGills, Wendy in her leather squirrel outfit, Everett rocking assless chaps and holding a cheese grater. Mr. Rooker in full clown paint, twirling his Whack-a-Doodler. The man with the primer-gray van, wearing an Asian woman's face for some reason. And finally, Harold and Jennica, the MotherFucker themself, dragging a sledgehammer across Stan's hardwood floors, Harold ducking low so piggy-backing Jennica didn't crack her head on the doorframe.

Jennica carried a foil-wrapped casserole dish containing leftover buffalo chicken dip. In case anybody got hungry, after.

Stan backed away, frantically looking from one former client to another. "What the hell is this about? I did everything you asked."

"Douglas Renner," Randall said. For once, his omnipresent smile had disappeared, his mouth now forming a thin, cold line.

"The new guy? The Tonguenapper?"

"That's *Daniel Renfield*," Jennica hissed with such venom her dentures popped partially out of her mouth. "And *he's* in prison."

Stan's face went pale beneath his newly acquired Caribbean tan. "Oh, fuck."

Randall Magree nodded to his neighbors, and together they converged on Stan Harvey. The MotherFucker sledgehammered his toes. Everett McGill sheared off Bahamas-tanned flesh with his cheese grater, feeding slices to Wendy. Phaedra borrowed a stolen scalpel from Nurse Nancy to carve P+S 4-EVA into the realtor's back, ringing it with a heart. Mr. Rooker Whack-a-Doodled. And the man with the primer-gray van began to slice Stan's face off.

As Randall watched each of them, with their own paraphilias, their own methods, their own victimologies, all tearing a sack-of-shit realtor to shreds, a warm feeling welled up in his chest.

Sure, they had their differences. But at the end of the day, they were a community.

That's what really counted.

CAN YOU HANDLE EVIL LITTLE FUCKS?

Evil comes in fun-sized packages.

Behind the facade of sweetness and light, there lurks a darkness that defies comprehension as the veil of innocence is cruelly stripped away to reveal something far more sinister. Journey through the twisted minds of evil children, those who are born not of childish whimsy, but rather sprout from the seeds of nightmares.

Presenting *Evil Little Fucks*, a curated anthology of horror stories penned by leading authors in the genre. Traverse a universe where humanity's own offspring unleash a level of brutality that surpasses the capabilities of most adults. Just remember, you brought them into this world, and you just might have to take them out.

Brought to you by Sinister Smile Press, a division of Crystal Lake Publishing.

EVIL LTTL FUCKS

Join the Crystal Lake community today!

Subscribe to our Newsletter!
(Scan the QR code or click if eBook)

Subscribe to our Patreon!
(Scan the QR code or click if eBook)

**Visit our Linktree for
all social media sites!**
(Scan the QR code or click if eBook)

Download our catalog!
(Scan the QR code or click if eBook)

ABOUT THE AUTHORS

Jay Bower is a horror author living outside St. Louis, MO, in the forest of Southern Illinois. He spends his time reading, writing, and convincing his wife the dark stories he writes do not involve her. Find out more about Jay at jaybowerauthor.com.

MJ Mars is the author of *The Suffering*, which was published by Wicked House in 2023. You can also find MJ's work in Dark Peninsula Press's *Negative Space and Negative Space 2 - A Return to Survival Horror*, Colors in Darkness' *Deadly Bargains*, and Silver Empire's *Secret Stairs*. She has featured on the *No Sleep Podcast* and *The Dread Machine*. MJ lives in Lancaster, UK, where the city's dark history of witches, ghosts, and monsters gives her endless inspiration. *The Fovea Experiments* and *The Suffering 2* coming soon. Find out more about MJ at mjmarsauthor.com.

Steven Pajak, a Chicago-based author, crafts stories that explore the depths of horror and the human psyche. With a pen that dances on the edges of darkness, Steven brings to life tales that challenge, terrify, and linger in the minds of readers. Drawing inspiration from the urban tapestry of Chicago, his work merges the pulse of city life with the eerie quiet of the shadows lurking within the darkest corners of our minds. Steven invites you into a world where fear meets courage, and the journey through his imagination proves as haunting as it is unforgettable. Find out more about Steven at stevenpajak.com.

Candace Nola is a multiple award-winning author, editor, and publisher. She writes poetry, horror, dark fantasy, and extreme horror content. Books include *Breach, Beyond the Breach, Hank Flynn, Bishop, Earth vs The Lava Spiders, The Unicorn Killer, Unmasked, The Vet,* and *Desperate Wishes.* Her short stories can be found in *The Baker's Dozen* anthology, *Secondhand Creeps, American Cannibal, Just A Girl, The Horror Collection: Lost Edition,* and *Exactly the Wrong Things,* with many more coming throughout 2023. She is the creator of *Uncomfortably Dark,* which focuses primarily on promoting indie horror authors and small presses with weekly book reviews, interviews, and special features. Find out more about Candace at uncomfortablydark.com.

Rebecca Rowland is a Bram Stoker Award–nominated editor (*American Cannibal*) of seven anthologies and a horror cocktail book and a Shirley Jackson Award–nominated author (*White Trash & Recycled Nightmares*) of three short fiction collections, one novel, and too many novellas and short stories, one of which, *Optic Nerve,* snagged a Readers' Choice 666 Award from Godless Horror. Despite her love of the ocean and distaste for cold weather, Rebecca makes her home in a landlocked and often icy corner of New England (USA). To indulge in her tomfoolery, follow her on Instagram at Rebecca_Rowland_books or visit RowlandBooks.com.

Gage Greenwood is the best-selling author of the Winter's Myths Saga, and *Bunker Dogs.* He's a proud member of the Horror Writers Association and Science Fiction and Fantasy Writers association. He's been an actor, comedian, podcaster, and even the vice president of an escape room company. Since childhood, he's been a big fan of comic books, horror movies, and depressing music that fills him with existential dread. Gage lives in New England with his girl-friend and son, and he spends his time writing, hiking, and decorating for various holidays. Find out more about Gage at gagegreenwood.com.

Mike Salt wrote a couple books and sometimes tries to write more. The day will come when he stops writing, but that day isn't today. He also has an army of raccoons.

Nick Roberts is a native West Virginian and a doctoral graduate of Marshall University. He is an active member of the Horror Writers Association and the Horror Authors Guild. His works include *Anathema, The Exorcist's House, It Haunts the Mind & Other Stories*, and *Mean Spirited*. He currently resides in South Carolina with his family and is an advocate for people in recovery from substance use disorder. Find out more about Nick at nickrobertsauthor.com.

Jeremy Megargee has always loved dark fiction. He cut his teeth on R.L Stine's Goosebumps series as a child and a fascination with Stephen King, Jack London, Algernon Blackwood, and many others followed later in life. Jeremy weaves his tales of personal horror from Martinsburg, West Virginia, with his cat Lazarus acting as his muse/familiar. He is a native of Appalachia, and you can often find him peddling his dark words in various mountain hollers deep within the wilderness.

R.E. Sargent is an editor, publisher, and author whose works delve into the sinister depths of horror, suspense, and the supernatural. His story "Lucy," featured in the Splatterpunk Award–nominated anthology *If I Die Before I Wake Volume 3 – Tales of Deadly Women and Retribution*, also resides among the dark tales in his collection, *Everything Went to Shit*. Nestled in the hauntingly beautiful Pacific Northwest, R.E. lives with his wife, their two granddogs, and the unyielding rain—a perfect companion for someone who revels in the eerie. Beneath the perpetual gray skies, he crafts stories that reach beyond the ordinary into realms best left undisturbed. Find out more about R.E. at resargent.com.

Nikki Noir is an author, editor, and publisher. She writes extreme horror, erotic thrillers, dark romance, and anything distinctly dark. Her fiction can be found on Godless, Blood Bound Books, and Amazon. Living in the Arizona desert, she finds any excuse to remain indoors hence why she became a writer with a full time job in IT & Security, hiding behind a computer all hours of the day. Besides working on a dozen projects at any given time, she is an avid reader, reviewer, dog cuddler (miniature dachshunds), baker/cake decorator, artist, gamer (console), and coffee connoisseur. Nikki can be found on Facebook, Instagram, TikTok, and Twitter @nikkinoirauthor. Find out more about Nikki at thatspookybeach.com.

John Durgin is a proud active HWA member and lifelong horror fan. Growing up in New Hampshire, he discovered Stephen King much younger than most probably should have, reading *IT* before he reached high school—and knew from that moment on he wanted to write horror. He had his first story accepted in the summer of 2021. His debut novel, *The Cursed Among Us*, was released June 3, 2022, and went on to become an Amazon bestseller. Next up, his sophomore novel titled *Inside The Devil's Nest*, released in January of 2023, followed by his debut collection, *Sleeping In The Fire* in June of 2023. In 2024 he released two more novels, starting with *Kosa,* which released to stellar reviews, and *Consumed by Evil* through Crystal Lake Publishing. Find out more about John at johndurginauthor.com.

Megan Stockton is an indie author who lives in Grimsley, Tennessee, with her two children and her husband, who is an indie filmmaker. She writes in a variety of genres that all have dark/horror elements, and all of her work is character-driven and immersive. She is known for delivering works that are raw, thought-provoking, brutal, and cinematic. She has been writing since she was a child and was always obsessed with horror and the macabre. When she isn't writing (or working her day job), she likes to work with the animals on their farm, read, play video games, and watch movies. Find out more about Megan at www.meganstockton-books.com.

Brian Asman Brian Asman is a writer, actor, and director from San Diego, CA. He's the author of *Good Dogs* and *Man, Fuck this House (And Other Disasters)*, both forthcoming from Blackstone. A film he co-wrote and produced, *A Haunting in Ravenwood*, is available now on VOD. Find him on social media (@thebrianasman) or his website brianasmanbooks.com.